A LITTLE FAIRY DUST

Mell Eight

A NineStar Press Publication

www.ninestarpress.com

A Little Fairy Dust

Printed in the USA
First Edition
January, 2021
Print ISBN: 978-1-64890-187-4

Also available in eBook, ISBN: 978-1-64890-186-7

Warning

This book contains sexual content, which may only be suitable for mature readers, and graphic wartime violence.

Table of Contents

Nine tales of magic, love, and a little fairy dust: A military posting at the Rapunzel Tower to avoid war in *The Tower*; a Brownie that just wants to do something right in *Cleanly Wrong*; a dream of love unfulfilled in *A Heart's Dream*; saving the victims of an evil witch in *The Red Apple Witch*; a boy who just wants to go to the ball in *Cinder-Elle*; a cursed kingdom and search for lost love in *The Curse*; a thief and his fairy godparent with different ideas about love in *Happily Ever After*; a lightning strike, a lost egg, an ancient battle, and love at first spark in *Thunderbird*; and a prince trapped, knowing his true love will never save him in *The Beast*.

Author's Note

I hope you enjoy my collection of reimagined fairy tales and are able to figure out which fairy tale each story is based on. Some are easy to spot like Cinder-Elle and The Tower and The Beast. Others may surprise you. Most importantly, have fun reading!

My parents introduced me to fairy tales as a child, and I've always dreamed of putting my own spin on a few of my favorites. I'd love to hear feedback on what you think.

You can reach me at:

> Facebook: www.facebook.com/MellEightFiction
> Twitter: @MellEight
> My website at: www.melleightfiction.weebly.com

THE TOWER

Chapter One

"And now, Prince Haines will pick the person who will be honored with the Rapunzel Posting!" General Darien called out loudly, his parade voice easily carrying over the noise of a few hundred men and women enjoying the annual feast. The room immediately quieted. Every year the officers and select few enlisted who were receiving an honor came together for a thank-you and award ceremony, but only every seven years was the Rapunzel Posting awarded.

Ishiah watched as Prince Haines stood from his place on the dais, where all the highest officers had been seated for the ceremony, and walked around the table until he was standing in front of the plinth holding a golden bowl. The bowl was easily deep enough for a baby to bathe, solid gold, and encrusted on the outside with gemstones, and it matched Prince Haines's outer appearance perfectly. Haines had golden-colored hair he kept pulled back from his face with a ruby-colored ribbon. His hand, as he lifted it above the bowl and hesitated there as if to drum up more drama, had a gemstone ring on every finger.

Those in the room held their collective breath as Haines dipped his fingers into the golden bowl. For the last seven days, the plinth and bowl had been standing in the entrance to the officers' mess hall where any officer interested in the Rapunzel Posting could drop a slip of paper into it with their name on it. Ishiah had walked around that bowl before and after every meal for seven days straight. He hadn't put his name in, but he hadn't needed to. He was just as capable of reading the winds of his political fate as anyone else in the kingdom.

It was with no surprise to Ishiah that Haines pulled out a piece of paper and read out: "First Lieutenant Ishiah Fitzsimons!"

The room didn't erupt into cheers as it would have for someone who actually wanted the post. Even the lowest enlisted man or woman in the room knew who Ishiah was. Fitz, meaning bastard child of royalty, and Simons, meaning the child of King Simon. Born to a mistress not even two months after Haines's own birth, Ishiah was a constant reminder of the king's infidelity to the political animals in the kingdom. He was also a second potential heir to the throne. With Prince Haines trying to solidify his status now that his wife was pregnant, Ishiah knew it was inevitable that he would be shuffled off somewhere. It was only a coincidence that the Rapunzel Posting had come due this year, and the convenience of it must have made changing all the slips of paper in the bowl to carry his name instead of the rightful candidates a worthy endeavor.

Ishiah stood from his seat at the back of the room and walked through the whispers and the tables toward the stairs that led up to the dais. He looked almost nothing like Prince Haines. Where Haines was golden, Ishiah was dark. His hair was black and was shaved tightly to his head on the sides according to military regulations, but he had allowed the wide strip on the top of his head to grow extremely long in the style of the eastern barbarians. The military allowed the enlisted barbarians to keep their ceremonial hairstyles or risk a potential uprising of the eastern territories, and many non-barbarian soldiers had chosen to copy them. Ishiah had originally done it to prove to the court that he was no prince—a prince wouldn't dare emulate the barbarians—and had ended up liking the hairstyle enough to keep it. Tonight, his long hair was thickly plaited and the tail of the braid rested between his shoulder blades. His skin was tanned like his mother's had been, the color of wet sand along the southern coast where his mother had been from before meeting King Simon. Only his eyes, gray shot through with blue streaks and wide in his face, proved his heritage. He shared his eyes with King Simon and Prince Haines.

Gray met gray as Ishiah climbed the stairs onto the dais and bowed to Prince Haines.

"Rise, soldier, and be honored," Haines said loudly enough to be heard over the soft whispers of the gossipers that had begun to fill the room. "First Lieutenant Ishiah Fitzsimons, you have been honored with the posting in Rap Tower in the Zel Mountains. You hold this prestigious duty to guard our lands from the western invaders. For seven years, seven months, and seven days, you will be watching for any sign of the returning hoard, and you will be studying. The tower has been provisioned with every textbook needed so when your posting ends you will be prepared to take on the mantle of colonel and lead this army to victory!"

He paused and it took Ishiah a moment to realize Haines was waiting for a response.

"I am honored to be chosen," Ishiah replied because that was the only thing he could say. "I will execute my duty faithfully and with diligence." He bowed again.

"Then come, join me for a toast and some dessert." Prince Haines gestured to the seat at the table that had remained ceremonially empty throughout the banquet. Ishiah walked over to it and stood behind the chair until Haines had retaken his seat. Ishiah sat and servants immediately entered the room bearing dessert trays.

"Congratulations, Lieutenant," General Darien said from Prince Haines's other side once the chatter around the room had risen enough that it would be difficult to hear what was being said on the dais. General Dairen was smiling at Ishiah, but there was a hard glint in his eye indicating he was aware of the political maneuvering that had gotten Ishiah the posting.

"Thank you, General," Ishiah replied.

They fell silent as plates of cake and glasses of champagne were placed in front of them. Prince Haines lifted his glass first.

"To Lieutenant Ishiah, who I know will be the most successful officer to come out of the Rapunzel Posting."

Those who could hear Haines also lifted their glasses in a toast. Ishiah took a long sip of the champagne, hoping to let the resentment he could feel bubbling up in his chest pop along with the bubbles in his drink. The dais was silent after that as they all applied themselves to their cake. Only once everyone else was distracted by other conversations did Haines fully turn toward Ishiah.

"I am sorry, Ish. I know this isn't what you would have chosen," Haines began, his voice soft so they wouldn't be overheard.

"Of course it's not, Hay," Ishiah replied, his voice tight with the anger he was trying to keep suppressed.

Haines shook his head firmly as if he needed to brush away Ishiah's feelings in order to finish what he had to say. "There were whispers at court. The malcontents unhappy with some of the policies Father and I have been implementing were talking about replacing us with you."

"Hay, those whispers started the day father announced to the court that I was his child," Ishiah replied, his anger making his words more of a growl than actual syllables. "Just admit that you're scared and instead of coming to talk to me about a solution you hatched this scheme instead."

"Fine!" Haines snapped, although his voice still managed to remain quiet. "Of course I'm scared. Victoria is three months pregnant and extremely vulnerable. I want my child to have a chance to be born, not murdered in the womb by some idiot who wants to put you on the throne instead of me. I only had a few options, Ish, to remove you as a threat. I could have killed you, of course, but that wasn't an option I was willing to consider. Father suggested making you an ambassador to one of our trading partners across the ocean, but I know you would have hated that. Think about it, Ish. Seven years and you'll come out of it a full colonel with a big enough salary and enough prestige you can settle down comfortably anywhere in the country. When General Darien suggested you as a good candidate for the posting, Father and I agreed."

After seven years of being out of the spotlight of the court, Ishiah would be all but forgotten by the malcontents. Haines would have cemented himself as the heir and his child as next in line. And, if Ishiah chose to live somewhere far away from the capital after the posting was over, his status as bastard son of the king would be all but forgotten.

And all of it had been neatly thrust on him in a way that left zero room for his refusal.

It took a moment for Ishiah to bury his anger again. Raising a fist toward Prince Haines would get him put in jail, which would be even worse than being put in the tower for seven years.

"You still should have talked to me about it first," Ishiah said once he was certain his voice could remain soft enough to keep their conversation private. "Instead of springing it on me like this. Treat me like a brother, Haines, instead of like the enemy you fear I'll be turned into."

"You're right." Haines let out a heavy sigh. "You are right," he repeated. "Forgive me?"

Ishiah frowned at Haines for a long moment before sighing himself. "Eventually, Hay. Let me be angry for a little bit longer. I expect you'll write me weekly and that my niece or nephew will start writing me as soon as they're able."

"I'll write you, Father will write you, and I'll make certain my child will write you. Ish, this posting is an honor, you know. We make sure not just anyone is picked for this. They have to be highly recommended by their peers and their superiors. If you hadn't been, you'd be on a ship heading for an ambassador posting instead. Please, I know you didn't want this, but be honored you are thought of so highly."

"I will be, Hay. As soon as the anger and betrayal fade, I will be." Ishiah cracked a tentative smile for Haines to show he meant it. "Besides, now you're going to have to figure out someone else for the court gossips to focus their ire on. Who will be the next family scapegoat now that they don't have my hair or the fact that I keep showing up to court events in my leather armor to harangue you over?"

"I'll be certain to let you know who they pick and why," Haines replied with his own hesitant smile.

Ishiah might be angry with him, but they were still brothers. They would get through this, and in seven years who knew what the political climate and their relationship would be like.

*

The tower came into view quickly enough. After only a day of riding out of the city heading due west, the pointed roof of the tower became visible on the horizon. For the next two days that's all Ishiah could see of it. By day four, he could make out the edge of the large window that opened to the northwestern mountains. For seven years, seven months, and seven days, Ishiah would be looking out that window as his only view of the outer world.

Day five of riding brought them well into the Zel Mountains, and the height of the tower was briefly hidden behind the high cliffs that bordered the narrow pathway, before quickly reappearing as the winding path climbed over those cliffs.

Sometimes he felt like the tower was taunting him. For seven years it would be his home—his prison—and for his last seven days of freedom it was a constant reminder on the horizon of what his life was about to become.

Midday on the seventh day brought them to the foot of the tower, and suddenly Ishiah realized just how massive a tower it was. It was ten stories high and wide enough around the base for an entire wing of the castle to fit inside. Built of thick gray stone, it looked ominous, nestled as it was in a shallow valley just before the path continued over the highest peak in the Zel Mountain range and began to descend into Faltiken, the land of the mindless hoard.

The most evident feature of the tower was actually what it was lacking, which in this case was any form of a doorway on the ground level, or even any level higher up the tower. The only entrance was that one window.

"Rapunzel, Rapunzel, let down your hair!" one of the guards called mockingly toward the top of the tower.

"Blow it out your ear!" a woman's voice responded angrily seconds before a long, braided rope of what did indeed look like hair came tumbling down from the top of the tower.

There was quiet for a long moment before the first guard who had spoken turned toward Ishiah. "Lieutenant, it's time to climb."

Ishiah's stomach clenched, but he swung off his horse and approached the rope despite the trepidation curling in his gut. His first impression was correct; the rope was made of some sort of hair, most likely horse, and it was easy enough to pull himself up the rope.

Ten stories had never looked so high before as he dangled from the rope, pulling himself up hand over hand with his legs wrapped around to keep him from slipping. He suddenly felt a tug on the rope and glanced up to see a woman hanging out of the tower window high above, pulling the rope as he climbed.

Ishiah's arms and stomach burned before he even reached halfway, and he didn't want to admit that the woman overhead probably did double the amount of work he did in getting him up the tower. He was a sweaty, exhausted mess by the time the woman hauled him over the windowsill and into the tower. He collapsed to the floor, panting desperately for breath. His heart was pounding in his chest and his arms shaking.

"It hits everyone like that," the woman said gently. She was standing over him, still looking out the window. He glanced up and saw she had tossed the rope back outside. "I know you're tired, but you need to listen to me closely because I'm getting out of here as fast as I damn well can."

He nodded to show he understood and, with a groan, got himself sitting upright so he could look at her.

"This rope is your only lifeline to the outside world. It breaks, the only way you're getting supplies or getting out of here is by climbing down the side itself. Check it every day for mold and for tears. Supplies and instructions on how to weave more hair into the rope to fix it are through that door over there." She pointed to a closed wooden door off to the right of the room, then glanced back out the tower before she started hauling up the rope again. "Supplies come every other week. They'll load up a basket and wait for you to bring it up." She didn't sound winded in the least as she pulled at what was no doubt a heavy weight. Ishiah was still panting. "You send your trash and any messages or supply requests back down in the basket." She tied the rope over a hook driven into the side of the window and bent outside to grab the handle of the largest basket Ishiah had ever seen. Actually, it was probably in proportion to the massive size of the tower, now that he thought about it.

She tipped the basket over, and Ishiah's belongings tumbled onto the floor in front of him.

"Bedroom's out here," she explained, and Ishiah finally looked around him to take in his new home.

The bed was pushed against the wall directly across from the window, and it was high enough that Ishiah would probably be able to see out the window without needing to get up. Along the left wall was a wide couch with a low table just in front of it. Along the right wall was a high table with two chairs, which was a little odd considering there was only one occupant of the tower at a time. Interspersed along those two walls were a number of closed wooden doors.

"Behind the kitchen table is the kitchen. There's a pantry in there with a cold box. Keep it clean or you'll get bugs. Or birds. They'll fly right in the window if there's something to attract them. The library is the door next to the couch. Trust me, you'll read every book in there many, many times, if only to stave off boredom."

While she was explaining, she was stuffing her own belongings into the basket. Once all of her bundles were inside, she carried the basket back to the window and heaved it out. It took a moment to unhook the rope, and she started lowering the basket down to the ground.

"Door right next to the bed leads to the bathroom. There's running water. Don't ask me how, because I have no idea. Damned tower is older than our great-great-grandparents, at least, and it's had running water longer than the barracks at the castle." The Rapunzel Posting had only been in use for the last two centuries, but the tower predated that by an unknown number of years.

Two centuries ago, the mindless hoard of Faltiken had invaded Monrath. Although the history books were always reluctant to admit it,

Monrath had been losing the war by a considerable margin. Then Private Gabby had gotten separated from her patrol and chanced on the tower. Somehow, she had climbed all ten stories without a rope and had seen that the mindless hoard wasn't so mindless. It had split in two, looking to catch the remaining Monrath soldiers in a pincer. Gabby had climbed back down the tower, found her patrol, and reported what she had seen. Monrath had won, and Private Gabby had ended up marrying into the royal family.

Twenty-one years later, Faltiken invaded again, and again Princess Gabby had climbed the tower. From the awesome height of the tower, she had seen every move Faltiken tried to make, and her pigeons had flown with messages for seven straight weeks. This time, Monrath beat Faltiken so badly there was little left of the mindless hoard, but Monrath wasn't willing to allow Faltiken the opportunity to amass again.

The history of the tower was researched, and in an old, dusty tome about the lost arts of magic it was discovered that Wizard Rap had owned the tower an unknown number of years before magic was lost to the world, and when magic was lost, Wizard Rap had vanished. Wizard Rap's tower in the Zel Mountains—Rap on Zel, as it had quickly come to be called—was chosen as the ideal location to keep watch on the Faltiken heartland, and the Rapunzel Posting was created.

Ishiah finally levered himself to his feet, shaking his arms out as he went. The view out the window was exactly as the stories indicated. He could see right over the last peak of the Zel Mountains, directly down into the wide valley below. All he could see was green grass. There were a few sparse trees, but aside from them there wasn't anything to impede his view should the mindless hoard suddenly decide to form ranks below.

The woman finally let go of the rope and turned toward him again. "The door on the other side of the couch leads to a training room. There's a seven-year training regimen in there for you. Make sure you do the arm exercises every day, or you won't be able to pull the rope up properly when your supplies come. Your only job while you're here is to train and to check out the window regularly. You see something out there, you light the fire." This time she pointed out the window toward the mountain peak on the Monrath side of the tower where a tall bonfire had been laid. Then she nudged a set of bow and arrows hidden in her shadow next to the window. "The patrol that comes with supplies every other week is tasked with checking on the wood. There's a shelter there to keep rain and snow off. You see something, you light the fire, and the entire Monrath Army will be here in seven days." The seriousness of that action wasn't lost on Ishiah. "Any questions?"

Ishiah shook his head wordlessly, unable to think of anything to ask. He couldn't help wishing he were on a ship, heading somewhere far away to be an ambassador across the ocean. As much as he would have detested every moment of it, surely it would have been better than this.

"Do your best not to go stir-crazy. Good luck, soldier." She nodded to him, then swung out the window and began climbing down the rope with a speed that spoke of a level of desperation Ishiah was just beginning to understand. He leaned out the window to watch her go, and when she reached the ground, she mounted the horse Ishiah had recently left. The patrol waved to him, before turning and heading back down the mountain.

"What do I do now?" Ishiah asked the empty room. When no one responded, he sighed and went to start putting away his belongings for what was already proving to be the most arduous task his life as a soldier had ever brought him.

Chapter Two

Ishiah lay on his back in the middle of the floor, his body resting in the sunlight pouring in from the open window as he panted for breath.

"Okay, maybe the last ten sit-ups were too many," he said aloud to himself, glad for the noise as it made him feel less like he had been completely alone for the last seven months. "Or the last twenty," he added when the idea of moving turned out to be one his body wasn't the least bit interested in.

"Rapunzel, Rapunzel, let down your hair!"

"I am going to slug that idiot the second I get down there," Ishiah grumbled.

He took a deep breath to brace himself and then, using his arms more than his stomach, got himself sitting upright. It took another second to get his feet under him, and then he had to bend to gather the long rope and toss it out the window. Ishiah let out a pained groan as his overworked muscles protested the movement. He stuck his head out afterward, desperate to see another face and hear another voice even for the ten minutes the patrol would be nearby.

"Any news from the crown?" Ishiah called down, loud enough to be heard all the way from the ground.

"Yes!" the same guard called back, "but His Highness ordered us not to tell you. He wanted to tell you himself in his letter!"

"Anything you can tell me that doesn't have to do with Prince Haines's news?" Ishiah yelled back.

"No. Everything's been quiet since you left." Which was, admittedly, the point of him leaving, so Ishiah was glad at least that had worked. "And everything newsworthy is in His Highness's letter."

The guards on the ground stepped back from the rope, so Ishiah let out a sigh and started heaving it up. The rope began to coil at his feet, and the big basket came into view quickly. It had definitely become easier to haul the basket up after seven months of arm exercises and basket hauling every other week, so it wasn't long before he was pulling the basket inside. He unloaded it without looking at what he was grabbing and rapidly refilled the basket with the things he was sending out. His bag of accumulated trash from the last two weeks went in first; the laundry he wanted professionally scrubbed rather than washed in the kitchen sink was the next bag, followed by the letters he was sending to his family and friends. After that, he squeezed in three blankets he had unearthed from the blanket chest at the foot of the bed.

It was starting to get colder at night as winter approached and the only three blankets in the tower smelled, were moth-bitten, and definitely didn't feel thick enough for a mountain winter. He had pinned a note to the top one requesting they be washed and mended, and asking for a proper quilt. Maybe he was acting like the spoiled son of the king instead of a proper soldier, but if he had to endure seven years of this place he would do so in comfort.

Once he was sure everything he wanted to send down was in the basket, he heaved it back out the window and started lowering it to the waiting soldiers on the ground. The soldiers grabbed the basket when it reached them, and Ishiah watched as they tied it to the waiting packhorse and headed off.

He was alone again for the next two weeks.

Well, at least he had his packages to check out for the next few minutes. Ishiah found his laundry first and put the folded clothes away in the chest of drawers next to the bed, and then he started to explore everything else he had been sent. There was food—all of it items that could last the weeklong journey to the tower—and that was easy to put away in the kitchen. He also found two new books, which meant he had to find somewhere to put them in the library.

Ishiah ran a hand through his hair and let out a sigh. He gripped the end of the long strands from the top of his head and yanked, then dragged his fingers through the shorter strands on the side of his head. There was no point in keeping his particular hairstyle for the next seven years if there was no one to impress with it. After seven months the shaved parts were a good two inches long.

The library was the biggest room in the tower, which Ishiah had been surprised to learn when he first opened that door to explore. There were easily a thousand books in a room that was double the size of all the rest of the rooms in the tower combined.

Ishiah liked to read and had welcomed the sight of all the books, until he realized that every single one of them had to do with his training.

Much like the exercise room only had the equipment needed for the outlined seven-year regimen, the books were exclusively geared toward turning him into the perfect soldier. Military treatise, strategy guides, and even biographies of influential military figures filled the many, many shelves. There wasn't a single fiction book to be found.

Even the two books he had been sent were solely for his training. The larger book was a strategy guide on best methods for gaining the higher ground and the smaller a biography of Queen Gabby the Second, the original Gabby's great-great-granddaughter, who had led the armies from the front against the barbarians, eventually conquering them and bringing them into the kingdom.

Ishiah took both books and his bundle of letters with him into the library. The books were alphabetized by author, which he had no doubt one of his predecessors had done to stave off boredom. Sometimes Ishiah had an urge to knock all the books down off the shelves just so he could spend the hours putting them back up correctly. It would fill some of the endless time he had at his fingertips.

It only took a few minutes to figure out which shelves the two books belonged on and to squeeze them both into their places. Afterward, Ishiah settled into the lone cushioned armchair tucked into a corner next to one of the lamps. He cracked open the letter with Haines's seal on it first.

Ish, amazing news. It's a girl!

Ishiah let out a happy hoot at the news, cheering for Haines's good fortune. He was an uncle! Ishiah would have to write a letter to his niece for the next patrol to take to her.

We have named her Gabby, so eventually she'll be Queen Gabby the Fourth. It's been so long since someone has used such a prestigious name. Victoria and I thought it was time.

Ishiah frowned at that bit of news. The last two girls to be named Gabby in the family had been born during extremely difficult times for the kingdom. Gabby the Second had fought against the barbarians, and Gabby the Third had dealt with severe pirate attacks crippling the coastal trade cities. Haines naming his child Gabby wasn't an omen Ishiah wanted to hear, especially since the issues with the malcontents were supposed to have been solved thanks to his being locked in this damned tower. Ishiah couldn't help wondering what he was missing.

She's the perfect little girl, but she screams like you did whenever I beat you at weapon's practice when we were kids. She has the family's eyes, of course, and your lungs, but I can't help loving her even when she's ruining my hearing. I wish you were here to hold her. I'll make certain she learns to love her Uncle Ishy even if she won't get the chance to meet you until she's seven.

We miss you here. I hope you're learning a lot. Let me know if there's some comforts from home I can send to make the posting more comfortable for you.

Wishing you the best,

Haines, Victoria, and Gabby

Ishiah was smiling as he folded the letter. He smoothed the paper flat on his knee, then put it on the small table next to where he was sitting. It was a reading table, so was only meant to hold a few books at a time. Ishiah had found writing supplies there instead. He pulled a fresh sheet of paper from the stack and dipped a pen in ink before writing his reply.

Haines,

I am so unbelievably excited for you! Gabby sounds amazing, and her having my lungs just means she's going to grow up to be awesome like her uncle. Give her my love and use some of my salary to buy her the softest blanket on the market. I don't care the cost; she deserves it.

I can feel winter approaching up here in the mountains, so anything you can send that will stave off frostbite in a tower with a wide-open window would be appreciated. I was also thinking that when spring comes the gardeners could send potted plants of things that I can grow and eat throughout the summer. Fresh food instead of the travel rations would be nice.

What news and gossip is going around the court these days? Certainly people must be talking about your choosing to name your daughter Gabby. Haines, that's not a name to choose lightly, given the women in our family with that name usually have to fight for much of their lives to ensure peace and the survival of our kingdom. I might not be able to do anything from inside this tower, but I would like to stay informed. Please fill me in on everything.

All my love to you, Victoria, and baby Gabby,

Ishiah

Ishiah folded the letter into thirds and slid it onto an envelope. He wrote Haines's name on the front, then stood to walk back to the main room where he had left his sealing wax. Except, as he walked past the bookshelves that lined the wall, the floor squeaked.

That was impossible. Ishiah froze in place and stared down at the floor, then rocked backwards on his heel and felt the sudden give under his foot. It felt like rotten wood, but the floor under his feet was built of the same thick stones as the rest of the tower. There were rugs scattered everywhere throughout the tower, covering all the floors including the library, but the ten-by-ten-foot rug he was standing on wasn't thick enough to bend under his feet.

Besides, Ishiah had walked over this section of floor dozens of times during his stay—he had walked over it just five minutes ago when he went to read Haines's letter—and it had never squeaked before.

Ishiah walked back to the sitting area and dropped his letter onto the table to deal with later, then knelt at the edge of the rug to begin rolling it up. The rug was old and filthy, sending up clouds of dust as he pushed it out of the way. Ishiah coughed, then held his breath for the last few feet. Once the rug was completely rolled up, he returned to the patch of floor that didn't feel right.

At first glance, all he could see was stone, but as he stepped onto the section that had squeaked, he could see that it was, instead, wood so old and dirty it had turned the same gray as the stone. It must be a trapdoor.

Excited because this was the first interesting thing to happen in all the months he had been locked in the tower, Ishiah looked for a latch or anything to help him pry the door up. He couldn't see anything, not even a divot in the wood where a latch might have once been.

Maybe he was wrong, and this wasn't a trapdoor. Maybe some of the stone had cracked and become dangerous, so it had been replaced by the wood. Still, Ishiah dug his fingernails into the edge around the wood and tried to yank it up.

"Open!" he growled at the wood, and with a loud groan the door popped up. A whoosh of stale-smelling air hit Ishiah in the face, making him cough again. Once his coughing stopped, he gripped the door and heaved it all the way open, and then stuck his head into the hole.

It was dark, but he could make out the start of a staircase just below his nose. Ishiah switched his body around so his feet went through the hole first, and he stepped down onto the top step. He found the next three steps by touch and was about to go back upstairs to find a candle when lights shimmered into existence below him, completely illuminating the stairs.

"What the..." Ishiah breathed to himself, gaping down at the stairs and the little bit of the room he could see below him. "Magic. Has to be magic."

This had been Wizard Rap's tower before Monrath took it over as a guard post, Ishiah reminded himself. It shouldn't be any surprise that there was some sort of magic inside. He ought to go back upstairs, close the trapdoor, return the rug to its spot, and forget this existed. Whatever was down there could be dangerous, and it would be at least two weeks before the next patrol, and therefore help, arrived.

Ishiah looked down at the sharply spiraling staircase his feet were resting on and the little square of stone-flagged floor he could see below and couldn't make himself leave. Going back upstairs to the same boring routine he had been following for the last seven months when there was a mystery right at his fingertips just wasn't possible. Ishiah started walking down the stairs before that thought even finished.

Once his head was below the upstairs floor, Ishiah could see the entire room, and it was huge. Unlike the upstairs, this floor didn't have separate rooms partitioning it. Instead it was one big room with different sections delineated by the different furniture. Ishiah was descending into what appeared to be another library equally as large as the one he had just left. There were two fluffy chairs in two different corners near shelves that from this distance Ishiah thought might actually be labeled. To the left of the library were two long wooden tables easily the size of banquet tables. They were empty, but Ishiah could see what appeared to be burn marks and gouges out of them both, so he felt safe in assuming they were work tables. Past that, Ishiah saw trunks and boxes of what looked like a storage area.

He headed to the books first since they were most likely to tell him what he was looking at. The shelf nearest the stairs was labeled "grimoires," and Ishiah couldn't help grinning at that.

Magic might be a lost art and the wizards of old gone, but this was a treasure trove he had every intention of exploiting.

Ishiah pulled down the grimoire labeled "beginner" and went to one of the chairs to start reading.

Chapter Three

"Rapunzel, Rapunzel, let down your hair!"

Ishiah rolled his eyes, but after two and a half years of hearing that imbecile say that same damned line every other week, in some ways Ishiah had grown to appreciate the familiarity of it.

Instead of getting up right away, Ishiah put the scrap of cloth he was using as a bookmark into the book he was reading—a treatise of warfare during the flooding of the spring rains—and closed his eyes.

"Bring the energy from the head, down to the feet, and back to the head," Ishiah murmured to himself, breathing deeply and evenly in meditation. "Then out through the hands with intent to focus the spell."

He held out one hand toward the waiting pile of rope and opened his eyes as his spell took shape. The rope drifted up into the air and tossed itself out the window. Ishiah grinned because he had gotten it to work.

Magic was as difficult to learn as all the books on warfare he was reading. Despite wanting to learn everything he could about magic as quickly as he could, Ishiah found himself needing to take a break all too often. The best way was to return to the books Monrath had supplied, and he read those until they started driving him crazy before returning to the magic ones. He was keeping up with all of the exercises he had been assigned, but adding the magic kept the tedium at bay.

Ishiah finally stood and headed over to the window. "Anything good for me?" he yelled down to the waiting soldiers.

"A few letters and the gardener sent a pot of potatoes for you. He said you can replant them yourself and included instructions."

"Thanks!" Ishiah called back. "Send it all up."

When the soldiers stepped away from the basket they had attached to the rope, Ishiah started pulling the rope back inside. He could still remember his first few times doing this and having to stop to shake his arms out. Now he wasn't even winded when the basket reached the top. He dumped it out like usual, careful of the wide pot with green sprouts popping out of the dirt, and refilled the basket with everything he wanted to send away. It never took long for the basket to get back to the ground, and the soldiers were practiced at getting the basket untied and hooked back to the packhorse. Ishiah waved as they turned around to head back to the capital.

He took his time pulling the empty rope back up, carefully coiling the horsehair so it wouldn't get knotted and making certain that all of it had safely survived yet another encounter with the basket. When he was sure the rope was secure, Ishiah rested his elbows on the windowsill and looked out into the spring afternoon.

The view hadn't changed in all the time he had been locked up in the tower. The last peak of the Zel Mountains was just below him, and beyond was the grassy plains of Faltiken. There were no enemy soldiers in sight, no one amassing for an invasion, and Ishiah let out a heavy sigh. He would never wish for war, of course, but company would be nice. If Faltiken did try to invade, Ishiah had no doubt that someone would be sent up the tower with him to act as a second set of eyes when Ishiah had to sleep, and that would be someone he could talk to. Ishiah was desperately tired of talking to the walls and not getting any response.

He turned away from the view slowly, and something suddenly sparkled out of the side of his eye. Ishiah spun back around, staring out at the grassy plain, but he didn't see anything. He looked away slowly this time, and as his head was turned sideways, he saw the strange sparkles again.

It had to be magic, but what kind he couldn't even guess. He was barely able to lift the rope successfully every time; knowing what sort of magic might be impacting his vision and pinpointing where it was coming from wasn't possible just yet. Still, he couldn't help leaning farther out of the tower to see just where the sparkles originated.

Ishiah looked down just in time to see a man walk into view from the Monrath side of the tower. He circled the tower underneath the window and then suddenly vanished.

That wasn't normal. Ishiah stared down at the spot on the tower where the man had vanished for a brief moment, before he suddenly heard footsteps coming from the magic library below him.

He wasn't alone!

Ishiah scrambled into the training room and quickly grabbed a practice sword and dagger, before hurrying into the library where he could stand protectively over the open trapdoor.

"Who's there?" he called down, half hoping and half dreading getting an answer.

"Who do you think?" a man's voice replied sharply. "Not many people know how to get into Wizard Rap's tower without having to climb up a bloody rope. In fact, that number is probably exactly one, especially since I'm going to make certain you don't remember this encounter."

Energy flowed from Ishiah's head, down to his feet, and back to his head, before flowing out from the tip of his sword. A surprised yelp echoed up the stairs, and Ishiah jumped down, carefully skipping steps on the steep spiral. He found a man standing in the center of the library, his arms crossed and a frown on his face. The man's hair was longer than Ishiah's, reaching his butt while Ishiah's was only just past his shoulder blades. It was also a vibrant shade of purple, which matched his wide lavender-colored eyes. He was beautiful, but despite the flower-colored hair, he also looked dangerous.

"Found my grimoires, did you?" the man asked, and while his voice was sharp, the aggressive tone from earlier was gone. "That was a fair attempt at a freezing spell. You show some promise, I admit, but you're two hundred years too young to be battling with me."

"How did you get in here?" Ishiah had to ask. He was still holding the sword and knife out protectively, but the excited beating of his heart had slowed. There was something dangerous about the man, yes, but after living most of his life in the army, Ishiah could tell when the aggression necessary to attack was missing.

"Please, I built this tower. Let me tell you, if you thought your little freezing spell was hard, try magicking up an entire tower from stones you magically mined from inside the Rapparees Mountains. Name's Zelimir, by the way. Call me Zel. Who are you?"

"I'm Ishiah," Ishiah replied. "I thought this was Wizard Rap's tower?"

Zel grinned and this time the excited beating of Ishiah's heart was caused by just how pretty Zel's smile was. Ishiah's sword was dipping toward the ground before he noticed his guard had dropped, but once he had, he leaned the sword against the banister and dropped the knife onto the bottom stair. There wasn't any point in holding them if he wasn't going to use them.

"It's amazing what gets lost in five hundred years and what doesn't. When I built this tower, the mountains were called the Rapparees because of how sharp the peaks are. Don't ask me when someone started calling them the Zel Mountains and decided my name was Rap instead." Zel fell silent and appeared to be studying Ishiah. Since Ishiah didn't know what to say in reply to that—and he was kind of afraid that something idiotic and besotted would come out—he kept his mouth shut. "You're obviously one of Gabrielle's get. She had those eyes too, and she had just enough of a magic touch to break the protections I had on my tower to keep intruders out. You've got a bit more than a touch of magic in you, which is why my fraying spells finally broke on me and you got into my workroom. I knew I should have come back to renew them, but laziness, you know."

What Ishiah was beginning to realize was that Zel couldn't abide by silence. His words weren't just chatter, but every time he closed his mouth on a finished thought, a moment later it was open and running again.

"And what with my accidentally knocking Gabrielle out of the tower when I came to see who had broken my protections, I was a bit embarrassed to come back. She fell on the brambles that had grown around the tower in my absence. Ended up blinding herself, among other injuries. Luckily her beloved prince found her quickly enough, and I used the magic from his tears to fix her up. I got rid of the brambles, of course, and then since I wasn't exactly using the tower when she came back twenty or so years later, I told her as long as she didn't destroy my tower she could use it as she liked. I'm guessing you're the result of that?"

Zel finally paused for breath, so Ishiah quickly cut in. "I've been assigned here," he explained. "On watch to ensure the Faltiken Army doesn't invade again."

"Oh, yeah. That was the war Gabrielle was involved with. Both times, if my memory serves. Nasty people, those Faltikens. Like to turn their wizards into slaves. I stayed out of that country for my first few hundred years until I could conceal what I am."

This time Ishiah didn't wait for a break, cutting in at the end of a sentence. "So, why are you here?"

"I already told you. You broke into my workroom."

"That was almost two years ago," Ishiah cut in before Zel could continue. The babbling was annoying, yet at the same time it was kind of endearing. That, and it had been so long since Ishiah had had any sort of conversation that he was enjoying every moment of it. Besides, the way Zel's face animated with happy eagerness when he was talking about the past, disgust when he was talking about the Faltikens, and shined with pleasure when he spoke about magic was absolutely beautiful to watch. If Ishiah didn't need to ask his own questions, he wouldn't have any problem with letting Zel chatter on uninterrupted.

Zel shrugged. "I was on the other side of the world working with another wizard on a project. She needed my expertise on shielding spells, which was about the moment when my shield on my workroom broke. I felt that you were only reading the books, and her project was far too interesting to leave just because you were curious. I knew you had to have some magic to break through my degrading spells, but I never thought you'd be able to teach yourself as much as you have. I'm glad I finally got over here. You need a teacher, and you need to have enough knowledge to make a decision. You've already elongated your life by about thirty years with the magic you've been using. If you want to continue working with magic, you need to understand that with magic continuously coursing through your body, you'll live until something kills you. That's not a decision you can make overnight.

"There's a reason magic became a lost art, you know." Zel continued speaking as if his last statement hadn't zinged through Ishiah, sending utter shock and a dozen panicked 'oh shit' lines running through his brain. Magic could really make a person live forever? Ishiah had to believe it, considering he was looking at the wizard that had personally built a tower far older than any human could ever hope to live, let alone how old Zel himself claimed to be. None of the grimoires he had been reading had mentioned that, but Ishiah thought that was because by the time anyone usually got to a grimoire, they had already been warned.

Thirty years wasn't too bad. He would definitely outlive Haines, but probably not baby Gabby. If Ishiah stopped using magic right now, he wouldn't have to endure seeing Gabby, and any of Gabby's children and grandchildren, live and die. If Ishiah ever had any children of his own—which he hadn't planned to, given how much political drama his own birth had caused—he would watch them die too. It was utterly horrible to think of.

But the magic felt so right, so pure. He loved working with it. Magic was hard, but so was sword work, and he diligently practiced that every day too. Stopping something he loved because of having to endure something so terrible made sense, and yet in some ways it also felt like giving up, and that was almost as bad.

"You see, when everyone knew about magic, bad people would learn it so they could subjugate others and live forever." Zel, oblivious to Ishiah's inner turmoil, was still talking. Ishiah latched onto his words as a convenient distraction. This wasn't a decision to be made in an hour, not when it could affect what could be a very, very long life. "The good wizards at that time—it was a few centuries before my time, you understand, but my mentor was there and she told me all about it—well, they got together and managed to defeat the evil wizards and place a spell of forgetting on the world. It didn't work so well in Faltiken. Magic is really weird over there. Don't ask me why—I hate traveling over there and have no interest in figuring out that mystery. Anyway, so most of the world forgot, but every once in a while, someone like you or me stumbles back upon it and we make the decision whether to study or to return to forgetting. You need to make a decision soon, before it gets to be too late to turn back."

"I need to think about it," Ishiah replied in a rare moment of silence. "I can't make a decision right now."

Zel nodded. "That's fine. If you decide to give up magic, I'll seal my workroom back up and make you forget both the room and magic ever existed. It's not too late for a spell like that to take hold. I'll continue on my travels, and you'll finish your posting here. You'll live a bit longer than most, but not considerably, and it will be a regular human life. If you want to keep practicing magic, I'll stay and teach you."

Ishiah's heart immediately jumped at those words. A companion to talk to during the long months of exile would be amazing, and looking at and listening to Zel would certainly brighten every moment. The man was far too beautiful.

"Until then, what do you have to eat around here? I'm starved."

Ishiah laughed. "Let's go to the kitchen and find out." He retrieved his sword and knife and started climbing the stairs back up into the main rooms of the tower, Zel right behind him.

Chapter Four

"Why do you keep twitching like that every time you walk past the window?" Zel asked on their third morning together. He had been watching Ishiah practice all morning, reading the seven-year training manual as Ishiah moved from warm-ups with push-ups and sit-ups to more complex sword movements. Today was all about footwork, so he had moved from the practice room to the main room where there was space for him to move back and forth.

Except, every time he happened to glance out the window there was that same strange sparkle he had first noticed the day Zel had arrived. If his noticing it had gotten bad enough that Zel was commenting on his reaction, then Ishiah clearly had to do something about it.

He lowered the weighted practice sword he had been working with and turned to face the window where he could see the empty grassy field of Faltiken where the sparkle was coming from.

"It's weird," he explained to Zel. "When I'm looking right at the field everything's fine, but when I turn my head to the side, the grass has gone sparkly." He turned his head to demonstrate, and sure enough the grass took on a strange sheen.

Ishiah expected Zel to laugh it off as some sort of side effect of his using magic for about two years unsupervised. Zel slamming the practice book shut and jumping to his feet so he could hurry to join Ishiah at the window wasn't expected at all.

"Out of the corner of your eye, you say?" Zel mumbled under his breath. A second later his purple eyes started glowing, and he squinted at the grass. "Shit," he added after another moment. "Looks like Gabby's plan to use my tower as a guard post was actually worthwhile."

"What is it?" Ishiah asked worriedly. He turned his head to the side again, but all he saw was the sparkling grass.

"Dirty magic," Zel replied with a snort of disgust. "The kind only used in Faltiken. Something's out there that they don't want you to see."

"What sort of something?" Ishiah turned his head again, trying to find a different angle that might show him whatever was there, but his view was unchanged no matter what he tried.

"Probably an army," Zel replied. He moved away from the window and retook his seat at the table. "I'm more concerned about the fact that you were able to see it. You're certain you only touched the early grimoires? You didn't go into anything more advanced?"

Ishiah wordlessly shook his head in denial, but most of his attention was still on the empty field. If any army was out there hiding behind some sort of magic spell, then he needed to act now before it was too late for Monrath to respond. Except, that field was still completely and totally empty. He couldn't call up the entire army just because he saw something that sparkled.

"Can you see the army? How many ranks are out there? Or is it just a scouting group?"

Zel let out a heavy sigh. "You're the one with the sight. My specialty is shielding. Yours is apparently with seeing. It's unbelievably useful, but it's also one of those magicks that will manifest inevitably. Even if you stop using magic and I help you forget its existence, one day you'll run into it again. You're going to be a wizard; you have no choice."

Distracted by Zel's words, Ishiah turned away from the window. "What do you mean?" He had been putting off making a decision on whether to stay with magic or return to his family simply because he honestly couldn't come up with an answer. Plus, he was enjoying Zel's company. The almost-constant chatter, the smiles, the ache in his heart whenever he looked at the beautiful man...Ishiah was well and truly smitten. The way he sometimes caught Zel looking at him made Ishiah think Zel might return his feelings, and yet, Zel was still planning to leave if Ishiah decided to skip choosing magic.

"I mean exactly what I'm saying. If you had never touched my grimoires, you would probably still see the sparkle. It might not be as bright, but you would have noticed it. Except, you would have no idea what it was you were seeing until you were completely overrun by whatever's out there."

"What is out there?" Ishiah asked, reminded that there might be an entire army sitting right at his doorstep. "What did you see?"

Zel shook his head. "I don't have much power with sight. All I could see was that there's some sort of concealing spell over that gigantic field.

From what I can see of how they set the spell, I'd say it's been in place for about a week now, but I couldn't tell you what it's hiding. Given it's Faltiken we're talking about, probably every single soldier and mage they have at their command, and Monrath isn't prepared for it at all."

"If I light the bonfire the army will be here in exactly seven days. I'm sure the first scouts will arrive sooner," Ishiah cut in. "We're ready for a fight."

"Against soldiers, yes, but mages? And an entire army that's concealed?" Zel fell silent, looking pensively toward the window and the view beyond. He didn't need to finish that thought, as odd as it was for him to stop speaking before everything in his head was out in the open. That, more than anything, told Ishiah how worried Zel was.

"At least we can call in the army. That's better than nothing, and they'll be able to give us time to figure out the rest."

Decided, Ishiah went over to the window where the bow and arrows were always kept. He pulled one arrow from the quiver and double-checked that the specially prepared wrappings around the tip were secure before heading to the nearest candle to light it.

Ishiah returned to the window and looked out at the empty field. "You're sure there's an army out there? I'm not making a mistake?"

Zel stood and walked to stand behind him. He put one hand on Ishiah's shoulder and squeezed comfortingly. "I'm certain, and if we turn out to be wrong, we can always pretend there was a lightning strike. All you have to do is figure out how to use your sight to break the concealing spell before your army arrives so they can see what they're up against."

Not an easy task, Ishiah knew, but if Zel was sure then Ishiah had to be too. He carefully put the arrow to the string of the bow, aimed, and let it fly. The arrow soared true, a flaming beacon in the bright spring afternoon air. Ishiah watched it, wanting to see it hit and light the bonfire, and gasped in alarm when the arrow suddenly turned ninety degrees and shot straight down to the ground.

"Damn, they're watching us," Zel hissed angrily. "Can you use your magic to get that fire lit? I want to see if I can spot where they're hiding."

Ishiah nodded, but aside from his hand still on Ishiah's shoulder, Zel wasn't paying attention to him. Ishiah closed his eyes to focus and breathed deeply just as he had taught himself.

Pull the energy from his head to his feet, then back up to his head, and out through his hands. He pointed his finger at the bonfire as he opened his eyes, willing the fire to light and burn brightly enough to summon the army. He had no doubts now that he had seen his arrow go down. They were under attack, and he needed to warn Monrath before it was too late.

With a bright flare of light, the bonfire lit, sending fire and smoke high into the sky before it settled down into a strong but calm fire. The relief of seeing the fire actually burning—and that it didn't suddenly go out with some other type of magic like his arrow had—was almost like a weight lifting off his shoulders. Monrath would be prepared. Now he just had to figure out how to make it possible for Monrath to actually see the enemy when the army arrived.

"Damn it, the watchers got away. Why is Faltiken magic so disgustingly slimy? I'm going to have to brush up on all my slime removal techniques for this fight."

Zel was muttering angrily under his breath when Ishiah looked away from the bonfire. His scowl was adorable and the way he was grumbling made Ishiah want to wrap a comforting arm over Zel's shoulder, but he knew there wasn't time for that now. The bonfire had been lit, and he had only seven days to figure the sparkly concealing spell out.

There was no question in Ishiah's mind now about using magic. He loved it and this time he was using it to potentially save his family. Yes, the consequences of what he would eventually have to endure were awful, but the benefits outweighed all of that. Ishiah left Zel to his angry muttering and headed downstairs.

For the first time since he had discovered the library, Ishiah headed to the far side where the advanced spell books were shelved. It only took a moment to find the labeled set of shelves for sight spells, and he took down a tall stack of books to start skimming through. He turned around to head to the sitting area and almost ran into Zel, who had somehow managed to silently sneak up on Ishiah.

"There are a number of different types of sight. You're looking for something called foresight, which is the ability to see things that are right before you, so through illusions and spells and whatnot. A book on farsight will be about seeing things that are far ahead in the future, so doesn't apply." He took the top book off the stack in Ishiah's arms and reshelved it.

As far as Ishiah knew foresight and farsight were synonyms. Apparently in magical terms they meant something different. He trusted Zel, though, so Ishiah put the stack down on the nearest table and quickly read the titles on the spines. Once he had removed all the ones that were blatantly not about the type of sight he was looking for, Ishiah took his smaller stack to the reading area. He would start by reading the indexing or chapter headings to find the sections that applied to him. Hopefully there would be techniques to hone his natural ability and spells to let him break through the Faltiken's concealment.

Zel sat down in the chair across from Ishiah with his own stack of books, and they started reading in companionable silence.

Chapter Five

"Now bring the magic to your eyes instead of your hands and hold it there," Zel instructed. His finger was on the crabbed handwriting of the journal he had found that explained the technique Ishiah needed to use, but his purple eyes were firmly focused on Ishiah. Ishiah was aware of that stare in every part of his being, but he pushed aside those feelings.

It had been five days and twelve hours since the bonfire had been lit. The monstrosity of a blaze had burned for two days before it ran out of fuel, and Ishiah was running out of time to have his explanation ready by the time the army arrived. All of his attention had to be focused on getting this technique right.

With his magic concentrated in his eyes, everything around him seemed to sparkle in the sunlight. There was magic in everything, and now he could see it flowing through the air and inhabiting everything in the tower. When he looked out the window, the entire field outside glowed.

"The book says you have to direct your magic through your eyes and toward the object you're trying to see. When the magic impacts the concealment spell, you need to forcefully push your magic through. Once you've broken through, the concealment spell should also break."

Zel put the book down on the kitchen table and focused on an apple sitting nearby. To Ishiah's magically enhanced sight, the apple seemed to sparkle like everything else in the tower, yet as Zel cast his magic, the sparkle became a glow similar to what Ishiah saw outside.

He had to send his magic out through his eyes instead of his fingers. Ishiah squinted and glared at the apple, trying to direct his magic that way.

"It's all about intent, remember," Zel said softly enough not to break Ishiah's concentration. "The action of pointing helps focus a normal spell, but the movement itself is irrelevant. You can do the same with your eyes without looking like your brain is trying not to explode."

Ishiah's concentration broke as he laughed, and he couldn't help grinning at Zel, who grinned sheepishly back.

This time when he looked at the apple it was somehow easier. Magic didn't go down his arms because that was the only way to cast a spell—Zel hadn't moved any part of his body to cast the concealing spell on the apple—it was just a prop to teach beginners. The magic probably didn't have to come out his eyes either. The idea of it coming from his eyes helped shape the intent. All Ishiah wanted was to see the apple fully.

Magic went from his head, down to his feet, and back to his head, and he used that momentum to keep the magic moving, exploding from his body like an arrow shot from a bow. The apple rocked on the table, the glow gone.

"You did it!" Zel crowed happily. He jumped from his seat and rushed over to Ishiah to throw his arms around Ishiah's shoulders and squeeze him tight. "A little too strong for the spell I used, but probably not quite strong enough for the spell outside. Try again." Zel fell silent and a moment later the apple was glowing again.

Ishiah breathed in and then out, sending his magic through his body with his breath. On the exhale the apple shot off the table and hit the wall with a thud. Zel cheered and his arms squeezed tighter. Ishiah turned his head to look at Zel just as Zel was leaning closer to say something. Their noses brushed and their eyes caught. Both of them froze in place, and Ishiah stared helplessly into Zel's bright purple eyes, utterly mesmerized by their beauty and by the emotion—the want—he could see there.

There was no way to know who moved first, but their noses shifted apart so their lips could press together. Ishiah had a fleeting taste of strawberries and cream before a voice yelled up through the always-open window.

"Forward scouts reporting!"

Ishiah pulled away from Zel reluctantly, but he knew he had to get to the window before the scouts called for him again. Once he was away from Zel's arms, Ishiah hurried to the window and stuck his head outside.

The scouting group had seven members. Two were looking up the tower at him while the other five were ranged in a semicircle behind them, looking outwards. Those five also looked curious. From their vantage, they could see enough of the fields of Faltiken to know it was empty.

"Tell them you'll be right there," Zel called. Ishiah obeyed, then pulled his head back inside. "We shouldn't yell everything we know down to them; there's no telling who's out there to overhear. Come on. We'll go the fast way." Zel led the way down the stairs into the workroom, and Ishiah followed him over to a blank area of wall. Zel flung his hand at the wall and then reached back to grip Ishiah's wrist. "The spell isn't keyed to you, so you'll have to stay close to me. Just keep walking and you'll be fine."

Zel stepped forward and through the wall, pulling Ishiah after him. Despite seeing Zel go through what looked like solid stone, Ishiah still couldn't help flinching away from the wall even as he was drawn into it, but he went through without any resistance. Ishiah found himself in a room so dark he couldn't see his hand even as he was tugged by it into a fast walk.

After a few seconds, Ishiah thought he could see a bare glimmer of light, and that glimmer grew the farther he walked until suddenly he was outside, striding along the grass at the foot of the tower toward the waiting group of scouts, all of whom jumped, gasped, or startled in some way when they caught sight of him and Zel.

"How..." one of the scouts murmured, but she shut up when the leader in the center of the group shot her a stern look.

"First Lieutenant"—the man said with a brief salute that Ishiah belatedly returned—"we're here for your initial report." Ishiah could see the man struggle not to give in to curiosity and look over at Zel. The rest of the scouts weren't so disciplined; one of them was openly staring at Zel's purple hair with his mouth hanging slightly open.

"This is Wizard Rap. I accidentally activated one of his personal beacons in the tower, and he came to investigate. We learned the Faltikens are using some sort of concealment spell on the field. We're working on breaking through it so we can see what we're dealing with, but it was prudent to light the bonfire just in case."

From the way the scout's eyes shifted slightly to the side to look at the visibly empty field just down the mountain, Ishiah could tell the scout didn't quite believe him. Still, the man saluted again.

"We'll return to the main army to make your report," the scout replied. Ishiah returned the salute, then watched as the group turned and headed back down the mountain.

As much as Ishiah wanted to lie down and luxuriate in the grass and the fresh smells of budding spring, he had a task to accomplish. After his fantastical sounding report and the skepticism he had seen, it had become all the more important that he be able to reveal the enemy by the time the army arrived.

Ishiah headed back to the secret passage, Zel in tow, so he could return to practicing.

*

It was possible to see Monrath's forces marching up the mountain range even from the awkward angle of the tower window. Their armor gleamed silver against the overhead sun, flashing brilliantly whenever Ishiah looked in their direction. Given the bonfire's lighting, the element of surprise on Monrath's side had long been lost, so it didn't matter Faltiken could definitely also see them coming. It still made Ishiah nervous—he expected an attack to come before Monrath could take the heights of the mountain range—but Faltiken remained hidden behind their spell.

Exactly two days after the scouting party had left, the army reached the foot of the tower. Only the command tents were set up in the grass around the tower—the rest of the army had found spots farther away—and Ishiah could see his brother's flag raised below. Of course Haines would have to come. As the crown prince who would probably be king in the next year or so, since Ishiah had heard their father was ill again, Haines needed to prove himself as a leader of men and women. In particular, the support of the military would help cement him as the next king.

And if Haines's bastard brother lit the bonfire and brought the army all the way out to the tower for no reason, that support would erode very quickly.

Ishiah let out a heavy breath.

"You've got the power figured out. I don't doubt you'll be able to do this." Zel's warm hand rested on Ishiah's shoulder and squeezed. "Prepare yourself. I'll bring your brother and the generals up to see." He squeezed one more time, then left Ishiah alone in the window.

Fifteen minutes later and the tower suddenly held more people than had probably ever been inside at one time. Ishiah could hear the angry grumbling at Zel from downstairs, mixed with the noise of soldiers who were shocked to see the second floor of the tower that they hadn't known existed. Haines came over to Ishiah and the window first.

"What's going on, Ish?" Haines asked. His voice was steady, but there were white lines of tension bracketing his mouth.

"Magic," Ishiah replied shortly. "Watch." He breathed in and out twice, trying to steady himself, and then called on his magic. It flowed from his head to his feet, back to his head, and then out his eyes. He pushed the magic forward and could almost see a sparkling stream of magic heading toward the glowing field below. He gathered more and more magic, flinging it from his head to his feet and back before adding it to the stream heading toward the field.

Ishiah felt the impact when his magic hit the shield. He staggered, but once he caught his balance again, he stepped back to the window, using his steps to thrust his magic forward. He formed a lance with the magic, the tip as sharp as any spear, and sliced and jabbed. Slowly, ever so slowly, he chipped away at the concealment magic.

At first, he could sense Haines's exasperation with him, and Ishiah could understand why. Magic was a lost art. The idea that Ishiah had stumbled on magic and had been able to learn it in so short a time was slightly ridiculous. Ishiah certainly wouldn't have believed that possible on the day he had first climbed the rope to get into the tower. Zel had also told him that his eyes didn't glow when he was using sight magic, which was probably because it was inherent.

It was easy to tell when his magic began to have an effect. The air of skepticism in the room vanished, and suddenly people needing to see what he was revealing surrounded Ishiah in the window.

He could see the effect his magic was having better than the rest. As the shield cracked under his onslaught, a hazy, wavering image began to fill the previously empty field. Two very large lumps filled the center of the field, and surrounding them were what his army-trained eye picked out as soldiers standing in their regiments.

The rest of the concealing magic slowly drifted away like fog on a misty morning, finally revealing what Ishiah knew had been hiding for a week or more.

The two large lumps in the center were humanoid in shape—men sitting on the ground with their two arms resting on the knees of their two legs—yet their size was easily that of any of the massive boulders that dotted the mountainous landscape around the tower. Ishiah could see a formation for at least two divisions of soldiers surrounding the giant men in the center, so about fifty thousand men were visible. Given he couldn't see any more sparkles or magical glowing, Ishiah was fairly certain no one else was hiding out there.

"We can handle two divisions." Haines had been taught to count formations just as Ishiah had, but his voice still sounded hesitant.

"Those are trolls," Zel said, predictably filling the silence. "Their skin is thick hide impervious to most weapons. By themselves they're not dangerous, but they're extremely susceptible to coercion spells, something for which Faltiken's corrupted magic has always been used. When directed, their immense strength can bring down an entire brigade in only a few minutes."

"How do we defeat them?" General Darien cut in.

"You won't be able to," Zel replied with a frown toward the window. "You have to find the wizards controlling them instead. I'll focus on that. Ish, you'll need to help combat any additional wizards Faltiken might have in that field. Keep their spells off your army while I distract the trolls."

"Begin your final preparations, soldiers," General Darien said to everyone in the room. "We attack in exactly one hour." He strode back into the library and the staircase that led below, quickly followed by the rest of the men and women Zel had guided into the tower. Zel hurried after them to show them the magical exit. Ishiah looked out at the now-filled field, wondering just how much death and destruction a magically coerced troll was capable of.

Chapter Six

Exactly an hour later, a threatening roar sounded from below, echoing through the mountain peaks. Swords pounded against shields, gauntleted feet stomped against stone, and horses shrieked and whinnied as the forces of Monrath psyched themselves up for the coming battle.

Ishiah, alone in the tower yet again, watched it all from above. The trolls didn't react, but after a few moments of the screaming, they lumbered to their feet and towered over the mountain. The Faltiken soldiers roared back, but they didn't draw their weapons or start marching forward. They were going to rely on the trolls for their attack. The soldiers were probably there for an invasion force after the trolls took care of Monrath's army.

Where were the wizards hiding? Ishiah sent more magic to his eyes so he could scan the Faltikens as he had been doing for the last hour. No one glowed or sparkled under his sight.

Monrath's army began to march down the mountain, and the forcible pounding of thousands of feet shook the ground until, as they picked up speed, they lost synchronization and the thudding beat faded away.

One of the trolls tried to respond. He lifted one leg as if he were about to stride forward toward the approaching army, and his toes smacked into an invisible wall. The troll hopped awkwardly backward on one foot, the other clutched in his hands as he whined at the pain of stubbed toes, and out of the corner of Ishiah's eye he finally saw a flash of light.

He turned his head to look, focusing the magic in his eyes to let him see the distance and...there! A woman had her hands raised and pointed toward the troll as magic formed between her palms in some sort of spell that Ishiah didn't doubt would do a number on Zel's shield.

Magic zinged down from Ishiah's head, back up from his feet, and out the finger he pointed at the woman. The spell was only half-formed, built more of intent than finesse—a battering ram instead of a rapier—but it did the job. The spell hit the woman, sending her flying off her feet. She landed in a crumpled heap on the ground, and the spell she had been forming dissipated in a shower of sparks. The woman didn't get up again.

Ishiah turned away, searching for someone else using magic. A second shower of sparks from the far side of the trolls told Ishiah that Zel had found one too.

The troll finally recovered, and he moved forward more delicately this time. His hands reached out until the palms rested on what appeared to be a flat surface. He dug his feet into the ground and started to push. There was no way Zel could hold that shield spell up under that sort of onslaught.

Monrath's army finally reached the foot of the mountain and the grassy field. Archers still high in the mountains let their arrows fly as the horses, which were finally on flat ground, lengthened their stride into a proper charge. The trolls hadn't started moving. The first was still fighting against the shield, but the second was looking around blearily, as if not sure why he was there and what he was supposed to do about it. Either Zel had already found the wizard controlling him, or because it took so much power to get the first troll to fight the shield, the coercion spell on the second troll had lapsed. Which meant Ishiah needed to find another wizard to neutralize before they realized what was happening.

A flash of light to the left made Ishiah turn to look, but it was only the glare of sunlight on a sword being drawn as the Faltiken soldiers realized their trolls would not be able to keep the fighting away from them. Ishiah kept scanning. He happened to notice an arrow flying through the air suddenly hit another invisible wall and fall to the ground. The person the arrow was aimed toward wasn't looking at the front lines where the fighting had already begun, but was instead glaring at the troll.

Ishiah formed his magic into a sharp point just as he had done to bring the large shield down and started chipping away. Apparently personal shields were easier because this one vanished within a few seconds. Ishiah thrust his magic forward, only to bounce back as he hit a second shield.

The wizard was looking around frantically, his attention completely diverted from the troll, and Ishiah knew he had to get the second shield down before the wizard could put up a third and fourth. Ishiah bore down with his magic, pushing against the shield like a drill. It cracked and he was through, only to hit a third shield, which only took half a second to crack. The wizard was tiring. Ishiah gathered more magic quickly, but before he could, a barrage of arrows came in and soldiers fell to the ground screaming. An arrow took the wizard in the throat and he collapsed to the ground.

Ishiah turned away from the grizzly sight. This wasn't his first battle—he had seen and given death to his enemies before—but it was never a pleasant task.

The magic was sluggish to his call as Ishiah started to look for his next target, and he realized he was tiring too. His body was hanging on the large windowsill of the tower because his legs didn't have the strength to keep him upright, and he was panting desperately for breath.

Still, this was war. As long as the magic still came when he called, he would keep fighting with it.

With a sudden pop that Ishiah could hear as well as feel as the percussive force bounced off his chest, even from so far away, the shield holding the troll vanished. The troll toppled forward as the resistance he had been pushing against disappeared under his hands. His arms windmilled for a brief moment, but he couldn't catch his balance. He hit the ground with a thud that shook the mountains. His chest still rose and fell, but the troll didn't move.

Had it been knocked unconscious by the fall? Ishiah couldn't tell from his vantage, but he thought that was a good guess. The second troll turned to look and blinked for a few seconds before understanding filled his dull eyes. One hand lifted into the air, waving around his head like he was trying to ward off flies. Ishiah thought it was probably a renewed coercion spell he was trying to ward off. Before it could take hold, the troll turned and ran, heading back into the depths of Faltiken and completely not noticing the soldiers he squished under his feet as he went.

Having the trolls out of commission was all Monrath needed from there. The air seemed to go out of the Faltikens' sails as it only took a mere hour before they had either been killed or surrendered. Ishiah sent spears of magic out whenever he thought he saw a wizard, but each attempt made it harder and harder to call on more magic. He had to use what little he had left sparingly, and by the time the cheer of victory went up, he was completely tapped out.

Zel found him collapsed underneath the window sometime later, and Ishiah vaguely felt himself be put to bed, and then he knew no more.

*

"What do you want to do, Ish?" Haines asked. Only General Darien was left in the tower at this point; Zel was escorting the last of the army officers out of the tower so they could begin the process of marching their men and their prisoners back to the capital for the start of peace negotiations.

"You have certainly earned the right to end the Rapunzel Posting early," General Darien added. "I have no problem with leaving one of my men for the two weeks it would take to send someone new here."

Ishiah did want to go home, of course. He wanted to see his niece and to not be alone in this blasted tower, yet he wasn't really alone any longer. With Zel here and with the excitement of magic at his fingertips, was the tower really that bad? Ishiah already knew he couldn't stay in Monrath for much longer. He wasn't going to stop using magic—he couldn't, if he understood what Zel had tried to explain—and he therefore wasn't going to age. Besides, all the spell books and the workroom for learning more magic were right in the tower. It made sense to stay here.

"I signed up for the full seven years, seven months, and seven days," Ishiah replied to them both. "Besides," he added as he remembered the real reason he had been sent to the tower in the first place, "the malcontents in your court don't need me around."

"Please," Haines scoffed. "I'm returning at the head of the forces that defeated the mindless hoard of the Faltiken Army. No one will have the political clout to go against me for the next ten years, at least. Come home or don't come home. This time it really is completely up to you, Ish."

Zel emerged from the library and joined them around the kitchen table. He stood just a little too closely to Ishiah, and the smile he gave Ishiah was genuinely happy.

"I'll stay," Ishiah said firmly.

Haines glanced quickly from Ishiah to Zel and back, and a small grin lifted the corners of his mouth. "Of course," he said. "I'll let Victoria know. Make sure you write if you need anything."

"You know I will."

Haines stood and General Darien pushed away from the wall he had been leaning against. "If you would show us the way out, we'll leave you in peace."

Zel nodded and led the way back into the library with Haines and Darien following behind.

This time when Zel returned the tower was blissfully quiet. Ishiah was still sitting in the second chair at the table. He was unsure if his legs would allow him to get up and crawl back into bed. Zel told him he had slept for an entire day after the battle thanks to his magic exhaustion, and he had needed Zel's help to get to the table in order to look at least somewhat presentable for the meeting that had finally ended.

"Come on, Ish," Zel said with a laugh as he gripped Ishiah's arm to help lever him to his feet. "Back to bed. I'm sorry I didn't warn you this could happen."

Ishiah stumbled to his feet and shamelessly leaned on Zel as they made their way the short distance to the bed. Zel gently dropped him down onto the mattress and then helped get Ishiah under the covers.

"Stay?" Ishiah asked, one hand reaching out to grip Zel's wrist.

The smile Zel gave Ishiah this time was wider and full of the promise of all the wonderful things they could do in the bed together. Ishiah wanted to smile back in the exact same way, but he was just too damned tired.

The smile didn't fade so much as Zel simply put it away to use later. He flipped the covers back and crawled in so his body was pressed against Ishiah's in all the best ways. The warmth of Zel's body and the comfort as his arms came to rest around Ishiah had Ishiah letting out a happy sigh. He drifted off to sleep knowing that not only would Zel still be there when he woke, but the promise of that wonderful, lascivious smile would be there too.

Epilogue

"And so, First Lieutenant Ishiah Fitzsimons from his posting in the Rapunzel Tower was able to discern the clever camouflage the mindless hoard had employed. He revealed the subterfuge to the Monrath Army as they arrived, and the battle was begun."

Ishiah closed the book he was reading and shelved it before looking up at Zel, who was kneeling over the closed trapdoor. There was a slight glow to the area to Ishiah's magical sight, but his regular sight only saw a stone floor. The trapdoor was gone. Zel stood and kicked at the rug so it unrolled to conceal the floor again.

"I'm amazed how quickly they've forgotten the magic," Zel said as he brushed off his knees. "The spell is supposed to do that, but it usually takes more than just a few years. Maybe it exerted extra influence because the war was being recorded in a history book that would be shared for generations to come. I wonder what they changed the trolls to?"

He didn't ask Ishiah to pull the book out again. They were heading to Ishiah's home for a few months first anyway so Ishiah could see his family and resign his commission, and Ishiah was certain he would hear the tale of his supposed exploits a few dozen times. He didn't doubt that at the end of the visit he would be extremely eager to embark on his and Zel's plan to explore the world so Ishiah could get experience with all the different types of magic the world could offer.

It was going to be a lot of fun, especially with Zel at his side.

"Rapunzel, Rapunzel, let down your hair!"

That had to be the most welcome sound Ishiah had ever heard. He hurried over to the window and stuck his head out to see who was there. The usual cadre of guards were arrayed below, but there was one empty horse and a young man—most likely Ishiah's replacement—was climbing off another horse.

Ishiah pulled himself back inside and bent to throw the rope out the window. When the young man started climbing, Ishiah started pulling the rope up to help him, just as he had been helped his first day.

"Haines remembered you, at least," Ishiah explained to Zel. "He sent an extra horse."

"He could hardly forget about me, what with you writing your letters from the both of us these last few years," Zel replied with an easy grin. He was waiting by their bundled belongings, out of the way of the now-exhausted man Ishiah helped through the window.

Ishiah sent the rope back down so the soldiers could hook the basket filled with Ishiah's replacement's belongings and started explaining everything the man needed to know about his new job. It was weird hearing the same words he had been told on his first day come out of his mouth, but it was nice to pass on everything he had learned. Hopefully the man was listening.

The young man looked completely overwhelmed, much as Ishiah must have looked back then, but unlike Ishiah, this man had definitely volunteered for the post. Ishiah continued explaining as he pulled the man's belongings inside. He gently dumped the basket and helped Zel fill it with their things, before heaving the basket back outside to lower it. Zel followed after the basket, climbing down with the aid of some magic. Once Zel was on the ground, Ishiah turned to the young man.

"Do you have any questions?" he asked.

The man looked around and then glanced at Ishiah impatiently. He clearly wanted Ishiah gone so he could start his assignment. Ishiah knew it wouldn't take long before he would regret not getting another five minutes of human contact, but for now Ishiah sat on the windowsill and swung his legs around. He grabbed the rope and started climbing.

After exactly seven years, seven months, and seven days—give or take a few hours—Ishiah swung himself up into the saddle of the waiting horse. Zel walked his horse forward until he was next to Ishiah. They shared a smile, and Ishiah signaled for his horse to start heading deeper into the mountains and home into Monrath.

He didn't bother looking back at the tower that had changed his life. His life was ahead, with Zel and a bit of magic.

CLEANLY WRONG

"Wrong! Wrong! Wrong again!" the other kids cheered gleefully. Rung didn't have to fight against a pout; he was used to this happening and could keep his own disappointment and sadness off his face from long practice.

"Wrong," Teacher Broom said disapprovingly. Rung hated when Broom called him Wrong. The other kids at the orphanage had perfectly good shortened names like Thimble or Dustbin. Rung's name was Ladder Rung, Rung for short, but the nickname Wrong had stuck so firmly Rung sometimes wondered if his teachers even knew his real name anymore.

"This is simply unacceptable," Broom continued, scrunching his nose and smartly groomed whiskers in unhappiness. Rung hung his head as he was supposed to while being chastised. He wished the other kids would stop giggling at his continual misfortune. "The eighth time you've taken this simple test and the room simply isn't clean, Wrong!"

Rung looked forlornly at the room he had spent the past three hours of the test cleaning. The test bedrooms in this wing of the orphanage were specifically mussed so the students could practice their hands at cleaning. Rung had swept and tidied until the place shone, and he had hidden himself perfectly whenever an instructor came into the room. Yet when it came down to the little things, he was always wrong. The books on the waist-high bookshelf were not in alphabetical order, nor had he color-coded them. Rather, Rung thought it more prudent to put the ones with the creased spines, obviously read much more often, on the top shelf within easy reach. The books that still smelled like the press they had recently come off were also put on the top shelf, because, clearly, the owner would want to find the new reads with ease.

Rung knew what his instructors wanted: alphabetical organization by author, genre, and if possible, cover color. Unfortunately, Rung couldn't do it. He tried, test after test, but that bookshelf always ended up his way. He couldn't manage to do it the way the teacher wanted no matter how much he attempted to organize the damned shelf. He couldn't help it!

"And the desk!" Broom went on as Rung picked up on the next bit of the teacher's rant. "How could you leave that stack of papers in such disarray?" Broom sighed. "Wrong, you are to go to your bed and contemplate what you have done wrong. Do not bother coming to dinner."

"Yes, sir," Rung said softly, knowing he had already missed lunch for another fault during class that day. Breakfast was a long time away.

Rung rounded his shoulders and walked through the crowd of students who had gleefully watched his punishment session. He ignored the jeers with long practice and managed not to gasp in pain when Needle shoved him into the wall on his way past.

The room where he slept housed six of the boys around the age of eighteen, and Rung was relieved none of them were present when he pushed open the door. He noticed his blanket was missing again when he walked past his bed on the way to the full-length mirror across the room to look at the new bruise forming on his shoulder. Needle's shoves were never soft, and Rung hadn't been braced this time.

The bruise was purpling, but it wouldn't be too bad. The mirror gave him an unvarnished image that Rung tried to overlook as he inspected his shoulder.

Brownies were relatively short creatures, the tallest topping five feet if they were unlucky. Being small meant it was easier to hide when the owner of the home they were cleaning unexpectedly entered the room they were in. Brownies were short and skinny. Rung was skinny, certainly, but he had gained bulk that sat on his shoulders despite always going hungry, and he was around five feet six inches in height.

Brownies had a layer of short fur covering their entire bodies. The fur was always some sort of shade of brown that would camouflage them well against the wooden walls of the majority of the homes they serviced. Rung's fur was a light tan color, not brown at all. He was human-colored, as Needle had so kindly pointed out when they had first seen pictures of the creatures who owned the houses that someday all good brownies would serve.

They had all declared that his father must have been human, which was something truly terrible, for it meant the human Rung's mother was serving had seen her—a mother who had died not long after Rung's birth. Parents were supposed to teach their children how to clean properly. When a brownie did not have parents, he or she was sent to the Orphanage for Cleanliness and Deportment, where the teachers would make the orphaned brownies into productive members of society.

And that, perhaps, was what was so wrong with Rung. He would never be a productive member of society if he couldn't learn to clean correctly.

Rung sighed and turned away from the mirror. If he went to sleep, he wouldn't think about his growling stomach. Also, if he was asleep by the time the rest of his roommates returned from dinner, they might give him his blanket back when they saw he wasn't available for whatever torture they had thought up this time.

Rung curled up in bed, hoping to quiet his empty stomach, and sighed. He would have to try harder to satisfy his instructors, but that could wait until the morning.

*

Rung woke, still hungry, and with the knowledge that the room was also empty. No one had bothered to wake him for breakfast, but Rung hoped there would still be some porridge left if he hurried.

He made it down to the dining hall without being seen—he had eagerly learned that lesson taught to all the students—and snuck into the dining hall to get his breakfast. That day Rung was lucky: not only was there porridge, but there was still a scone left too.

Rung took his bounty to a corner table, keeping his head down as he went. If he were shorter, he could blend in better, but Rung had found that if he pretended not to exist he could still avoid a good deal of trouble.

"Another one?" someone gasped at a table as Rung passed by. "How horrible! To be thanked!"

"An edict," Broom was saying as Rung brushed past the teacher's table. "The prince will have no more brownies in his castle."

"Six of us he's disgraced, the poor thing," Rung's orderliness teacher, Tea Cup, continued. "If he keeps thanking us, there will be no one left to clean for him!"

"You don't understand, Tea Cup," the first teacher said earnestly. "The edict states that brownies are not allowed to clean the castle ever again. Prince Lionel will thank anyone who comes within his halls as a matter of course."

"No!" Tea Cup gasped. "That poor boy!"

Rung moved out of earshot and found a place where he could enjoy his scone and porridge. He had just put his spoon down in his empty bowl when Needle found him.

"So, Wrong," Needle said with a cruel laugh, "have you heard?"

"Heard what?" Rung asked quietly.

"You've failed the test eight times. Once or twice, sure; that's happened before. But eight? You'll be tossed out!" he crowed. "But the teachers here can't send out a brownie who can't properly clean. I bet they'll kill you instead." Needle's cold smile agreed with his words. He had passed every test with flying colors and was still at the school to get preferential training so he could serve someone of importance. Needle would probably replace an aging brownie at a lord's manor when he graduated.

"How can you know that?" Rung asked, afraid Needle might have been telling the truth rather than pulling a cruel prank.

"I asked," Needle said, his tone saying he thought Rung was stupid for not knowing. Needle put on an innocent face before continuing. "'Teacher Broom, what will happen to that poor Wrong? Someone should help him!'

"'I don't know if that is possible at this point,'" Needle continued in a deeper voice that imitated Broom's perfectly. "'Wrong's clearly not teachable. He can't stay here and take up space another orphan needs, but we certainly can't send him out into society.'"

Needle's voice switched back to his own faux innocent one. "'But what will happen to him?'"

"'Imprisonment, certainly. He can't be allowed to roam as he is: an embarrassment to brownie society.'" Teacher Broom's voice came through despite Needle's malicious smile. "'Or worse, if the Council decides it would be too much hassle to care for him indefinitely, he'll face death.'"

Needle's evil grin didn't fade as he loomed over Rung.

"Thanks for the warning," Rung said softly as he looked into his empty bowl sadly. It was all over now. He would never be allowed to clean again.

"Then what are you still doing here?" Needle asked with what seemed like genuine curiosity in his voice. "Run away before they catch you!"

Rung glanced at Needle, who looked confused. "I guess," Rung said softly. It might be better to leave now than to be locked up and never allowed to clean again.

"Your blanket is under my bed. Go get it, and I'll get you some food from the kitchens. Let's meet by the garden door in five minutes," Needle said helpfully.

"O-okay," Rung agreed, and he stood to return his bowl and go find his blanket.

Needle was waiting by the garden door with a small bundle in his hands when Rung got there with his blanket, his few personal items, and a change of clothes.

"Here," Needle said as he thrust the bundle of food into Rung's hands.

"Thank you," Rung replied. He pushed the door open and stepped out into the world, knowing he had to hide quickly because the instructors would be looking for him when they realized he wasn't in his first lesson.

*

A week in the real world, and Rung was hungry, cold, and tired. He knew he would be found if he settled into a house, so he had been traveling nonstop the entire time. Being on his own like this was frightening, but it was also somewhat exhilarating. Still, Rung knew he had to keep moving in order to find somewhere to keep properly hidden. His goal was to make it to a city. He had been told often enough how human he looked. If he could blend in with the humans, no one from the orphanage would be able to find him.

Rung stared up at the huge wall and the open gates that led into the first city he found on his journey. A brownie's initial inclination was to hide from humans, but Rung was about to boldly walk into their city.

He took a deep breath, steeled his nerve, and stepped forward. That step was followed by another step as his feet brought him into the crowd of humans and through the massive gates.

A guard was stopping people at random while they passed and asking them questions. Rung hunched his shoulders and pretended he didn't exist when he walked past. It didn't work this time.

"Hey, boy!" the guard called. "I just have to ask you some questions before I can let you in."

Rung froze and slowly turned toward the guard.

"You're looking for work, then?" the guard asked, not unkindly.

Rung nodded.

"Hng," the guard grunted. "Well, you're not the first one I've seen today. I'll give you the same advice I gave the rest of them, yeah? The castle stable and kitchens are looking to hire some boys about your age. Go on up there for work. And don't be causing a mess in the city, boy," the guard admonished. "Thieves are not welcome in the capital, yeah?"

"Thanks," Rung whispered as he turned away to walk in the direction the guard was pointing.

The castle was perfect! The teachers had been talking about some edict against brownies in the castle. Surely they would think that even Rung wasn't so stupid as to break that edict. If he could stay hidden in the huge building, which he could see on the horizon on the other side of the city, Rung could stay there forever without worry of the orphanage finding him!

Rung went toward the giant stone edifice on the top of the hill and, instead of following the humans inside, found his own way into the building.

*

Rung liked the basement he had found and made his home. There were a lot of basements in the castle; every time a new addition to the gigantic building had been built, a new basement had been put in too. Rung's basement was in one of the oldest sections of the castle. When he found the area, it was filled with cobwebs and had a rank smell of disuse about it. Rung fixed that and made himself a comfortable living area. All he had to do was sneak into the kitchens every few days for food.

Rung was somehow even able to keep his need to clean and organize at bay whenever he was sneaking about. Initially, he had spent days cleaning his new home and doing it in such a way that a human would not notice the changes unless he or she walked all the way into Rung's basement. He had then occupied himself with making new furniture. If his wooden bed and side table were more ornately carved than any other bed in the castle, at least the time spent smoothing the wood into exotic shapes had helped keep Rung from reorganizing the spice rack in the kitchens whenever he ran out of food.

And the best part was that Rung was never wrong in his own home. His blankets were tucked into his bed based on comfort. The soft wool blanket in which he enjoyed curling up at night was first rather than a top sheet as he had been taught at the orphanage. Rung didn't even need to organize his food stores alphabetically or by color and size.

It was wonderful and freeing to finally be able to live as he wanted. Rung very firmly ignored the fact that he was lonely, and that the knife rack should really have the bread knives closer to the cutting board and the paring knives closer to the sink so that the poor chef and his assistants would stop blindly grabbing for the wrong knife when they were cooking.

Rung had escaped to the castle to find a safe haven, not to clean. If he cleaned and was discovered, bringing further shame to his race, he would be tried and executed. So Rung forced himself to ignore the knives. He tried to find something new to dust or carve for his home instead.

Ultimately, he knew he would fail. He was still a brownie after all, even if he was Wrong.

The day came when he was sneaking through the kitchens. He walked past the balding chef mixing some sort of marinade for the night's dinner and into the pantry. Rung loaded a day-old piece of bread into his recently woven basket, added some smoked meat, and wished he had a way to keep milk or eggs fresh as he bypassed the cooler.

Once he had taken all he dared, Rung retraced his path out of the kitchen. One of the assistants was cleaning chicken at the sink; the meat was probably going to be paired with the marinade the chef was finishing up. The assistant cleaned either a leg or thigh in the water flowing from the pump and took a knife to remove fat and excess feathers.

As Rung watched, the knife the assistant was using fell to the floor. With a curse, the young man tossed the dirtied knife onto a counter and reached for a new one. Only the knives weren't organized the way they should have been.

The bread knife was sharp and serrated and in the wrong spot. The assistant wouldn't lose his finger, but even stitches and time to heal would not be enough to repair the damage. As blood splattered onto the cleaned bird and the assistant cried out in pain, Rung ran from the room.

He could keep himself to out-of-the-way places, like the kitchen, unused guest rooms, and other disused basements, Rung thought to himself as he rushed back to his basement. He wouldn't anger anyone if he stayed in those places where he wouldn't be noticed.

Resolute in what he would be doing in the morning, Rung put away his food and got into bed. That knife rack would be organized, perfectly, so no one else would ever cut themselves by accident again.

*

The Lord Seneschal asked the Lord Steward to stay behind after their weekly organizational meeting. Once the room emptied, the Lord Seneschal pulled the other man into a quiet corner away from where a passerby could overhear.

"There's a brownie in the castle, Rufus," the seneschal, Gerald, murmured quietly.

"I've been wondering, Gerald. All the wool and wood going missing, it couldn't be anything else," Rufus, the steward, replied in an equally soft voice. "Weird sort of brownie though. Within the first day, the last one got into all my papers and began organizing them by date until I couldn't find a single one. The wool went missing weeks ago."

Gerald nodded. "This one's keeping to itself for some reason. Hasn't caused any ruckus with its cleaning yet. I've had reports that some things have been moved around the kitchen. After that poor boy cut his finger, the knife rack was put to rights. The chef swears by how it's been organized."

"No!" Rufus gasped. "The last brownie organized them by size and sharpened all the knives that are purposefully kept somewhat dull for different types of cooking. The chef would have killed the creature if he had gotten his hands on it. Maybe it isn't a brownie, especially since the chef actually likes something that's been done."

Gerald shook his head. "It's a brownie. Go into the green guest wing, and you'll have no doubt."

"The wing that was put into disuse when we had to fire most of the maid staff for stealing? No one's been in there for over a year!"

"And that is what's so peculiar. This brownie clearly has the same need to clean as all of its kind, but it's really trying to be helpful and stay out of the way." Gerald sighed and ran a hand through his graying hair. "And what is more perplexing is that a brownie would dare come to the castle after the edict."

"The poor thing must be hiding from something," Rufus said with a sharp nod. "Why else would it not advertise that it's here by cleaning everything in sight? So do we tell Prince Lionel his edict's been broken?"

Gerald shook his head. "The creature isn't causing any harm, and after what he did to clean the green rooms, I'm inclined to let him stay. As long as he does nothing to alert Prince Lionel that he's here, I think we should just ignore him."

Rufus looked relieved. "I was hoping you would say that. My wife just got this wonderful new blanket from somewhere—she won't say where—that keeps her warm enough at night that she doesn't wake with aches in her legs. With all the evidence of a brownie...well, the creature made my wife complain less!"

The Lord Seneschal echoed the Lord Steward's laughter as they left the room to go back to their duties.

*

Rung's nose twitched as he held back a sneeze through sheer force. He had found a set of secret passages two days ago that had fallen into such disrepair that Rung knew no one would ever notice his presence. The only issue was that the main passage ran along a set of bedrooms, and the human occupants would easily overhear any loud noise he made.

The urge to sneeze passed, so Rung returned to his careful sweeping. He would finish clearing the layer of dust and cobwebs from the passage this afternoon, and tonight, after his dinner, he would sneak to the well to draw water for mopping.

Rung gathered another five feet of dust into a pile, uncovering a wood floor in desperate need of polishing—another job he was looking forward to—when he heard the sound of someone swearing in one of the bedrooms up ahead. Rung abandoned his broom and crept forward. He found one of the spy holes in the wall and uncovered it slowly to mitigate any squeaks. He hadn't yet had the chance to oil any of the spy holes or secret doorways, but he would. Rung pressed an eye to the hole and glanced into what looked to be an office. He must have reached an area of the castle that had suites of rooms.

There was a young man inside the room rifling through a desk so covered in papers that it didn't surprise Rung to see him having such difficulty finding whatever document he was searching for. The man looked to be about Rung's age, but he was considerably taller, as well as fully human, with shoulder-length brown hair and finely tailored clothes. He was someone of high station to have such a nice suite of rooms and fine clothing, but Rung couldn't understand why the place was such a mess! The papers on the desk were the least of the issues: there were books scattered across the floor, clothes in need of washing or ironing in random piles, and a general sense of untidiness about the room. Why clothing was even in the office Rung would never understand, but he assumed the bedroom and dressing room would no doubt be in equally disgraceful shape.

The man swore again, louder this time, and Rung winced when he saw that a hidden inkbottle had been accidentally tipped over. The cap had clearly not been properly fastened, and ink was slowly leaking onto the many piles of papers.

The man threw his hands into the air in exasperation. "I give up!" he growled. "The report clearly doesn't exist. The captain will have to rewrite it for me."

The man stomped out of the room, slamming the door and leaving behind a desk dripping ink onto the floor. Rung took one look at the mess and swallowed. He wanted so badly to fix it, but he knew he shouldn't. He was only allowed to hide in unused passageways and clean unused rooms. Cleaning this man's things was completely against the rules Rung had set for himself. Yet he couldn't look away from the dripping ink slowly staining the carpet an ugly black.

Maybe he could just take a quick peek, see that the mess really wasn't so bad. Once he knew his touch wasn't needed, Rung could back away and leave the mess for someone else to clean.

With that thought firmly in the forefront of Rung's mind, he made his way to the secret entrance that led into the office. A panel next to the fireplace popped open with a squeak Rung couldn't suppress. He froze in the opening for a second, listening for the sounds of movement from outside the closed office door. He heard nothing.

First, before he even moved farther into the room, Rung investigated the secret doorway. A brownie always had to have an avenue of escape prepared ahead of time in case humans suddenly appeared. There was a simple design of vines and small flowers carved into the wood along the wall. Rung quickly found the latch hidden in one of the carved swirls. Pressing the latch would spring the door open, allowing Rung to escape to freedom swiftly.

With his escape route completed, Rung felt comfortable walking over to the desk. He walked around a pile of two, or maybe three—it was hard to tell pieces of clothing apart in the mess—sets of dirty riding leathers, a pile of clothes that still smelled like fresh laundry but was unfolded and wrinkled, and a pile of clothes that desperately needed washing. Each pile was carefully separated from the other. Even the books seemed to have been left around the room with a sense of organization: the ones closer to the desk had to do with matters of state, the ones left by the lone armchair beside the fire were pleasure reading, and the ones tossed near the doorway pertained to very specific subjects and had probably been used for research and left by the door with the intention of returning them to the library at some future point.

Rung reached the desk and glanced over the papers. He wasn't surprised to see that there was some organization on the desk as well. The papers pertaining to the castle itself were scattered across one corner while papers about laws and the running of the country covered the entire left side of the desk. International papers held court in the final corner, and in the center of the desk, all these careful piles had met and mixed. The ink had almost totally destroyed all the papers about the inner workings of the castle.

The carpet under the desk wasn't ruined yet, but it would be if left uncared for. Rung bent down and chanted a small cleaning spell over the area. It was just a little ditty they had taught at the orphanage that made stains easier to remove. It didn't replace good scrubbing, just made the effort needed a little less. Rung could return that night and still be able to remove the stain.

He could also do quite a lot to make the man's life a little easier. He wouldn't disrupt the organization style already in place, but if he added a bookshelf by the door for library books and built a small table with a bookshelf underneath to go with the armchair by the fire...well, the man wouldn't feel the need to leave his books all over the room. Plus, if Rung were to relocate the desk to the far corner of the room, he could put in two bookshelves along the walls behind the desk and tuck a small set of shelves directly into the corner to connect the bookshelves. That would open up the room considerably and remove the sense of untidiness Rung felt pervading the space.

It would have to be done quickly, in one swoop, but there was good wood on the woodpile right now. It could be done.

Rung bit his lip as he surveyed the room one last time before heading to the secret entrance. It was totally against the limits he had set for himself, but Rung couldn't just abandon the man living here to disaster.

He finished cleaning the secret passage over the next few days. Rung spent a good bit of time with his eye pressed to the peeking hole of the messy office while he worked. The man would spend hours meticulously reorganizing the layer of papers on his desk only to knock one stack over in his haste to grab something later in the day. Nothing ever really seemed to be accomplished either, since any papers he wrote on inevitably burrowed to the bottom of a stack and were lost.

The man even held meetings in his office. Rung had watched the Lord Seneschal pick his way delicately across the floor, grimacing at the ever-increasing piles of dirty laundry and jumping when he accidentally stepped on a book and slid forward a few feet. The captain of the guard had refused to enter the room at all, much to Rung's disconcertion. He thought that a man who spent his days sweating and riding smelly horses should have been very used to walking through a big mess.

The furniture Rung planned to sneak into the room began piling up in the secret passage. He had both bookshelves and their corner-shaped connecting piece right next to the secret door. The bookshelf for the library books was pushed along the wall to make room for Rung to walk. Only the proposed side table for the sitting area was incomplete, but Rung still didn't feel right about fixing the office just yet. He had realized two things while watching the man these past few days.

First, if Rung didn't find a proper way to organize that desk, all his efforts to get the office clean would be superfluous. Having the books organized did not mean the productivity of the office would improve as well.

Second, Rung had noticed that the piles of laundry seemed to be increasing. This made the office smell a little unpleasant, and it perplexed Rung to no end. Why would an office be the appropriate place to leave dirty clothing?

Rung decided that he needed to see the rest of the suite of rooms before he finished fixing the office. If he could figure out what was wrong with the dirty laundry basket in the bedroom, perhaps he could also save the office from drowning under piles of stinking clothes.

There wasn't a secret passage into the rest of the suite, though—Rung had checked. That meant he would need to sneak through the office, out into the sitting room beyond the doorway, and into whatever other rooms were attached to the sitting room. He was good at sneaking—that was what brownies did best—but being sneaky and being stupid were two different things. First, he would need to make sure he wouldn't be caught.

Rung would have to keep his ears open while he was about the castle. Hopefully something would occur to ensure the set of rooms would be empty. Until then, he would continue with creating a compact, easy-to-use filing system.

*

Rung relaxed in his bedroom, very pleased with the day's efforts. Yet another disused corridor was finally spotless. This particular one had been far back in the winding castle, up on the top floor, and it had very clearly not been touched for at least two generations. The hardest task had been finding a way to remove all the dust without attracting attention. Dust flying out the top-floor windows into the back gardens would have drawn too much notice, as would a sudden increase of the size of the midden pile. But Rung had figured it out in the end.

Now he could take a well-deserved rest in his new chair. He had built it himself out of scrap wood that would not be missed. When he had been moving things to the trash pile, he had noticed four old cushions with stuffing hanging through the ragged shreds of cloth and had taken those cushions home. With some new cloth covers and some fluffing, those old cushions were now the best part of his new chair.

It was a great place to relax after a hard day of work. Rung particularly liked to whittle while sitting in his chair. The piece he was working on now was a horse standing strong with its head held high. It would look lovely on one of the shelves behind the desk in the office he was remodeling. From the number of dirty riding outfits that littered the office floor, he knew the occupant liked horses.

Taking the time to relax and de-stress that night was also important because there was some sort of hullabaloo in the grand ballroom the next night. It was someone's birthday, and this birthday was important enough to have hired musicians and set the kitchen into a cooking frenzy. Rung had almost been seen in the kitchen earlier that day because of the number of people and flurry of activity going on there.

What the craziness meant was that everyone of any sort of import in the castle would need to attend, including the occupant of the office. The office and attached rooms would be empty for hours. Rung wished he could take this opportunity to start moving in all the completed furniture so he could finally clean the office, but he knew he couldn't make any further moves toward cleanliness until he was certain his efforts would permanently stymie the growth of the disaster. If there was something wrong with the bedroom that needed to be fixed first, or something in one of the other rooms, Rung needed to know about it before he put his beautiful new furniture in harm's way.

Rung sighed and put down the small knife he had carefully been running over the emerging horse's body. The urge to just go into that office and start scrubbing was growing every day, and Rung was getting a bit twitchy about it. No one should be forced to live under such horrifying conditions, and Rung now had an opportunity to do something about it. Only he couldn't. The office and the connecting rooms needed to be cleaned and reorganized in one swoop—doing otherwise would not solve the problem.

Rung gently put the horse aside and headed over to his bed. He would go to sleep and force the twitching need to clean aside. He had to focus so he could be prepared for tomorrow night. Rung slid under his covers and resolutely shut his eyes, hoping he wouldn't dream about the growing piles of dirty clothes.

*

Rung slipped through the secret doorway into the office and cringed. Technically, there was still a path to the door amid the piles of filth, but it was narrow and quickly vanishing. Rung felt the need to fix it run through his fingers, just the littlest bit. He put his hands in his pockets instead.

The door to the rest of the suite was cracked open. Rung crept silently along the pathway to the door, and then he carefully peeked through the opening and froze in shock. He was clearly looking into the outer sitting room. There were two more doors in the walls, one of which was too sturdy to head anywhere but into the castle while the other door was similar to the one Rung hid behind.

However, what made him freeze in place was the total lack of mess. There were two couches situated around a coffee table, carefully organized shelves of books and knickknacks along the one wall without a door, and absolutely no signs of dust or debris. Someone cleaned this room often; yet why was this room kept up while the office, quite clearly, was not?

The room was empty, so Rung pulled the office door open just enough that he could slip his body through. He didn't close the door as he stepped from dirty carpet to clean, just in case he needed to make a run for the secret entrance. Fighting with the door in his flight would not be optimal.

Rung took a closer look at the coffee table and the ornate miniature stone statue of a man holding his sword in the air. From the way the cleaning polish had been rubbed into the wood of the table, Rung could tell that the castle maids were allowed into this room. Why, then, were they not allowed into the office? It just didn't make any sense to Rung.

The other door was closed. Rung put his ear to the surface as he had been taught back in the orphanage and listened for a long time. There weren't any sounds of movement, nor did he hear any breathing that could indicate a person asleep. Cautiously, Rung turned the handle and pushed the door open.

This time, the sight that greeted him was much more expected. There was a bed somewhere in the mess, Rung assumed, but it was totally covered in a disarray of blankets and sleeping clothes. Along the far wall was an open armoire with unfolded clothes spilling out of the shelves onto a large pile on the floor. Those clothes might actually have been clean, but the clothes and other belongings, like a rusted set of armor scattered across the rest of the floor, were definitely not. There wasn't a clear path through the debris in this room. Rung did what the man who lived there must do every night: picked his way over the mess, stepping only on clothes without anything underneath that would make him lose his footing and send him sprawling. Rung really did not want to fall onto what must have been months of dirty clothes.

Rung picked through the piles, trying to ascertain just what furniture was actually present in the room. There was a bed and an armoire, plus an armor stand in the far corner by the dirt-encrusted windows. Next to the armoire was a doorway that led to a tiled washroom and changing area. The washroom wasn't vile, but it could still use a good scouring. Someone obviously took a scrub brush to the bathtub every so often. The changing area had more clothing strewn about, except these were mostly nicer outfits and jewelry. The set of shelves for the velvet-lined boxes was full, but the boxes were left open and empty. Rung was careful not to step on anything priceless as he poked through.

The issue was clear: there was simply no receptacle where dirty clothes could be left for the maids to take to the laundry and there was also insufficient storage space for the clothes once they were cleaned. Rung needed to carve a hanging rod for the changing room where the nicer items of clothing could be hung neatly and easily. He also thought the jewelry issue could be resolved if the boxes were labeled. It looked to Rung as if the owner had actually tried to put the ruby cufflinks—still attached to a dirty shirt—away, but could not find the proper box and so had put the shirt on the shelf instead.

The main room would need a storage chest for the excess blankets. Rung knew there was enough available wood for him to build one. However, there was no possible way for him to build another armoire, which the room sorely needed. There had been a nice pair of large-sized armoires in one of the rooms in the wing he had just finished cleaning, though, now that Rung thought about it. He could move both of those in and take out the small one. All he needed to do was add some carvings to the wood so they would match the bed, which had been masterfully carved at one point in time. The bed did need a polish, but that couldn't be done until the rest of the room was fixed up first.

Rung closed the bedroom door behind himself very firmly, resisting the urge to go back and gather some of that discarded clothing so he could start washing. The pristine sitting area mocked Rung as he moved through the space. He firmly kept his mind on the two large baskets he could begin weaving immediately, one for dirty clothes in the bedroom and the other for the dirty clothes in the work area. Since the man clearly got undressed often there, a basket would probably be beneficial.

After Rung returned to the office, he pushed the door back to where it had been before he moved it. No one would know he had ever been poking about when he left. The path through the clothes led by the desk, and Rung couldn't help sneaking a look. The piles of papers had grown. Rung could see one page marked "urgent" beneath a large stack of papers titled "library appropriations": a paper that needed to be seen to immediately beneath something that should have been at the very bottom of the to-do pile.

Rung's fingers twitched again. He could move just that one urgent paper to the top where the man could see it, just the one to help him out a little. Rung's hand reached out and found that paper, but he knew he couldn't move it without moving the stack on top. So he picked up the library stack and put it aside. The urgent paper was easily visible, but there wasn't any knowing what Rung had just inadvertently hidden instead by shifting the stack of papers. He picked up the stack again and was glad he had. Another urgent paper was now visible beneath a short report on the stables.

Rung bit his lip. It would be so easy to temporarily fix this. Urgent papers organized by date and necessity. Other papers organized by relevance and the date the information needed to be completed. It could be done, and it wouldn't take long. With the party going on downstairs, no one would ever see him.

Rung's hands trembled while he bit his lip, trying to fight the urge but knowing he was failing. He let out a sigh and set to clearing off the desk. It might get him in trouble or get him thanked, which would be equally awful, but it had to be done. It had to be.

*

The Lord Seneschal and the Lord Steward met outside the office door and grimaced at each other. Luckily, the door was closed so the occupant couldn't see them.

"Shall we brave it, Gerald?" Rufus asked with trepidation in his voice.

"We must, Rufus," Gerald replied with his fear also made quite clear. He reached forward and knocked politely before pushing the door open.

"Ah, gentlemen," Prince Lionel said genially. He was sitting behind his desk, clearly inured to the general stench of the room and the piles of things that generated the terrible smell. Prince Lionel was remarkably sober. After the grand ball last night celebrating Lionel's twentieth birthday, most residents of the castle were nursing hangovers. Prince Lionel was not.

"Your Highness," Rufus said as he and Gerald bowed. "You summoned us?"

"Yes," Prince Lionel replied. "You see, I'm afraid I must hand you a bit of a mystery. Last night while I was at the ball, someone snuck into my office and rearranged all my papers."

Both Rufus and Gerald looked appalled. "Our apologies, Your Highness," Gerald murmured. "I shall have the culprit apprehended and arrested."

It was well-known around the castle that daring to touch Prince Lionel's things was a firing offense. Prince Lionel had grown up with maids and nurses constantly touching him and moving his things around without his permission. They liked to take advantage of the fact that they had the opportunity to manage Prince Lionel's life so completely, and they had done so without first consulting the young Lionel about what he wanted. Lionel hadn't taken it well from his nurses as a child; now he couldn't stand having anyone in among his things, even just to clean.

Additionally, the brownies that kept moving into the castle always zeroed directly in on the messiest room in the castle, Prince Lionel's, and cleaned it. It drove him particularly mad to walk into his bedroom or office to see everything suddenly spotless. Suits were organized into their separate parts, jackets hung apart from their accompanying pants, which made it nearly impossible to rematch the two. Papers were alphabetized by sender and made even more incomprehensible when the crabbed writing on the papers from the captain of the army was rewritten very neatly with absolutely no indication included of who had originally penned the document, because the man never bothered to sign them. Prince Lionel had been incensed and had promptly banished all brownies from the castle after the sixth one tried to "help."

"No, no," Prince Lionel said thoughtfully. "I do want you to locate the individual, but I was thinking I could hire them as my secretary."

"Your secretary, Your Highness?" Gerald asked sharply.

"Yes! Come look at what they've done!"

The Lord Steward and the Lord Seneschal both moved closer to the desk and looked at the organized piles of papers.

"It's been set by what I need to do first, not by any alphabet," Prince Lionel explained. "I need to get the garden budget done before I can authorize adding the new pond my mother wants, and whoever cleaned this put those papers exactly in the order I needed them. It's marvelous!"

Gerald caught Rufus's eye, who nodded back. "We will start searching at once, Your Highness," Gerald said. "We will bring you the maid or manservant responsible immediately!"

Both men gladly left the office and took deep breaths of the clean air in the sitting room.

"This brownie really is a bit of an odd one," Gerald murmured as they moved into the castle hallway. "Cleaned the red wing that was closed up during King Lester's time seventy years back. It's so pristine we could use it to house our most distinguished guests right now if we wanted. Yet he hasn't so much as touched any of the rooms that are occupied."

"Probably saw this room and couldn't help himself, the poor thing," Rufus agreed, knowing from his experience with the last few brownies in the castle that Prince Lionel's rooms were enough to send the creatures into palpitations. "But the creature managed to actually help Prince Lionel! We need to do something to encourage it. If it can touch Prince Lionel's things without issue, maybe we can get it to do something further? Those rooms..." he finished without needing to give a description. Gerald could easily fill in the blank himself. His echoing grimace was all the confirmation Rufus needed.

"More good wood out by the woodpile," Gerald said thoughtfully as he held his office door open for his friend.

"Wasn't there a set of knives gone dull the chef wanted to have replaced? Good ones that could be sharpened by a careful hand?" Rufus asked.

"Yes! Those can go to the top of the trash pile, and I'll bet you they'll vanish within a day. Can you think of anything else we might have?"

They put their heads together and began to plan. This brownie might actually help the situation with Prince Lionel, and they were going to give it every possible opportunity.

*

Rung hummed quietly to himself in the room he had appropriated for his workshop. The knife he was holding slid along the wood of the armoire he was carving, copying the whorl in the design he remembered from the bed frame. He had chosen a good pair of furniture pieces to reappropriate; both had thick wood to carve into and were large enough to hold all the clothing that would eventually be cleaned up.

Rung blew the wood shavings away and studied his work. It was almost perfect. The design matched what Rung remembered from the bedroom almost exactly; however, the carvings of wolves howling up at the ring of a moon weren't quite right. Rung remembered they had full, winter-length coats, but he could not recall whether their tails had been pointed up or down.

He needed to return to the bedroom to have a closer look at those designs.

Decided, Rung began to clean his workspace. He carefully swept up all the wood shavings and polished every piece of furniture so that there weren't any splinters or loose bits of wood remaining behind. He pulled out his cart, a sturdy thing he had put together in order to move all the heavy pieces of furniture around the castle.

Aside from the wolf tails, Rung was finished. He loaded the wide blanket trunk onto his cart, checked the hallway to see it was empty, and headed out to the nearest entrance to the secret passageways. He could easily finish the carvings in the secret passage, and it would be that much sooner he could begin cleaning that awful office and bedroom.

When Rung got to where he was storing all the furniture for the office, he unloaded the trunk and peeked through the spy hole. The man with the lovely brown hair was bent over his desk, snarling at the disarray of papers. Rung was dismayed to note that his careful organizing of the desk had barely lasted a week. The owner of the office was buried under unimportant forms again while the important ones vanished.

Rung shook his head with a sad sigh and left. He checked the office after every item he carted down the secret hallway, but the man still struggled through his duties. Finally, after Rung had begun to wonder if he would need to wait until the next day, a polite knock sounded on the office door.

"Enter!" the man called. The door creaked open, and a young man in a servant's uniform poked his head around the frame.

"Your Excellency," the youth said with a small bow, "your honored mother wishes to speak with you."

The man sighed. "Of course she does. Is she in her solar?" he asked as he put down the paperwork he had been ineffectively filling out and pushed his chair away from his desk.

"Yes, sir," the servant said with another bow. Both humans left the office moments later. Rung listened while the owner of the office walked through the sitting room and into his bedroom for a long moment before returning to the sitting room. The thump of the heavy door leading into the castle as it closed told Rung it was safe to explore.

The secret door opened silently, and Rung crept out into the mess of an office. The path through the mire had gotten thinner over the past week; Rung knew he had to hurry his plans to get this place fixed up before there wasn't a path at all. Still, he took a quick moment to shift some papers into proper order on the desk before taking that path—he couldn't help himself after seeing the man struggle for so long.

The sitting room outside was as immaculate as always, but the bedroom made Rung cringe again. It took him only a quick moment to study the carvings on the bed frame. The tail was pointed triumphantly upward; this wolf ruled the hill he stood on.

Rung made sure to close the bedroom door as he stepped back into the sitting room. When he turned around, he stopped short and dove behind a chair. He wasn't alone!

"Oh, come out of there," a familiar voice said pleasantly. Rung was used to hearing jibing tones from Needle, so the nice request threw him.

Needle was standing in the perfect sitting room with his hands on his hips as he surveyed the area.

"This isn't as bad as I was told it would be," Needle said thoughtfully. "I suppose you've managed to keep this clean, then?" he added, and now Rung heard the familiar hated scoff.

"Why are you here?" Rung asked instead of answering.

Needle sneered. "I got special commendation at my graduation. A graduation that would never have happened had you stayed at the orphanage," he added coldly. "But when you ran off, they could finally give us our degrees without worrying about the embarrassment of needing to find somewhere to send you to."

Rung blinked, confused. "You said they were going to kill me?" he asked.

Needle laughed. "Of course I did. I am the best brownie to ever go through their training. I wasn't about to let my future suffer because of filth like you, Wrong. I got you out of the way, and now look at me! Special assignment to the castle, specifically to help the poor prince. And what with the other benefits from those who requested my presence here, this job will keep me on the very top of brownie society! I just didn't expect this room to be clean already." Needle shrugged. "Makes it easier, I guess, but first I have to get rid of you. Can't have you destroying my future again."

Needle advanced toward Rung, and Rung couldn't help backing away. All those childish pranks back in school—stealing his only blanket, knocking him around, and everything else Rung had endured—none of it had prepared him for the idea that Needle would lie and connive in order to get ahead.

Rung squeaked and dove to the side when Needle lunged forward. While Needle had the proper small and wiry build for a brownie, he was more used to fighting than Rung. It wasn't long before Rung couldn't dodge in time.

Rung's back hit the floor with a cracking thud, and Needle's fist hit his face seconds later. Rung felt his teeth cut his lip, blood already dripping down from his nose, and he knew the carpet would need a very deep scrub to get the blood out. When Rung cried out and clapped his hands to his face, Needle shoved away from him. Rung never saw the foot that hit his left forearm, sending an ominous snapping sound into the air, or the knee that cracked some of his ribs.

Needle was laughing as he backed away from Rung's huddled form. "You understand now?" Needle crowed. "I belong here, and you don't!" He turned away with a sneer and threw open the nearest door—the one leading into the bedroom. "Oh, so this is what they were talking about," Needle breathed. "Well," he added with a smirk over his shoulder at the crying Rung, "I'm off to work!"

Rung whimpered, both from the pain and from the knowledge that Needle was going to destroy everything. He was going to touch things and move them around, and the owner of this suite was going to hate it.

But there was nothing Rung could do right now. His broken arm throbbed, and he sobbed as he rolled over onto his one good hand and his knees. Blood dripped from his face onto the carpet, leaving a trail as Rung crawled his way toward the office. He needed to get away before the owner returned. Brownies were never caught, and he wasn't going to be, no matter how hard Needle tried.

It felt like hours before he finally made his painful way through the slightly ajar office door and through the tangled piles of clothing. It was agony to reach upward and press the catch for the secret door, but he got it open. He didn't have the strength to close it behind him again, but everything was already ruined, so what did it matter if a human found all the furniture he had so meticulously been working on?

Rung knew he passed out several times before he finally made his way to his basement room, where he had a small stash of bandages for any carving accidents. He used some to stop up his nose, and whatever was left he wrapped around his broken arm. He knew it was ineffective, but there wasn't anything else he was capable of doing.

It took the very last of his strength to crawl into bed. His good arm was able to pull the covers over his head, but before he could start sobbing again, he passed out from the pain.

*

For the second time in just over a week, the Lord Steward and the Lord Seneschal were summoned to Prince Lionel's office. They hurried through the castle hallways, meeting up just outside the suite door.

"Do you know what this is about?" Rufus wondered.

Gerald shook his head. "Do you think the brownie did something again?" he asked.

"Probably," Rufus agreed. He reached out and pushed open the door. Both men stepped into the sitting room and stopped short.

Prince Lionel was standing in the middle of the room, arms crossed over his chest and a deep scowl on his face.

"Call in the hounds," Prince Lionel snarled.

Rufus sighed and shot his counterpart a quick look. He didn't really want to hunt for the poor brownie. He stepped over to Prince Lionel and blinked at the scene in front of him.

There was blood on the sitting room rug, droplets of it leading from one larger puddle through the open office door. The bedroom door was also open, but inside there was a floor and a neatly made bed. None of the mess remained. The office was still a disaster, however.

"I returned in time to stop the menace," Prince Lionel snapped. "He hadn't gotten to my dressing room yet, but my bedroom has been totally destroyed. I want this creature found before he touches my office as well."

Rufus looked back at Gerald, who also had a quizzical look on his face.

"This doesn't make sense," Gerald murmured as he glanced at the immaculate bedroom.

"Of course it makes sense!" Prince Lionel snapped. "There is an obnoxious brownie in the castle, and I want him found and removed at once!"

"Maybe there are two?" Rufus asked Gerald.

Gerald nodded. "That might explain it. And they were fighting, hence the blood."

"Explain. Now," Prince Lionel said in his most officious tone.

"Your Highness," the Lord Steward began, "we believe there are two brownies currently in residence in the castle. One has been here for months, quietly cleaning the disused rooms and making the kitchen staff quite happy. We believe this brownie is the one who organized your desk last week."

"This brownie has never shown any inclination toward meddling in someone's belongings," Gerald agreed. "He somehow managed to enter your office and all he touched was your desk? Impossible, I would have thought, but that is all this brownie has been doing."

"This," Rufus added as he pointed to the clean bedroom, "is not our brownie's work. A second one must have come here, seen the mess, and started cleaning."

Prince Lionel listened to their explanation with a stony expression. "Or," he added in a scathing tone, "the brownie you have allowed access to my castle for so long has finally shown its true colors. Find it—or them, if you still think there are two—and bring them to me."

Prince Lionel stomped off into his bedroom. Rufus could see him walk directly to his bed, grip the covers and sheets tucked under his pillow at the head, and yank the entire ensemble down the bed and onto the floor.

The Lord Steward looked over at the Lord Seneschal, and they both sighed in agreement. They quickly left Prince Lionel's suite and called out the search parties.

*

Gerald went with one hunting dog as it followed a scent trail from Prince Lionel's rooms into the castle hallways. The troop of guardsmen following weren't wearing armor because the sound of the metal parts clanking would alert the brownie. Rufus stayed with the dog that was sniffing at the blood in the carpet. The animal followed the trail into the office where Rufus and his contingent of guards found an open door in the side of the fireplace.

"Did anyone know this was here?" he asked the lieutenant, who just shook his head in equal surprise.

The dog led them through the door and into a hallway that must have been traveled by the brownie—it was perfectly clean. It was also filled with furniture. Bookshelves and dirty clothing baskets, armoires and hanging rods—it looked like the brownie had a system almost ready to go to fix Prince Lionel's mess rather than just clean it. The solution was what Rufus expected from the friendly brownie.

The dog led them through the secret passageway and back into a disused wing of the castle that had also seen recent care by the brownie. They went down three flights of stairs until they were in the oldest of the basement sections.

Rufus had an idea of what signs to look for as the dog led them unerringly through the twisting basement rooms. There were still spider webs in the corners, but it was obvious the webs had been purposefully left there to cultivate the illusion that the basement was untouched. The walls and floors were too clean and the door hinges in too good repair for this to be anything but a brownie hideaway.

Finally, they rounded the last corner and were met with a wooden door left partially open. The door was the equal to any gracing the king's personal rooms. There were fanciful carvings across the entire surface that made the guards with Rufus gape at the extravagance.

The lieutenant finally gathered his wits and pushed open the door, his other hand on his sword. Rufus followed behind.

The bedroom was well appointed with a bed, a clothing chest, and a rocking chair that were just as beautiful as the door. In the middle of the bed, buried under the covers, was a breathing lump.

Rufus waved the lieutenant away. If this was the good brownie, he didn't want to scare it. He drew the blankets down with a gentle tug and gasped at the black-and-blue creature huddled there. There was blood staining the bandages pressed to his nose, and his left arm did not look right. Those injuries plus the bruising indicated this brownie was highly disliked by someone.

"Call a doctor immediately!" Rufus said to one of the waiting guards. The man saluted and spun away, heading back into the basement at a quick jog.

"What should we do, Excellency?" the lieutenant asked, clearly upset by the broken image lying unconscious in the bed.

Rufus sighed. "Leave him be. The doctor will attend him, and when he is better, we will bring him to Prince Lionel. Just hope that the Lord Seneschal can find the bastard brownie who caused these injuries."

"So there are two of them?" the lieutenant asked curiously.

Rufus nodded. "I believe so. You can tell from how elaborate this room is that this poor fellow has been here for months, and not once has he interfered in such a manner as I saw today. There must be a second creature; it is the only explanation."

"I'm afraid I don't understand why I must travel so quickly to the basement!" Rufus heard the crotchety doctor hiss, his voice echoing from a few hallways down. That was quite the defense mechanism; being able to hear anyone encroaching from a long way off gave the brownie ample time to scurry away. If only he weren't unconscious at the moment.

Soon enough, the doctor was being led into the bedroom. The man was older and deserved his fame as the head doctor. The second he saw his patient, the doctor stopped complaining and got to work.

Rufus flinched when the doctor reset the broken arm, and the brownie moaned and sobbed despite still being unconscious. The rest was just bad bruising, possibly cracked ribs, and a few cuts on his face.

The doctor had just finished wrapping those hurt ribs when the brownie finally stirred and blinked his eyes open. He squeaked in fear when he saw he wasn't alone and would have tumbled off the bed to run and hide if he hadn't put his injured arm down first. The resulting cry of pain kept the brownie in one place for long enough that Rufus could rush forward.

"You're safe," Rufus told the whimpering creature, who was switching between clutching his splinted arm and staring wildly at all the humans surrounding him. Now that the brownie was awake, Rufus could see there was an odd discrepancy to his features. The brownie could probably pass as a human, his layer of fur was so light and thin, and his facial features almost seemed more human in appearance than brownie—he totally lacked a set of whiskers and had a full, human-sized nose instead of a snub one. Maybe this was a half-breed?

"Can you tell me your name or what happened?" Rufus asked gently, careful of startling the brownie again.

The creature hung his head. "I'm Ladder Rung," he whispered, "and I'm sorry I couldn't stop Sewing Needle from messing everything up."

Rufus smiled grimly, glad to finally have concrete proof that there were two brownies in the castle and this one was innocent of any wrongdoing. Hopefully he would be able to convince Prince Lionel of that.

"If you're feeling able, do you think you could come speak with Prince Lionel about what happened?" Rufus asked politely. The brownie still cringed and ducked his head.

"Don't let him thank me," the creature whispered, but he was carefully climbing out of his bed and shuffling over to Rufus.

"Ladder Rung, I want to hire you. If that was your work we saw in that secret passage, then I want to assign you permanently to cleaning up after Prince Lionel."

Rung ducked his head, trying to hide a blush. He shuffled slowly after Rufus as they and the guards finally left the basement to return to the castle proper.

*

Rung followed silently while he was led out of the basement and into the castle. He had been caught, and the cold shivers running up his spine told him he was about to be thanked. He had finally made a real home for himself where he was safe and comfortable, and Needle had to ruin it! The thought almost made him sob aloud.

He avoided the curious looks of the castle residents as the group of guards surrounding Rung and the Lord Steward walked through the main hallways. They stopped outside of an unfamiliar door, but when it opened, Rung knew exactly where he had been taken. The sitting room they walked into was almost immaculate, but Rung could still see the bloodstains dotting the rug. Someone had given the stains a scrub, but it had been totally ineffective. Rung's fingers twitched as the desire to go find a proper cleaning cloth and attend to that stain crossed his mind.

Instead, he was herded toward the office. The steward knocked on the door politely before opening it. Rung let out a relieved breath. The office had not been touched, which meant the owner of the rooms had returned before Needle could do too much damage.

"Your Highness, we found the good brownie," the Lord Steward said politely.

Rung bowed his head, his ribs aching too much to allow a proper bow, before looking up at the man who owned this office—at the prince—and froze. Logically, seeing all the wolf carvings in the furniture when the symbol of the ruling family was the wolf ascendant should have tipped Rung off. Or the fact that not only was the clothing strewn about so fine, but there was also such a multitude of it that the cost would have been debilitating for anyone of a lesser station. Rung should have easily been able to guess whom he had been trying to clean up after. Maybe he had just not wanted to think about it, because if he had taken the time to put all the facts together, he would have been forced to abandon his efforts to clean these rooms.

Prince Lionel was the one who had declared the edict refusing all brownies entry into the castle and could therefore thank Rung at any moment, but that wasn't the real reason Rung stood in frozen surprise. Prince Lionel wasn't just regal; he was beautiful. His brown hair offset a pair of vibrant green eyes set in a face that was so symmetrical Rung wanted to carve it.

"Y-Your Highness," Rung forced out when Prince Lionel quirked an eyebrow at Rung's blatant staring. Rung felt his face going red and ducked his head.

"I'm to believe that you are the brownie who has been poking about my desk?" Prince Lionel asked.

Rung nodded miserably.

"And you are the brownie who has taken the time and effort to build all those marvelous pieces of furniture out in the secret passage?"

Rung nodded again, ducking his head farther away from Prince Lionel's scrutiny.

"You did say you wanted to hire a secretary," the Lord Steward added when Prince Lionel continued to stare at Rung.

"So I did," Prince Lionel murmured musingly.

Rung lifted his head slowly, glancing up at Prince Lionel through his eyelashes. Did this mean he wasn't going to be thanked?

A loud commotion sounded from the sitting room. Rung could hear more guards swearing and Needle's voice threatening them. The entourage pushed into the office.

The Lord Steward gently pulled Rung off to the side of the room as the Lord Seneschal stepped forward.

"Found the culprit, Your Highness," the Lord Seneschal said with a bow. "This is the one who dared clean your bedroom."

Prince Lionel stepped forward and loomed over Needle's much smaller form. "Do you know the laws and edicts of the country in which you reside?" Prince Lionel said in a hard, officious voice. "Do you?" he added sharply when Needle just glared.

"I know the laws," Needle sneered.

"And the edicts?" Prince Lionel pressed.

"And the edicts!" Needle yelled. "Now, let me go!"

Prince Lionel ignored Needle's outburst. "So you do know that I have declared an edict that no brownies are allowed residence in this castle?" He didn't wait for an answer. "Why, then, are you here?"

"Because this place is filthy. I needed to clean it!" Needle answered with his usual snarl. "You're disgusting."

The two guards holding Needle in place shook the brownie in retaliation. Needle hissed at them.

"He said the Orphanage Council sent him here," Rung said, softly but firmly. Needle was finally the one in trouble; Rung wasn't about to let him get away this time. His broken arm throbbed in agreement.

"The council?" Prince Lionel asked. "That's foolish, because I sent a copy of my edict directly to that council. They know better."

"They got paid better," Needle finally sniffed. "We send someone in to keep Prince Lionel's rooms cleaned, the edicts are dropped, and we can move entire families into the castle. No more homeless brownies."

"That's interesting to know," Prince Lionel replied calmly.

"Is Sewing Needle telling the truth?" the Lord Steward asked Rung.

Rung nodded. "I think so. Needle said that someone had requested him to clean here."

"Fine," Prince Lionel said firmly. "Sewing Needle, thank you very much for your service to me, to the castle, and to the crown. We appreciate your efforts to the utmost."

Needle seemed to shrink into himself as the words of thanks were spoken. He glared up at Prince Lionel. "What about Wrong?" Needle snarled, sounding devastated and petty at the same time. "Wrong deserves to be thanked too."

Prince Lionel looked down at Needle with a frown. "You are something else, brownie. I will be writing a letter to your council about your horrible conduct and disposition. They never should have allowed you to graduate from the academy." Needle shrunk in on himself even more, but his sneer never faded from his face.

Prince Lionel turned toward Rung. "Is Wrong your real name?" he asked gently.

Rung shook his head, but it was the Lord Steward who replied, "Ladder Rung, Excellency."

"Very well, Ladder Rung," Prince Lionel began. Rung could feel his shoulders rounding as the thank-you was about to be said. "I would like to hire you on a temporary basis as my personal secretary and manservant. If your improvements are effective, that hiring will become permanent."

Rung could feel his jaw drop in surprise. Instead of a thank-you, he was being hired? Needle looked equally shocked.

"You'll hire the half-breed failure who dropped out of school because he couldn't do anything right?" Needle gasped. "I hope you suffer," he added.

Prince Lionel nodded to the guards holding Needle in place. "Escort that miscreant out of the castle and out of the city," he said. Rung watched as Needle was dragged out of the office.

"You want me to clean for you?" Rung finally gasped once the noise from Needle's unwilling departure had faded.

"Clean, organize, anything you can think of. After the way you've cleaned my desk, I think you're necessary," Prince Lionel explained.

"Even with my arm like this?" Rung asked, giving Prince Lionel another chance to back away. Hiring Rung, Wrong, to do something might end up being a disaster.

"I want you, no one else, and until your arm heals, you'll have servants dealing with anything heavy or strenuous." Prince Lionel turned to the Lord Steward and the Lord Seneschal. "See that my orders are carried out."

Prince Lionel walked past Rung on his way out of the office, totally ignoring the small path through the debris as he stepped on clothing and books alike on his way. He nodded to the Lord Steward and clapped Rung on the shoulder before leaving the room.

"So," the Lord Steward asked, sounding excited, "what do you need a servant to do first?"

Rung blinked at the Lord Steward in shock for a moment before his wits returned. He had permission to clean this disaster and, broken arm or not, he wasn't wasting a single moment.

"There are two large laundry baskets in the secret passageway," Rung explained.

Servants were called quickly. One held a basket while another servant and Rung gathered the dirty clothing from the office and dumped it inside. When one basket was full, it was carried down to the laundry and emptied. It took five full baskets before the floor was cleared of dirty clothing.

Two male servants began dragging the bookshelves in next. Rung happily directed the servants where to place the shelves and which books went where. One servant heard that the shelves put by the door were specifically for books to be returned to the library, and he went ahead and took those books there directly.

It only took a few hours before the office was immaculate. The desk had been moved to the corner, and the three shelves behind it made the space look very official. The new side table was next to the armchair, and a tea set had been unearthed and placed on top. All the pleasure-reading books were now safely on the shelves beneath it. The office was now both an official and a comfortable space that would be easy to keep organized. All the old furniture needed to be polished and dusted, but overall the improvement was palpable.

They moved into the bedroom next. Needle had cleaned the space properly; there was nothing wrong with him in that area. The floor was empty of clothing, but Prince Lionel had stripped his neatly made bed at some point. Rung had two footmen bring in the trunk first and set it at the foot of the bed. While Rung filled it with all the blankets Prince Lionel had purposefully removed from his bed, three maids emptied the old armoire. After the footmen had carted that piece of furniture out of the room and the two replacements back in, Rung and the maids carefully reorganized all the clothing inside.

They moved to the changing room, where one maid was set to the task of matching jewelry with jewelry box and then affixing the labels. The footmen installed the hanging rod while the other maids began carefully hanging the expensive suits. Rung was glad when another maid began scrubbing the bathroom without needing him to direct her.

"You did all this in one afternoon?" Prince Lionel's voice called from the bedroom door.

Rung stepped out of the changing room and nodded. "Yes, Your Highness," he murmured. "But it's not done yet. I need to dust and shine, and the carvings aren't quite complete yet."

"And you think all these changes will help keep these rooms clean?" Prince Lionel asked sharply, wincing slightly as all the maids, footmen, and manservants finally finished their tasks and left the back rooms, bowing and curtseying to Prince Lionel as they left the bedroom. "I don't like having people going through my things uninvited," Prince Lionel explained.

"Um," Rung began, worried for a moment that Prince Lionel included Rung in that distinction. It was clear, though, that for some reason Prince Lionel had no problem with Rung's presence. "If you put all your dirty clothes in the baskets by the door, all a maid has to do is take it first thing in the morning. She won't have to do more than open a door, and she won't have to touch anything. I'll take care of keeping up after the rest of it."

Prince Lionel glanced around his bedroom before moving into his office. Rung followed behind, worrying his sore lip between his teeth as Prince Lionel studied all the improvements. "There is still something missing in here," Prince Lionel said finally.

"Sir?" Rung asked, looking around to see what Prince Lionel could possibly mean.

"My secretary needs a desk as well. Find one that will suit you, and have it brought here in the morning. Your job will be to keep my papers organized and to take care of anything trifling that needs my signature but shouldn't be taking up my time."

"Yes, Your Highness," Rung said with a happy nod. It didn't matter what tasks he was set; Rung had been specifically asked to clean up after the messy prince. What could be better?

"And call me Lionel, since we're to be working so closely together," Prince Lionel added.

"Yes, Lionel," Rung replied. "I'm Rung. Nice to meet you."

*

Rung loved his new job. Every morning, he received the day's mail and sorted it according to a very strict formula. All the mail that was formal correspondence stayed on Rung's desk. He would read it and write a proper reply on behalf of Prince Lionel. The personal letters and the project letters giving Prince Lionel more information or requesting information from Prince Lionel went into a specific spot on Prince Lionel's desk. Any letters that were marked as urgent or that Prince

Lionel was waiting for were put on top of the stack. Any other letters were sorted based on urgency and whether Prince Lionel was the only one capable of taking care of the issue.

Rung also took direct delivery of all paperwork. Much of it he could actually fill out on his own and then have Prince Lionel read through and sign afterward. The rest he put into their places on Prince Lionel's desk.

Not only was the entire process much more organized, but Rung had also greatly decreased the sheer number of papers on Prince Lionel's desk simply by taking care of many of them himself. Prince Lionel was very appreciative.

There were some drawbacks to the job, of course. Rung was continuously thanked whenever he interacted with most humans, which made him very twitchy. Prince Lionel and the Lord Steward had hired him, and he had very succinctly been informed that only thanks from one of them actually constituted a dismissal. Still, any thanks was one too many by Rung's brownie sensibilities.

It was also very disconcerting to be visible all the time. Brownies were prized for their ability to fade into the background and be unseen; sitting at a desk in the middle of an office where everyone who entered saw him made him flinch toward hiding underneath the desk until the visitor was gone.

These problems made Prince Lionel laugh though. Every time he saw Rung eyeing the space beneath his desk he chuckled, which made Rung blush. Still, he found spending so much time with Prince Lionel to be a lot of fun. He could organize the office work to his heart's content, and he could have a very pleasant conversation with a man who was quickly becoming a friend at the same time.

When he wasn't buried under piles of disorganized paperwork, Prince Lionel liked to smile and chat about nonsensical things that made Rung laugh. For the first time in his life, Rung knew he had a friend. He particularly cherished the evenings when Prince Lionel would relax with a pleasure book and Rung could clean around him. Rung's efforts to solve Prince Lionel's cleanliness issues had been largely successful, but there was always something fun to pick up or scrub during the evening. Rung even got to finish his carvings on the furniture once his arm healed. It wasn't back to full strength just yet, but his carving abilities hadn't suffered because of the break.

At night, he could scurry unseen down into his basement bedroom, climb into bed, and go to sleep with the knowledge that his skills weren't wrong.

Rung loved it. He should have known from long experience that it wouldn't last.

*

"Well, this is nice, at least," a voice called from behind Rung when he stepped into his bedroom late one night two weeks after his arm had finally healed. Rung spun around and saw Teacher Broom studying the carved front door to Rung's bedroom. "An interesting setup you've created, Wrong," he added as he followed Rung into the room.

Rung took a deep breath and straightened his spine. He was the personal secretary and manservant to Prince Lionel. No one else could say they had ever held the position for any significant length of time, but Rung had been working hard for months. There wasn't any reason Teacher Broom couldn't get his name correct, particularly since Rung was no longer a student.

"My name is Ladder Rung," Rung said as sharply as he could. He still felt a desperate need to duck his head and cringe, because he had never dared speak back to a teacher in such a direct way. "My familiar name is Rung, and since we have a history, I will allow its use in your case. Now, Teacher Broom, may I ask why you are here?"

Broom stared at Rung for a long moment, his eyes carefully taking in Rung's smartly dressed form—Prince Lionel refused to have a secretary dressed in secondhand fabrics, so he had supplied Rung ample, high-quality cloth to sew his own outfits—and Rung's direct glare.

"I see you have grown up finally, Rung. As you must know, every student to pass through the Orphanage for Cleanliness and Deportment is evaluated two months after they first enter the real world and find a home to settle into. We must be certain our teachings are being used to their utmost potential. Your case is a peculiar one, Rung, because of your unfinished schooling and your chosen home."

Rung nodded. He remembered wondering what happened when a brownie failed their two-month evaluation while he was still at the orphanage but hadn't thought about it since running away.

"I will be shadowing you for the next few days to ascertain your fitness in taking care of this castle," Broom added.

"Teacher Broom, please keep in mind that there are more unique circumstances at play than just my lacking a graduation certificate," Rung explained. "Because of the edict against brownies, I have been officially hired in a visible position that allows me to complete my duties as a brownie while not breaking the laws of the kingdom."

"I will keep everything under advisement," Broom agreed. "Now let me inspect your living quarters."

Broom looked at everything Rung had built for his bedroom and asked invasive questions about where Rung had located certain fabrics and pieces of wood in the castle without being seen and how he had reappropriated the old scraps into something usable and comfortable. Rung thought Broom left impressed with what Rung had been able to create, and he hoped the rest of his work would be just as pleasing to the members of the Orphanage Council.

The next morning Rung pretended he didn't feel Broom staring at him from wherever the teacher was hiding. He did his usual rounds of the castle, checking that the kitchen didn't need reorganization and that none of the disused hallways and rooms he had cleaned over the past few months were in need of a new dusting. He moved to the wing of the castle that must have been the royal wing when the building was first constructed. The suites of rooms were large and heavily decorated, but the construction was clearly dated. Bit by bit, Rung was cleaning decades of dust and debris. Once he was finished, he could start working on modernizing the rooms.

By eight in the morning, Rung had completed his daily goal of cleaning. He tidied himself up and headed into the more populated areas of the castle.

"Good morning, Ladder Rung," Lord Perkinsmythe called as Rung turned the corner into the grand hallway containing the staircase upward toward Prince Lionel's rooms.

"Good morning, my lord," Rung responded with a polite bow. Lord Perkinsmythe was a rotund man who lived by the philosophy of whatever he couldn't have done by someone else didn't need doing.

"I was wondering," Lord Perkinsmythe began tentatively, as if he were actually hesitant about asking—he wasn't in the least bit. "I was wondering if you might be able to bring me the bimonthly financial reports? I believe the ones pertaining to the gold mines and the jewelry businesses under the oversight of my duchy contain the information I am seeking."

"I'm sorry, My Lord, but I'm afraid you will need to speak with the Lord Seneschal or Prince Lionel about obtaining those documents," Rung replied as nicely as he was able. This wasn't the first time some lord or lady had tried to ask a favor or curry a bit of preferential treatment from Rung. "I'm sorry I can't help you," Rung added.

Lord Perkinsmythe frowned deeply. "That is very inconvenient. You're sure you cannot pull a few strings for me? I would be in your debt."

"Again, I am sorry, my lord," Rung repeated. He bowed to the still-frowning Duke and hurried off before he was late to work.

"There you are, Rung!" Prince Lionel called as Rung pushed open the door to the office. "I was getting worried."

Rung smiled shyly at Prince Lionel. "I'm sorry. I got waylaid by Lord Perkinsmythe wanting some papers on gold and jewelry."

"Please," Prince Lionel laughed. "One minute late to throw off an annoying noble? That's an excusable tardiness." He grinned to show he was joking, which made Rung smile back.

Rung settled in behind his desk and picked up that day's stack of mail to begin sorting. He now recognized the handwriting of most of the people who wrote to Prince Lionel, so it was easy enough to toss aside items like Lady Fornwith's most recent attempt at betrothing herself to Prince Lionel without needing to read them.

"It is interesting that Lord Perkinsmythe was the one to approach you about it," Prince Lionel mused as he flipped through the carefully organized stacks of paper on his desk. "I have the gold mines and jewelry reports here, and I don't notice anything out of place. I wonder if I was supposed to?"

Prince Lionel was clearly talking to himself, a habit he only had when someone else was in the room to hear him, so Rung tuned him out. Carefully sorting the other missives waiting on his desk was more important.

"Hey, Rung, when you've finished with that, do you think you can find the Lord Steward and go into the archives?" Prince Lionel asked. "I think I want to take a look at the reports on gold over the past few years."

Rung nodded. "I can do that. Give me five minutes to finish sorting this, and I'll be off."

"You're not allowed to think about cleaning the archives, just so you know," Prince Lionel added gently. "I don't want you getting lost down there."

Rung bit his lip and nodded. He could resist the urge if he had to, particularly since he already had a fulfilling job. He set the letters Prince Lionel needed to take care of on the proper corner of Prince Lionel's desk before heading out to find the Lord Steward.

The Lord Steward was in his office and welcomed Rung inside when he knocked.

"Hello, Rung. How can I help you?" the Lord Steward asked after Rung had taken a seat in front of his desk.

"I had a run-in with Lord Perkinsmythe this morning," Rung explained. "He wanted me to get him the paperwork on his gold mines and jewelry businesses. Now Prince Lionel wants me to go into the archives to find the reports for the last few years."

"Lord Perkinsmythe?" the steward asked. "Now that's odd. I wouldn't think he would be part of any conspiracy." He put down the pen he was holding and stood up. "I think we should have a look at more than just Lord Perkinsmythe's accounts. He may be a duke, but he's small fish. We need to hook the shark leading them all," he explained as he led the way from his office down into the archives.

Rung had come down this way once before, when he had first come to the castle and been looking for things to clean. The archives were a dusty, disorganized mess. One perusal through had told Rung that it would take years before he could make any headway into the clutter. Cleaning the rest of the castle first had seemed like a much more practical use of his time.

Scrolls and stacks of papers greeted Rung the second he stepped through the doorway after the steward. There were shelves for scrolls, books, and papers, and those shelves were organized to a degree, but a sense of horrid disarray pervaded despite that. Perhaps it was the inches of dust on top of those shelves, or the feeling that time had forgotten about the secrets contained within, but the archives were in desperate need of care.

They walked to a shelf not far from the door, where the Lord Steward began pulling stacks of papers down. He handed the first stack to Rung. "This is five years ago: the compiled reports on the gold industry for the year." He continued to pull down stacks until they were both holding every bit of information on gold mines and jewelry sales for the last five years.

They left the archives, and after the Lord Steward had locked the door, they headed upstairs to Prince Lionel's office.

"Rung, can you take notes?" Prince Lionel asked after the papers had been carefully stacked on one of the shelves behind Prince Lionel's desk. Both he and the Lord Steward took a year's stack and began rattling off names and numbers to Rung, who quickly jotted all the information down in shorthand.

After one year was done, they took a break, which gave Rung time to take his shorthand scribbles and write out a proper chart. Each noble family got a row, and each column held their revenue and expenditures by year on gold. After a few minutes, Prince Lionel and the Lord Steward began again.

It only took two hours to finish going through the reports and for Rung to copy all the information onto his chart. Prince Lionel took Rung's chart but had to turn his head and cough before he could really look at it.

"We need to ring for tea before we can continue this," the Lord Steward said attentively.

"I'll go get it," Rung said, happy to be able to move around after bending over a piece of paper for the last few hours. He hopped to his feet and hurried out the door. The kitchens always had water over the fire for tea.

*

"Scrappy little thing, isn't he?" Rufus asked after the outer door to the suite had closed behind the brownie.

"I like him, Rufus," Lionel replied firmly.

Rufus snorted. "A bit too much, I'd wager," he agreed, gratified to see Lionel blush a bit at the admission.

A knock sounded on the office door, cutting any further conversation short.

"Come in!" Prince Lionel called.

Three adult brownies walked into the office. They bowed and the oldest one stepped forward.

"My lords, we are part of the evaluation committee from the Orphanage Council sent here to investigate Ladder Rung's performance.

We would like to ask you a few questions about his job here. We understand the unique position he is in because of the edict, but proper protocol must be enforced," the eldest brownie explained.

"Ask your questions," Prince Lionel said sharply, "but keep in mind that Rung is the best personal secretary I have ever had. Nothing you say will refute that fact."

"I find that strange to hear, Your Highness," the brownie said thoughtfully. "We have received letters of the utmost urgency requesting his immediate removal. That, coupled with the statements given by our most promising student, Sewing Needle, led us to believe that Ladder Rung had found some way to blackmail or manipulate Your Highness. As the worst student the orphanage has ever seen, we cannot deny these claims have significant merit. Such a terrible thing must be stopped!"

"Rung should have been the best student you've ever had," Lionel snapped, standing in fury behind his desk. "That Sewing Needle came here and cleaned, but he did it in such a way that he was invasive to my life, which I believe is something you brownies strive to avoid. I thanked Sewing Needle at once—I don't need interference like his disrupting my duties to the kingdom. Rung is the opposite. He accomplishes his duties as a brownie without getting in the way or causing irreparable harm. If I were you, I would reevaluate the grading system, because that Needle needs a serious attitude adjustment, as I'm sure you read in the letter I sent about his deplorable behavior," Prince Lionel finished with a snarl.

"What I find particularly compelling," Rufus added with his own cold tone, "is that neither His Highness, nor I, nor the Lord Seneschal, have been writing any letters to the council. We certainly wouldn't write anything bad against the one person who keeps His Highness's duties and obligations so organized. I would be interested to know who exactly is writing to your council."

"Lord Five-Stones was very informative in his letters," the second-oldest brownie exclaimed. "Ladder Rung is disrupting the proper running of the castle at every turn! We haven't seen any evidence to dispute that."

The third brownie, the youngest, looked a little uncomfortable to Rufus's eyes as his colleagues spoke, but he didn't speak up in Rung's defense.

"Regardless," Prince Lionel snapped, "I will not allow you to take away my secretary. Now leave!"

The three brownies bowed again and quickly backed out of the office. Rufus didn't hear the outer door open and close, but that wasn't surprising when brownies were involved.

"Lord Five-Stones, the Duke of Plemont," Prince Lionel mused. "Now that's a man whom I would expect to have a hand in this. He's wanted my father's trust and the prestige that comes with it for years, but my father has never been duped by false praise and lobbying."

"The duke's certainly not above claiming that connection to those who wouldn't know it for a lie, like those brownies, and he's been implicated in fraud before," Rufus agreed, "but we could never prove his involvement before this. But what does writing to the brownie council have to do with whatever is happening with the gold?"

Rung returned a few minutes later with tea and scones. He hurried about the office, tidying up after their intense study session, while Lionel and Rufus went through his carefully compiled chart.

"Every few months?" Rufus murmured.

Lionel nodded. "It would appear so, but it's not on any real schedule. I wonder why I never caught on to this before. These reports come across my desk every two weeks."

"Because your desk was a disaster," Rung answered dryly from where he was sitting at his own desk writing responses to Prince Lionel's mail.

"That's certainly true," Rufus agreed with a laugh at Prince Lionel's slightly shamed pout. "But every once in a while you would work your way through most of the mess."

"Yeah, until a brownie moved into the castle and any chance I had of finishing my work vanished under his scrubbing thumbs," Prince Lionel grumbled. Both Prince Lionel and Rufus stared at each other for a long second after those words faded away.

"That's the connection!" Rufus gasped. "Whenever you actually got work done, Lord Five-Stones would no doubt send a letter to the brownies asking for someone to come clean. Your office would get into massive disarray thanks to the creature, and he could move forward with whatever embezzlement plans he had!"

Prince Lionel nodded his agreement. "Find the Lord Seneschal. I'm putting you both in charge of this investigation. I want Five-Stones stopped and everyone he's coerced into helping him uncovered as well."

"At once, my lord!" Rufus said sharply as he stood. He bowed and hurried out of the office.

"That's terrible!" Rung whispered from his desk. His head was hanging low over his papers, so he couldn't look at Prince Lionel.

Prince Lionel stood and walked around his desk over to Rung. He gently pressed a hand onto Rung's shoulder. "You've redeemed your entire race, Rung," he said softly. "Without you, we never would have figured all this out. You have no idea how pleased I am that you snuck into my castle."

"Really?" Rung asked with a sniffle as he glanced through damp eyelashes at Prince Lionel.

"Really," Prince Lionel agreed. "Now, I don't want you to think about any of those problems any more. I've got the best possible people investigating. I need your excellent work organizing my life. Have you got anything for me to sign yet?"

Rung lifted his head and wiped off his wet cheeks. "I've got two letters needing your signature, and that stack of papers is stuff only you can take care of."

"Of course, Rung," Prince Lionel said with a smile as he took the papers and returned to his desk. Rung smiled back quickly, before turning back to the letter he was writing. How could he convince Lady Fornwith that Prince Lionel had no interest in her marriage proposal and insist she halt her foolish plans without alienating the eldest daughter of an earl?

*

That night, Rung returned to his room deep in thought. He knew he wasn't supposed to worry about the fraud investigation, but he couldn't help thinking about the way the brownies were being used so terribly to further the human's plans. It was horrible, and it was frightening that the brownies would follow a human's decrees so blindly. The man may have been a duke, but he wasn't a prince or king—the brownie council wasn't held accountable to Lord Five-Stones.

"Rung," Broom's voice hissed. Rung spun around and found his teacher ducking behind a statue just beyond the entrance to the secret passage that led down to the basement.

"Teacher Broom?" Rung asked, hurrying over to where Broom was hiding.

"Go sleep somewhere else tonight," Broom said sharply as he glanced around furtively. "Picture Frame and Banister are planning on forcing you out of the castle tonight. You need to stay hidden from them."

"What?" Rung gasped.

"I've misjudged you," Broom continued softly. "You've found yourself a beautiful home where you can clean to your heart's content. Keep hold of it!" Broom turned and dashed away down the hall, leaving Rung behind to stare after him in shock. The teacher who had so enjoyed failing Rung had just congratulated him? Then Rung remembered Broom's warning. Picture Frame and Banister were two highly placed members of the council. If they were here, it was only to remove Rung from the castle. He really did need to find somewhere else to stay for the night. Rung could only think of one place the elder brownies wouldn't dare search: Prince Lionel's bedroom.

Lionel would be asleep by now. Rung had taken a few hours to do some more cleaning in the old royal wing after work, and it was fairly late. He could easily sneak in and find somewhere to spend the night.

Decided, Rung set off back into the castle. He took the secret passage that exited through the fireplace in Prince Lionel's office and snuck through the suite until he was pressed against the outside of the bedroom door. He listened through the wood for a long moment but could only hear the sounds of someone sleeping. The door opened silently, and Rung slipped inside.

As usual, one of Prince Lionel's pillows had fallen to the floor. Instead of putting it back on the bed, as Rung did whenever he cleaned the room, he took the pillow and climbed underneath Prince Lionel's bed. He curled up in the darkness, listening to Prince Lionel breathe, and fought back a sob. First the brownie council was being exploited. Now they were trying to take him away from the only home he had ever had. Rung didn't want to leave the castle. He enjoyed cleaning the large building, and he loved keeping up after Prince Lionel, but mostly he wanted to be able to see Prince Lionel smile every morning when Rung joined him in their office.

"Come out from under there," Prince Lionel's sleepy voice called, causing Rung to jump in surprise. He quickly scrambled out from under the bed and stood at Prince Lionel's bedside.

"Sorry," Rung whimpered. "But Broom told me not to go home tonight, and this was the only safe place I could think of. I don't want to be taken away!"

A match flared as Prince Lionel lit a lamp. His beautiful, sleep-tousled face came into view.

"Come here," Prince Lionel said softly. Rung climbed into the bed next to him and felt Prince Lionel's arms circle around his chest. Rung fell into the warm embrace with a sob.

"I don't want to be taken away," Rung hiccupped, pressing his face into Prince Lionel's nightshirt. "Broom says they're going to take me away!"

"Those brownies can't take you away. I hired you, and only I can send you away. My life has never been so organized and clean before. I've never been able to tolerate someone touching my things or me. Yet here you are, and suddenly my life works. Why would I ever want to send you away when you've given me so much?"

Rung looked up at Prince Lionel and saw the earnest expression on his face. Rung could see honesty in Prince Lionel's eyes and, perhaps, a touch of love. Rung hoped his own eyes showed Prince Lionel the same emotions in return, because his heart was certainly feeling it.

"Let's take care of this," Prince Lionel said finally, kissing the top of Rung's head. He helped Rung climb off the bed and held his hand as they walked from the bedroom into the sitting area. Prince Lionel pulled the cord to summon a servant.

The main door opened a few seconds later as a servant slipped into the room with a bow.

"Summon the Lord Steward and the Lord Seneschal. Tell them to call out the dogs. There are three unwelcome brownies in my castle," Prince Lionel said in an authoritative voice despite wearing his nightshirt and clutching Rung's hand in his.

The search took hours, but one by one the council members were unearthed. Rung was curled up on the couch, trying to get a little sleep, when the knock on the door came.

"Your Highness," the Lord Seneschal said formally as he entered the sitting room. "We have located all three brownies in question."

Rung sat up as Picture Frame, Banister, and Broom were escorted into the room.

"You have stated your case to me," Prince Lionel said formally to the brownies. He had gotten dressed hours ago in order to be better able to coordinate the search. "But you have not heeded my dictates. Ladder Rung is the only brownie welcome in this castle. The fact that you want to forcibly take him away tells me that you care too highly for your own prestige and the might of your council. You have forgotten that my older brother, my father, and I are the only three people in this kingdom who have a final say in such matters. I thank you, all three of you, for your time in this castle, but you are no longer welcome here. See that they are escorted out."

Picture Frame and Banister walked out of the sitting room with looks of horrified shock on their faces. Clearly, they had never been thanked before, and the fact that Prince Lionel had been the one to deliver it hurt. Broom hesitated after the other two were led out.

"Treat Rung right," he said sharply. "He's still my student, and it's still my job to watch over him."

"I will," Prince Lionel said gently. "I'll watch over him for the rest of our lives, and I know he'll want to keep cleaning up after me for that long too."

"Good," Broom said with a nod. "I do feel bad about all this. Is there anything I can do to make reparations?"

The Lord Steward had remained behind while the Lord Seneschal escorted the other two brownies away. He stepped forward and spoke when Rung remained silent. "If you could send us a copy of all the letters Lord Five-Stones has sent your council, we would be very appreciative," the Lord Steward said. "If we can use those letters to tie him to a good deal of money missing from our gold revenue, we can clear up a lot of the mystery around why your council thinks Rung is doing a poor job."

"I'll do it," Broom said with a formal bow. He left the room with the Lord Steward following behind.

"Is that true?" Rung asked softly as soon as the door closed behind the Lord Steward.

"Is what true?" Prince Lionel asked. "That with those letters we shouldn't have any issues proving Five-Stones' involvement in the mess, and we can end this farce quickly?"

Rung shook his head. "That's important and good to know," he replied, "but I meant about you wanting me to clean for you for the rest of our lives. Was that true?"

"Oh, Rung," Prince Lionel said with a soft smile. He quickly walked forward and pulled Rung into a hug. "I knew from the first moment I saw you, looking so cute and bashful, that you would become special to me. Do you want to stay with me that long? It will mean a lot of cleaning up after me."

Rung smiled. "I would like that," he responded with an answering smile.

"Good," Prince Lionel said. He bent down and gave Rung a gentle kiss on the lips before backing away. "I'd like that too."

A HEART'S DREAM

The stone really was the most perfect thing in the world. Mina sighed happily, still looking down at the small stone clutched in his claws.

Admittedly, the stone wasn't anything to laud. A simple river stone, smoothed and rounded by the flowing water, it was plucked from the depths by a pair of children looking for something pretty. An ordinary shade of dirt brown with white and black streaks marbled throughout, a dozen similar stones could be found all along the banks of the Nanteri, the great river that bisected the city and brought the grand trade ships in from the distant ocean. That was where Mina and Paxton had found the stone.

The stone kept Mina enthralled because of what it represented: memories. To Mina, the stone meant friendship, and that was the most precious thing he had ever had.

At one point his hoard had been the envy of every other dragon his age in the neighborhood. Now, all he had left was the one stone, overlooked by his aunt and cousins when they had moved into the house and sold everything. Mina knew what had happened, of course. People didn't fall from the Nantax Bridge by accident, and his father going over the high railing and falling into the water below had definitely been no accident, especially since his father could fly.

The Nantax Bridge spanned the width of the Nanteri River and kept the two halves of the city connected. It was high enough that the trade ships didn't need to lower their masts to sail underneath, wide enough that four carriages could cross side by side, and had a pedestrian section carefully fenced off so those on foot would not get in the way of the carriages.

Father hadn't fallen—it just wasn't possible—but no witnesses had come forward to attest that he had been pushed. Mina had already known Father's will left everything to Father's younger sister. Mina had only been eleven years of age at the time, but he had understood that he was still too young to run the business and the house. Aunt Jubilee was to be his caretaker with the understanding that someday she would hand everything back to Mina. Instead, she had taken everything away from him permanently.

Except for the memory the stone represented, of course. She could take the physical things—the jewelry, the furniture, and even his clothing—but taking his dreams wasn't possible.

Mina loved his hoard. He could sit up in the rafters, stone in hand, for hours and hours just dreaming of what could have been had Father not been killed, had Paxton remembered that one day on the banks of the river, or had any number of lovely things occurred.

Sometimes he dreamed of simply flying away. He didn't have any worldly possessions in his sorely depleted hoard. Mina could take wing and go downriver to the ocean, or up into the mountains. This was one city in the middle of a vast country. Perhaps even the capital city nestled into the footholds of the mountains he saw every day on the horizon would bring adventure.

But reality always reared its ugly head before a dream could become something more. He had responsibilities to Father's memory. Besides, if he left, then Aunt Jubilee won. She got the shop, the house, and the money. It was all technically Mina's, and when he had turned eighteen, it should have been given to him. Aunt Jubilee had gone to the local magistrate instead, insisting that she had full rights to all of it since for seven full years it had been her efforts that had kept the shop alive and thriving. Mina didn't have any money to hire someone to help him—not money he wanted his aunt to know about and try to take, at least—nor did he have any standing to fight with. A protest had been lodged on his behalf by the court, but only because the law required that both sides of the issue be properly aired, not because Mina himself had done anything.

The case had been on the docket for two years at this point. Criminal matters always took precedent in the courts, so civil matters had to wait for an opening. It could be as long as another year before the court heard the case, and by then it really would be too late. Ten years of successful ownership was the minimum for a business transfer in these cases.

Really, there wasn't anything he could do except leave. Mina sighed heavily, knowing that his few moments to hide in the rafters and dream with his little stone had been ruined by the knowledge of what was to come. Aunt Jubilee couldn't throw him out of his own house at the moment, but once the case came to a close she would ensure it.

Was it better to leave now, tail tucked between his legs, or to be forced to leave later, but with his head held high?

The stone in Mina's claws didn't have an answer. It represented dreams, not fears and worries.

Mina let out yet another sigh and carefully put the stone down. He was high in the rafters in the attic, a place only he could reach. The stone would be safe on the wooden support beam.

He let gravity do its job as he rolled off the beam. Mina's wings flared out, catching the air and slowing his descent. When he reached the floor, his small-form receded, quickly replaced by his human one. Mina straightened the rough brown shirt he was wearing before he opened the hatch in the floor and climbed down the stairs into the rest of the house. It only took him a few minutes to walk the hallways and down two more flights of stairs, but by the time he reached the kitchen, breakfast had already been cleared away. One of the servants had discreetly left a roll on a shelf holding the bowls, and Mina grabbed it to eat as he hurried through the kitchen, into the backyard, and across the yard to the kennel.

Mina wasn't allowed to eat with his aunt or cousins in the morning, but sometimes if he timed it right, he could get to the kitchen before the bowls of food could be scraped clean. His musings this morning had taken too much time, but the roll would suffice. He had lived on less before one of the servants had started taking pity on him.

The smell of the animals greeted him as Mina pulled open the door to the kennel. He could hear at least one dog barking and the low hiss of the unhappy chimera in the corner. The business prided itself on being capable of boarding all sorts of creatures, magical and not. When someone went on vacation and couldn't take their pet, they came here. Mina's role was to keep the kennel clean, which was a nasty job at times, but someone had to do it.

Mina went along the row of cages, hitting the switch to open the door for the animals that needed to go outside. There was a bit of concrete under the sun outside every cage, but if Mina let the chimera out, for example, it would simply climb the walls with its thick claws and escape. The dogs and the manticore went outside, though, which made it easy to go into their cages to clean.

It took a long time to clean every cage, especially the ones where he had to coax a cat or the chimera into a separate box for the few minutes it took. Mina made certain every animal had food and water when he was done, and then he went outside to clean concrete slabs.

*

The double sun was high overhead when Mina was finished. He was hot and sweaty, his brown shirt sticking to his back and itching, but if he turned the hose on himself, his aunt would scold and carry on. Instead, Mina headed back to the house where the large stone sink in the kitchen afforded enough space to dunk his head under the faucet. Mina found a rag to dry himself off with; then he took a long, bracing breath before heading back outside. This time he didn't go into the kennel, instead heading to the front of the shop where one of his cousins worked as the receptionist and his aunt and other cousin worked as...Mina didn't actually know what they did, to be honest. Maybe they were receptionists too? They seemed to mostly spend the day lounging around and smiling whenever a customer arrived.

Mina went directly to the closet where the cleaning supplies were kept, grabbing the broom first to begin sweeping up the accumulated dust and pet hair. He couldn't help doing the back hallway first, stalling, but eventually he had to push through the doorway and into the front room.

There weren't any customers. Angelina was sitting in one of the waiting chairs, studying her nails in the light from the front window. Her hair was blonde, which emphasized the dark tanned tones to her skin. As a part ogre, the skin tone made sense, but the hair looked unnatural. It should have been brown with shades of green, but Angelina had decided to dye it instead. Audrianna was behind the long desk, moving papers around. Her hair hadn't been dyed and was instead pulled back into a formal-looking bun at the top of her head. That, combined with her spectacles, made her look very severe. Where Angelina had their mother's vanity, Audrianna had their mother's stern and unbending personality.

Aunt Jubilee wasn't in sight, so Mina hurried with the broom. His cousins ignored him entirely, and it wasn't long before Mina was heading back to the closet.

Unfortunately, the next step was mopping, which eventually brought him back to the front of the shop. Aunt Jubilee had arrived sometime in the interim, Mina noticed the second he pushed through the door. He ducked his head and focused on the mop, hoping Aunt Jubilee would be too engrossed with whatever conversation she was earnestly having with Angelina.

"It's this weekend. Can you believe the short notice?" Mina couldn't help overhearing Aunt Jubilee say indignantly. "How are we supposed to get proper dresses in time?"

Aunt Jubilee was only half-dragon and had been Mina's father's half sister. Her heritage was clearly evident in the width of her shoulders and hips, since dragons were built on strong lines like ogres, but her mother had been a fairy, which gave her body long lines and a graceful bearing. She was utterly gorgeous with hair a soft golden brown curled around her face and wide eyes that glimmered in the light. Her marriage with the ogre that had fathered her daughters had been for money—even years afterward Mina's father had still expressed his dislike of the union—and when the ogre had died, and the money was eventually used up, Mina's father had taken his tumble off the bridge.

"The prince has been stopping in every large town and city on his route and hosting a luncheon or a ball in each," Audrianna cut in sharply. "The larger the city, the larger the event. Common sense would have told you weeks ago that when he arrived here a grand ball would be held. I ordered my dress last month," she added smugly.

"Well good for you, brat," Angelina snapped with an angry toss of her hair. "What about for those of us that had more important things to worry about last month? This is the king's younger brother we're talking about, and he's single! I only have the few days he's in the city to make an impression."

"Rumor is, the king's plan wasn't merely for his brother to tour the country to meet the people and find out what the people needed the king's help with." Aunt Jubilee sneered as she spoke, her opinion of that clear on her face.

Mina actually knew what they were talking about. Even he, with his almost hermit-like existence, had heard about Prince Paxton touring the country. The official reason for the tour was the one Aunt Jubilee was so unimpressed with, but rumor said the king wanted Prince Paxton to marry and hoped an eligible bride would be found at one of the many luncheons and balls.

"One of you, my beautiful daughters, will surely catch his eye," Aunt Jubilee continued after she had recovered from her disgust. "Audrianna, since you already have a dress, I will leave you in charge here. Angelina and I will be out for the day." She stood and waited for Angelina to stand as well. They both headed to the door and Mina held his breath in the hope she wouldn't notice him, but Aunt Jubilee paused in the doorway. "The front windows need washing, inside and out; there are cobwebs in the corners of the ceiling that need removing, and I think the kennels could do with an afternoon cleaning as well today." She didn't turn to look at Mina as she spoke, but Mina knew that if those chores weren't accomplished she would take out her anger on him.

Aunt Jubilee and Angelina left. Mina continued mopping, hoping that Audrianna wouldn't notice how tightly he was gripping the broom in order to keep his anger in check.

*

Mina was almost too exhausted at the end of the day to think, but he had managed to work his anger out by scrubbing things all day. He trudged up the stairs toward his attic room, his plate of dinner—left for him on a counter in the kitchen while his family ate in the dining room—in his hand. He pushed the trapdoor open over his head and climbed the last few steps into his room. The door closed behind him with a thud, and Mina was finally free to let out the heavy sigh he had been holding in all day.

Prince Paxton. Mina had always known who he had met down at the river all those years ago. They had been two children escaping from the rigors and expectations of demanding parents wanting them to stand still or act polite. At five years old, all Mina had wanted to do was play in the water. Running into Paxton—who had the same wish—had simply made the day better. The river had been shallow where they had inadvertently met, and they had spent hours splashing around. Pledging eternal friendship at the end of the day over Mina's rock had sealed the day into perfection, at least until Mina's father and Paxton's caretaker had found them both after a day of desperately searching for them.

The chances that Paxton actually remembered that day were slim and the chances that he would recognize Mina fifteen years later even slimmer, but Mina couldn't help wanting to go to the ball just to see. However, he could already picture Aunt Jubilee's disgusted face should he ask her for the time off to prepare.

If Mina wanted to go to the ball, he would have to figure out a way that kept his aunt from knowing.

He had an option, Mina knew. Using that option would be difficult, especially since he had to make doubly certain Aunt Jubilee never found out, but it might allow him to get to the ball.

Going to the ball to see Paxton trumped all the difficulties involved, Mina decided quickly. If Paxton didn't remember him, then at least Mina could have a nice evening away from the house and kennel.

Mina sat down in the lone chair he had in the attic to eat before his plate got any colder, but as he ate his eyes kept straying hopefully upward to where that one last important bit of his hoard remained hidden.

When he was finished eating, Mina napped in his chair for a few hours, waiting until he was absolutely certain he was the only person awake in the house. He shifted into his small form and pumped his wings eagerly. Mina flew upward, through the rafters and past his rock until he reached the exhaust fan that only ran in the hottest summer days to cool the house.

His claws scrabbled on the latch for a brief moment before the fan unhooked and swung open like a window. Mina took a moment to close it behind him, making absolutely certain it didn't latch so he would be able to get back in, before flying off into the night.

What Aunt Jubilee didn't know about was the house and money Mina's mother left when she passed away when he was four. Mother hadn't been particularly wealthy, but Father had invested well and Mother's money had grown enough that he could afford to keep her house and her belongings for when Mina was older. Mother and Father had divorced when Mina was two, but she had left everything to Mina in the care of his father. Father, in turn, had left everything of Mother's to Mina in care of Aunt Jubilee. Except, Aunt Jubilee thankfully had no idea about Mother's accounts. When Mina had turned eighteen, they had become his, but Mina was deeply afraid that if he revealed them to Aunt Jubilee before the court case was decided she would claim to have been the caretaker all along and take Mother's money too.

It was exhausting just to think about, especially after such a long day. Mina couldn't help yawning as he flew across the city and over the Nanteri. He landed on the front stoop of his mother's house and transformed back into his human form before knocking loudly.

It took a few minutes to hear the clicking sound of the door unlocking. The door swung open slowly to reveal Sebastian looking grumpy in his sleepwear. Sebastian was part drow, a type of fairy with beautiful dark skin and shining white hair, and part tree elf, which made his eyes blaze green in the reflected street lamps. His eyes widened in surprise when he saw Mina, and he threw the door open wide so Mina could walk inside.

"Master Mina!" Sebastian gasped. "How can I help you? And so late?" he added in admonishment.

"Sorry, Sebastian. I had to wait for my aunt to fall asleep."

Mina waited for Sebastian to close the door and then followed Sebastian into the kitchen. He took a seat at the table, and a few moments later, Sebastian brought tea over for them both.

"I want to go to the ball, Sebastian, but I haven't got any appropriate clothing. I was hoping some of Mother's things might be altered in time?"

Sebastian looked thoughtful for a moment. "Well, your mother didn't spend much time in formal settings as a man, but I can see if one of her suits is still in good condition."

Mina shook his head. "Sebastian, if I go as a man Aunt Jubilee will recognize me immediately."

"Your mother had plenty of dresses that would work. She preferred her female form just as you prefer your male form." Sebastian might be speaking to Mina, but his eyes were unfocused as he no doubt mentally ran through all the dress options still tucked away in Mother's closet.

Mina had some suspicions that Sebastian and Mother had been lovers before Mother's illness, and since Father had kept Sebastian on as caretaker of Mother's house rather than selling it, it made sense.

"Change into your female form and let me take measurements. I'll have a couple dresses altered for you to try on by...Wednesday should be fine."

Mina took a deep breath and dug deep inside. Changing between his small form, his human form, and his large form was easy. However, changing genders was a little more difficult. Dragons generally had a preference for which gender they liked best and Mina definitely preferred being male, but it wasn't something set in stone. Opening the inner pathways that allowed the change took a moment, and then he suddenly had breasts straining the front of what had been a fitted shirt.

"Stand up," Sebastian ordered. He rummaged through a nearby drawer before pulling out a tape measure. He took all the measurements he needed, swinging the tape around Mina's hips, chest, the length of his arms and legs, and a dozen other places on Mina's body. By the time he was finished writing down the last measurement, the first sun was beginning to rise in the eastern horizon. Dawn, and the start of Mina's workday, didn't officially occur until the second, larger sun began to rise, but any light that made it difficult to hide his return was too much light.

Mina shifted back to his male form, thanked Sebastian, and flew off as quickly as his wings could take him.

*

Mina yawned his way through his morning chores, which had Audrianna scoffing at him as she glared over her glasses. By lunchtime he had completed everything he had been assigned and there had been no sign of Aunt Jubilee, so he retreated to his attic room for a few hours' nap. As long as he was downstairs early enough to check the kennels and make sure everyone had enough food and water for the night, he wouldn't get in trouble.

The next few days passed much the same way until Wednesday arrived, and Mina stepped into the main office with his broom to find Aunt Jubilee and Angelina had returned.

"My dress is the color of the Nanteri after the first frost, white and blue with sparkling crystals woven onto every inch," Angelina was explaining to Audrianna as Mina began to sweep. "What color is your dress?"

"Green," Audrianna said shortly.

"Bah, you're so boring. Mother's dress is rose pink with golden thread for the stitching and embroidery. You know," Angelina continued in a faux whisper, "I think Mother is hoping to snare Prince Paxton herself. She is single, after all."

"Honestly, Angelina, I would be much happier if you...or Audrianna," Aunt Jubilee added after a brief pause, "won his hand. Still, perhaps there is another rich man looking for a wife who might be interested in me. I must make as strong a showing as my two beautiful daughters. Now, Audrianna, please tell me your dress has more embellishment than just green."

"Yes, Mother. The dressmaker was insistent. It will be quite fashionable."

Aunt Jubilee nodded firmly. "I should hope so. Now, I have scheduled hair and makeup appointments for us all on Saturday morning. The shop will be closed that day. Audrianna, make certain our customers know not to pick up or drop off their filthy animals that day. And, Mina," Aunt Jubilee continued, her sharp gaze fixing on where Mina was brushing the pile of dirt into a dustpan, "you will, of course, stay here that day to watch over the shop. I expect the kennels and the shop cleaned properly."

"Yes, Aunt Jubilee," Mina mumbled. It wasn't as if he ever got weekends off. If he didn't feed and clean the animals, no one would, and the poor things didn't deserve to starve. As long as all he had to do were his regular chores, he ought to have plenty of time to get ready too.

"Good. Now get back to cleaning. This place is filthy."

Mina escaped down the hallway with his full dustpan just as the bell on the front door rang to announce they had a customer.

Luckily Aunt Jubilee and Angelina were gone by the time Mina came back with the mop, so Mina spent the rest of the day peacefully cleaning the shop. They didn't come back to the house until late too. Mina could hear the clatter as they walked up the stairs to their bedrooms a little after midnight, but it didn't take too long for the house to quiet. Mina flew up to the fan and unlatched it and within a few minutes was flying over the Nanteri toward his mother's house.

Sebastian was waiting by the door for Mina and hustled Mina inside to a nearby sitting room. The dress Sebastian had chosen was lilac with silver embroidery at the low collar and wrists.

"Long sleeves aren't really in fashion this year, but they really complete the dress so I didn't remove them. I took in the waist a tad and was able to add a few inches to the length. Try it on and I'll pin the last few alterations."

Mina shifted to his female form and quickly took off his too-tight clothes. Sebastian held the dress up high so he could drop it over Mina's head, then carefully tugged it into place. Mina tried not to fidget as Sebastian laced up the corset back, pulling the bodice tight around Mina's breasts and cinching his waist.

"Gorgeous," Sebastian insisted as he stepped around to Mina's front to take a critical look at Mina in the dress. "You look just like your mother." He smiled fondly at Mina for an awkward moment before apparently remembering he had a job to do and turned away to grab his supplies.

"Did you alter any of Mother's other dresses?" Mina asked. Purple was probably a good color for him, but without a mirror to look into, Mina couldn't say for certain.

"The orange one," Sebastian replied as he returned with a box of pins in hand. "But the color makes it look a little too casual for a ball, I think. Had this been a luncheon for the prince, I would have chosen that one instead. Did you want to try it on?"

"Just in case someone declares purple to be illegal or something ridiculous," Mina answered with a small shrug so he didn't mess up Sebastian's work on the hemline. "I'm trying to keep my bases covered."

Sebastian paused and looked up at Mina with a worried expression on his face. "I'm sure it will be fine. Now, have you thought about how you're getting into the ball? I believe invitations were sent out last weekend to any households of means in the city. As a prominent business owner, the widow of Mr. Donington"—who had been one of the wealthiest men in the city until Aunt Jubilee had spent it all—"and your father's sister, your aunt received an invite. Now," Sebastian continued before Mina could start to panic. He hadn't realized the party was invitation only. He had figured just showing up in a dress would be enough to get inside. "Your mother was also fairly well to do when she was alive, so I made some inquiries as to why her estate hadn't received an invitation, even just as a courtesy. I hinted that some of your mother's political donations that I make on her behalf might be in jeopardy, and an invitation arrived in the mail yesterday. I have also hired a carriage to take you to the hotel where the ball is being hosted. You shouldn't have any difficulties meeting up with your prince. What time do you think you might be able to get over here to prepare?"

Mina shook his head. "I have no idea. I know my aunt and cousins have makeup and hair appointments in the morning, but I need to clean the shop and kennels then. If I think I can escape while they're getting their dresses on, I'll come over then, but Aunt Jubilee usually has some sort of demands for me whenever she goes out. If I'm not there to hear what she has to say, I might be discovered, so I probably won't be able to come over until they've left already."

Sebastian let out an unhappy snort. He stood and began pinning the waist a tad tighter. "I will have a bath and your mother's makeup and hair products ready to go. You'll be late, but that's still fashionable these days so no one should comment. Just make certain you leave the ball before your aunt, should she decide to check on you when she gets home."

"I'll make sure, Sebastian." In fact, Mina would leave the fan unhooked that night just in case he needed to sneak in.

Sebastian completed the dress fitting at quickly as possible. The orange dress was lovely, but Sebastian was right that the lilac one would be much more appropriate for the ball. Mina shifted back into his male form and got dressed.

"Thanks, Sebastian," Mina said softly. He hugged Sebastian at the door before changing into his small form and flying home.

*

"Where is my pearl necklace?"

"What about my hair!"

Mina rolled his eyes and sighed, trying to focus on getting the last few kennels clean. The fact that he could hear his stepfamily all the way over in the office, when they had been sequestered in their rooms getting ready for the ball since after breakfast, was sad. All the animals still deserved to have a clean place to sleep, food, and water, but as usual, Mina was the only one who noticed.

He finished with the last kennel and went to find the broom to get the rest of the shop clean too. Aunt Jubilee might not care whether the animals were being taken care of today, but tomorrow morning she would definitely notice if a speck of dust had accumulated, if only to give her something to harangue Mina about.

It took the rest of the morning and most of the afternoon to finish. Mina was just returning to the house via the kitchen, hoping to find some scraps left over from lunch or a late snack served to his family, when he heard the clacking sounds of wheels on the street.

As far as Mina was aware, the doors to the massive central hall where the ball was being held weren't supposed to open for at least another two hours, and even then, it was more likely to be another hour after that before the royal family arrived. It didn't make sense that the carriage was already here.

Although, knowing Aunt Jubilee, she had concocted a plan to be in the very front row when Prince Paxton arrived in order to show off her two daughters from the best vantage. That would require getting to the ball early, but not this early!

Mina found some bread and cheese and ate quickly over the sink so he didn't make a mess. Once he was done, he snuck upstairs as quietly as he could, carefully placing his feet on every stair and holding his breath as he stole past his stepfamily's rooms on his way to the attic. The last thing he wanted was Aunt Jubilee assigning him more chores to complete "to keep yourself busy while we're away."

Thankfully he made it to his attic room unscathed, and then it became a waiting game. Mina didn't dare leave before his family, for fear they would call him for something and discover his absence, but he wanted so badly to change form and fly off. He ended up pacing back and forth the length of the attic as the minutes slowly ticked by.

In the end, Aunt Jubilee made the carriage and Mina wait for a full hour. Mina finally heard their voices coalesce in the hallway below him, then move father away as they headed downstairs and then outside.

Mina shifted forms and flew upward to carefully stick the tip of his snout out through the air vent. He could just barely see the street from his vantage, but he could make out the carriage rocking as his family climbed inside. A few moments later, the carriage took off. Mina forced himself to wait until the carriage had turned the corner and was out of sight before he clambered out of the air vent. He closed it carefully behind him to make sure it wouldn't latch and then flung himself into the air to fly to Sebastian as quickly as possible.

A bath was waiting for Mina when he arrived, as promised. Mina scrubbed as quickly as he could, getting the day's sweat and grime off with the heavy sponge Sebastian had also provided. Sebastian was waiting in Mina's mother's old dressing room when Mina emerged from the bath. He had hot curlers ready to steam out the water and set Mina's hair properly. Mina sat on a low stool in front of the makeup mirror and let Sebastian work. Mina also put a little line of darkener on his lower eyelid to accent his eyes and a bit of gloss on his lips.

Once they were both done with their primping, Sebastian brought in the dress. Mina draped his dressing robe over a nearby chair and held up his arms to let Sebastian carefully drop the dress over Mina's head without mussing his artful curls or makeup. Sebastian tugged the corset ties tight and then stepped back.

"You really do look just like your mother," he sighed.

Mina turned to look in the mirror. He had always looked more like his mother than his father, but with his features softened in his female form, it was unmistakable. The magnificent dress also helped. Sweeping skirts and a trim, embroidered waist did amazing things for Mina's body.

"It fits perfectly," Mina told Sebastian.

Sebastian sighed again, his nostalgic smile not fading, before he abruptly shook his head and strode across the room. "Right, the invitation is in here, as are a few coins to tip the carriage driver." He held out a small black clutch for Mina to take. "You'll show the invitation at the gate, which will allow the carriage to enter the drive for the hall. You shouldn't need it after that, and you'll tip the driver when he returns you here after the ball. Leave the clutch in the carriage so you don't have to carry it all evening."

Mina nodded to show he understood even as Sebastian waved for Mina to precede him out of the room. Mina headed to the carriage, which had only been waiting a few minutes, but stopped at the door.

"Thank you, Sebastian," Mina said, his voice soft as he tried to keep from tearing up. He was going to get to see Paxton thanks to Sebastian's help. That meant everything to Mina.

"I'm so glad you asked me for help," Sebastian replied, and his nostalgic smile was back. "I might not be able to save you from your aunt, but please let me know if there's ever anything else I can do for you."

Mina hugged Sebastian, who then helped Mina climb into the carriage. The footman shut the door, and he was off.

*

Mina had never been to the grand hall before. The organizers had chosen the fanciest hotel in the city, which had a massive ballroom known as the grand hall. Every time a member of the royal family came to visit, they stayed at the hotel, but Mina had never had the opportunity to go. The place certainly lived up to its reputation.

Gold and silver accented everything Mina could see, from the sconces on the walls to the mirrored panels reflecting the light. Even the dark-stained wood plank floor looked like it had gold veining. The people were also amazing. Everyone was wearing beautiful dresses or suits, glittering jewels, and had an air of opulence. Mina looked the part, at least, but he still found himself standing on the edge of the room, unable to step forward into the throng.

Gigantic banquet tables of food were in the other room where small tables were set up for diners. Rich smells of roasted meat and chocolate floated in the air for Mina to appreciatively sniff. A high balcony held a full orchestra and dancers filled the center of the room, twirling happily along to the strains of some sort of waltz. There was no sign of the royal family.

Well, Mina had come to see Paxton, not dance, although the food was starting to tempt him after only a quick lunch a few hours ago. He was just gathering the courage to step away from the wall to go try some of what he was smelling when the waltz came to a halt. Instead of picking up a new tune, the instruments remained silent. It took a few seconds for the milling crowd to realize this meant something, but once they had begun to quiet, the great doors opened and a crier stepped into the room. He pounded his staff against something on the floor that rang like a bell.

"His Royal Highness, Prince Paxton, Duke of Verrity, Heir Presumptive..." The rest of the crier's announcement went through one of Mina's ears and out the other as he caught sight of Paxton.

The boy he remembered was gone, of course, yet there was still something about the arch of his cheeks and the round of his chin that spoke of the child's face from so long ago. Then Paxton turned his head to look over the crowd, and Mina caught sight of his eyes. They were still the brilliant green of a spring afternoon, the most prominent part of his elfin heritage almost glowing in the light of the hall. Mina remembered those eyes most of all.

The riverbank had been only moderately more interesting than the meeting Mina had snuck out of. Father and some other men had been locked deep in conversation, and Mina doubted they had noticed Mina slip out the balcony door and climb down the rose trellis, thankfully empty in the early spring. He had somehow found himself at the bank of the massive river. The water was cold, too cold to do more than trickle his fingers through it. And then he had turned his head at the noise of someone else disconsolately splashing at the water nearby and had gotten trapped by those eyes.

Paxton nodded regally to the room when the crier finally finished. Mina hastily curtseyed back along with everyone else, but he couldn't take his eyes off Paxton, who turned and walked into the room with the food. He rather rudely brushed past the governor of Nanteri, almost as if he didn't notice the woman gesturing to him. Given she was a half giant and therefore huge, it seemed weird to Mina.

Mina helplessly trailed after Paxton, watching every movement Paxton made. Could he have grown into a selfish, uncaring adult? Mina certainly knew firsthand what a lot of spoiling could do to a person, given how awful his stepsisters were. Had that happened to the bright, wonderful boy Mina had known for so brief a time?

Paxton stopped in a corner and stood there, looking out across the dining tables. His face was completely blank. Mina could not tell what he thought about the hall, the dining area, or the ball itself. He waited for Paxton to move, maybe to get some food or to accept one of the invitations of the women who just happened to casually be drifting by him as the current song ended, yet Paxton just stood there, motionless.

Mina drifted closer, trying to look like one of those women begging for Paxton's attention. Ten minutes had passed since Paxton had entered the room, and still he didn't move or show any interest in his surroundings. Mina finally got close enough to see his eyes, and immediately froze in place from shock. Paxton's eyes were still that vibrant elf-green, but they were empty. Soulless. As if whatever personality Paxton might have once had had somehow been drained from inside him, leaving black holes in his eyes where Mina had once seen joy and happiness. There was no emotion whatsoever.

Someone bumped Mina from behind, jolting him back to reality, and Mina scrambled away to find his own corner to hide in.

People didn't lose their emotions like that. If Paxton hated the ball or his life, or anything that was making him depressed or had hurt him, there would still be something shining out from within him. Boredom, maybe, or pain still would have been reflected. To have nothing inside him meant a spell.

Mina had done his best to study spells after his father's untimely death. Mina had hoped to figure out why his father had been unable to shift forms and fly to safety, and a spell would have prevented that. One of the spells he remembered reading about was called a stone heart. When someone removed your emotions, the book had said, sometimes when death arrived you didn't bother to fight for survival. You couldn't fight for anything, because nothing meant enough to you to be worth putting in the effort. Those cursed with a stone heart would eat and sleep as their body demanded, but had no will to do anything else on their own. They were essentially a puppet piloted by the spell caster.

Mina figured someone had bashed his father over the head, and then tossed his unconscious body over the railing of the bridge, rather than go to the effort and cost of using a spell, but you couldn't just kill a prince. With Paxton they needed to go the extra step. But that left the questions of who was piloting puppet Paxton, and for what purpose had they taken control of him?

And it left the question of how to save Paxton. Mina wracked his brain, trying to remember that spell he had read about so long ago. He hadn't really been interested in the cures at that point, but he had read them. There had been something about overwhelming the spell, Mina remembered. Paxton had to experience an emotion so strong the spell couldn't suppress it, and that initial chink would grow until the spell shattered.

Mina let out a shuddering breath full of defeat. His shoulders were slumped, and even the tight corset couldn't keep his back from bending slightly. What did Mina know about the last fifteen years of Paxton's life? Nothing. He didn't know Paxton's likes and dislikes, or about anything that made him feel passionate. To overwhelm the stone-heart spell, Mina needed to know all of that and more, but in reality, Paxton was a stranger to Mina. He had nothing that would help Paxton, nothing more than one shared afternoon playing together by the river.

Mina bit his lip in thought. That was a memory that kept Mina going in his darkest moments. Could it be something like that for Paxton too? It was the only avenue for Mina to try, which meant he needed to go get his precious river stone to show Paxton.

He wanted to shift forms right then so he could fly off and get the stone immediately. Instead, Mina turned his back on Paxton and forced himself to take a couple of deep breaths. He had just publicly run away from Paxton. If the puppet master were nearby, which he had to be to keep Paxton under his control, then he had probably seen Mina's reaction. Mina had to pretend to have had a fit of nerves when daring to approach Paxton to ask for a dance. He couldn't run off, as that would give the puppet master reason to catch him, and if Mina wanted to save Paxton, he couldn't be caught. No, Mina needed to stay at the ball for a while longer. He needed to keep himself occupied, as if his only purpose for the night was to attend the ball and have a good time, as if he hadn't noticed anything amiss with Paxton.

To that end, Mina let out another heavy, bracing breath, before turning around and resolutely heading toward the banquet tables. He grabbed a plate and filled it, not really paying attention to what foods ended up on the plate, and then headed to one of the tables on the far side of the room to eat and relax. A waiter came by with wine, and Mina took a glass, settling comfortably into his seat as if he were simply enjoying his dinner.

He took his time emptying the plate, mostly because it was hard to swallow with a throat tight with worry and nerves. He definitely couldn't taste anything, which was almost a mercy given how it sank into his stomach like a lead weight. When his plate was finally empty, Mina forced himself to continue sitting calmly at the table for a few minutes more, delaying until after the waiter had come by to clear the dishes. Mina stood, heading toward the dessert table, trying to act as if he only wanted an after-dinner sweet, but he paused halfway there, made himself frown briefly, and then turned to his left to head down the side hallway toward the bathrooms instead.

Mina walked right past the bathroom door, continuing down the hallway where he hoped to find an open window or a door. He was in luck. The door at the end of the hallway was propped open, and the sharply unpleasant stench of cigarette smoke blew inside. Mina pushed his way out the door, holding his breath to keep from breathing in the nastiness, and hurried past the smokers to the low wall that surrounded the courtyard. It took a bare moment to shift shapes into his small form and fling himself into the air.

Flying at night wasn't the best time. There weren't any air currents from the heat of the day to help buoy his wings. He had to fight for every wing beat, and it was exhausting. It took forever to fly all the way across the city, and when he finally landed on the roof of his house, his wing muscles ached. Still, he shifted to his human form and unhooked the vent so he could clamber inside. He lowered himself down onto the nearby rafter and picked up the last piece of his hoard.

Could the memories the stone represented save Paxton? Was it worth bringing the last bit of his hoard out of a safe location on an off chance Paxton remembered that one afternoon as fondly as Mina?

Mina resolutely closed his hand around the river stone. It had to be.

He shifted back to his small form and flew back onto the roof. He carefully closed the vent, just in case he needed to get back inside in a hurry, and threw himself back into the air, the stone clutched securely in one claw.

Every wingbeat made overused muscles ache. Only his resolution to get the stone to Paxton as fast as possible kept him in the air when his body would much rather walk as a human at the moment. He definitely didn't fly enough—when did he actually have time to fly, what with him taking care of the shop and being exhausted at the end of each day—and he was regretting that lack right now. His stamina was nonexistent and his muscles far too weak. It had been two hours since he had first seen Paxton in the hall, and as he struggled to keep flying, two hours quickly became three, and then three and a half. It was still faster than walking would have been, but Mina was panting desperately for air and badly in need of some ice when he reached the hotel again.

Thankfully the smoker's courtyard was empty when Mina landed. He hobbled inside and went straight to the women's bathroom where he wet a towel with cool water and blotted at his face. His makeup was ruined from the sweat, but he tried to gently run the towel under his eyes to get rid of the raccoon look while still keeping some of the color where it was supposed to be. The rest of the makeup came off on the towel, but that was better than going back into the ball looking sweaty and nasty. Mina got a fresh towel, wet it in the iciest water he could, and draped it along the back of his neck, hoping to relieve some of the muscle aches in his back. It didn't help, but he did finally catch his breath.

When he was ready, Mina threw away both towels, shook out his skirts to try to get some of the wrinkles to come out, and headed back toward the ballroom. He could only hope no one saw how out of sorts he looked, but Mina didn't have time to stress about that now.

No one noticed his return to the ball as far as Mina could tell, but he was mostly looking for Paxton. He wasn't in the dining room—his corner from before was empty and he wasn't sitting at any of the tables—so Mina walked into the ballroom, but he didn't see Paxton there either.

Could something have happened to Paxton in the hours Mina had been gone? No, Mina realized quickly. If something had publicly happened to Paxton, the room would be full of buzz and gossip instead of the soft strains of music and drunken chatter. Maybe, hopefully, the puppet master had tired of piloting Paxton and sent him to bed.

Mina did one last circuit of the ballroom to double-check Paxton wasn't one of the dancers in the middle of the room, before slowly making his way back down that too-familiar hallway toward the smoker's courtyard. It was still empty, so Mina didn't bother being discreet as he stared upward.

The nicest rooms in hotels were always on the top floor, or so Mina had heard his aunt say before. On this side of the hotel was the two-floor ballroom, but from his vantage Mina could also see the other wing of the hotel, which was also two stories, but the second-floor rooms all had personal balconies. One of those rooms had to contain Paxton, and the balconies gave Mina somewhere to land as he searched.

The country was at peace with its neighbors and the royal family was well liked by the populace, so Mina wasn't surprised when he didn't see any guards on the roof or on any of the balconies as he slowly and painfully circled overhead. There would be guards inside the hotel, likely outside the hotel room door or blocking off an entire hallway if Paxton's retinue needed that much space.

Mina landed on the first balcony and cautiously approached the wide double doors. The curtains weren't pulled shut, and thanks to the street lights, Mina could just barely make out two white-headed figures sleeping on the bed. No Paxton, so Mina moved on, quickly hopping over to the next balcony. The second room appeared to be empty; there was no movement and no sounds coming from the room, and the bed was neatly made. Mina moved on. A young woman brushing her hair. Next room. A child sprawled out on the bed, asleep, while an older woman worked at the desk. Next room. Empty. Next room. Three older men, hair just going white at the temples, were lounging in the sitting area, drinking. Mina quietly moved to the railing, ready to hop over to the next balcony when voices filtered out the cracked open balcony doors.

"It has to be someone from this city. All the rest of the stops on the prince's procession are smaller towns and villages. If we're going to find someone to marry him to, it needs to be from here."

Mina froze in the shadows, trying not to move or breathe too heavily. He remembered his stepsiblings gossiping about why Paxton was on procession—that he was looking to marry and might choose one of them as his bride—but this discussion sounded like it was leaving Paxton completely out of the loop on that choice. Could one or all of the three men inside be the puppet master?

"There are a few likely candidates," a second man said, sounding thoughtful. "Someone weak willed, yet ambitious enough to eagerly serve our needs. I met a couple of such women tonight. Perhaps we can invite them over one by one tomorrow and see which lady would work best for our needs, and we can have the prince at the altar by tomorrow night."

Someone weak willed probably meant someone who either wouldn't notice or wouldn't care about the stone-heart spell because all they wanted was the power. Mina shuddered because he had two such women as stepsisters, and Angelina in particular would be all too happy to fill that role.

"We will have to wait a few months before figuring out how to kill the prince and the king, to give the marriage some credibility, of course," the first voice added, "but it should be easy to then marry her to one of your sons and give him enough legitimacy to claim the crown."

"Which women were you thinking about?" the third man finally spoke.

Mina stopped listening. He had to save Paxton now, before those men managed to execute their terrible plan. Even if Mina couldn't break the stone-heart spell, he knew he couldn't leave Paxton at this hotel, not when those three men wanted to force Paxton to marry tomorrow.

He scrambled over to the next balcony and carefully peeked inside. Finally! Mina let out a relieved breath. Paxton was sitting stiffly in one of the chairs near the door, staring blankly at the wall. The balcony door had been left open to let in some air, and Mina carefully pulled it wide enough that he could walk through. Once he was inside, he changed into his human form.

"Paxton," Mina said softly, cognizant of the men in the next room who would be on the lookout for strange noises coming from Paxton's room.

Paxton's head turned very slowly to look at Mina, and he blinked, but otherwise no emotion like surprise that Mina had come in from the balcony flickered across his blank face.

"Stand and walk over to me," Mina explained, trying to keep his instructions simple so Paxton's spelled mind could process them. Paxton obeyed immediately. "Walk out to the balcony." They walked outside together. Now came the tricky part. "Paxton, don't make a sound. Climb over the balcony railing and carefully lower yourself down."

While Paxton was still throwing a leg over the stone rail, Mina quickly shifted to his small form, flew to the ground, and shifted back to human. He stood under Paxton's dangling body, hoping to ease the drop.

"Let go," Mina called as loudly as he dared so Paxton could hear him. Paxton dropped the last few feet, right into Mina's arms. Mina grunted at the impact, but got Paxton back on his feet. "Follow me," Mina said finally, taking off at a quick walk through the hotel garden, heading for the closest building where they would be out of sight of any of the puppet masters looking out the window.

Mina didn't know where to take Paxton now. They had to go somewhere safe, but also somewhere where Mina could show Paxton the river stone. It would help if Mina could do something to boost the memory that stone represented too. Mina bit his lip in thought as he hurried around the building and out into a side street, where he slowed their steps to a sedate walk so they didn't alarm anyone still awake at such a late hour. The riverbank where they had played together was an obvious choice, but Mina didn't know whether it was safe. If the puppeteers discovered Paxton was missing, the entire guard would get called up; standing in such a conspicuous place would get them caught. Yet, it was more important to try to break Paxton's spell, and the puppeteers had looked like their discussion was going to go on for a while. There would be enough time to try the riverbank and then find somewhere to hide, Mina hoped.

"Walk with me, but keep your head down," Mina instructed Paxton even as he looped their arms together so they could look like two lovers out for a late-night stroll.

The walk was not short, but Mina didn't have the coin to hire a carriage, and anyway, a driver might recognize Paxton and ruin everything. Mina jumped at every sound, expecting to hear the emergency bells start tolling at any moment, but they mercifully remained silent. After a long forty-five minutes, they finally reached the park that led down to the river path.

Another five minutes of walking had them at the river's edge. The sound of the water splashing against the banks was soothing, and Mina needed all the calming influences he could get right now. Still, he had to focus on his task.

"Hold out your hands," he told Paxton, who obeyed immediately. "I'm going to place a stone in your palm. Don't drop it," he added firmly. If Paxton dropped the river stone now, the last of Mina's hoard would be gone forever. Paxton obligingly clutched the stone tightly as Mina slowly let go of it. "Think, Paxton. Think really hard about what that stone represents and why I brought you to the riverbank to give it to you. Think with all your might."

Mina stepped back and all he could do was hope for the best. Paxton was staring down at the stone in his hands, and a second later, he slowly looked up at the river. He took the initiative to look up! Mina held his breath, then let it out with a cough when he realized he needed to breathe in again.

Were Paxton's hands shaking? Mina squinted, trying to see, but then Paxton's shoulders started to shiver and Mina knew for certain. Something was happening.

Slowly, ever so slowly, Paxton wrenched his eyes away from the river and turned to look at Mina.

"Mi...na...?" he breathed out, his voice as shaky as his body.

Paxton's knees collapsed and Mina dove forward with a yelp to grab him before Paxton fell into the water. They landed tangled in a heap on the soft grass.

"Wha—" Paxton shivered, huddled in Mina's arms.

"You were cursed with a stone heart, turned into a puppet," Mina tried to explain.

"Bast...ards," Paxton said. His free hand reached up to grasp the folds of Mina's dress. Mina was happy to see Paxton's other hand was still locked in a fist around the river stone. Mina wrapped his arms around Paxton, holding him close, and closed his eyes.

In every daydream of that long-ago day when they were children, Mina had longed for something more, but he had never dared put those wishes into actual visions of what could be. This, though—hugging Paxton tight, feeling Paxton clutch at him in return—it was close. But, at the same time, Paxton was suffering and Mina was the closest form of comfort. Although Mina knew he shouldn't read into this as anything more, it was hard to resist, as all dreams were.

Bells started tolling from far away, and Mina sat up with a jolt. He couldn't tell whether he was hearing the clock bells tolling the hour, or the alarm bells. When the smaller, emergency bells on the bridge started to ring, Mina knew it was the alarm bells.

"We have to get out of here, get out of the open," Mina told Paxton. "Come on, lean on me." He helped Paxton struggle to his feet and wrapped Paxton's arm over Mina's shoulders.

They couldn't go back to Mina's house. Even with the privacy of the attic, Aunt Jubilee would notice the sounds of a second person and wouldn't hesitate to turn Paxton in. Besides, they would need to cross the bridge to get there, and there was no way Mina would be able to sneak Paxton past the guard post there. Mother's house was Mina's only option, and luckily it was only about a ten-minute walk from the park.

Mina and Paxton walked, Mina helping keep Paxton steady when he stumbled. They managed to get out of the park in the lee of the bridge before the guards mobilized a search, and Mina resolutely turned them in the direction of his mother's house. He took back roads as much as possible, staying out of the glow of the street lamps.

The guard would seal all the main exits out of the city and would inspect everyone who tried to cross a main thoroughfare like the bridge, but Mina hoped they would start their door-to-door search immediately around the hotel, which would give them more time.

So late at night, no one else was around, especially on the side roads. Mina was glad to be unobserved as he dragged a shivering Paxton the last few blocks. He banged on the front door. There was a clatter inside and then the sound of running footsteps before the door was flung open.

"Are you okay?" Sebastian asked breathlessly. His eyes were wild as he studied Mina, who no doubt looked horrible: exhausted, makeup running, dress dirty. "No, don't answer now. Come inside."

He ushered them both inside, and Mina saw his eyes widen in shock when Mina helped Paxton across the threshold. Still, Sebastian shut the door and firmly locked it and made sure they were both settled onto a couch in the nearby sitting room before starting to ask questions.

"Mina, I heard the bells. What's going on? Why's the prince here?"

Mina shook his head. "You know I went to the ball to see him, Sebastian?"

Sebastian let out a sly grin. "I figured you were going to see some boy. I didn't realize you were going to kidnap the prince in the process," he added as his grin turned into a frown. "What happened?"

"Paxton was under a stone-heart spell," Mina explained and felt Paxton shiver against him at the reminder. "I had to break it. Do you remember the day Father took me to one of his meetings and I ran off?

Father had half the city searching for me, and the only reason he couldn't get the entire city searching was because Prince Paxton had also chosen to run off?"

"And the guard found you both, playing together at the river." Sebastian nodded. "Your father decided not to take you to any more meetings until you grew up, but he unfortunately died before then."

Mina nodded. "I took Paxton to the river," he said, and he couldn't stop one hand from reaching out to cover the river stone still clutched in Paxton's hand. "But when I was flying around the hotel, trying to figure out where Paxton was stashed, I overheard some men talking. They said they were going to marry someone of their choosing to Paxton, then kill the king. After Paxton was crowned, they were going to kill him too. Then, Paxton's widow would marry one of their sons—who I guess must be in line for the throne too—and that would give that son more legitimacy to become the next king. Sebastian, I had to take him away from there."

Sebastian nodded again and opened his mouth to reply, but Paxton cut in.

"He calls himself the grand duke," Paxton said softly. He finally looked up from their clasped hands around the stone, and his green eyes were dull with exhaustion and sadness. Mina was happy to see any emotion at all, but he couldn't help tightening his hand to try to comfort Paxton a little. "He's my father's younger brother, so he received the honorary title of duke when my father became king. An honorary title is...lackluster." He laughed dryly. "I don't think my uncle appreciated not being king, so he did everything he could to elevate his standing at court. The problem with an honorary title is it can't be passed down; it can only be bestowed. When my brother has children, one of the younger ones will get the title, just as my uncle did."

"So he's trying to make his son king instead?" Sebastian asked. He was pacing in front of them as he spoke. "A stone-heart spell is incredibly illegal, but it's effective. You would have married whomever you were told to, and killed yourself when they told you to. It's completely untenable that someone was willing to try it." He stopped walking and looked at them both, then shook his head wryly. "Enough of my nattering. You both need a bath and some rest. Come, I have a safe place for Paxton to stay."

Sebastian waited for them to struggle to their feet, then led the way down the hall and up a back staircase. He paused on a landing where a large portrait of one of Mina's maternal relatives was hanging. Sebastian pressed the center of one of the flowers in the carved wood frame, and with a click the painting swung open like a door. He held it open for Mina and Paxton, then followed them inside.

Mina gasped, staring around at the room. "My...my hoard," he whispered out through lips that suddenly felt numbed. It was all here. His bedroom furniture, his jewelry box—which looked as full as it always had before Aunt Jubilee arrived—and even some of his childhood toys were all set around the room.

"I saved as much as I could," Sebastian said as he gently rested a hand on Mina's shoulder. "As soon as I realized what your monster of an aunt was doing, I bought it all using various shell companies and straw buyers." He walked over to Mina's jewelry box and carefully lifted the lid. It was full. Mina could see all of his childhood jewelry—at least the items Aunt Jubilee hadn't decided to keep for herself—tucked inside. Sebastian reached into a smaller compartment and took out a ring. "Of course, as soon as I realized your father's death was suspicious and your aunt was getting custody, I broke into your house and stole this before she realized what she could have gotten her hands on." He held out the ring to Mina, who took it in shaking hands. His signet ring, silver with a blooming rose engraved on the front.

"You're nobility?" Paxton asked. He had collapsed on the edge of the bed where his body sagged with exhaustion, but he looked with interest at the ring.

Mina shook his head. "Not really. My mother was the fourth daughter of a baron with far too much money. He had eleven children total, and he didn't care who my mother married so long as they were well off enough to take care of her. My father was a very well-to-do businessman, and my mother made her fortune on her own thanks to savvy investments, so he was happy enough to let her be. One day, he decided he was going to have family rings made for all of his grandchildren, and this showed up."

"Lord Indagreet," Sebastian said with a laugh. "He's the court eccentric, but I learned never to let his odd beliefs distract me from his very shrewd mind. That ring might only be a connection to a barony, but it still affords you access to far more places than you'd expect. If this aunt of yours I keep hearing terrible things about had gotten her hands on it, well, it very likely would have been bad."

"Which is why I stole it," Sebastian added. "You were too young at the time to protect it from her, Mina, so I protected it for you."

"Thank you," Mina said, and his voice was shaking as he tried to suppress tears. "I thought all of it was gone."

"Yes, well," Sebastian said gruffly. "Let me find sleepwear for your prince. I suggest you remain here, Your Highness. This room is well hidden, so you should be safe from the grand duke should any searchers come calling. Mina, should I make up a room for you too?"

Paxton's shoulders stiffened, and he looked up at Mina, his eyes pleading as if to say he didn't want to be alone. Mina smiled gently back.

"I'll stay with Paxton, Sebastian."

Sebastian didn't look surprised. "I'll collect sleepwear for you too. Will you be returning to your male shape?"

Mina nodded through a yawn. "Yes."

Sebastian left. Mina focused on his inner self, pulling his magic along the pathways that changed his gender, and let out a sigh of relief when his male form took over. The corset sagged against his flat chest and slimmer hips, but Mina ignored it. He couldn't help slowly walking around the room, gently brushing his fingers over everything.

His hoard was safe. Mina couldn't believe it. The necklace his parents had given him for his third birthday, with its thumbnail-size ruby surrounded by diamond chips, lay on top of the jewelry in his jewelry box. He had thought he would never see it again.

Paxton let out a soft grunt, and Mina looked over to see he was struggling to remove his formal jacket. It was stiff with embroidery and didn't want to bend to allow Paxton to contort his shoulders to slide it off. Mina hurried over and helped Paxton with the jacket and with the buttons on his dress shirt underneath. Gravity took care of the pants with even more formal embroidery after Paxton undid the ties holding them on.

Mina liked the idea of finally getting out of his formalwear. Once he was sure Paxton was set, Mina reached behind himself to try to get the ties holding the corset tight, but the strings kept slipping through his fingers.

Paxton let out a soft laugh, which made Mina's heart soar, but then Paxton's fingers gently pushed Mina's aside, and Mina's heart started thumping heavily for another reason. Paxton loosened the corset quickly and the entire dress fell to the floor. Mina stepped out of the dress and sank onto the bed next to Paxton.

They were both in their underwear, but Mina didn't have the energy to care. When Paxton let out a yawn and lay down, Mina followed suit.

"Thank you for saving me," Paxton said softly.

"You're very welcome," Mina replied even as his eyes were slipping closed as sleep grabbed him and pulled him under.

*

The sounds of someone puttering around, the clink of dishes, and the smells of hot coffee and fresh bread woke Mina.

He had thought he wouldn't remember what sleeping on a proper mattress would feel like. Mina had been using a straw pallet on the floor or sleeping up on the rafters in his small form, for so long. Yet his old bed from childhood, stuffed with down feathers, had welcomed him back into its warm embrace as if he had never left. Mina was also comfortably curled around Paxton, with one arm thrown over Paxton's torso holding him close. Paxton's puffed breaths caressed against Mina's collarbone.

Mina carefully craned his neck to see who was making the noise and saw Sebastian putting down a cloche-covered plate on the table at the little dining area Mina had used to have in his bedroom suite back home. Sebastian must have heard Mina move because he looked up and smiled at Mina.

"Breakfast," Sebastian explained, his voice soft since Paxton was still sleeping. "I've left out some clothes for you both. When you're dressed, please come down to the sitting room. I have some ideas of how to set things right."

Mina nodded. Now that he was awake and could think straight, Mina knew they couldn't put this off any longer. The guard was no doubt going door to door, searching every nook and cranny. Even with a concealed room to hide in, Paxton wouldn't be safe until they dealt with the grand duke.

Sebastian left and Mina gently untangled himself from Paxton. He rolled over onto his back and hissed as the pressure ignited muscle pain. When he stood—which was a slow process as sharp bolts of pain shot up and down his spine—Mina hunched like an old man and hobbled his way into the washroom to get clean. By the time he was dressed in one of the two sets of men's clothes Sebastian had set out, he was standing a little straighter as his muscles warmed up and stretched out, but Mina knew he wouldn't be flying anywhere for the next few weeks, at least.

Paxton was sitting up and blinking owlishly as he gazed around the room. At the sight of Mina, his confused expression faded into a smile.

"Breakfast," Mina said. "There's clean clothes for you too." He waved toward the washroom. Paxton climbed out of bed and walked into the washroom. Mina went to explore their breakfast options.

He was just settling into a cup of coffee, wondering when the last time he had been able to enjoy the luxury of hot coffee first thing in the morning had been, when Paxton joined him.

Fresh eggs, soft boiled and still steaming, and actual buttered toast cut into points to dip in the runny yolk; Mina had to close his eyes for a long moment after the first bite just to keep the tears at bay. He opened his eyes just in time to see Paxton let out a shuddering breath of his own.

"I know I ate when I was under the spell," Paxton explained when he noticed Mina looking at him in concern, "but I couldn't taste any of it. This is the first real food I've eaten in..." He trailed off and swallowed hard.

Mina watched Paxton for a moment, wondering how he could help. Paxton mostly needed the chance to feel things again, and starting with a good breakfast certainly seemed to be helping, but Mina also thought Paxton needed to know he wasn't alone in his pain.

"I don't know the last time I was actually able to eat hot food," Mina said, and if his voice was a little strangled from his own tears, Paxton was kind enough not to comment. "Usually I ate whatever scraps were left over from my aunt's meals, or, if I was lucky, one of the kitchen staff would leave me a small plate to eat once meal service was over and I wouldn't get in their way."

"But you have this place?" Paxton asked, his voice gentle as if he didn't know whether his question might be painful for Mina.

Mina laughed dryly. "When my father, erm, died, my aunt got custody of me. She immediately started spending my inheritance—the money she was only supposed to use to provide for my upkeep—on herself and her two daughters. She destroyed my father's business, ended up selling most of his various investments and such for the hard cash, until all that was left was the house and the animal shelter that shares the back courtyard. Given she started the process by selling off my hoard, I realized pretty quickly I had to hide whatever she didn't already know about. I've visited Sebastian a few times over the years, but it wasn't until the ball that I used any of my mother's resources."

"You're of legal age now. Why not leave?" Paxton looked curious, but there was a hard set to his chin that said Aunt Jubilee wouldn't be happy with life after Paxton was finished with her.

Mina shook his head and ate a few more bites of toast dipped in egg before he replied. "She filed a civil suit on my birthday, claiming because she had put all the work in for so many years, my father's businesses and assets should be transferred fully to her name. It's been stuck in the legal system ever since. I was afraid if she learned about my mother's money, she would try to claim that too in the suit."

Paxton nodded. He took a delicate sip of coffee and wiped his mouth with a napkin before sitting back in his seat. Mina ate the last few bites of his own breakfast. He poured himself more coffee and offered the pot to Paxton, who waved him off with a smile of thanks.

"My problems will handle themselves eventually," Mina finally said after a few long minutes of silence while he enjoyed the coffee and Paxton seemed to enjoy sitting across the table, watching him. "Yours are more pressing. Sebastian said he has some ideas. Let's clean up and go find him."

Mina waited for Paxton's nod of agreement. He finished the last gulp of coffee in his cup and started collecting plates. Sebastian had left the tray on the small table by the door, so Mina used that to carefully stack the dirty dishes. After a moment of watching, as if Paxton didn't know how to clean up after a meal—which, given he was a prince with servants who had always done that chore for him, he probably didn't—he lent a hand. Mina hefted the full tray in his arms, and Paxton hurried ahead of him to get the door.

They walked to the kitchen together, where Mina left the tray on the counter by the sink, and then headed to the sitting room where Sebastian was waiting.

"There you are," Sebastian said with a smile as he stood from the armchair at their arrival. He gestured for them to take seats on the couch before returning to his chair.

"You said you had some ideas?" Mina asked.

"I do, but let me start with the situation here, first. Guards are going door to door conducting thorough searches of every house. They're claiming Prince Paxton fell madly in love with a girl at the ball last night, but she was kidnapped. The prince is desperate to save her, so he ordered the extensive search and the city gates closed." Paxton opened his mouth to comment, but Sebastian held out a firm hand to stop him. "I have an idea of how to get around that, before you start worrying," Sebastian continued. "You see, Mina, your mother had a number of business interests in the capital, and I am known to travel there a couple times a year to oversee them. A lone man on horseback on a regularly taken journey would not raise suspicion. I can therefore get out of the city and reach the capital."

"You can get word to my brother!" Paxton said with a gasp.

Sebastian grinned at him. "I'll need a letter from you though," he told Paxton. "Something that will let your brother know I am not delivering a ransom demand."

Paxton smiled back and stood from the couch. He walked over to the writing desk in the corner and pulled out a piece of paper. "I've got just the thing."

While Paxton was writing, Sebastian turned back to Mina. "The maid who comes to the house every day was here this morning. She said the grand duke is leading the search himself, but he's only going near the noble's estates. You should only get the guards in this neighborhood. I told her I was going to the capital to escape the ruckus, and that she should stay home until I return so she doesn't get caught up by the guard for questioning. You and Prince Paxton should be undisturbed until the guard arrives."

"Do I let them search the house?" Mina asked. The doorway to the secret room was very well concealed, but it seemed silly to just allow the guard into the house.

"Read the situation when it happens. If they're busting down doors, then let them in, let them search, and let them leave. If they're knocking politely and asking for permission?" He paused and a slow smile grew on his face. "Let them casually see your ring. I'd be interested to see if they even bothered to search your house, or based on the ring, were willing to believe your word that no kidnapped women were being held here. Certainly, if they do search the house, they'll likely be a bit politer about it; they probably won't go around ripping expensive paintings off the walls."

Mina twisted the signet ring around his right pointer finger and bit his lip. All he had to do was act like a noble's younger son—entitled and expecting deference—and the guard wouldn't try as hard when they searched this house. Mina could do it; he had to in order to keep Paxton safe.

Paxton hurried back to the couches, a folded piece of paper in hand. "If you give this to my brother, he'll know it's from me and that you're not the cause of my troubles." He handed the letter to Sebastian, who stood and took it from him.

"Your Highness, I will go with all haste. My fastest horse will get me there in two days, and hopefully I'll have completed my audience and be on my way back by day three." Sebastian bowed to Paxton, nodded to Mina, and hurried out the door. The click as the front door closed and locked sounded a few seconds later.

They sat in silence for a few long moments. Mina kept twisting the ring on his finger and could feel Paxton's eyes on him.

"What do we do now?" Paxton asked, his voice shattering the silence abruptly.

Mina released the ring and looked up, immediately caught in Paxton's brilliant green gaze as Paxton looked earnestly at him.

"We wait," Mina replied easily. It was all they could do. Sebastian was racing north to the capital to get help. Until then, it was Mina's responsibility to keep Paxton out of harm's way.

Mina stood and reached his hands out for Paxton to take so he could stand too. "Come on. Let's get the chores done."

"Chores?" Paxton asked, even though he followed Mina out of the sitting room and back towards the kitchen.

"Yes, chores," Mina replied, cheekily grinning over his shoulder at Paxton. "If we leave those dishes for days until Sebastian comes back, he'll have every right to scold us. Come on, Pax, it'll be fun."

Paxton's frown said he didn't agree with Mina, but he still continued following him all the way into the kitchen.

"First, water."

Mina used the pump by the sink to fill a kettle, which he then hung over the fire. While that heated, he filled the sink most of the way with cold water and started carefully dropping the dishes inside to soak. He didn't want boiling water, just nicely hot, so when the kettle started steaming, Mina grabbed a cloth to protect his hand and poured the water from the kettle into the sink.

"See, Pax, now we take a cloth, get it nice and soapy, and scrub the dishes clean. You get a clean cloth from over there, and you can dry."

Paxton went over to the drawer Mina was pointing to and pulled out a fresh dishcloth. "What do I have to do?" he asked. He sounded genuinely curious, and when Mina glanced over, he was looking down at the cloth as if unsure what he was holding.

Mina reached into the depths of the sink and pulled out the first dish he found, a plate, and started scrubbing off the leftover butter and crumbs from the toast points.

"Dry off the water, and stack them on the counter. Once we're done washing, we'll put them away. See. Fun."

"I don't know that I'd call this fun," Paxton said. He took the clean plate from Mina and started drying it earnestly, but then he looked up and a smile lifted his lips and brightened his eyes.

That smile, so beautiful and welcoming. Mina remembered that smile as a child on the banks of that river, when Paxton realized he had a brand-new friend to play with. Mina couldn't help doing now what he had done then: he flicked some of the wash water at Paxton, who immediately gasped when the warm drops got his shirt wet. He put the dish down, then snapped the towel at Mina, who flicked more water at him.

Mina didn't know exactly what happened after that, just water everywhere, giggling, and Paxton chasing Mina around the kitchen until Mina tripped and Paxton landed on top of him. Their faces were inches apart as Paxton stared into Mina's eyes. And then, as if it was choreographed, both of their heads tilted perfectly and their lips met with a flash of heat. A feeling of rightness swept through Mina, warming him from the inside, and he helplessly lifted his arms to twine them around Paxton's neck to pull Paxton closer.

The dishes didn't get washed that morning. Or that afternoon.

When Mina's stomach rumbled late that evening, they finally rolled out of bed and returned to the kitchen to explore the, thankfully full, larder. While Paxton fumbled to put together a plate of cheese, dried fruit, and crackers, Mina quickly finished the dishes. They returned to the hidden room to eat and enjoy being together for just a little bit longer.

*

Two days later, the inevitable knock on the front door echoed through the house. A forceful *bang, bang, bang* done by someone with authority, who expected to be obeyed, had Mina and Paxton both jumping in their seats. The pack of cards Paxton was holding flew out of his hands and fluttered to the floor.

"Guess I should go answer that," Mina said, aiming for cheeky, but his voice quivered too much to pull it off.

He stood and took in a deep breath, before grabbing the jacket he had left draped over the back of his chair—his father would never have greeted visitors in his shirtsleeves, and Mina wasn't about to either, not when he was pretending to be nobility—and headed for the door.

"I'm going to lock you in," Mina reminded Paxton, although at this point neither of them needed the reminder. The words were comforting though. "Stay quiet. I'll come back once they're gone."

"Mina—" Paxton stopped as if he didn't know what he meant to say.

Mina turned at the door and eagerly took the two steps back into the room so Paxton could wrap his arms around Mina to pull him into a hug.

"You'll do fine, Mina," Paxton said softly. "Just keep your head up and your back straight, and they'll listen to everything you have to say." Paxton slowly unfolded his arms, but only so he could grip Mina by the shoulders and smile at him. "Now go."

Mina went. He heard the click as Paxton closed the painting behind him, but then the sound was eclipsed by another *bang, bang, bang* from the front of the house. Mina hurried to the front hall, then slowed so he could make sure his lapels were straight as he walked the last few steps. He turned the lock and pulled open the door, then stepped onto the threshold.

"Good afternoon, gentlemen," Mina told the six guardsmen arrayed in front of him. "My apologies for the wait. I had forgotten I sent my staff home to avoid all the ruckus and had to come answer the door myself." Mina rested one hand on top of the other on his abdomen, and was gratified to see the eyes of the man with sergeant's patches on his uniform flick downward at the movement. "How can I help you, Sergeant?"

"My lord, we come to search for His Highness's missing bride. Are there any young women in your household?"

"I can save you the effort of searching here," Mina replied, hoping the fact his heartbeat was thumping in his throat and his fingers were tingling with nerves was not visible to any of the guard. "There are no women in residence here, and I told the maid who comes every morning to clean not to bother until after your search is completed."

"There are no women in your household?" the sergeant asked, his voice disbelieving. Yet, Mina could see some of the other guards shifting impatiently behind the sergeant.

"Be good to not have to search this big house," one of the guards muttered to another.

"I'll get home to my wife that much sooner tonight," the other guard joked back with a rude snigger.

Mina and the sergeant both ignored the chatter, Mina because he was too nervous to take his full attention away from the sergeant, and the sergeant was too busy staring down at Mina as if waiting for Mina to crack and change his story. Well, Mina wasn't going to crack, not when Paxton was relying on him.

"I'm afraid not," Mina replied. He switched his hands, so his left one was on top where he could show he did not have a wedding band on his ring finger.

"We would like to search anyway," the sergeant said.

Two of the guards behind the sergeant groaned. "Come on, Marcus," one of them whined. "He's just some noble's brat. At most, he's got last night's whore still in bed. Let's let him go back to her, and then finish this street so I can go home too!"

The sergeant closed his eyes briefly, as if trying to find the strength to handle the rude insubordination, but then he simply let out a breath and shook his head.

"Have a good day, my lord," he said to Mina with a shallow bow. He turned and walked away, cuffing the loud guard on the back of the head as he went by.

Mina held himself together somehow as he calmly walked back into the house, closed the door, and turned the lock. Only once the door was completely secure behind him did Mina's knees start shaking. He sank to the ground, both hands raised to cover his mouth as he panted and shook helplessly.

He did it! Mina had convinced the guards not to bother searching the house. He couldn't believe it. He needed to tell Paxton!

Mina scrambled back to his feet and scurried through the house until he reached the painting. He pressed the switch to open the door and stumbled inside.

"They're gone," Mina gasped happily, out of breath but smiling widely.

Paxton was sitting stiffly upright at the table, but his shoulders relaxed at Mina's words. He stood and walked over to Mina, his hands held out for Mina to grab.

Mina held on to Paxton's hands and squeezed gently. "I showed them the ring, told them no women were in the house, and they left just like that. Can you believe it?"

Paxton smiled. "It's because you're so earnest. It's hard not to believe in you." He drew Mina farther into the room, and the painting swung shut behind them. "And now we return to being patient," Paxton added.

He released one of Mina's hands so he could move some of the hair that had fallen free from the previously neat tail Mina had pulled it into. Paxton's fingers trailed over Mina's forehead and brushed down to tuck the strand behind Mina's ear. Except, Paxton's hand didn't move away afterward.

"You keep saving me," Paxton said softly, his words as much of a caress as his fingers. Mina couldn't help leaning his cheek into Paxton's hand.

"I'm pretty sure it's saving me too," he replied, his own voice soft.

"Let's keep saving each other then," Paxton murmured even as his face drew closer to Mina's. Their lips touched, and Mina let out a sigh and he leaned forward to press against Paxton.

Warmth bloomed in Mina's chest, spreading through his body until even his fingertips were tingling with it. Mina felt so right, with Paxton in his arms, surrounded by his hoard, and he wouldn't change anything about this moment. Well, almost anything, Mina realized, when Paxton angled his head just so and the warmth turned into wonderful, burning flames.

Paxton slowly pulled away, and the grin he shot Mina was full of promise. Mina couldn't help grinning back, and happily went with Paxton as Paxton gently tugged Mina toward the bed.

*

The next two days passed much more easily than the first. With the worry about the guard taken care of, and what with the change in their relationship, the hours seemed to pass Mina by without notice. Isolated in their secret room, neither Mina nor Paxton knew how the grand duke's search for Paxton was going, but Mina honestly wasn't thinking too much about it. He had Paxton to distract him, and Paxton was a truly lovely distraction.

Midmorning on day five, however, Mina knew they needed to start thinking about the real world again.

"Sebastian could be back today," he said to Paxton. They were both fresh from the bath and almost done eating a late breakfast.

Paxton set his tea cup back on the saucer and nodded. "Yeah. We should probably clean up a little." He looked around the room and winced, and Mina winced too.

Dirty clothes were strewn everywhere, the bed was unmade, and stacks of used dishes covered every available flat surface. The room looked like a hedonistic den, and Mina didn't want Sebastian to see it.

"I'll start bringing the dishes down to the kitchen," Mina said. He gulped the last bit of his tea and found the tray he had used to bring breakfast upstairs. Mina stacked plates, cups, and silverware onto the tray until it was as full as he thought he could safely carry. Paxton had already started gathering the dirty clothes from the floor, throwing them in the direction of the hamper. Mina left him to it.

The walk to the kitchen was short, and it wasn't long before Mina had unloaded his dishes next to the sink for washing and was heading back upstairs to get more. He was about to press the switch to open the painting when an imperious *bang, bang, bang* sounded from the front door. Mina tumbled into the room, gasping.

"Someone's at the door again," he told Paxton, even as he dropped the tray onto the table and rushed to grab a jacket. He had his ring, a stop in front of the mirror showed he looked presentable—although his hair was still damp, but there wasn't anything he could do about that—and he couldn't stall any longer.

Paxton straightened his lapel at the door, and Mina tried not to look at the worried wrinkle that had appeared between Paxton's eyebrows. Their last few days had been so happy. Why did someone have to ruin that now?

Mina couldn't help hugging Paxton before letting himself back into the hallway. He double-checked the painting was firmly closed and then hurried down the stairs toward the front door.

Bang, bang, bang.

The knock was more forceful than earlier; likely Mina's visitors were getting impatient. Sebastian had the key, so he wouldn't be knocking. It had to be the guard. Mina still couldn't make his feet move any faster. The longer the guard waited, the longer Paxton was safe. Still, the house was only so big and a few minutes later Mina was turning the lock and pulling open the door.

"May I help you?" he asked the waiting guard politely. It was the same sergeant as before, but this time he had double the number of companions, all of whom looked far more sharply dressed than the guard that had knocked last time. An ornate carriage waited on the drive, made of gold and gilt, with carved wood and a team of four identical gray horses. Mina didn't know who was inside, but the sight had his heart rate skyrocketing. The grand duke would certainly ride in such a fancy carriage.

Mina fought to keep the worry off his face, and his hand from clenching into a fist. It was a lovely morning, and this was a simple social call, Mina tried to tell himself even as the sergeant studied him.

Instead of speaking, the sergeant stepped aside and nodded toward the carriage. A footman immediately sprang into motion, popping the door open and holding out a hand. A woman's gloved hand reached out and rested on top of the footman's, and she gripped it delicately as she climbed outside.

Aunt Jubilee studied the house first, and Mina saw the flash of greed that lifted the corners of her lips in a cruel smile. He had no doubt she was already imagining herself living in the house and how that would raise her social status, let alone what riches she could find inside to sell or exploit. Then her gaze fixed on Mina.

"Mina, darling! I've been so worried!" She gushed with sincerity, her hands clasped against her chest as if she were relieved to see him.

Mina knew her ploy, had known it the moment he chose to keep his mother's assets hidden from her, and now she had found out. He had to keep her away from the house; not just because of Paxton, but because she would ruin everything Mina had suffered for. All those years of slaving under her, waiting for the court case to finish so he could finally leave her behind, and she was calling him "darling"?

No. Mina couldn't let her win; for his own sake and for Paxton's safety, Aunt Jubilee could not be allowed to take one step into the house.

"Do I know you, ma'am?" Mina asked, his tone as cutting as he could make it. "I certainly never gave you leave to address me so informally." He was the grandchild of a baron—title-less and penniless at the moment, but a child of royalty nevertheless—and she was a glorified shopkeeper. He had to act his part and forcibly put her in her place.

Aunt Jubilee froze in place, her jaw dropping open in surprise. "But, Mina, dear, I raised you after your father's unfortunate death." She was pleading with him, still desperately trying to coerce him into playing into her scheme.

"You mean after my father's murder?" Mina asked coldly. That stopped her again as she stumbled to find words to reply. Instead of waiting for her next sally, Mina turned to the sergeant. "This woman is not welcome on my property. She is a thief and quite possibly a murderer. Please remove her at once."

The sergeant's body twitched as he forcibly suppressed the urge to obey Mina, and he looked to the carriage. Apparently, someone important enough to command the sergeant was inside.

Mina wanted to call whoever it was out, to get everything out into the open and get it over with, but he knew he couldn't. The longer he stalled, the more time Sebastian had to return and add his own authority to Mina's.

"The order is every house must be searched," the sergeant finally said, breaking through the awkward silence. "She claims to be this home's rightful owner and has given permission for a full search to be conducted."

Mina clenched his jaw, then forced himself to relax. Aunt Jubilee had no legal basis for her claim.

"When my mother passed away, she left her home, businesses, and money to me, but kept in the care of her lover until I turned eighteen. This woman has never seen this house before, and has absolutely no claim on any of my mother's assets. That she says otherwise only reinforces my statement that she is a thief."

Mina could see Aunt Jubilee open her mouth and the fiery glare in her eyes that said she was about to lose her composure, but then the footman sprang forward again. He pulled the carriage door open, but this time didn't offer his hand. A man stepped out onto the drive and started walking over. He also took a moment to study the house, but Mina couldn't read anything off his blank face. Then he focused on Mina, who had to hold back a gasp. The stranger's eyes were the exact same shade of green as Paxton's, but where Paxton's were warm and open, the stranger's were cold and hard. He had to be related to Paxton, and since this wasn't the king, he had to be the grand duke.

Aunt Jubilee curtseyed extremely low to the ground and held it there as if she were standing in front of the king. The sergeant and the rest of the guard saluted, holding their hands by their foreheads without moving.

Mina knew what was due to a member of the royal family and to a duke, especially from someone of his negligible station, but Mina just couldn't make his back bend in a bow. Everyone else continued their genuflections while Mina stood still, and the grand duke tried to stare him down. Finally, after another few moments in which Aunt Jubilee started to wobble, the grand duke waved his hand, and everyone else relaxed.

"As a citizen of this great nation, you are ordered to hand over Prince Paxton immediately." The grand duke's voice boomed, as if he were used to using its power as yet another way to subdue others.

Mina fought to keep both his knees and his voice steady as he replied. "On whose orders?"

The grand duke's eyes opened wide in surprise, then narrowed with calculation as he studied Mina.

"The king's orders, of course. Who else's?"

Mina forced himself to look away from the grand duke, over toward the carriage where the door remained open next to the attentive footman.

"Is the king here too?" Mina knew that was an asinine question to ask, but he was running out of ideas. With the grand duke here, nothing Mina said would prevent them from eventually searching the house, which meant the only thing really keeping Paxton safe at the moment was one measly painting. Mina could only hope the longer he stalled, the more impatient the guard would get, and the less attentive they would be in their search. Plus, the longer he stalled, the more time Sebastian had to get back to the city. Mina could only hope he had gotten to the king as planned by day three, and was almost back to the city by now. Maybe he would get back before the grand duke clapped Mina in chains.

"If you will not release Prince Paxton, then we will be forced to save him ourselves!" the grand duke roared again, his voice echoing powerfully from house to house.

"Can I see this supposed order?" Mina asked, slightly amazed at how audacious he was being. "Actually seeing the king's signature on the order might convince me it's real."

The grand duke turned to the sergeant, apparently done dealing with Mina. "Sergeant, arrest this miscreant at once on charges of insubordination and impersonating the nobility."

The sergeant looked uncomfortable, but still reached for the pouch that held his restraints. He had to obey the duke, Mina understood that, but he couldn't help wondering what the sergeant would do if Mina dashed back inside and locked the door. Probably break it down, unfortunately, which would certainly stall for time, but likely wouldn't help his cause in the long run. Mina took a step to the side, away from the sergeant so the sergeant would have to lunge to grab him.

The grand duke was glaring and waiting expectantly, the sergeant was gathering his restraints, and Mina was trying to decide his best course of action when the *clip-clop* of at least a dozen horses started getting closer. Everyone turned to look—Mina glad for further distractions, although he could guess by the darkening countenance on the grand duke's face that he wasn't happy about it at all—and it was only a few seconds before the group rounded the corner and came into view.

Sebastian was leading them, and Mina let out a sigh of relief, except Sebastian was wearing heavy armor and a stern expression, neither of which Mina thought he ever used. Mina looked around the group and found a second Sebastian, this one much more familiar in regular clothes.

Sebastian had a twin? Mina hadn't known that, although he had to admit all he really knew about Sebastian was that he was Mina's mother's lover and the caretaker of her estate. Mina hadn't had the time to spend with Sebastian to really learn about him, so for all Mina knew, Sebastian could have dozens of siblings.

A man in the middle of the group rode forward, and Sebastian's twin moved to the side to let him through. This new man had the same green eyes as the grand duke and Paxton; Mina didn't need the coronet on his head to show him this was the king.

Mina immediately bowed.

"I received a missive from you, Uncle, saying Paxton was kidnapped," the king said. His voice was soft, yet it somehow managed to have the same amount of power as the grand duke's yelling. No one missed a single word. "I immediately traveled here to aid in the search, and yet I find you accosting Paxton's fiancé instead of searching for him?"

"F-fiancé?" Aunt Jubilee stuttered.

"Of course. Paxton and Mina have been betrothed since they were children. Now, Uncle, I am waiting for an explanation, if you please."

The grand duke had an ugly expression on his face, full of hatred and anger and a lot of jealousy. He wiped it away the second he realized the king was looking at him, replacing it with a smarmy smile.

"Your Highness, I was merely trying to ascertain Prince Paxton's health. He left the ball in secret, without informing any of his secretaries of his plans. We could only assume the worst."

"I see. Except, we stopped by the hotel in question prior to coming here, and I was informed all of Paxton's secretaries had been fired about three days after he left for his grand tour. The guards told me Paxton was lifeless for much of the trip. One even said he remembered Paxton saying how excited he was to see the Nantax Bridge again, but by the time Paxton arrived here, that excitement had mysteriously vanished. I have to wonder, Uncle, why that might be? I told myself no one in my family would do something as cruel as curse Paxton, but then I remembered how much you like to boast about your prowess with curses. I also know you haven't been training Paxton to take over as the grand duke, which you should be."

The grand duke was completely white in the face, but his chin was set. "How dare you chastise me, the grand duke! I am—"

"I am the king! Of course, I dare. And you are no longer the grand duke. I filed the paperwork to strip you of the title and give it to Paxton the moment I realized what you were about. Unlike you, I know Paxton will pass the title on to one of my younger children. Captain?"

Sebastian's brother dismounted and strode forward. The ex-grand duke had gone from white-faced to purple, and although his mouth was moving up and down, no words were escaping. Suddenly, he flung his hands outward, gesturing toward the king. Sebastian's brother threw one of his hands forward. A concussive blast punched Mina in the chest, sending him staggering into the sergeant, who helped steady him.

When Mina looked up again, the ex-grand duke was sprawled on the ground, and Aunt Jubilee was crouched with her arms up to protect her head. No one else had moved, or they had all recovered faster than Mina. Sebastian's brother knelt at the ex-grand duke's side, two fingers pressed to the pulse point in his neck.

"He's alive, Majesty," he said.

"Then we'll cart him back, and he'll be tried in traitor's court."

A flurry of movement started at the king's words. Soldiers dismounted, someone put cuffs on the ex-grand duke, and a group of soldiers lifted him and carried him away. Aunt Jubilee was helped to her feet and let out a disbelieving shriek when her own arms were cuffed behind her back. She was led away too. Sebastian pushed through the melee until he reached Mina's side.

He gestured for them both to go inside. "I'm happy we arrived in time, but you did a damn good job holding him off."

"I was hoping you were on your way," Mina replied, glad to hand back responsibility to Sebastian for the moment.

"Turns out, one of the guards was suspicious of how Prince Paxton and the ex-grand duke were acting. When Paxton went missing, he went outside the chain of command here and sent a carrier pigeon to his superior back at the capital. I met the king's retinue about a half day's ride from the capital, and when I handed over Paxton's letter, they doubled their speed to get here on time. We would have been earlier if we hadn't needed to stop by the hotel to get the full story, and then the king had to draft the papers to strip the grand duke of his title." They stopped walking in the foyer, and Sebastian gestured toward the back stair leading to Paxton. "Speaking of the king, why don't you go tell Paxton he's here. I'll make us some tea. Come to the sitting room."

Mina winced at the reminder of the kitchen. "The kitchen isn't exactly...clean," he said sheepishly.

Sebastian laughed. "I expected as much. I'll manage. Go get Paxton."

Mina went, hurrying through the hallways and up the stairs to the painting. He pressed the switch and stepped inside.

"You're okay!" Paxton gasped, dashing forward to yank Mina into a hug. "I heard yelling. What happened?"

Mina fell into Paxton's arms, glad for the security and warmth in his embrace. With only Paxton here to see, Mina could burrow into that comfort. He was shivering as adrenaline began to wear off, and Mina remembered everything he had so brazenly done.

"It's okay. I've got you," Paxton murmured into his hair.

Calm came slowly, but with Paxton there to hold him, Mina was finally able to take a deep breath.

"First it was just the guard. I was able to hold them off just like last time, except the second it got heated my aunt joined the fray. I don't know how she found out about me being here, but she pretended to be worried about me. I could tell what she really wanted was my mother's money, and I've been hiding that from her for so long, so I was able to stop her. But then the grand duke got involved."

"Uncle is here!" Paxton gasped. He tried to pull away from Mina, as if he was going to personally go scold the ex-grand duke, but Mina held tight. Paxton settled back into Mina's arms. "Tell me what happened."

"He yelled a lot and threatened to have me arrested; he was winning and would probably be tearing this house apart brick by brick to search for you, but then the king arrived."

"Gregori? That idiot. He shouldn't have come all the way out here." Paxton pulled away from Mina, but only so he could grab Mina's hand and gently pull him outside and down the stairs.

"He was worried about you," Mina explained, although he willingly went where Paxton was pulling. "When he found out what happened, he stripped your uncle of his title and gave it to you."

Paxton stopped in his tracks, and Mina bumped into his back. "He did what?"

Mina couldn't tell if Paxton was angry or shocked, or both, but a second later he continued moving, except this time it was more of a stomp than a walk. Paxton threw open the doors to the sitting room and stomped right up to where the king was sitting, a cup of steaming tea in one hand.

"What asinine things are you doing, Greg?"

King Gregori slowly took a sip from his cup, and carefully returned it to the saucer waiting on the nearby table.

"I received a missive stating you had been kidnapped, only to find the truth even worse. The stone-heart spell is not something even my best mages could have removed. You're lucky your fiancé was able to come to your aid."

Fiancé. King Gregori had mentioned that earlier, but Mina had assumed it was a ploy to distract the ex-grand duke. He wouldn't be mentioning it again if he weren't serious though.

"Paxton, are we..." He couldn't get the words out, but as Paxton turned and saw Mina's hopeful face, he smiled.

Paxton reached into his pocket and pulled out the river stone. He held it out for Mina to see. "I know you remember the day we met. We had both snuck away from boring meetings our fathers were attending and found each other at the river. It turns out, our fathers were meeting each other to see if we might be a good match, except when they went to find us to conduct a formal introduction, we had both vanished."

King Gregori laughed and cut in. "It was the talk of the court for months. Prince Paxton escaped from all his keepers, evaded the guard who were supposed to watch him, and ran off before he could meet the potential fiancé that had been so carefully chosen for him. And where do they find him, hours later? Having the time of his life with said fiancé. He cried for two weeks when we made him go home, demanding to know where his Mina was."

Paxton shot his brother a look, and King Gregori stopped talking, but his grin said he had plenty more stories to tell, and Mina would likely be hearing all of them later.

"Our fathers signed an initial contract that evening, contingent on us still being willing in twenty years," Paxton continued. "Except, things seemed to go wrong from there. First, your father died, Mina. We thought to give you a while to grieve and then approach you about coming to live at the castle with us, since you only had your aunt left. But then our father died, too, and the mourning period and then the coronation for Greg took all of our attention. By the time we tried to look for you again, you had vanished. We searched, of course. Part of the reason I set up the excuse to travel from city to city was in the hopes you would hear about it and come see me."

"That—that day by the river. You really remember it as strongly as I do?" Mina had to ask, and if his voice was a little shaky with tears, no one commented.

"Why do you think the sight of this stone was able to break the stone-heart spell?" Paxton asked, and his voice was just as rough. "It's one of my happiest memories." His hand holding Mina's was so warm, and as Paxton lifted his other hand with the stone in it to cup Mina's cheek, Mina couldn't help leaning into it.

"Right," King Gregori said with a clap of his hands. "Clearly, this means you still consent twenty years later. I'd say that contract is fulfilled. First, we have traitor's court. And, of course, we have to throw out that civil suit against you, Mina. I'll see that whatever is left of your father's trading and business empire is returned to you."

"More of it is still alive than you think, Mina," Sebastian added. "I've been doing what I can there, same as I did for your hoard."

"Even better," King Gregori cut in before Mina could close his mouth and formulate some sort of reply. "Once all the legal crap is completed, we'll start planning your marriage. I hope you're both willing to wait a few months?"

Mina looked away from Sebastian and back to Paxton, who immediately smiled at him. Paxton knelt on one knee and held out the stone again. "Mina, will you marry me?"

Mina's own knees hit the ground before he realized they had given out, but he barely noticed the impact as his shaking hands reached out to clasp Paxton's and the stone. His answering smile was bright with happy tears. This was the dream he hadn't dared dream, up in the rafters of his attic room with only memories to sustain him. How could he answer anything other than "Yes?"

THE RED APPLE
WITCH

"Mirror, mirror on the wall. Open your eyes, hear my call!"

Marcel stepped away from the magic mirror and waited. Slowly, ever so slowly, a pair of colorless, opaque eyes formed on the surface of the mirror. Nothing else was left from his mother's time. The soldiers had destroyed her spell books, her cauldrons, and even her ingredients—decades of knowledge and hard work gone to the fires in an instant just because she had tried to kill one measly princess. But they had missed the magic mirror hanging on the wall during the cleansing. It looked innocent enough; its body-length size was wrapped in an ornately carved golden frame—and his mother had been known for her vanity so having a mirror in such a place wasn't too odd. Luckily it was too heavy and cumbersome to move, so it remained in the dank basement his mother had used for her evil spells.

"What is your bidding, my master?" the mirror intoned in a flat, emotionless voice.

"Where are my grandmother's spell books?" Marcel roared at the mirror. "I've asked you time and time again, and you haven't given me an accurate answer yet!"

"Through the woods, dark and bleak, lies the house of candy which you seek," the mirror replied, totally unfazed by Marcel's anger.

Marcel growled, his fingertips lighting up with sparks as he pointed furiously at the mirror. As always, the magic impacted against the glassy surface before fading away and leaving behind unmarred glass.

"That's the same riddle you gave me last time!" Marcel moaned. "I've searched the Dark Forest endlessly, and the only house I've found belongs to those damned dwarves!"

The mirror's eyes crinkled, as if it were laughing silently. Still, its voice was just as blank as always when it spoke again.

"Have you thought about searching any of the other woods?" the mirror asked. "Perhaps your grandmother did not live in the Dark Forest."

"But the riddle says dark and bleak," Marcel replied. "What other forest fits the description nearly so well?"

"Go forth, search north," the mirror sighed in another riddle before its eyes closed.

Marcel sighed as the mirror went into hibernation again before turning and taking the secret passage that led out of the castle and into the nearby town. He had another journey to prepare for.

Left behind in the dark basement, the mirror opened its eyes again. This time, there was no doubt of the smile in its eyes, although whether the smile was comforting or malicious couldn't be seen.

The mirror watched Marcel as he snuck out of Snow White's castle and smiled before finally closing its eyes and falling into true hibernation again.

*

"You've met my stepmother," Hansel laughed. "Of course, she would do something like that!"

Johann just sighed. "I still can't believe she purposefully took you and your sister and left you both deep in the forest to collect kindling for your father the woodcutter. She wanted you both to get eaten by that witch, didn't she?"

Hansel tilted his head, his longish light-brown hair flopping into his green eyes. His hair wasn't as long as Johann's waist-length blond curls that partially covered a pair of vibrant blue eyes, but it reached past his shoulders and he was proud of that fact.

"Well...yes," Hansel replied. He had come to terms with his stepmother's actions years ago, but Johann was new to the area and was just hearing the village stories for the first time. "There wasn't enough food for five of us, and her own son was more important than her two stepchildren."

"I don't think I like your stepmother very much," Johann finally decided with a firm nod.

Hansel didn't like the woman all that much either—and he had reasons beyond being sent to die with his sister when he was a child—but even though he liked Johann a lot—a little more than he ought to (but he was keeping that bit to himself for the moment)—there was no reason for Johann to malign Hansel's family.

"Well, Grethel had the brilliant idea to crumble our bread to leave a trail behind us." Hansel continued, "Only she never realized something besides ourselves would find the crumbs palatable. The birds had them gone before I figured out what she was doing. And then only the birds were fed that night because she used up everything we had to eat. So, we were hungry and lost when we found a gingerbread cottage."

Johann snorted. "That's one of the easiest spells in the books. I could make this room look like it's made out of cheese without overexerting myself." He gestured toward the wooden walls and heavy wooden table that comprised the back room of Hansel's shop. The walls were covered in wooden cabinets filled with potions ingredients, but Hansel kept his workroom clean and organized.

"So could I," Hansel agreed with a tone to his voice that said if Johann wanted to hear the rest of the story he needed to stop interrupting. "But we were kids, and no one teaches kids magic, so we had no idea. The old lady who greeted us was kind and gave us plenty to eat. What were we supposed to think? But she was blind and not too bright."

Johann nodded—a witch whose strongest spell was a simple illusion over a house couldn't be too intelligent—but he didn't say anything.

"She forced Grethel to work and locked me up, but every day she would come to see if I had fattened up enough for cooking. I gave her a chicken bone to feel instead of my finger. Grethel had the chance to shove the witch into her own oven, and we escaped. Only, it turned out the gingerbread illusion wasn't just to make a bland cottage look inviting to innocent children, it was also to hide the fact that the walls were packed with stacks of gold coins."

"That explains so much," Johann said with a nod of understanding. "So that's why your family is so rich for no apparent reason!"

Hansel nodded. "Grethel and I came back with our pockets filled with the coins, and our stepmother sent our father out with a wheelbarrow to collect the rest once she heard our story. Now our house is the biggest and our family the best dressed in the village. If Stepmother didn't spend all that money in the shops here, we might have had an issue with our neighbors," Hansel laughed, "but she's never had a problem with spending the coins and sharing our prosperity in her own selfish way."

"I still don't like your stepmother," Johann repeated with a grumble.

"Yes, well, join the club," Hansel sighed. "Remember that she tried to kill me and my sister, and the only reason she let Grethel and I back into the house was because we made her wealthy. Now, show me how to do that animation spell again."

Johann laughed. "You'll have to show me that house of golden coins sometime," he said as his fingers began to glow. "Now pay attention," he added as a carved wooden duck began to waddle across the table.

*

The magic lesson ended twenty minutes later just as Hansel was beginning to understand the particular twist he needed to form the magic into in order to animate the wooden duck without Johann's help. Grethel knocked loudly on the workroom door, her squalling child on her hip, and pushed into the room without waiting for a reply.

She and Hansel looked like twins, but Grethel was ten months younger than Hansel. They shared the same shade of light-brown hair and green eyes, but Grethel lacked the spark inside that gave Hansel the ability to control magic. His eyes were just a touch brighter than Grethel's, something she could only replicate with drops of belladonna. Johann had that same spark in his blue eyes, which was how Hansel had known Johann was a witch too.

Hansel let the magic dissipate from the tips of his fingers, the wooden duck falling still on the table, before turning to look at his sister and nephew.

"The guards are here again," Grethel grumbled. She dropped her unhappy son onto the wooden table, pushing the duck into his grasp to get the child to quiet down. "They're asking for the town witch to meet with them," she continued.

Hansel sighed. "What does the guard want this time? I'm not joining their magic brigade, and the town has paid all its dues."

"I'll clean up here," Johann offered, half his attention on keeping the baby from getting a grip on his long hair.

"They're in the square," Grethel finished, swooping down after her son and leading the way out of the back room, through the small magic shop Hansel owned and ran, and out to the street.

The square was just a block away; Hansel could see the soldiers watering their horses at the well there and the captain impatiently standing in the road staring at Hansel as Hansel finally stepped onto the street.

"There you are, Hansel," Captain Arno said with a wide grin as Hansel walked up the road to join him. "Have you reconsidered my offer?"

Hansel tried to hide a grimace as the smelly man draped a friendly arm over Hansel's shoulder. Captain Arno's hand was a little too free with touching, and it made Hansel unbelievably uncomfortable.

"My answer hasn't changed," Hansel replied. He stepped forward quickly, forcing Captain Arno to either grab hold of Hansel or let go. Hansel breathed a quiet sigh of relief when that heavy arm dropped away.

"Too bad," Captain Arno said with another grin. His pale-blue eyes were not focused on Hansel's face as he spoke, rather somewhere much lower, which made Hansel shiver in disgust. "Well, I'm to inform every northern town and village that Prince Marcel was spotted heading in this direction. He is a very powerful witch and is considered to be extremely dangerous. We would prefer to apprehend him alive, but if death is unavoidable then Queen Snow White will understand."

"What are Prince Marcel's crimes?" Hansel asked, wondering what the witch could have done to merit such a harsh sentence. True, there had been a rash of evil witches living in the area in the past. Hansel and Grethel had destroyed one a mere decade ago, and a second had ensnared and eventually killed the king and tried to kill Snow White repeatedly. Hansel had heard other stories from neighboring kingdoms, too, about stolen children and ladders made of hair and princesses sleeping for a hundred years, but he hadn't heard of anything this Marcel had done.

"Nothing yet," Captain Arno said. He sniffed loudly and spat onto the ground. "But he's from an evil bloodline, and there have been rumors."

"There's always rumors," Hansel grumbled. "I'll keep an eye out, Captain," he finished. "Thank you for passing on the information."

Hansel was very happy to leave behind Captain Arno and head back to his shop. He didn't care what Prince Marcel had or hadn't done. Johann was almost finished teaching Hansel that spell, and Hansel was much more interested in learning magic than chasing after Snow White's younger, eviler, half brother.

*

Marcel was tired. This was the third forest he had traipsed through over the last month. Once he finally got to the center of every forest, he found everything to be dark and bleak just as the mirror had promised. Still, Marcel headed north.

He traveled as close to the road as he dared, but he feared being seen by the guards so was forced to trek through the trees, avoiding roots and low-hanging branches as best he could. Marcel was scraping leaves and dirt off his grazed hands and knees more often than not, but it was yet another hardship he was willing to endure. When he dared to make camp, he had to travel well into the woods where a fire wouldn't be visible from the road. Marcel had found yet another dank wood to search through. Hopefully the mirror hadn't steered him wrong.

At the moment the sun was quickly setting. If he hadn't known the road was off to his right, he would be totally lost. He needed to find a place to camp before it got dark, though, somewhere where he felt secure enough to actually sleep. An overgrown clearing would be perfect, where no one had visited in a long while, or an ancient loggers' shed where his only company were a few wild squirrels.

Or, Marcel paused in his fervent wishing, an old cottage in great disrepair exactly like the one in the clearing he had just stepped into. The wood was rotting, and he could see from where he had stopped to study the building that the roof had holes. But it was an actual building with a chimney. He could have a real fire and sleep on an actual floor.

Within moments, Marcel was at the front door. The heavy wooden frame hung askew, the actual door long taken by the elements, but one glance inside showed Marcel that no humans had been into the cottage in at least a full decade. The heavy dust and debris showed plenty of small paw tracks, but not one human-sized footprint.

The best part of the cottage was the total lack of happily whistling dwarves. How his sister had put up with that bunch for so long was beyond him.

Marcel found a space to lay out his bedroll and collapsed onto it with a groan. His feet hurt, his palms were scratched, and his knees were bruised. Those tree roots were merciless, especially after he had been walking for so many hours. It was almost too much effort to build a fire and make dinner. His protesting stomach told a different story, so Marcel forced himself back to his feet and dug into his pack.

He had plenty of water from a stream he had passed a few hours ago, so it was the work of moments to fill his small pot with dried meat and vegetables. He left the dried ingredients to soak while he wandered back outside into the forest to find brush and sticks for a fire. Marcel was happy to see that the chimney looked straight and unbroken from the outside of the cottage, but when he returned inside, he still gathered a bit of magic to send a puff of wind through the hearth to see if the smoke from a fire could also escape. He didn't want to suffer from smoke inhalation on top of everything else that was hurting him right now.

The puff of air made it through unimpeded, so Marcel laid out the kindling and with another touch of magic caught the small pile of dried sticks and bark alight. Marcel added sticks of larger and larger size until he had a merrily burning fire. The pot of soup fit nicely between two of the larger branches Marcel had found, and with the addition of some spices from a small pouch in his pack, the smell of a rough stew soon began to permeate the dilapidated cabin.

Marcel went to sleep that night warm and full for the first time in a week. He had already decided to stay at the cabin for a few days to rest and let some of his bruises fade before he curled into his bedroll next to the still crackling fire.

Morning came and the sound of birds leaving their nests in the eaves of the broken roof woke Marcel from deep sleep. Usually sleeping outside meant keeping an eye open for predators or passersby, but the cabin was considerably safer. Breakfast was the remains of the now-cold stew from the night before.

Once breakfast was cleaned up, Marcel was at a loss. There were chores he could do, like mending some of the holes in his clothing or collecting more firewood, but he was also curious. Who would build a cabin so far into the woods that sunlight barely reached through the heavy leaves to the ground? And why had the cabin been abandoned? Perhaps he could find an old table or a chair so he wouldn't have to sit on the ground.

With that happy thought firmly in mind, Marcel got off of his bedroll and headed toward the shakier-looking portion of the cabin. He had slept in an area in front of the fireplace that was mostly free of debris and had few holes in the roof over his head. The other half of the cabin was a disaster. One of the heavy support beams for the roof had fallen in, and the forest had started to reclaim the wood as seedlings and moss sprouted all along the beam.

Marcel found a thin path under the beam and through the saplings growing around it. It looked like an animal had tried to burrow and had given up halfway, but it had cleared enough room for Marcel to squeeze through. He found a staircase that must have led to a storage or sleeping loft, the floor of which had long rotted away. Beyond the staircase Marcel began to find old and cracked bricks scattered all along the floor. There must have been a second chimney, he realized as the path of bricks led him to a massive iron oven. One of the hinges had fallen off, leaving the oven door hanging open and askew. It was unusable without the chimney, but Marcel wondered if he could store his foodstuffs inside to keep any wildlife from stealing it from him.

The oven door was rusted into place, but he put his back into his shoving, and with a loud screech the lone hinge turned and the door opened. Marcel cautiously stuck his head inside, wary of bats, and gasped in dismay.

There were bones inside the oven. Large-sized bones that could only belong to a human. He could see the remains of a hand, and the way the bones were thickened at the knuckles told him the body belonged to an elderly person.

Marcel gathered his magic and let a questing puff drift across the bones. What his magic encountered made him feel immediately ill, and he let go of the spell before the roiling in his stomach made him lose the meal he had just enjoyed. The old woman lying inside her own oven had been a cannibal, feasting on lost children until one of those children overcame her and she died.

He felt sick, looking at those bones, but Marcel was also excited. He could only think of one witch who had been so hungry for children that she had started eating them: his grandmother. With new eyes, Marcel looked frantically around the cabin. Those spell books had to be somewhere.

Aside from what nature had reclaimed, the place looked untouched, as if the children who had killed his grandmother had fled and never returned. The chances of those spell books remaining unharmed on a shelf were high. He walked past the old oven, using his human eyes and his magical ones to search. He stumbled over an old rug, partially saved thanks to a blanket of roof covering it. Next to the rug was a rocking chair in fairly good shape. The find went unnoticed; Marcel had more important things on his mind instead.

He was in a sitting area, Marcel hoped, as what was left of a small side table appeared. It was crushed into three pieces and a large nest was tucked underneath, but it made the section of the cottage he was searching unmistakable. There must be a bookshelf nearby. Marcel yanked leafy branches to the side so he could find the walls, the most likely place for a bookshelf. Finally, finally he found it.

The bookshelf was knee high, with only two shelves, but those shelves were stuffed full of spell books. His grandmother's cramped writing was on the spines, and Marcel read the titles and dates hopefully. He tried to find the earliest journal, and when he found one dated nearly a hundred years ago, he laughed out loud in relief. The mirror hadn't steered him wrong; he just hadn't been searching far enough north.

Marcel reached out to gently take the journal down from the shelf. The answers to everything he had been searching for were inside. His fingers touched the cover. He felt the old and cracked leather and the layer of dust that threatened to make him sneeze. And lastly, he felt the powerful spell web laid on the bookshelf.

It was too late to counter, Marcel realized as he struggled vainly with his own magic. The spell wound around his body until he was completely immobilized. All Marcel could do was analyze the spell, hoping he could find some way to break it. The spell had settled onto his body the previous night when he had first used magic in the cabin. It was an inert spell, which was why he hadn't noticed it. Had he left the cabin without touching the books, the spell would have faded away as if it had never been. Instead he had touched the books and the spell that had been hiding for hours was activated. It had been laid too long ago for him to stop it.

Marcel's body was frozen in place, on his knees with one hand reaching futilely for the book he so desperately needed. He was so damned close, but all he could do was wait for the person who had so cleverly woven the spell to return to see what they had caught.

*

Hansel was sleeping in. A rare occurrence for him and he wanted to enjoy it fully. He had a shopkeeper and a young witch in training running his shop, his sister was busy with her child, and his idiot stepbrother was no doubt still drunk in his cups. Only Johann wouldn't be busy and might wake Hansel up for a bit of early morning fun.

But it wasn't Johann that finally got Hansel out of bed. There was a persistent tugging in his magical awareness. He tried to bat it away as he rolled over and buried his face into his pillow, but it continued to poke at him. It took Hansel a few long seconds of sleepy grumbling before he realized the direction of the spell.

The woods. A very strong spell of his in the woods had been activated. There was only one spell that qualified, which made Hansel grimace. The witch's cabin, or more specifically, the witch's evil spell books.

When Hansel had first gone back to the cabin all those years ago to collect the extra coins with his father, he had come upon a small bookshelf filled to the brim with old magical diaries. One look inside a book told of death, pain, and magic. Destroying spell books required magical fire. Anything less and either the books would be unharmed or they would violently explode.

Hansel had already known after days and days of sitting helplessly in a witch's cage while Grethel worked hard to save them both that he had to do something to ensure he would never be caught like that again. He was going to become a good witch, using his spells and potions to help people. Good witches were welcomed in every town, and the army had an entire unit made up of them specifically to battle the threat of bad witches.

Their town hadn't had a good witch back then, which was why they had been plagued with the child-stealing witch for so many years. Finding those evil books had only cemented the plan in Hansel's mind. He would learn how to make magical fire so he could destroy the books and all the horrible things they represented.

When Hansel was fifteen, he realized there was another option for those books: bait. An evil witch had heard a rumor of powerful spell books left abandoned and she had traveled to the town to terrorize them until the townsfolk handed the books over. Hansel had taken care of her—he had the scars to prove it—and once he had recovered he put his spell web onto the books instead.

Every few years a rumor whispered through the taverns about an abandoned cabin in the woods containing spells of power no evil-minded creature could resist. He had caught a half dozen evil witches that way, much to the pleasure of the guard when he hauled them into the guard station.

Hansel hadn't sent the rumor out in a few years though, so it surprised him that someone would be looking for the cabin and the books. Perhaps someone had heard the story and couldn't travel until recently. Either way, Hansel knew he had to change his afternoon plans with Johann. Instead of working on spells, he needed to check out just what, or who, had gotten caught.

With that in mind, Hansel climbed out of bed and started his day. If he was going to go confront an evil witch, he ought to be clean. He lugged buckets of water from the small well behind his house to fill the tub and then dipped his fingers into the water to call heat to his bath. He soaked for a while, letting the stress of studying float away while very firmly trying to listen to what Johann was saying instead of staring at his full lips as he spoke. He didn't let worry about the witch he was going to capture infect his bath. If the witch was strong, Hansel would have to fight, and fighting often meant getting seriously hurt. Hansel didn't enjoy it, but he would do it for the good of everyone in his village. He couldn't allow another evil witch to terrorize them again.

Hansel dressed and headed to the center of town. Johann liked to read in the sun, and he frequented a decorative park Hansel's father had commissioned for the town to honor the mayor a few years back. Sure enough, Hansel could see Johann lounging on a wooden bench underneath a large oak tree. He was reading his book, totally unaware of the picture he presented to Hansel.

The bright morning sunlight made his already blond hair look like strands of pure gold, which was bent over his book, the braid containing all that hair hanging over one shoulder. The tip of the braid was brushing the ground, but Johann was too engrossed in his book to notice. He was even biting one plump lip in thought as his blue eyes moved quickly back and forth over the page. Even Johann's long legs were splayed out in front of him, as if inviting Hansel to step close, bend down, and take a deep kiss.

Hansel pushed those thoughts away. He almost had to wave his hands in front of him to force his daydreams aside, they were so firmly entrenched in his mind. He wanted Johann; he was absolutely aware of that. Hansel had wanted Johann from the very first moment Johann had stepped into his shop, looking for a fellow witch to trade spells with. That Johann was also nice and funny and so caring was a bonus Hansel couldn't overlook. Johann had the entire package, and Hansel wanted to take him home forever.

But there was a very good reason Hansel hadn't allowed himself to fall in love, one that he also shouldn't be dwelling on at the moment.

He cleared his thoughts and, before he drifted away again into daydreams, purposefully strode forward.

"Johann!" he called as he reached the bench without Johann noticing. Johann jumped, startled, and accidentally snapped his book shut without replacing the bookmark lying in his lap.

"Hansel! You startled me," he gasped. He flicked the book open again and turned a couple of pages before he found his spot and slid his silk bookmark into place.

"Sorry," Hansel replied while trying to swallow a laugh. He wasn't actually sorry in the least. Johann always got caught up in his books, and it was hilarious to see him jump every single time Hansel managed to surprise him. "I was just stopping by to tell you that something has come up and I'm going to have to skip our lesson this afternoon."

Johann frowned, his lower lip jutting out invitingly. "You were going to show me that spell you use on Dame Martha's garden to help her grow such big vegetables."

Hansel sighed. "I know. It's my turn to share a spell, but I promise when I get back I'll look for you."

"You're not going to be gone long?" Johann asked.

Hansel shook his head. "It's just through the forest. I should be back before suppertime."

"Fine," Johann grumped, but Hansel could see the hint of a smile peeking through despite his feigned ill attitude. "But I expect you to come straight to me the second you return," he added with a pointed wink.

If Hansel hadn't already been falling for Johann, those words might have made him swoon. Instead, he was used to Johann's flirting and through sheer force of will kept his knees from buckling, his heart from beating out of his chest, or his lips from descending to meet with Johann's. Okay, so maybe he did love Johann, but Hansel still kept his thoughts to himself. There was something he had to make sure of first.

"If you insist," Hansel replied loftily with a wave of one hand, trying to show that Johann's flirting didn't actually have an effect on him. "I'll see you later then."

Hansel walked off. He wanted to stop by his shop first to check in— that ought to take enough time—and then he would head into the woods.

*

Hansel was barely a hundred yards into the woods when he noticed he was being followed. He had known that would happen, but it made his heart sink all the same. He let himself be tracked as he walked through the woods along a path that was unfortunately very familiar to him.

The first time he had walked down the path had been an accident, fueled by youth and ignorance as well as a hungry stomach and a whining younger sister. The second time had been with his father, explaining that the cottage was filled from floor to roof with shining golden coins. Then the evil witches had started to arrive, chasing after those terrible spell books, and Hansel had walked down the path to stop them. Now there was another witch waiting at the end of the path; plus, there was a witch following behind him. Hansel had had his fill of walking down the damned path.

The way was winding, and there were protective spells along the path that Hansel had to disable in order to get by. He left the spells inert; he wanted his follower to reach the cabin, too, and forcing him to play with Hansel's protections might scare him away. Finally, the clearing came into view, and Hansel walked toward the dilapidated cabin centered in the middle.

His fingertips glowed as he chanted softly. The witch in the house could no doubt sense him, and the one following Hansel was watching from behind a tree. Hansel ignored them both, focusing on his spell work instead. The destroyed house appeared to shimmer for a few moments before a quaint cottage appeared instead. This was the house that had appeared once the witch and her spells were dead. Inside the walls had been packed with gold coins, but outside it looked like a normal home. The house that had drawn him in as a hungry child had been covered in inviting gingerbread, which had been just as much an illusion as Hansel's illusion of the dilapidated house. Without any concealing spells, it looked so ordinary even an adult wouldn't have hesitated to knock and ask for help. The witch, despite being senile, had known what she was up to.

Once the magic had dissipated from his fingers, Hansel strode to the front door. It was unlocked and he pulled it open with a forcible yank. He left it open behind him, an invitation for his follower to snoop, and strode inside.

Next to the main fireplace was an unwashed pot filled with what looked like the remains of stew. A worn pack lay next to an equally worn bedroll, situated near the fire for warmth. It was odd that the witch had chosen to camp before beginning the search for the spell books, but it wasn't unheard of. Most were so greedy that their first inclination was to find the books and then find dinner, but that didn't mean every witch was the same.

In the back of the house was the sitting area. The evil witch had liked to sit in her rocking chair and read her evil books while the children cooked in the massive oven behind her. Kneeling on the floor, one hand outstretched and fingers barely touching the spine of a book, was a young man approximately Hansel's own age.

His skin was white as snow, his lips as red as blood, and his hair as black as ebony. There was no mistaking the witch his spells had caught. Prince Marcel, the most wanted evil witch in the country, was helplessly bound in Hansel's trap, and, Hansel remembered, another witch had been following him. He turned around just in time to see Johann step through the doorway, his hands raised and fingertips alight with magic. Johann took two steps forward before his magic flickered out, and then he struggled with the spell web Hansel had weaved over the doorway until he, too, was caught.

"There was once a witch who was desperate for children," Hansel said coldly. "So desperate that her evil deeds to accomplish her goal were known far and wide. But the evil witch began to age, and her lust for children grew into a form of insanity. When she settled into this house, she had already destroyed two villages. Children in my village quickly began to go missing, and when my own crazy stepmother decided that Grethel and I were too great a burden, she abandoned us in the woods to get eaten. But Grethel and I defeated the witch instead. I knew there was evil here. I knew that other evil witches would lust for the spells contained in those journals. But I never expected to catch Prince Marcel and Prince Johann."

"You knew," Johann rasped through the spells keeping him still. "You knew who I am and why I was at your village."

Hansel nodded. "The entire time. There is only one reason a witch will travel this far north, and it isn't to exchange spells with me."

"You led me here on purpose," Johann snapped.

"Yes," Hansel snapped back. Johann was still so beautiful, even though he was angry. Hansel couldn't stop himself from recognizing that fact. Johann was his friend, and Hansel honestly thought he was a good person. Had Johann been an evil witch, bad things would have started occurring in the village. An evil witch was always so consumed by their power that they couldn't help themselves. When people hadn't started vanishing from their beds, Hansel had allowed himself to hope that Johann was telling the truth. Instead, Johann had finally revealed his lust for the evil books and Hansel's heart had started breaking.

"Let me tell you a story," Johann hissed through a jaw clenched in anger. His eyes flashed with magic that Hansel's web prevented from lashing out. "Let me tell you a story about an old crone desperate for children."

He started his story in the exact same way Hansel had. That should have been warning enough for Hansel to realize where the story was going, but he still felt betrayed and hurt.

"An old woman moved into a house with a large, walled garden in the backyard. There she grew beautiful Rapunzel lettuce. When she learned the family living on the other side of the wall was expecting a child, she put an evil spell on that lettuce. The expectant mother had craved strange things before due to her pregnancy, so her husband didn't think twice about scaling the wall to pick Rapunzel lettuce to appease her. But the mother fell terribly ill, and the crone appeared on their doorstep and revealed herself to the family as an evil witch. In return for her healing the mother, the witch would take their newborn child. And so, it was done, and the evil witch disappeared with her new baby girl.

"The girl grew up eventually, as all children do," Johann continued with a sneer on his face. "But the evil witch wouldn't allow her child to become an adult. She dressed the young woman in children's clothes and tried to pretend that womanhood wasn't quickly arriving for the child. But then the girl met a boy and they kissed. The evil witch went ballistic. She killed the boy and ate him raw, then took the girl and locked her up in a tall tower with no exits save one window. There she confined the girl and put a spell on her hair so it would grow long and strong enough to be used as a ladder.

"The rest of the story doesn't matter. A prince came to rescue the girl, the evil witch found out, and prince and girl were banished to opposite sides of the world, the prince blind and the girl lost. Eventually they found each other again, and Prince Handsome and Princess

Rapunzel lived happily ever after. Until they had kids and realized the spell on Rapunzel's hair was hereditary. My sister almost killed her husband in her sleep one night when her hair grew triple the length and nearly smothered him. I have to cut my hair daily or I'll end up dragging a tail of it along the ground. And somewhere in those spell books," he finished with a pointed glare at the small bookshelf, "is the evil spell laid out that will allow me to begin unraveling the spell on my hair!"

The story was so very strange, Hansel thought. Hair that never stopped growing was an odd spell to worry about. Yet, the ferocity and the sincerity in Johann's eyes were unmistakable. Hansel had spent enough time staring into Johann's eyes to know when Johann was lying or playing a joke, and Hansel didn't think this was one of those times.

"Why these spell books in particular?" Hansel asked, feeling defeated. Was he really considering freeing Johann from the spell web and allowing him to look through the evil books?

"I followed the old stories," Johann explained, his shoulders drooping in what looked like defeat to Hansel. "The evil witch went completely crazy when my mother betrayed her by growing up. She started eating children village by village, so her trail was easy enough to follow. It led me here, to a village that had been plagued by an evil witch eating their children until one day Hansel and Grethel walked out of the woods unharmed."

"You only made friends with me to trick me into showing you where the books were?" Hansel asked sharply, the feeling of betrayal growing in his chest again.

Johann bit his lip, a familiar gesture that almost made Hansel relent and forgive. Johann was upset and contrite, but until Hansel heard the full explanation he wouldn't allow himself to give in.

"At first that was the plan," Johann said softly, as if the weakness of his voice could hide the hurt his words were causing. "I thought that would be the fastest way—become friends with the man who as a boy defeated the witch, and I knew I would eventually learn the location of the spell books. But then I met you," Johann insisted in a stronger voice. "And I spoke with you, and we shared spells, and I realized all of a sudden that we were friends in truth. I never lied to you about that. But Hansel, you—" He paused, blushing much to Hansel's surprise. "—you're amazing; you know that? You survived the evil witch and gained a purpose in life to defeat evil that I have never seen before. You're wonderful and I really did grow to like that...and you. I like you."

*

The dilapidated cottage was shimmering around Marcel. Despite being trapped, he could feel the magic swirling around him, and he swore at himself. It was the easiest spell in the world, putting a simple illusion on a house to make it look like something it wasn't, but because of the ease it was also a deceptively subtle spell. Marcel, in his arrogance, had totally missed it.

The broken-down house had been so inviting to a weary traveler and the space in front of the fire perfect to spend a night and move on. Had Marcel done just that, he would never have been caught. It was genius to leave just one viable pathway through the clutter. The path led past the old oven with the witch's bones, a warning to any intruder of just what would happen to them should they attempt to steal the evil spell books just beyond. A warning Marcel had ignored.

The spell work had been so clever and so delicate he had never realized he was caught in a trap until after it was sprung. Watching all of that perfect work purposefully unravel around him was illuminating and humbling. It was also damned impressive, but if it got him turned in to the guard, Marcel would have to be impressed after he escaped.

The witch who walked inside the house once the spell had settled was young, but power and competence exuded from him. His green eyes missed nothing as they studied Marcel, and recognition flashed there after a few moments. Then a second witch walked into the cottage. Marcel thought about warning Prince Johann about the trap. They had grown up together, two princes tucked safely away for fostering until Snow White had taken the throne and Marcel had been called home. But Marcel saw the web of spells Johann had unwittingly walked into when he stepped through the open cottage door. It was far too late for Marcel to say anything to help Johann.

And then the sob stories began. The same crazy evil witch had tormented both men, and they were also apparently in love with each other. The anguished looks of hurt and betrayal that as Johann's story progressed grew into relief were not fun to watch. When Johann, that romantic idiot, began to confess his feelings, Marcel had had enough.

"I've been stuck here for hours," he interrupted. "Before you start kissing, do you think you could let me go?"

The stranger Johann was so enamored with spun around to glare at Marcel. He twirled his glowing fingers behind his back, and as simply as that Johann was freed. Johann stumbled on unsteady feet for a second before taking a few wobbly steps and sinking into the rocking chair next to Marcel.

"Why are you here?" Johann asked.

"For the same damned reason you are," Marcel replied. All of a sudden, he just felt exhausted. All of his searching had led him to this debacle, and his anger over his failure was useless. "Let me tell you a story," he said instead, since that seemed to be the theme of the day. He even started with the same words, since his story was connected to theirs. That also seemed to be the theme of the day; three terrible stories from three different lives that were all somehow connected by the same damned witch.

"There once was an evil witch who desperately wanted a child. She was young and beautiful, but despite all the usual methods and the spell-augmented ones, she could not get pregnant. Toward the end of her life she would go insane, stealing baby girls to lock up in towers and traveling from village to village to eat children." He saw the recognition in their eyes as he referenced their stories in conjunction with his own. The evil witch had traveled far and wide, spreading her poison, and somehow, they had all been impacted.

"But in my story, she was still young and, while she was still evil, she hadn't quite gone crazy yet. She traveled the world searching for something that would allow her to have a child, and one day she encountered an evil fairy looking to curse a baby recently born in a nearby kingdom. They traded spells. The baby would grow up and then prick her finger on a spindle and instantly die while the evil witch could have exactly one child. And so, the witch gave birth and the child grew into a very beautiful, very vain young woman. The evil witch was forced to watch as the child she had fought so hard for married a king and left her behind, which was, I believe, when she started going insane. The beautiful daughter had inherited the evil witch's inability to bear children, but she had heard a story of a spell wrought by a queen that brought to life a daughter with skin as white as snow, lips as red as blood, and hair as black as ebony. She married that king and studied the spell left behind in the queen's bower, and eventually she gave birth to me. The rest of Snow White's story is widely known, but the story of that baby girl from nearly a hundred years ago has been forgotten.

"My mother told me with glee about how she had been conceived thanks to an evil fairy. But, I later found out that the good fairies had managed to counter that evil spell, and the girl had pricked her finger and fallen into sleep instead of death. Further research led me to believe that after a hundred years the power of the good fairies would fade and the girl would die. It has almost been a hundred years, and somewhere in these spell books is the answer to how to unweave that spell and save her."

Johann sighed. "Damn, but we're all screwed up."

"My mother used a similar spell against Snow White, you know," Marcel continued. If he was going to keep Johann and the stranger from turning him in to the guard, he knew he had to keep telling the truth. "A bite of a poisoned apple sent her into deadly slumber. Had Snow White actually swallowed the apple instead of it getting caught in her throat, she would have died outright. But they destroyed every single one of my mother's spell books after her death. Only my grandmother's books, these books, hold the key."

"And you want to save this forgotten princess," the stranger said skeptically. His arms were crossed over his chest, and his face was set into a hard frown.

"Hansel," Johann implored. "This is Prince Marcel. I grew up with him, and I know he's not evil."

Hansel shook his head. "Of course, he's not evil. People haven't been dying mysterious deaths all across the kingdom while he's been running from the guard. Even the most distracted evil witch would stop to take a few beating hearts for some spell or another. I've been keeping my ears open, and I haven't heard anything. But there's always a starting point for each evil witch, and I don't want reading these awful books to be it. For either of you!"

The spell on Marcel swirled slightly around his body and somehow managed to dissipate as swiftly and secretly as it had appeared. Marcel finally let his arm drop to his side, and he sat on the rug in front of the bookshelf with a thump.

"Your spell work is very impressive," Marcel couldn't help saying to Hansel. He had honestly never seen such fine and delicate control before.

"Yeah," Johann agreed. "All this time I've been teaching you paltry animation spells when you could weave capture and nullification webs?"

"I hadn't tried an animation spell before you showed me one," Hansel defended himself. "These webs are my specialty, since I've spent a lot of time and effort trying to capture evil witches using the spell books as bait."

"Makes sense, I guess," Johann sighed, but Marcel could see the teasing twinkle in his eyes. "So, what are you going to do now that you know we're also after the books?"

Hansel shook his head and groaned. "Honestly, I don't really know. But I think if I watch you both carefully to make sure you're not drawn into any evil spells aside from the ones you're interested in I can keep the books from corrupting you."

"I would appreciate a chance," Marcel interjected, looking for any possibility that he could try to find the spell he needed.

"Then I hope I don't regret this," Hansel replied. Hansel reached directly into and through the complicated protection web around the bookshelf. Somehow, he could read the web and avoid the traps that would stop even the man who had designed them. Marcel knew he would never have even the slightest bit of that advanced sight and control, but then he didn't think Hansel would ever be able to master Marcel's specialty either.

The first book Hansel removed from the web was the one Marcel had been reaching for. It dated back nearly a hundred years and would most likely be where the spell was written down. The second book he pulled free was from forty years ago, when Queen Rapunzel had been a child. He handed both books over and then began to weave a new web. Marcel allowed the web to settle over him, and when he opened the book, he found he couldn't actually read what was on the pages. He flipped though the book, carefully because of its age, until he found a spell in the middle that was perfectly legible.

"That's a very nifty spell. You'll have to teach it to me," Marcel murmured as he began to read pure evil.

"I've found it very useful," Hansel agreed.

*

Hansel refused to leave Marcel and Johann alone when two of the evil books were out of the spell web. Just because he had put his search spell onto the books didn't mean that something bad couldn't still happen. Hansel thought he had judged both men correctly—neither seemed facetious when telling their story—but it was good to be safe just in case.

"Ohh," Johann moaned. "Mother forgot to mention the part where the witch bathed her hair with the blood of a virgin on her wedding night."

"That requires at least two violent deaths to nullify," Marcel murmured absentmindedly as he ran his finger down the page he was reading.

Johann moaned again. "You think I don't know that?" He took another long moment to reread the spell before shutting the book firmly. He handed the book back to Hansel and then shuddered theatrically. "I feel like I need a bath, a very hot bath."

Hansel returned the book to the shelf, glad there was only one evil book still out. "At least you know there's nothing you can do," he said gently, hoping to return the usual grin to Johann's face.

Johann rubbed his face with tired hands and let out a groan. "I hope I don't end up like my sister. Every morning her maid has to chop off the three feet of hair that grew overnight. The wig makers love her, but it drives her crazy. I just give the ends a trim every few hours to keep it under control."

"I'd be happy to help you with that," Hansel said gently, reaching out to lay his hand over the thick braid of blond hair hanging over Johann's shoulder. "Maybe I can try to create a spell web that will take care of it for you. You and I can experiment and then send it to your sister for a birthday present?"

Johann's smile finally returned to his face. "She would like that. But you'll have to come home with me to give it to her in person. She'll want to meet you."

The last time their faces had moved so close and their voices so husky with lust, Marcel had interrupted before their lips could actually press together. Marcel didn't disappoint, speaking just as Hansel could feel the heat of Johann's breath against his own lips.

"What do you know about true love's first kiss?" Marcel asked. Hansel could tell he hadn't interrupted again on purpose; he had been so absorbed in studying the spell that when he looked up to see Hansel and Johann pressed close a touch of surprise flitted across his face.

"That would be nice," Johann muttered under his breath, albeit with a pointed look at Hansel that made his face heat up.

"Everything I've read says 'true love's kiss' is a catch-all phrase made to sound fancy and intimidating," Hansel answered thoughtfully.

He didn't know how to respond to Johann with anything more than a shy grin, so he focused on Marcel instead. "It's really the intent that matters, so if you want to save the princess, you give her a kiss while keeping that thought firmly in mind, the spell should break."

"Are you sure that's the solution?" Johann asked. His hand crept forward to grip Hansel's, as if he wanted to reassure Hansel that he understood why Hansel hadn't answered with words. Hansel squeezed his hand and didn't let go.

"I think so. Looking at the components to the original spell, plus what I know of how the good fairies mucked with it, I think that could be the only solution." Marcel held the book out to Hansel, who was forced to let go of Johann in order to take the book and put it safely away. He added another layer of spells just in case and couldn't help letting out a sigh of relief to have the books finally back on their shelf.

"So now you have to go free a princess and we'll..." Johann trailed off, looking over at Hansel again. Hansel could read the indecision in Johann's eyes. He had been friends with Marcel and wanted to help him. Hansel wanted to help too. Anything to defeat the last of the evil witch's influence.

"The castle is guarded by great enchantments. I could use your help with those," Marcel added.

Hansel glanced over at Johann one more time, and then sighed. Johann was going. Well, Hansel didn't mind the idea of a bit of adventure. Maybe now that they didn't have any secrets to hide, he and Johann could form a relationship.

"I need to go back to the village and pack some supplies," Hansel said in answer. "I'll be back in an hour. Johann, do you need to grab anything?"

"Some supplies would be good. Marcel, will you be okay if we leave you here for a bit?" Johann asked.

Marcel shrugged, looking irritable again. "Not like I have a choice. I have to stay hidden from my sister's idiotic guards, and this place is as good as any for that."

Hansel hesitated, looking at the bookshelf for a moment before pinning Marcel with a hard glare. His meaning was obvious enough, so he didn't elaborate. "How far away is this enchanted castle? I need to know how much food to pack."

Marcel frowned in thought. "I think my grandmother was actually journeying there. In her crazy mind, she wanted to return to the very first child's life she ruined, I think. It'll take us about two days to walk that far north, as long as we don't find any obstacles on the way."

"So, enough food for a week, at least, and we can forage to supplement it if we have to." Hansel walked across the cabin to where Marcel's bedroll was still laid out. "I'm going to put some of the protections back up on the cabin while I'm back in the village," he warned.

Marcel and Johann joined him by the bedroll, and Hansel plucked and twisted with his magic until the spell webs on the cabin were back in place. The neat and orderly cabin vanished, replaced with the ramshackle and rotting version. The less visible webs also settled into place.

"An hour," Hansel said in reminder before he led the way out the door and back into the forest, Johann following behind.

They reached the village quickly and went their separate ways to start packing. Hansel hurried to his house to grab a bag to hold another set of clothes and some food supplies, then stopped in his shop to warn them he would be away for a few days.

Fifteen minutes later, he was waiting outside by the well in the central square for Johann.

"Going somewhere?" Captain Arno asked. He stepped out of the doorway to the pub and walked across the green to where Hansel was standing.

"You said Prince Marcel was spotted nearby," Hansel replied, quickly coming up with a plausible lie. "I was going out to set some traps to keep the village safe, just in case."

Captain Arno grunted. He leaned in toward Hansel, giving Hansel a terrible whiff of an unwashed body combined with the stench of old alcohol. "Need another hand?" he asked, and his leer was both suggestive and slightly drunken.

"I think I can manage. I have Johann to help, anyway," Hansel tried to explain as he took a step backward. Thankfully, Johann stepped out of the inn doorway, which was the building directly adjacent to the pub. Johann saw Hansel and Captain Arno and headed over.

"You think the two of you can handle the greatest dark witch of our times?" Captain Arno exclaimed, his words mostly slurred. "I think I should join you instead of this fop."

"We'll be fine, thanks," Johann cut in sharply. "Hansel?"

Hansel hurried to Johann's side, skirting around Captain Arno who was blinking at them stupidly, and fell into step with Johann as they both headed back into the forest.

"Let's go quickly before he thinks to follow," Hansel hissed under his breath. Once he was certain the trees hid him from Captain Arno's view, Hansel started jogging. "We have to get out of this forest before he thinks to come after me." He reactivated all of his traps as they went past them, making certain each one was functioning correctly before they moved on. No one could be allowed to find the cabin while he was away from the village, including weary travelers his spells usually let through so they could have a safe place to spend the night.

They practically burst back into the cabin, startling Marcel, who jumped to his feet and grabbed his pack after one look at their expressions. He didn't ask questions, instead following them back out of the cabin and into the woods.

*

Marcel led the way through the forest since he was the one who actually knew where they were going. Hansel and Johann's frantic expressions when they had returned to the cabin had told him all he needed to know about speed, so he kept them at a pace that would get them to the enchanted castle in a little over a day. After an hour's walking, however, Marcel knew he had to ask.

"What happened?"

Johann let out a low grumble under his breath. "There's this nasty captain of the guard who's enamored with Hansel. He offered to come with Hansel to set some traps to catch you."

"That's the excuse I used when he cornered me to ask why I looked like I was going to be traveling for a while," Hansel added.

"Which means he'll be expecting something when we return," Marcel finished with a sigh. "Well, fine. It's about time I confronted my sister anyway. I just need to rescue the sleeping princess first."

The rest of the day was spent in silence, as they all needed their breath to keep up with the pace. Marcel was pushing himself and he was used to traveling at this point, but Hansel and Johann were managing to keep up without complaint. There was so much compelling Marcel onward. The time limit on the princess's life was the most urgent one, of course, but he also needed to stay a step ahead of the people working for his sister. She couldn't know what direction he was headed in, given the enchanted castle was hidden by magic, but there was always the chance someone could get lucky and find him. The sooner he finished this rescue, the sooner those worries would stop chasing him.

They camped in a clearing deep in the woods that allowed just enough moonlight that they didn't need a fire to see each other as they ate the travel rations they pulled from their bags. The next morning, they packed quickly and started off again, but this time Marcel kept the pace more manageable. There was no reason to be exhausted from walking when they reached the castle.

It was a hidden enchanted castle, so they didn't actually see their destination until they basically walked into it. Johann was in the lead, and he abruptly stopped short and threw out a hand to keep Hansel from walking into whatever he had found. Marcel hurried to catch up.

A wall of thorns greeted him as Marcel stopped walking next to Johann.

"This is the first barrier," Marcel explained. He called on his magic to explore the wall and could sense the telltale prickle that said Hansel and Johann were doing the same.

"It's a very intricate web," Hansel murmured. His eyes were closed, but the fingers in his outheld hand were twitching as if he were counting.

Webs were Hansel's specialty, Marcel now ruefully knew, so he stepped back to let Hansel work. Johann backed away as well.

"I'm better with illusions," Johann admitted. "I was teaching them to Hansel while he was teaching me spell webs."

All while Johann waited for Hansel to reveal where he had hidden the spell books, of course. If Hansel didn't already have a serious crush on Johann, Marcel would feel bad for them, but he could tell Hansel had been able to already forgive Johann for the slight. It would be nice to have someone like that in his own life.

Hansel opened his eyes and slowly let out a breath. "This is probably the most complicated web I've ever seen."

"Can you get us through it?" Johann asked seconds before Marcel could ask the same question.

Hansel grinned over his shoulder at them both and then closed his eyes again. He held out both hands toward the wall of thorns, and all ten fingers began twitching. Marcel could not make out any discernable rhythm. After a few moments some of the thorns right in front of Hansel unfurled like they had simply been flower buds instead of deadly spikes. More and more thorns followed until the entire space in front of Hansel was full of beautiful red flowers. It looked almost like a doorway in shape and size.

Hansel took a step forward until his fingers were touching the soft petals. He paused there for a moment and then stepped forward again. Johann followed, no doubt because he wanted to stay close to Hansel to guard his back, and Marcel made sure to stay close as well.

The wall of thorns was no more than three feet deep. After only a few strides, Marcel emerged on the other side where he had to stop short again. A dry moat was about two feet in front of the tips of his toes. He could see sharp spikes on the bottom, thrust deep into the earth so their deadly points were angled exactly in the right place to impale them should they fall.

"It's an illusion," Johann said. It was his turn to close his eyes, and before Hansel or Marcel could jump forward and grab him, Johann stepped out into the moat. Marcel knew Johann wasn't stupid, but that didn't stop his heart from jumping into his throat at the sight of Johann's booted foot reaching out into empty air. Except, his foot hit a solid surface of some sort, and he completed his stride until both feet were standing and he was totally suspended over the moat with nothing visible under his feet. Johann turned to look over his shoulder and grinned cheekily at them. "There's a path across. Follow me exactly where I step."

Since Marcel had zero interest in falling to his death this close to the end, he obeyed. He wasn't about to admit to the other two that nervous sweat dripped down his spine or that his hands may or may not have been shaking slightly, but he took that first awkward step into thin air and felt solid ground under his feet. Johann began to walk very cautiously, and Marcel marked the exact spots his boots touched down so he could carefully follow.

The bridge didn't actually lead straight across the moat, of course, so they had to very slowly and precisely zigzag their way. Marcel's breaths were shallow from fear the entire time. Looking at his feet was scary; to his eyes it appeared he was standing on air with those sharp spikes just waiting for gravity to finally catch up with him. Needless to say, it was quite disconcerting. Yet, he had to look down to ensure he was placing his feet in the exact same spot as Johann, which had his heart pounding with nerves at every step.

All three collapsed to the ground when they finally reached the other side of the moat. Hansel was shaking and leaning on Johann, who was gripping Hansel back just as tightly. Marcel dug his fingernails into the firm ground just to reassure himself it was actually there. He took a few deep breaths to try to calm the frantic beating of his heart.

As distracted as they were, they almost didn't hear the roar reverberating overhead. The sound was unmistakable, though, and had them scrambling to their feet as the dragon swung into view. Marcel knew better than anyone what a dragon sounded like. It was how the evil fairy who had helped his grandmother had died. When Marcel had enchanted the evil fairy's spirit into an object so he could question her, she had still been in dragon form. Thanks to that, Marcel was an expert on how dragons sounded. The sound of the roar ratcheted his previously calming heart back up into a frantic pace as he desperately looked side to side in the hopes of seeing some sort of cover they could hide behind.

He couldn't see anything except the wide moat behind them and what appeared to be an endless expanse of green lawn in front of them. The wall of thorns had vanished at some point, but that wasn't what was important right now.

A second roar sent them running aimlessly, desperately, into the green lawn. Marcel kept looking for somewhere to hide, but the illusion or whatever was surrounding them was too good.

"We have to get away from the edge of the moat, at least," Hansel called from ahead of him. Marcel agreed with that wholeheartedly, but at the same time, there wasn't anywhere to go. All running would do was exhaust them when they would no doubt need everything they had left to fight the dragon that was coming for them.

There was no need for the third roar that sounded because the dragon dipped down from the clouds overhead. It was a beautiful creature, but scary at the same time. Bright red in color and powerful-looking as it dove at them with sharp fangs in its wide mouth and large horns over its eyes, and it was heading directly toward Hansel and Johann, likely because the pumping of their arms and legs as they ran attracted its attention. It banked sharply to get a better angle, its wings huge and covered in fire-red scales, and as it turned Marcel caught sight of something gold around its long neck.

Webs might be Hansel's specialty and illusions Johann's, but like his mother and grandmother, Marcel specialized in enchantments. That collar could only be one of two things: a controlling collar to force the dragon to attack anyone who got past the moat, or an enchantment collar making something innocuous look like the dragon.

He had never met a real dragon before—the evil fairy might have looked and sounded like a dragon, but she was still a fairy underneath the spelled façade—but Marcel was pretty certain dragons were too smart to get stuck as a guard dog for a hundred years. This was probably a hawk or even a sparrow spelled to look like a dragon.

Marcel called on his magic, letting it zip between his fingertips for a brief moment before he sent it flying upward to investigate that collar. Hansel and Johann were yelling something, and he could feel the impact of their spells as they fought off the dragon, but he ignored it all. The real magic was on that collar, and he had the best chance of ending this fight if Hansel and Johann kept the dragon distracted until he figured out the spell.

It was extremely intricate, which he had expected. Spells were woven around even more spells in layers and twists that were dizzying in their complexity. All of it had been compacted into the size and shape of the collar, which made it even more difficult to decipher. Still, just as there was a physical clasp holding the collar in place around the dragon's neck, there would be a magical equivalent hidden somewhere in the spell. He just had to find it.

Hansel and Johann were still yelling, and the dragon let out another roar. Marcel didn't dare look away to see what had happened. He hoped they were okay.

Marcel picked through another layer of the spell and dug deeper into the collar. His magic was straining to cover the distance and to keep up the contact with the dragon, but even as he locked his knees to force his body to remain upright, Marcel still kept frantically searching.

Until...there! It was an odd little knot of magic buried in the middle of the mess of the rest of the spell. He used his magic to carefully pick apart the knot, separating the individual strings of the magic, and then suddenly it fell apart.

The roaring and the yelling abruptly stopped. Marcel carefully let his magic dissipate and looked down to see what had happened. Johann was pointing at a much smaller bird of some kind that was high in the sky and flying away as quickly as its wings would take it—it had flown too far away at this point for Marcel to make out exactly what type of bird it was. The dragon had vanished, which meant his assumption that it had been an enchantment on a different animal had been correct. In the dragon's place, the castle had finally appeared.

Built of wide gray blocks of stone, the building was lovely. They were standing in the inner courtyard, so it was difficult to make out the full extent of the castle, but Marcel could only see one tall tower. The princess would be there. He marked its location at the back left side of the castle.

"I assume you were the one who broke the spell on the dragon?" Hansel asked as he and Johann joined Marcel at the foot of the stairs leading into the front hall of the castle. They looked okay, which was a relief. They were only slightly singed around the hems of their clothes.

"I knew you could hold it off long enough for me to break the enchantment," Marcel answered simply.

Waiting for more chitchat or taking the time to explain his actions would be a waste. Instead, Marcel started walking up the stairs to the front door. Hopefully, the dragon was the last of the protections, but Marcel still kept an eye out for another trap.

"Where is the princess?" Hansel asked. He and Johann were following Marcel closely, no doubt so they wouldn't be separated.

The expensive glory of the entrance hall was hidden under what appeared to be a gloomy fog. Marcel had no doubt it was magical in nature, likely to prevent thieves and such from touching anything that belonged to the princess. As long as he stayed away from the brief glimpses of gold or silver he occasionally saw, he should be fine. Ahead of them was another room that appeared to be either a grand ballroom or a throne room. A double staircase framed the entrance hall, one on either wall, that led up to the second floor.

"She's supposed to be in the tower," Marcel answered. He chose the stairs on the left and turned left on the second floor to head deeper into the castle.

Johann let out a laughing groan. "Of course, she's in the tower. What is with evil and magic that convinces them to use towers?"

Marcel's grandmother had certainly liked towers, but his mother had preferred dank basements. It depended on the witch, to be honest, but he couldn't blame Johann for making that generalization.

They eventually found a set of stairs leading to the third floor, and from there it was simple enough to find the tower and the entrance. The strange fog seemed to be guiding them along by obscuring side hallways. The door leading into the tower opened as they approached.

The staircase inside wound its way upward to a lone room at the top. Marcel took the stairs slowly. He was tired from the journey here and from all of the magic he had used up. It took a while to get to the top, but neither Hansel nor Johann pressured him to move faster. They appeared to understand just how important this was to Marcel.

Years of hard work and study had gone into this moment. Dozens of forests searched for the correct spell books, all the miles he had traversed to get here, and now he was finally about to achieve his goal of saving the princess helplessly sleeping at the top of the tower.

The fog cleared away as they climbed the last couple of steps into a room lit from large windows set into each of the eight walls. A bed was situated in the center of the space, and on the bed lay a figure shrouded behind gossamer bed hangings. Marcel paused at the top of the stairs, unable not to take a moment to stare at his goal.

Hansel and Johann slid around him, and Hansel reached forward to pull the bed hangings back.

"Um, Marcel?" Hansel said hesitantly as he got a good look at the person in the bed. Marcel took one last steadying breath and then forced his feet to step forward toward the bed.

She was as beautiful as the stories had said. Her hair was the bright gold of sunlight and her lips the pale pink of the softest rose. She was lying on top of the covers and her dress covered her feet. For having been asleep for a hundred years, her beard didn't look like much more than a five-o'clock shadow.

"Her parents desperately wanted a baby girl," Marcel murmured as he looked down at the princess. "When she was old enough to understand the choice her parents had made, she tried being a boy for a few years, but she didn't enjoy it. Perhaps she might not have made the same choice to be a girl had she been raised as a boy, but it was a choice she stuck with until the day her curse took hold."

Kissing her without her permission wasn't something Marcel would normally ever do, except it was the only way to break the spell before she died. Hopefully she would forgive him for being so forward.

Marcel carefully sat on the side of the bed, then leaned over and gently pressed his lips to hers. There was an audible snapping sound, and then a rush of air as if one of the windows had suddenly opened.

Marcel sat up straight just in time for the princess to slowly blink open her vivid blue eyes.

They immediately found Marcel and widened as she looked at him, and then her pink lips slid upward into a smile.

"My name is Aurora," she said. "It's nice to finally meet you, my handsome prince."

*

Hansel didn't know what he should have expected when he arrived at the castle after being exhausted by the battle with the enchanted dragon, but the layers of spell webs that covered absolutely everything were almost more beautiful than the furnishings. He couldn't say what Marcel saw as he led the way through the castle and directly to the tower, but Hansel could see the spells that were making that possible.

The magic didn't seem malicious, at least. It was as if now that they had overcome all three tests they had proven their worth and were welcome here. It would take days, if not years, to unravel all the intricacies of the webs in the castle. Hansel really wanted to stop and study it all, but one smile from Johann at his side reminded him they were on a rescue mission. They could study the spells after the princess was safe.

Except, love's first kiss had swept through the entire enchanted castle, dispelling all the magic as it went. The chance to study the webs was gone, but the princess was awake and safe, which was just as important.

Aurora was definitely beautiful, if a bit unconventional, and the way she smiled at Marcel brought a sparkle and joy to her eyes. Marcel was gazing back at her like he had never before seen something so wonderful. It was totally unlike how Hansel had fallen for Johann, which had been slowly over the long days they spent together practicing magic, and yet Hansel couldn't help reaching back to take Johann's hand in his. Johann squeezed back and stepped forward so their shoulders were pressed together.

"I've been dreaming about you—about all of you," Aurora added as she turned her head to include Hansel and Johann in what she was about to say. "I know what the evil witches have done to you and how you have all still managed to live your lives despite the burdens you have been forced to carry. I know how the world has changed while this castle and I have been sleeping, but I am ready to take my place in the waking world again. Will you all help me?"

That was a far more layered question than Aurora's simple smile implied. Hansel was used to evil witches trying to cajole his support by sounding like they were only trying to do what was best. As much as he doubted Aurora was the evil witch in this case, Hansel still couldn't allow himself to immediately give his support.

"If you have dreamed about my life," Johann answered before Hansel could formulate his own reply, "then you know that there are very few decisions I am allowed to make without consulting my parents or my sister first. Giving my support to Prince Marcel for this mission to save you might have overstepped the line, but I know that Marcel is the victim of a terrible misunderstanding, so once that is cleared up my actions will be deemed worthy. I cannot do the same for you until my family and I better understand your situation."

"I do see why your personal situation prevents you, but I hope that I might be able to change that as you get to know me better." Aurora turned to Hansel for an answer, but her eyes caught on their clasped hands, and she instead smiled gently at him and then turned back to Marcel.

There was a knock on the door before Aurora could say anything else. "My lady," the servant said with a bow after she bid him to enter, "there is an armed force of guards at the gate demanding we turn over the evil witch Marcel so he might be brought to justice for his crimes. Your father asks if you know what they are talking about."

Aurora swung her legs over the side of the bed and slowly stood up, leaning on Marcel for support as she carefully steadied legs unused to holding her weight for so long. "Tell my father that Prince Marcel is a welcome guest in our home and that if Queen Snow White wishes to speak with him, she will need to send a proper emissary to our court to discuss the situation. Let me get dressed properly, and I will come down to explain it in full."

The servant bowed again before hurrying back out the door and down the stairs. Hansel and Johann followed to give Aurora privacy to change, although Marcel stayed behind, which would likely raise some eyebrows if anyone found out.

It didn't take long to find a window overlooking the front courtyard. The first thing Hansel noticed was the moat, the wall of thorns, and even much of the thick forest surrounding the castle had vanished. The trees of the forest were still visible in the distance, but a long, manicured lawn led up to the main gate, which was closed and manned by men and women in armor. Outside the gate was a small force of what looked like thirty men on horses, and Hansel was pretty certain Captain Arno was standing in the center of them.

"He followed us," Hansel said, swearing softly under his breath.

"But he can't get in, at least, not yet," Johann replied. "Marcel is safe as long as Snow White doesn't send an entire army to the gates." Which wasn't outside the realm of possibility.

As they watched, there was some commotion inside the gates. The soldiers at the top were lowering what looked like a letter down to the waiting guards, and a few moments later two of Captain Arno's men galloped off in the direction of the forest.

"And now, we wait," Johann murmured.

He wasn't wrong. It took six days before those two soldiers came galloping back, and the message relayed to the gate guards was that Snow White herself was on her way.

"She never leaves her prince or her castle," Marcel said, his voice breathy with surprise, when the message was delivered at breakfast that morning.

"Then we shall have to prepare handsomely for her arrival," the queen exclaimed. She stood from her chair and clapped her hands twice. Servants and vassals surged to her side as she strode from the room, listening as she spoke and then peeling off to go accomplish whatever she had ordered.

Hansel watched it all happen from his place at the table, still somewhat bemused a mere shopkeeper was invited to sit at the table with royalty, even if two of those princes were his friends, and he was fast becoming friends with Princess Aurora too. Still, his knowledge of spell webs had been invaluable in figuring out what had happened to the castle a hundred years ago. While the spell had been broken, Hansel had been able to locate enough of the remnants to decipher the entire tale.

The evil fairy had cast a spell to kill Princess Aurora using the prick of her finger on a spindle as the catalyst, but the good fairies had managed to twist the spell web enough that they could stave off death. Then, they had added another web which had put the entire castle to sleep—right down to the mice in the walls.

The fairies had apparently explained much of the rest of the tale Hansel hadn't been able to figure out to Aurora in her dreams, which they had given her as a window to the outside world while she slept. It was only supposed to take five years at most for rescue to come, but princes and peasants alike—good people all—had tried and failed to rescue her until the years started piling on. One prince had even managed to kill the evil fairy, but though he had kissed Aurora, there was no love for her in his heart, and the curse was not broken.

As the years passed, the good fairies had despaired of ever finding someone for Aurora until the day they found Prince Marcel. A little push here and there and suddenly he was on a quest to right the worst of the wrongs his family had committed, including rescuing Aurora from imminent death.

Which led them to today, sitting together at a breakfast table waiting for the pending arrival of Queen Snow White.

Breakfast was long over and Hansel fidgeting in the entrance hall when the blare of horns announced Snow White's arrival. A beautiful golden-colored carriage pulled up to the foot of the stairs outside, and a footman jumped down from the back to open the door and set out a stool. A silk-slippered foot stepped out onto the stool and was followed by the rest of a woman Hansel would have pegged as Marcel's sister even if he hadn't already known.

Her hair was braided and knotted at the back of her neck. It was the color of ebony, and against her snow-white skin, it almost seemed to glow. Her lips were the red shade of fresh blood. They had the same father, and their mothers had used the same spell to conceive them, but until he actually saw her he hadn't know just how much alike they looked.

She smiled at the waiting crowd as she climbed the stairs and stepped inside the castle.

"I had heard stories of the lost kingdom," she said as she held her hands out toward the queen in welcome, "but I had not realized it was on my lands."

And just like that, the gauntlet was thrown down. Aurora's kingdom was situated on the northernmost tip of Snow White's and had likely been subsumed into Snow White's a hundred years ago when the kingdom had vanished beneath the fairy's spell. According to modern borders, Snow White technically owned the castle they were standing in.

"Come, cousin," Aurora's mother said as she took Snow White's hands. "We have much to talk about, especially since my daughter and your brother are looking to wed."

That had Snow White pausing in place, and her serene expression faltered for the briefest second. Her eyes slid sideways toward where Marcel was standing, but they stopped on Aurora, and a small smile lifted her very red lips.

"So I see. Shall we sit somewhere and discuss?"

Aurora and Marcel led the way up the nearest flight of stairs and into a sitting room just off to one side. The queen and Snow White followed behind with everyone else trailing them. Hansel was swept along with the group, but he was the only peasant present. Johann rested a hand on Hansel's shoulder, and when Hansel looked up at him Johann was smiling.

"It's fine. You'll see," he whispered before leading the way to a love seat and sitting down beside Hansel. It was comforting having Johann so close, especially when Snow White's gaze passed over them from where she was sitting in a nearby armchair.

"It seems I have two issues to handle while I am here. I would like to see to Marcel first, if you do not mind."

"Please." The queen sat back in her own chair and waved her hand in the air. Servants hurried into the room bearing trays of tea and finger snacks. Snow White waited until she had a cup of tea in her hand and the servants had left before she spoke again.

"I see Prince Johann here, as well as Hansel, the premier witch hunter in my kingdom." She knew who he was. Hansel couldn't believe it. "I have a hard time believing two good men would willingly sit in the room with purportedly the evilest witch of their generation."

She paused as if waiting for an answer. Hansel didn't quite dare open his mouth, but luckily Johann was willing to step up.

"Where did you get the impression that Marcel was an evil witch? I've known him since we were fostered together, and he never once made me think he might be evil."

Snow White frowned to herself. "Captain Arno was quite specific."

Of course, it was that idiot. Hansel couldn't help rolling his eyes, but he kept the scoff inside.

"You do not like Captain Arno, Hansel?" Snow White asked him.

This time he couldn't get out of answering. Hansel swallowed to clear his throat. "No, my lady. He is not very...nice...to me."

"He is hoping to bring you my heart in a box before you think to ask for it," Marcel added.

Snow White appeared to understand what Marcel meant because her brow furrowed. She didn't explain, instead taking a long moment to have a sip of her tea and to nibble on a bit of pastry. Hansel didn't know that Marcel knew Captain Arno, but maybe he knew that type of unpleasant person well enough.

"It will be handled. Ugly rumors led my husband, the king, to put out an edict he should not have. I will see Captain Arno interrogated and the truth of the matter brought to light. I suspect someone was trying to discredit me by reminding the kingdom that my stepmother tormented them for so long. Which brings me to my next point—this old kingdom reappearing within my borders."

"We are aware that the world has continued turning without us," Aurora said softly. "We have no wish to cause chaos and strife by demanding control over lands that have long been lost to us, but perhaps a compromise could be reached." She held out one hand, and Marcel immediately took it in his.

"When I married, you were going to give me a bit of land to be steward for, just as dukes, earls, or barons are stewards for their lands under your rule. Let me have this bit of land here with Aurora at my side. We can't have children of our own, but we would love to foster one of yours and perhaps make them our heir."

"My sister is looking to foster her youngest son," Johann added. "I know my fostering with Marcel worked well for me, and I have no problem recommending this as a safe place to send my nephew."

"After the wedding, I will think about it. There is much to do beforehand, including ferreting out the extent of the traitors trying to force me to turn against my only brother. If I can have your support," she added directly to Aurora, "I can ensure your kingdom will have the same autonomy as any dukedom."

Aurora glanced over at her parents, who both nodded regally. "You have our support."

"Wonderful!" Snow White smiled, and suddenly Hansel knew why she was considered to be the most beautiful woman in the world. It was easy to understand why a vain, self-indulgent woman had decided to kill her. "Now, if you don't mind I think I would like freshen up after my journey here. Shall we reconvene after lunch?"

She stood and everyone jumped to their feet. The queen rang a bell and a servant hurried into the room.

"Show Queen Snow White to her room and plan lunch for her convenience."

The servant bowed and politely gestured toward the door. "This way, my lady," he said softly. Snow White swept from the room.

"Well." Aurora let out a heavy breath, but she was smiling. "I think that went well."

"I told you, she's got too good a heart. That's why she doesn't leave home much—she's too soft-hearted for politics, even though she has quite the head for it." Marcel shrugged, but he was smiling at Aurora. "I think it will go well."

They stayed in the sitting room for about ten more minutes to finish the tea and snacks, and then the queen, king, and Aurora all left to get organized for the next meeting. Marcel was about to follow when Johann lifted a hand to stop him.

"Hansel?" Johann said leadingly.

He knew what Hansel was feeling without his having to say anything out loud. Hansel squeezed Johann's hand to convey his thanks.

"Do you need me here?" he asked. "Not that I'm not happy to stay if you do, but I have duties and a shop to run back home."

"We'll be back for the wedding, of course," Johann added, "but it's long past time for us to return home."

He meant Hansel's home. The little magic shop with his annoying sister. Their sharing magic spells during the day, a meal in the afternoon, and a smile at night. It sounded wonderful. Hansel wanted to go home so badly, but he knew his duties as a subject in this kingdom, so if Snow White needed him he would stay.

Marcel grinned at them. "You just want the privacy of your own bed without servants popping in and disturbing you. Go ahead; just get back here for my wedding." He continued his aborted walk to the door, but he paused just inside. "And, thanks for believing me and helping me." He vanished before Hansel could reply.

"Shall we go home?" Johann asked Hansel softly.

Hansel tilted his head upward, and Johann leaned down obligingly. Their lips connected briefly at first—just the barest brush of skin against skin—but Hansel wanted more. He surged upward, demanding Johann's mouth and claiming it with his own. It was wet and perfect, and he was eager to touch bare skin with his fingers too.

"When we're home," Johann murmured, his lips feathering against Hansel's as he spoke.

Hansel took another kiss in answer and only reluctantly pulled away a moment later. "Let's gather our things and get going, then," he replied before taking Johann's hand and leading him out the room to start their journey home.

*

The magic mirror was definitely smiling now. It was visible in the crinkle around its eyes as he looked out into the dark basement that was his home for the moment. Soon enough another witch would need him—be it for good or evil—but for now his task was done. He could finally sleep until the magic words called him forth again.

This time when the eyes slid closed there was a sense of finality about the gesture. Some sort of element of magic in the air of the basement that had held on despite all the magical implements being properly destroyed all those years ago faded away.

The magic mirror on the wall slept.

CINDER-ELLE

Prologue

When Elle was six years old, his father remarried. His mother had died from illness two years before, and society had finally deemed it time for the widower to find a new wife. The woman he chose was barely a dowager baroness; much to the surprise and horror of the gossiping society, she was only the daughter of the fourth son of the Earl of Beedlin. She was a widow herself, her husband having died five years previous in a hunting accident and had only been the wealthy Baron of Vellei whose courtesy title was tied with his dwindling fortune rather than with peerage. The marriage of the two widows may have been one of convenience, freeing both adults from the watchful eyes of a society unused to unwed parents, but both Elle's father and his new stepmother seemed quite pleased with the arrangement.

The wedding was lavish; Elle's father could afford it, and no expense was spared for the new bride.

She was beautiful and willowy, and the white dress she wore made her look ethereal. Her blonde hair was styled to fall like water skipping down the back of her ornately embroidered dress. The white veil covering her face made her look mysterious in such a way that only emphasized her stunning looks.

When she stood next to Elle's father at the altar, everyone in the audience sighed at the lovely picture they made together. Elle's father was tall and muscular, with straight brown hair and piercing blue eyes. The wedding of the Lord Elleron, Duke of Marchcant, to the Lady Sadia Vellei was spoken about for weeks afterward.

Elle's new stepmother brought two sons to the marriage, both near Elle's age, and Elle was excited to finally have playmates. His father financed himself with a large merchant company and was constantly traveling, leaving Elle alone in their manor. With two new boys to play with, Elle thought he wouldn't be lonely anymore.

The oldest stepbrother's name was Sil—or Silvester, but his mother was the only one who used his full name—and he was two years older than Elle. Sil was a miniature male version of his mother. He had the same blond hair, and his nose was already showing signs of growing into the pert little upturn that, on his mother's face, made men sigh.

Everett was the younger stepbrother. He was barely five years old and had been born just a few months after his father's death. Elle assumed Everett looked like his father because his hair and eyes were dark brown, something neither his mother nor older brother shared.

Elle stood out next to his fairer stepbrothers. His hair was a deep shade of black cut fashionably long to his shoulders and tied into a small tail at his neck. His eyes were green. His father used to call Elle a miniature version of Elle's mother until Lady Olivia had died. Since then, Elle's father had just quietly helped Elle tie his hair back every morning instead.

After the vows were said and dinner eaten, the adults went off to dance in the ballroom. The children were sent to their own small party out on a side veranda where they could still hear the music and chatter from the adults but were not actually underfoot. Elle didn't really know what to do to keep his two new siblings and the invited children of the guests entertained, but luckily, many of them seemed to already have their own group of friends to be with.

"Such a lavish garden," Sil said imperiously as he joined Elle at the railing overlooking the back garden. "Why the cost of those azaleas..." He trailed off as he stared over at the vibrant purple bush. "Everett, we really must go have a closer look."

Everett was standing behind Sil, sucking on his sleeve and looking at the small outdoor reading nook tucked into a corner of the veranda wall. Sil sighed in an exasperated tone and reached out to slap at his brother's hand.

"You are disgusting," Sil told Everett, turning his nose in the air as if he had seen something vile on the ground below.

Everett dropped his arm to his side and hid the wet sleeve against his hip. "Sorry, Sil," Everett squeaked and ducked his head. "But it looks comfy over there," he added as he pointed toward the set of chairs and small table in the little nook.

"I'm sure it does," Sil scoffed. "But we were going to go see the azaleas now, not look at some ratty old chairs."

Elle looked over at the bushes Sil was still pointing at and shrugged. His mother had liked the brightly colored flowers, so there were azaleas all over the garden, but if his new brother wanted to see the bushes, then Elle didn't mind showing him. Elle wanted Sil to like him, after all.

"There's a staircase down into the gardens over here," Elle said as he gestured just past the nook Everett was admiring.

"Very well," Sil said imperiously. "Show the way."

Elle led Sil and Everett past the reading chairs and around the corner where a stone staircase led from the veranda down into the garden. The staircase went downward until it reached a short landing where the stairs made a sharp left and hugged the wall until they met the ground. A stone railing ran along the outside, and Elle used to enjoy putting his feet through the spokes on the landing and watching his parents stroll along the carefully kept garden paths below.

Everett was holding back behind them to take a longer look at the nook, which made Sil sigh as if he was being terribly put upon.

"Oh, go have a look then," Sil grumbled with an imperious sniff of distaste. He let Elle lead the way to the top of the stairs while Everett scampered off, clearly trying not to look too happy to have been given the chance to get away from Sil for a while. "So this is the way down?" Sil asked as he turned back to Elle.

When Elle thought back on that day, years later, he was never sure if Sil had done it on purpose.

Elle had just put his foot out to take the first step downward when Sil seemed to trip. His arms came out in front of him and impacted against Elle's back. Sil's knees hit the veranda, but Elle wasn't as lucky and lost his footing.

Elle fell. He could feel the bruising force of the steps as his side and arm hit one stair and felt the skin on his leg scrape against another. His momentum wasn't halted until he reached the small landing, which he skidded across until his back crashed into the supporting spokes of the railing.

Elle's head whipped backward from the sudden stop and cracked against one of the railings with enough force to make him cry out in pain.

When he first felt the impact to the back of his head and his vision flickered out, he still had some hope that Sil would rush down the stairs to help him. But when Elle looked upward, all he saw was Sil's face. Sil was biting his lip hard enough to draw blood, but his eyes held a vindictive light. Elle looked away as dark spots ran across his sight.

Was it an accident?

Elle tried not to think about that day overly much.

*

When Elle woke, he was in his bed in the manor. He felt the silk of his sheets and the soft down mattress and pillows behind his head like usual. Then he tried to open his eyes.

Elle was sure they were open, but he rubbed them to be sure. Yes, his eyes were open. Maybe it was night, and no one had lit the fireplace in his room or left a candle burning? That would explain the total darkness enveloping him.

Something rustled at his side, and Elle turned his head, trying to peer through the darkness.

"Elle?" his father asked. "How are you feeling? It's a lovely morning, so once you're up we can go have breakfast on the veranda."

That was when Elle began crying. It would not be the last time he cried, but it would be the only time he cried where someone else could see him.

Elle was blind, and the doctors couldn't figure out how to fix him.

*

A week later, Lord Elleron left to join one of his caravans on a month-long trip, promising to speak to every doctor he found on the way about Elle's condition. Elle heard the horses leave the manor drive through his open window, and his heart and hopes went with his father.

Elle spent the month of his father's absence in his bed. The doctors who came by periodically to check on him tutted and told Elle to go out and play, but were never able to treat his injury. Whenever Elle did get out of bed to follow their orders, he bumped into things or tripped, and Sil and Everett would laugh at him. It wasn't long before Elle finally decided not to leave his bed at all. His father would bring the cure back, and Elle wouldn't need to worry about misplaced chairs or bunched rugs. His jammed toes and barked shins appreciated the rest anyway.

Everything was sharper now. The pain in his body from falling down the stairs slowly healed, but the ache of knowing his eyesight was missing persisted. Sil's jeers, followed by Everett's quiet compliance, twisted that ache until Elle buried his head under the blankets where he could cry without anyone knowing.

But there were other, happier, things that kept Elle going. He had never noticed the singing and chirping of the birds outside his window in the morning before. Nor had he ever been aware of just how comforting the sound of the morning maid setting out his breakfast tea was; he liked hearing her feet pad across the carpet because he knew he wasn't alone. The clink of the tea pot and cup was a sound he could easily recognize without needing any explanation, like he had after all the banging and shuffling outside that time when a man had come to fix the cobbles in their drive. Elle could hear things now that he never would have given any credence to before his fall, and it gave him an entirely new perspective on the things around him.

Elle's father returned at the end of the month with a cough and no answers. Elle lost some hope that day, but his father assured him that on one of the stops on his next trip there was a doctor who professed to be an expert on sight. Next time, Elle's father would no doubt locate a cure.

A week later Elle's father was coughing blood, and the week after that Elle stood at his father's grave as the priest spoke his last rights. Elle didn't cry. He stood between his two stepbrothers who were equally dry-eyed, though they had barely gotten a chance to know their new father. Elle just couldn't summon the tears for his father because he had already cried his own hopes into his pillow the night before. There would be no cure now.

Elle sat quietly through the carriage ride home while what remained of his family chatted around him. The second they stepped through the manor doors, what had already become a sad life turned for the worst. His fine clothes and belongings were stripped from him at his stepmother's order. Her hand fisted around Elle's upper arm, the nails digging into his skin uncomfortably as she dragged him through the corridors toward the servants' quarters.

"You're useless to me, boy," Lady Sadia snapped in a voice he had never heard her use before. It was cold and cruel, with just the right amount of disdain to make Elle shiver. "Just a mouth to feed as you are. I can't even marry you off in a few years because what family would want a blind boy? You'll work for your keep in my house!"

With that, she shoved him toward the waiting head servant and stormed away; Elle could clearly hear the sharp, quick click of her shoes echoing off the walls over his own shocked gasps for breath. He had help changing into his new sackcloth garments his first time, the material hard and scratchy against his soft skin, and one of his father's friendlier servants saved his childhood blanket, knitted by his mother before she passed away, when his stepmother sold everything in his rooms to pay for her new wardrobe.

Elle started his new life as a servant in his own home. He was six years old, blind, unused to his new duties, and he was left alone for the most part.

He was not a true servant of the house, as the other servants knew he was the rightful heir to the manor and the title of duke, no matter how often Sil was addressed as the duke. The servants knew this and kept away from Elle—at least until they were all fired. Then the new servants kept away from Elle because he was disabled and because Sadia treated him so much more callously than any other servant; they didn't want anything that was wrong with him to have any effect against them.

Elle was most often found cleaning the fireplaces of soot—what else could he be trusted to do?—so Sil and Everett called him Cinder-Elle, teasing and abusing him at every opportunity.

As the years passed, Cinder-Elle became used to his new station and to his disability. Those who should have been his family were quick to forget he was any relation of theirs. They hid him away in the bowels of the deteriorating manor where society could conveniently forget about him as well.

And that is where our story begins.

Chapter One

Elle walked into the market with his basket of fragile eggs under one arm and his walking stick clasped firmly in his other hand. The stick tapped along the ground, alerting Elle's ears even over the clamor and bustle of the market to where the ground was uneven or a step had been carved into the dirt road. He was careful of his burned finger holding on to his walking stick. He had accidentally touched the red-hot side of a teapot just that morning while preparing and delivering his stepfamily's breakfasts to their rooms.

Elle wound his way toward his house's stall; they sold everything they could these days as it was the only way to keep up with his stepfamily's expensive lifestyles. The back garden of the manor was now a small farm, and they took everything that did not end up on the table to be sold.

"Watch where you're going, blind boy!" a voice snapped as the man it belonged to shoved past him. Elle felt his long braid of hair thump against his back as he stumbled. He was tall and very thin, but muscular from working hard and eating too little. His hair had not been cut since his injury; at first no one had ever taken enough interest in his well-being to care, and then Elle had come to like the weight of it running down his back. Elle thought he was distinctive enough that the man should have been able to avoid him, but he ignored the man's comment with the ease of long practice. Any attacks against his lack of sight had ceased to bother him a long time ago. Besides, he had been making this trip every morning for the past ten years, and at twenty years of age, Elle knew when to keep his mouth shut and just walk.

He followed the tapping sounds of his stick. A clank here meant he needed to veer right, the big rock on his right meant he had gone too far that way, and the three steps down the hill meant he had reached the well and needed to carefully circumnavigate the circle or get wet.

When the group of kids playing by the well threw rocks and mud at him, Elle just smiled and shielded his basket carefully from their onslaught. He had no other choice, after all.

"Rotten kids," a voice snarled loudly before a second wave of rocks could come at Elle. Elle heard the kids scatter and turned his head to smile at the helpful man.

For four years Elle had been hearing the soothing tones of Theo's voice and smelling his sharply wonderful scent in the morning—a welcome change to the usual stench of a market filled with animals, people, and yesterday's rotting refuse. At first Elle had been sure the man had wanted to make off with his goods—Elle was a fairly easy target for thieves—but at their first meeting he had simply held the basket for Elle and guided him through the throng of people until they reached the correct stall. All of the carrots Elle had been carrying that day had still been in the basket when Theo left.

Now Elle looked forward to every morning when Theo would join him for the last bit of his walk through the market. It made the fact that Elle was forced to fight through the crowds because he was ordered to stay at the manor for breakfast service and was therefore unable ride the cart with Macy first thing more than bearable.

"Good morning, Theo," Elle said happily.

"And good morn to you, Elle," Theo replied with equal levity in his voice.

Elle felt his basket being gently tugged from his arms, so he let it go and took Theo's arm when it brushed against his side. They began to walk along the street with Theo gently guiding Elle. Elle relished this short time they had together where he could stop tapping his stick and instead let someone he trusted guide him.

"How has your day been so far, Elle?" Theo asked, despite the fact that the sun had barely been up an hour.

"The usual," Elle replied. "My stepmother fired all but two of the servants in the kitchen over the weekend, so I've been learning how to cook. Did you know that there is a different smell when the food is cooked correctly? It's really amazing. I've only burned a couple things so far, and it's much more fun than mucking out the cow stalls or cleaning more fireplaces."

Elle hadn't told Theo all of the truth, of course. He was fairly sure that Theo was under the impression that Elle's stepmother was the head servant of his household and the other servants were all a lazy bunch that deserved to be regularly turned out.

After two months of living as a servant, Elle's stepmother had decided to fire every single one of his father's servants. The first two new servants she had hired had been a mother and her twelve-year-old daughter. Somehow they had both remained on staff despite his stepmother's frequent change of servants. Their newest financial woes meant that the only servants besides Elle still in the manor were Macy and her mother, Lucy.

When the two women had first moved into the manor, they and Elle had not crossed paths very often. He was too young for Macy to be interested in playing with him, and both children had work to get done anyway. Only after they had all realized that they were the only three servants who appeared to have permanent positions had they become friendly. Elle was nine years old by then and so used to being ignored that it had taken weeks of a constant barrage of friendliness before he had opened up to the women. Elle still held them at arm's length, because he knew there would come a day when Lucy and Macy no longer worked for his stepmother, but neither Lucy nor Macy accepted this distance.

They reached the stall and Elle told Theo where to put the eggs.

"Will you come out drinking with me tonight?" Theo asked Elle suddenly as he was taking an egg from Elle. Elle turned his head toward Theo, confusion written across his face.

"Yes, he will!" Macy's high-pitched voice chirped from across the stall where she was stocking cabbages. At Elle's disgruntled look, she elaborated quickly. "The man's been helping you for years, Elle. You really ought to thank him properly by agreeing to go out with him."

"But the nightly chores," Elle began.

"Oh! I'll do your chores," Macy said with a laugh. "It's just the kitchen and main hall fireplaces you need to clean out and lay for the morning's fire, right?" she asked.

"Yes, but—" Elle tried again.

"No buts!" Macy said imperiously. Elle heard her skirts rustle as she turned to Theo. "We close an hour after sundown."

"I will be here!" Theo said with a laugh. He said goodbye to Elle as if something unusual hadn't happened and left.

Macy joined Elle in putting away the eggs as she giggled. "He's handsome, just so you know," Macy said.

"I don't think his looks matter all that much, in my case," Elle said jokingly, even though the reminder that Macy could see Theo when he never would did sting somewhat.

"Oh, pish," Macy snorted. "You want to know anyway, don't you? Well, he's got this light-brown hair, almost blond really, and it hangs to his shoulders. His hair is styled and it really makes his eyes stand out." She sighed to herself quietly. "Such blue eyes. Well, if he wasn't so interested in you, I'd be going after him!"

She was called away to help a customer, so Elle finished placing the eggs on their stand. Macy was right; he did wish he could see Theo. There wasn't a day Elle didn't wish that he could still see, of course, but seeing the man who so gently helped him every morning would be a truly special treat. Not that Elle was holding his breath. He enjoyed being able to hold Theo's arm and feel the tight muscle covered by stiff fabric that could only belong to some sort of guard uniform, so while his sight returning would be nice, he was more than pleased with what he could feel now.

But what Elle really wondered about, even more than the eye color of his helpful friend, was why Theo had suddenly asked him out. After four years of their friendship consisting of an amiable morning walk together, why now did Theo decide to change their routine?

As the day aged, Elle put aside his questions to handle the busy work of running their stall. Through long practice, Elle was perfectly capable of handling orders. And, because copper had a very distinctive smell and each coin amount had a different picture stamped into the metal for his fingers to feel, he could handle money too.

It was a busy day and they had sold quite a number of goods, leaving less than half their normal stock to be packed back into the wagon. In the morning, Macy would bring the wagon back to the market while Elle served soft-boiled eggs and hot tea. Elle would join her with a basket filled with whatever had been harvested by Lucy after Macy had left.

"Ready?" a warmly familiar voice asked behind Elle as he was helping Macy load the last bundle onto the wagon.

Elle jumped and turned around. "Hello, Theo," he said shyly. He had come to a decision while working. It didn't matter why Theo had suddenly changed their routine; Elle was going to enjoy their time together anyway.

"He's ready!" Macy replied as she climbed into the driver's seat of the wagon. "I'll leave the back gate unlocked for you, Elle," she added before clucking at the mule and heading off.

Theo held out his arm, which Elle took. "Do you have a preference of taverns?" he asked as they walked out of the marketplace. Elle could hear the happiness and excitement in Theo's voice, particularly once the sounds of the market closing up for the night faded behind them.

Elle felt his face flush. "I've never gone out drinking before. I've always been too busy with chores and such."

"You've never been out drinking?" Theo said, sounding incredulous. "We'll have to go to a couple of different taverns then!"

"I've snuck drinks before," Elle defended himself, thinking of the rare times when his stepmother hosted a party and there was a bit of wine or spirits left in someone's glass for Elle to sneak as he cleaned up the dinner table.

"All right," Theo laughed.

At the first place they went to, Elle had two drinks Theo bought him. He wasn't exactly sure what was in the mugs Theo pressed into his hand, but the taste was heady and bubbly, fizzling against his tongue in a way that made him giggle. The company was even better. Theo kept up a happy conversation with Elle; his voice never once slipped from sounding interested to bored, so Elle knew Theo was having just as much fun as he was. By the third tavern, Elle was swaying and babbling happily.

Theo sat them down on a nearby stoop when Elle's listing almost brought them to the ground as they traveled between taverns.

"Don't take this the wrong way," Theo said softly. Elle felt him lean close, gasping when Theo's warm lips pressed against his own. The kiss was soft and chaste, but Elle could feel the passion in how gently Theo pushed against Elle and how Theo's lips trembled just slightly from how much feeling was being released from just the small contact. Theo drew back after a few long seconds, and Elle, feeling sober for the moment, pressed his fingers against his tingling lips.

"Why?" Elle asked, surprise and a fair bit of excitement slurring his words even more than the drinking had. No one had ever kissed him before!

Theo sighed. "My mother is planning something and expects me to be with her. I don't know when I'll be able to see you again, and I couldn't leave without at least trying to tell you my feelings."

Elle was quiet for a while, still feeling the phantom of Theo's lips against his own. "So this is goodbye?" he asked, reaching out to touch Theo's shoulder.

"No!" Theo cried. "It's a promise that I've got a plan to save me from my mother. I will be back soon."

Elle fisted his hand in Theo's shirt, the effects of too much drink making him a bit reckless. Leaning forward, he pressed his lips against Theo's.

"I'm holding you to that promise," Elle said when he finally pulled away.

Theo laughed happily. "All right! Well, let's go to one more bar, and then I should get you home."

They took their time at the last bar, each slowly drinking one final mug and equally reluctant to acknowledge that the time when they would have to part was quickly approaching. Elle sat with his head resting on Theo's shoulder the entire time.

Too soon, they said their farewells, and Theo watched Elle slip through the back gate of the manor. Sneaking around the edges of the vegetable garden and through the kitchen door, Elle let out a sigh of relief and made his way to his bed for the remainder of the night.

*

When Elle woke up the next day, he immediately wished the roof of his small servant's room would fall in and relieve him of having a head. After almost half an hour of sitting on his sleeping pallet without moving, the nausea began to pass.

"Elle?" a worried voice called through the curtain that separated his room from the servant's hallway.

"Yes?" Elle croaked.

The curtain swished as Lucy, Macy's mother, entered Elle's room. "You should be glad you can't see, with a hangover like that," she clucked kindly. "The light in here would kill you, no doubt."

"Okay, Lucy," Elle groaned out.

Lucy clucked again. "Here, drink this and get yourself up," she said as she pressed a cup into Elle's hands. "The missus is going to be calling on you soon, what with this morning's excitement."

Elle gasped, thinking of his morning chores still undone. "What time is it, Lucy?"

"Oh, shush. Don't worry. Macy and I took care of it all ourselves. With half of this manor closed up, there's really not that much to do anyway. Macy's just hitching up the wagon now, so you have plenty of time to wash up and bring breakfast around to the family."

"I'll get to the garden then," Elle said as he thought about Macy loading all those heavy bundles into the cart alone. There was still enough time to help her before his stepfamily woke and demanded he bring them breakfast. He stood with a groan, his head threatening to fall off his neck.

Lucy steadied Elle with one hand and handed over his walking stick. "No, no, listen for a moment. A letter came this morning from the palace. There's to be a set of three balls and all eligible ladies are invited! They're trying to get the second prince married, of course, now that the Crown Prince has an heir on the way, but the missus has it in mind to get her own sons hitched to those rich, eligible ladies too."

"And she's going to need someone to run to the dressmakers in a few minutes," Elle guessed, knowing his stepmother's needs from long experience.

"And the jewelers, no doubt," Lucy agreed. "You're going to be busy for a while, boy."

Elle sighed and went to get ready to meet with his stepmother.

*

Lucy was right; Elle didn't go to the market stall the entire week. Instead he went to the tailors for Sil and Everett, the dressmaker for his stepmother, the jewelry store to have her pearls reset and then back again when she decided that it was inappropriate to wear white jewelry and wanted her rubies and sapphires reset instead.

The day before the first ball had Elle running up and down the stairs, frantically trying not to trip, in response to his stepmother's demands. Only once she, Sil, and Everett had been handed into the carriage hired for the night did Elle finally relax.

He walked back into the manor, plans of an early dinner and a nap while he waited for his stepmother to return running through his mind.

"Elle," Macy called, alerting him to the fact that the two other servants in the house were waiting for him.

"Yes?" Elle asked carefully. Why weren't Lucy and Macy already in the kitchen enjoying their dinners?

"Your Theo stopped by the stall today and left a package and a request behind," Macy said. "He's been invited to the ball and would like you to join him."

"Me?" Elle asked incredulously. "Why would I be invited to a ball?"

Lucy snorted. "Because he's besotted with you. If he's going, then you should join him as his date. Now, come along. We have a bath waiting for you."

In something of a daze, Elle was bathed, his hair was brushed to a shine, and he soon found himself thrust into unfamiliar, expensive-feeling clothes.

"Um, why am I wearing a dress?" Elle asked as he realized just what he was being helped into. The stiff fabric of the skirt brushed against his legs with a soft swishing sound as Lucy brushed the folds into order.

Macy laughed as she carefully pulled the bodice of the dress into place. Elle could feel that it was a little loose up top from the air that flowed through, but when Macy started tightening the ties up his back with a hum of concentration, he felt the stiffly embroidered fabric stiffen properly around his chest.

"Theo said invitations were carefully regulated to avoid any counterfeits, so he couldn't get you an extra one, but since every eligible lady was invited, you wouldn't be turned away if you showed up in a dress. Besides," Macy continued as she leaned over to giggle in Elle's ear, "I think he wants to muck up those plans of his mother's."

"And me in a dress would do that?" Elle asked dryly.

"Psh," Macy snorted. "Like he would tell me? But I have my own mother to annoy, so I do understand." Macy giggled, and Elle heard Lucy grunt in familiar exasperation with her boisterous daughter from where she was tugging on the hem of Elle's skirt.

Lucy stepped back from her handiwork with the dress and Elle's hair and sighed. "You're too beautiful not to wear something this fine anyway. Now if only we had some jewelry. That would finish the dress quite nicely."

Elle bit his lip. He trusted Lucy and Macy to a small extent. They were his only friends aside from Theo, and they did seem to care for him. The real question was, did Elle feel safe from his stepmother's wrath if he told them? "There is some jewelry I could use," he finally said.

"You're not thinking of using Her Grace's jewels," Lucy admonished, worry touching her voice.

Elle laughed at that absurd idea. "I've felt what she calls jewelry. It's all heavy. I'd hate wearing that. No, there's a safe full of the first Duchess of Marchcant's jewelry that the current duchess doesn't know about."

Elle led the way up the stairs into one of the living corridors of the manor that had been closed and unused for years, careful of tripping in the unfamiliar skirt as he went. "This wing was closed before the old duke remarried. When Lady Olivia passed away, he put all of her things in storage or in the safe in her room and never came back. The duchess doesn't know Lady Olivia's things exist."

"And how do you know all this, Elle?" Lucy asked as she followed him into his mother's room.

"My mother died when I was four," Elle said softly. He smelled dust, rather than his mother's sweet and flowery perfume he faintly recalled. "My father remarried when I was six and died a few months later from a lung disease. My stepmother decided she wanted her son to have all the perks of being duke, so I became a servant in my own house."

"You're the duke, not that spoiled bastard Sil?" Macy gasped, surprise and a fair bit of incredulity in her voice. "But, why haven't you done anything about it? I understand you couldn't when you were a kid, but why not now?"

Elle laughed sadly. He was blind. How could he properly hold any title if he couldn't see? How could the rest of the nobility allow someone with his disability to come to power? No, Elle hadn't fought Sil for his rightful position because Elle was deeply afraid that once they realized he was blind, Sil would be given the position anyway. That would hurt so much more.

He walked over to the dressing table and pulled out a drawer. Lying amid the rest of the odds and ends in the compartment was the key Elle needed, and he felt around inside until he found it. Moving to the painting that hung next to the dressing room door, he pushed it aside. The safe had years of dust on it that Elle brushed away with his fingers. When his searching fingertips found the empty space that was the keyhole, he slipped the key inside.

"You look like her," Macy said softly, any uncertainty or disbelief leaving her voice as the key clicked and the safe slid open. She put something down on the dressing table with the gentle click of metal on cloth, and Elle vaguely remembered a small portrait of his family being there at some point.

Elle just shrugged. He couldn't know exactly what he looked like, and his mother was more a memory of that light, floral scent than of features.

"Well, let's see if we have anything to match your dress," Lucy said as she reached into the safe. She and Macy twittered over the jewels they uncovered, eventually setting aside the prefect compliments to Elle's dress. Soon Elle was wearing the jewelry. He could feel the delicate metal filigree and hard stones pressed around his neck and left wrist as well as an unfamiliar weight that hung from his ears. The safe was packed back up and locked.

Elle wore his regular cloak, old and patched as it was. It covered his dress completely, which was good as he climbed onto the driver's seat of their farm cart next to Macy. His dress would remain clean, and no one would start gossiping about the girl in the fancy dress riding through town in a cart.

"I'll be keeping an eye out for when the missus leaves and come find you," Macy said. "Leave your stick in the cart with your cloak. I'll guide you to the ballroom, and hopefully Theo will be waiting for you there."

"You're sure this is okay?" Elle asked, worried. "Even if the duke should be invited to the ball as a matter of courtesy, my current station as a servant says otherwise."

Macy laughed. "Oh, hush. You look lovely in that dress. No one will think you're a servant with Theo there as your date, so why should anyone even ask?"

They parked the cart, and Elle shed his cloak and walking stick. If his grip was too hard on Macy's arm as she guided him up the drive and to the main doors of the palace, she didn't comment. Of course Elle was nervous. This was his first high-class social event since his father passed away fourteen years ago. Fourteen years was a long time.

"If you would take my arm, my lady," a guard said gently as they reached the doors. "I will guide you to the ball."

"Thank you, sir," Elle said softly. He gave Macy's arm one last squeeze before taking the guard's arm and heading off to meet with Theo.

Chapter Two

Elle could hear the ball well before he arrived on the guard's arm. There were instruments already playing a gentle waltz tune over the din of hundreds of voices, and Elle couldn't begin to decipher all the different noises he heard.

"You're a bit late, my lady," the guard said apologetically. "I'm afraid the dancing has already started."

"Oh," Elle replied hesitantly, frantically trying to come up with a believable excuse. Why would someone dare be late to the biggest social event of the season? "My carriage broke," he finally came up with. "Something with the wheel or the axle, so my maid and I walked. I'm glad to have gotten here at all." He smiled shyly, hoping his feeble explanation would assuage the guard's curiosity.

"Of course, my lady," the guard said, much to Elle's relief. He gently dropped Elle's arm, and Elle heard fabric rustle as the guard bowed quickly and left the way he had come.

"Your name, my lady," another man said from near the doors.

"Elle, sir."

"Very well, Miss Elle. If you will come this way," he said, and Elle slowly followed the sound of the man's voice, hoping he wouldn't trip on something and embarrass himself. "I will announce you and you will make your way down the grand staircase. Do not forget to curtsey to Their Majesties at the bottom. Once you finish with that, do as you like."

"Thank you, sir," Elle said quietly, trying to hold back his worry at the thought of stairs. He was more apt to fall down the stairs from missing a step than walk down them to curtsey.

"You're very welcome, Miss Elle," the man replied. "Now be ready."

Elle felt a rush of wind on his face as the doors were opened in front of him. The cacophony of noise he had been hearing lost the little muffling the doors had provided and blasted Elle. Stirring up his courage and hoping his ears would recover their full hearing soon, Elle stepped forward as the man announced him, and was glad that no one was likely to have heard over the sounds of the music and chatter. If Elle fell down the stairs, at least no one would know his name.

Elle had to pause once he was through the doors to try and get his bearings. He waved his hand out in front of him, trying to find a banister and avoid any embarrassment.

"Elle!" Theo's voice called, and Elle immediately turned toward him, glad to have someone to guide him safely. He took Theo's arm and hoped his relief didn't show on his face too much. They made it down the stairs without any mishaps, Theo murmuring when the steps began and ended into Elle's ear as they went.

It was easy to curtsey to Their Majesties with Theo holding his arm; Elle couldn't be worried next to Theo's strong presence. The sounds of the waltz and the murmurs of the other attendees faded away every time Theo bent to ask Elle a question or point out a set of tables and chairs to his left that Elle needed to sidestep.

This experience was greatly different from their walks together in the market. Besides the rich dress Elle wore, rather than his usual rags, Theo wore a heavy coat with a thick braid down the sleeve that Elle could feel under his fingers. Perhaps he was a guard captain? It would explain why Theo was in the market so often if he had patrol there every morning.

Besides their clothes, Elle felt a sense of lightness to their steps. He had felt the stirrings of something similar at the beginning of their drinking date the prior week, but once the first mug of alcohol had gone into Elle's stomach, other concerns had taken precedent. Now, though, with music in his ears and Theo at his side, Elle floated.

"Do you dance?" Theo asked softly.

Elle bit his lip. At six he had begun lessons in the most basic of steps, but as a servant the most he had done was tend the ballroom fire while his stepbrothers learned. Still, Elle wanted to dance with Theo; this was a ball, so they should dance.

"If you lead," Elle responded finally, "I will try my best to follow."

Theo laughed. "This is the first waltz of the night. They always try to give many slow dances at the beginning for the older couples before they tire. The next dance will be slow and easy, so follow me as best you can."

When the musicians stopped, Elle heard much rustling of skirts as those finished dancing left the floor and others moved to replace them. Elle was gently pulled into place on the dance floor by Theo.

"Start with your right foot. This is a four-step waltz, one, two, three, four," Theo explained, counting off the timing for the steps as he arranged their hands and feet into the starting positions. While the musicians reset for the dance, Elle absorbed as much of Theo's instructions as he could. "Curtsey, Elle," Theo added when Elle heard a pause in the uncoordinated noise from the musicians. Elle curtseyed in response to the fabric rustle from Theo's courtly bow. When the first stirrings of the violin sounded, they were off.

Floating was an apt term for the experience, Elle thought. His feet did tangle with Theo's plenty of times, but Theo laughed every time until Elle's blush would fade. The steps to this dance were simple, and it wasn't long before they glided along the floor, hand in hand with their steps seemingly perfectly choreographed to Elle's senses.

Elle's head was in the clouds even though his body was quite aware of whose arms held him close. It was a wonderful experience as one dance melded into two, then four, until Elle couldn't remember how long he had spun in Theo's arms.

"Are you having fun?" Theo had asked at a pause in the dancing as the old musicians retired for the night and new ones set out their instruments.

"Oh yes," Elle breathed happily. "Thank you so much for inviting me!"

Theo's laughter led them into the strains of the next dance, a much faster one, but by this time Elle was so used to following Theo's whispered instructions and expert leading skills that he hardly noticed the speed.

When their final dance of the night ended, Elle was able to tell it would be their last before Theo began leading them from the dance floor. There was a sense of disappointed hesitance in Theo's arm, as if he didn't want to let Elle get away.

"Your friend from the market is hovering by one of curtains covering the balconies," Theo explained.

Elle bit his lip with a frown. "It must be time for me to go," he said vaguely, not wanting to explain the details. His stepmother must have some reason to leave before the end of the ball.

"There you are!" Macy called when they had pushed through the curtain and onto the balcony. "Her Grace has ordered for her carriage, so Elle and I have to be going."

"Elle can't stay?" Theo asked sadly. "He could stay out when we went drinking."

Macy must have shaken her head because Theo sighed.

"The missus will be calling for Elle to light fires and hang dresses first thing," Macy explained, no doubt in response to Theo's disappointed expression. Elle knew his own face was set in sad lines, but he also knew that his stepmother would ask after him upon her return from the ball.

Theo sighed again, and Elle could hear mirroring sadness in his voice. Theo was as disappointed by the night's abrupt end as Elle was—it was good to know that Theo had enjoyed their time together as much as Elle had. "All right," Theo said. "But there's another ball being held next week. I don't know if I'll be able to get you a new dress, but you must come."

"I'll be there!" Elle said excitedly. Another chance to dance with Theo? Elle wouldn't miss it!

"And don't worry about the dress," Macy added with a wicked note in her voice. "We have that taken care of already."

Elle's arm was passed from Theo to Macy, but not before Elle felt Theo bend and place a gentle kiss on his wrist.

"Until next week, Elle," Theo said softly, in a voice that melted Elle's insides. His inner wrist was tingling and his face felt hot.

"Oh the look on your face," Macy giggled.

As Macy led Elle away, Theo left to reenter the ball. Elle strained his ears to follow the retreating footsteps.

"Where is that lovely lady you had with you?" a male voice called. Theo must have pushed back the curtain.

"She got away," Theo's rich voice answered. Any other response made was lost to Elle as the heavy curtain dropped back into place.

"Stairs!" Macy hissed. "I know you're totally in love with the man, Elle, but listen to me before you break your neck!"

"Sorry," Elle said, feeling his cheeks flush once again. The bells in the clock tower began to ring midnight as they reached the bottom of the stairs and headed into the night.

*

Elle was whisked into the servants' portion of the house by Lucy the second his feet crossed the threshold.

"The missus's carriage was spotted in the main square moments ago," Lucy explained. "One of the baker's sons ran to tell me. Hurry, hurry."

Elle's dress and jewelry were removed, and he felt one of the women tugging his hair into a braid as the other handed him his sackcloth shirt and breaches to put on.

"He's still clean, Mother," Macy grumbled worriedly.

"The main hall fireplace hasn't been swept out for the night yet," Lucy said as she pushed Elle down the corridor. "Run there quick and get yourself properly dirty, then get to cleaning it."

Elle nodded and rushed off, trying to tap his stick in front of him but barking his toes on a few steps and walls anyway. He had just buried himself in the ashes when the sound of carriage wheels echoed off the drive.

"Your hair, Elle. Don't forget your hair!" Lucy called as she rushed by to get the door for Her Grace and her sons. "Oh, I hope Macy has that mule and cart put away, or the lady will let me hear it."

Elle quickly poured ashes over his head, wincing as a half-burned piece of wood thumped him on the forehead. He rubbed some into his long braid, but when he heard his stepmother's heels on the front step, Elle pulled the bucket and rake over to begin gathering the old ashes for disposal.

"Send the boy to my rooms at once," Lady Sadia said imperiously to Lucy as she swept into the house.

"Not a good idea, Mother." Sil's nasally voice followed his mother's sharp staccato footsteps into the house. "Cinder-Elle's gotten himself dirty just for the occasion. But filth should be with filth on such an auspicious night." He laughed cruelly.

Elle ignored their words and continued to gather the ashes from the hearth. If they didn't call him to attend them, he knew he wasn't to approach no matter what they said about him in his presence.

"And on a night when I need my dresses hung and pressed?" Lady Sadia sneered. "The boy isn't allowed meals for the next day."

"Yes, my lady. I'll send Macy up at once," Lucy said without a hint of agreement in her voice.

"See that the girl is clean," his stepmother agreed, before the sound of her skirts sweeping away, followed by the two sets of footsteps belonging to Sil and Everett, told Elle his disguise had passed their inspection.

Elle finished cleaning out the hall fireplace and laid the wood for the morning's fire. He washed his hands and face roughly in the kitchen before gathering a new stack of wood to take to his stepmother's rooms.

Lady Sadia and her sons were lounging in her personal sitting room, sipping tea while Macy brushed her hair. Elle quietly shuffled to the fire to add more wood.

"And did you see the girl the prince spent the entire night dancing with?" Sil sneered. "She was too tall and too thin. And it looked like she worked for a living—did you see her shoulders?"

"She really was unkempt, wasn't she," Lady Sadia agreed, derision in her voice. "The way she just stared so awkwardly, even though Prince Drin ran to greet her like that! But you, Silvester, did well for yourself. Two daughters of prominent nobility dancing on your whim all night."

"Yes, Mother," Sil said, as if having women at his beck and call was a usual occurrence. At twenty-two, Sil should have been married with children already. The nobles' daughters must have been from out of town, to not know of Sil's reputation for cruelty and selfishness. Either that, or they were second or third daughters looking for any available option to marry and start their own household.

"But you, Everett, are a disgrace!" their mother continued. "Did you leave the buffet tables at all tonight? Silvester must be married, but you ought to have prospects too. If you marry well, Silvester will have a better showing at his own wedding."

"I apologize, Mother," Everett said softly. There was a soft thump as he put aside the book he habitually kept with him and a clink as he reached for his tea. "But I did have a conversation with the lovely Lady Estelveld."

"That horrid woman?" she screeched. "Her daughters are not good enough for Silvester, and I won't have you associating with such riffraff."

Elle had to hide a smirk at Lady Sadia's words. The Duchess of Estelveld had formally denied Sil's attempt to court her daughters years ago, and his stepmother had never forgiven the slight against her precious son.

"Luckily, tonight went well regardless," Lady Sadia continued. "Silvester made a good showing, and we left exactly at midnight. You will have ladies crawling at your feet at the ball next week, asking after the air of mystery you've managed to project."

"It really is a wonderful plan, Mother," Sil agreed with his usual haughty tone.

"Anyway, off to bed. We must start planning for the next ball in the morning!" she said with a happy sigh.

Elle quickly finished banking the fire for the night and left the room before anyone noticed him. He finished the rest of his nightly chores and went to bed dreaming of dancing on the clouds in Theo's arms.

*

The following week was as hectic as the last, Elle once again visiting the dressmakers and the tailor and the jewelers.

Two days before the ball Elle was helping his stepbrothers with their final fittings. Lady Sadia had purchased Sil yet another suit that fit him perfectly. Elle was fastening the buttons of Sil's brocade shirt, when his hands were sharply slapped away.

"Mother," Sil said nasally. "I really must have an actual manservant. Having a blind oaf attempt to do my buttons correctly is too much!"

"Of course, dear," Lady Sadia answered from where she was standing in front of a mirror as Lucy held up different jeweled necklaces for her consideration.

Properly chastised for being unable to suitably button a shirt, Elle moved to help Everett with his jacket. Everett brought his arm to Elle's searching hand and stood still while Elle pulled the shoulder into place.

"The sleeves are too short, Mother," Everett complained as Elle tried to move the cuffs into position and instead ran out of fabric.

"You received a new set of pants for the occasion, Everett," Lady Sadia snapped. "Be glad you are able to wear one of Silvester's older jackets."

"Yes, Mother," Everett sighed with his usual resignation. As the second son and the second person in his mother's heart, Everett was used to getting the short end of the stick. Still, Elle could sense an unusual amount of disappointment when Everett clapped Elle on the shoulder in a quiet thank-you for trying to help him with the jacket.

Elle went to help Macy finish making dinner and setting the table after the family was again dressed in regular clothes and off on their own pursuits.

Later that night, Macy and Elle snuck into the abandoned wing of the manor.

"I've been working on it in secret," Macy said in an excited whisper. "Of course, your mother's dresses are all out of style, but luckily I'm fairly good with a needle and thread!"

She led Elle to the bed and placed his hand on a silk dress with what felt like very ornate embroidery.

"I chose this one because it matches that beautiful sapphire necklace I saw the other night," Macy explained excitedly. "You will look absolutely stunning in this."

"Thank you so much, Macy," Elle said quietly, somewhat overcome with how much his friend had been helping him.

"It's all in the name of love!" Macy replied with a giggle. "I figure that when I fall in love with my handsome man, you'll return the favor."

Elle nodded. How could he not? But, speaking of love—Elle's thoughts turned toward Everett and his too-short jacket sleeves.

Elle knew that his younger stepbrother was used to secondhand clothes; this wouldn't be the first time he had worn a cast-off jacket of his brother's that was too small. So why had Everett voiced a complaint this time when he knew from long experience that Lady Sadia didn't care? Elle thought it had something to do with Lady Estelveld and her eldest unmarried daughter, Lady Marina. Elle had a suspicion that Everett was trying to woo a lady of his own, despite his mother's disinterest in the matter, and Lady Marina was his choice.

"Could you help me with something else?" Elle asked before he lost his resolve to help his less terrible stepbrother.

"Sure," Macy replied easily. "What do you need?"

Elle walked to the door that led to his mother's dressing room and opened it. Inside were dozens of dresses for all occasions. In the back, if Elle remembered correctly, was a door that connected to his father's dressing room. It had been Elle's favorite hiding spot when he was avoiding lessons as a child.

The door was there as he remembered, and beyond it Elle's searching hands found where suits and slacks were carefully hung. Elle began fingering the sleeves of the jackets. He needed one that was the correct length for Everett.

"How does Her Grace not know about all this?" Macy asked in awe when she joined Elle in the closet.

"I told you," Elle explained. "When my mother died, my father had this wing closed. He moved to the other side of the manor and never looked back. There are tons of things left behind. I used to come here to play before my father remarried."

Elle pulled out a jacket that felt like it was the right length and held it up for Macy to see.

"Do you think you could make this fashionable for Everett to wear?" Elle asked.

"The style of jackets hasn't changed much over the years," Macy mused. "A snip of the ruffles and a stitch here or there to fit it properly and it would work perfectly. Why are you helping him though?" she asked curiously.

"I think he's trying to get married so he can finally move out from under his mother's thumb," Elle explained as he led the way back into his mother's room.

"Well, anything to help someone escape from the missus," Macy said with a laugh. "I'll have this done in time, don't worry."

*

"Where did you get this?" Everett asked as Elle helped Everett slide on his new jacket. His voice was quiet and held a touch of incredulity, as he was aware that his self-absorbed brother and his brother's new manservant were just across the room and any noise of surprise would alert them to the fitted jacket Everett now wore.

"Don't ask," Elle replied in an equally soft voice. "Just enjoy talking with Lady Marina."

"Elle—" Everett began, but he was interrupted when the door opened.

"Ready?" Lady Sadia asked imperiously as she swept into the room and over to Sil on a swirl of skirts and clicking heels. Elle could hear her fussing over Sil's jacket collar and wasn't surprised when she never bothered to glance over to see how her younger son looked.

"Yes, Mother," her two sons replied.

Elle's stepfamily left the manor, entering their rented carriage quickly. The moment the carriage left the driveway, Elle, Lucy, and Macy rushed to Elle's mother's room.

Elle was bathed and primped and dressed. Macy helped him with his jewelry while Lucy did something artful with his hair. Elle could feel individual strands being pulled and tied on the back of his head into some sort of bun, while the rest was brushed gently to hang down the back of the dress. Soon enough, Elle found himself holding tightly to Macy's arm as she led him to the main doors of the palace, thoughts of finally being near Theo again running through his mind.

The second ball would be as wonderful as the first, Elle hoped, as his arm was passed from Macy to the waiting guard's.

As Elle ascended the steps into the palace on the guard's arm, his excitement grew. When Theo met him at the top of the long stairway leading down to the dance floor, Elle couldn't stop the huge smile that slid across his face. Theo seemed equally enthusiastic, as he was quick to sweep Elle into his arms and onto the dance floor.

Chapter Three

"You look magnificent," Theo said with excitement and warmth in his voice as he led Elle onto the dance floor.

"Even though I'm in a dress?" Elle quipped with a smile.

"Even so," Theo agreed, his own smile evident in the lightness of his voice. His steps were quick and sure as he led Elle into their first dance.

They danced quite a few songs together. Elle listened to Theo's whispered instructions just like the last ball and was pleased that he didn't step on his toes nearly as much this time. The wonderful floating feeling from being held so gently in Theo's arms as they spun around the ballroom returned, and Elle enjoyed it immensely. Elle could tell by Theo's voice as he laughed and talked that he was having a very good time as well.

After their sixth dance, Elle was panting and laughing. The floating feeling had faded, but levity had replaced it and Elle barely felt its loss. Somehow when Theo had instructed Elle to turn left, Elle had gone right instead, and they had ended up bumping into each other.

"All right," Theo said, amusement in his voice as he steadied Elle before leading him off the dance floor. "Let's take a break. Would you like a drink and a snack?" he asked.

"Yes, please," Elle said, still giggling from his mistake, but happy that Theo was happy. In his rush to get to the ball on time, he hadn't had time for a bite of dinner and was hungry, so Theo's suggestion was eagerly met.

Theo laughed once more and led Elle over to a small table. He smoothly sat Elle in one of the seats before setting off for food and refreshments.

Elle sat quietly, listening to the music and the soft sounds of people talking. The ball seemed like such a happy place, although Elle made certain not to listen to the content of what people were saying. He didn't want to listen to cold gossip or political wheeling, as that would ruin the euphoria. His head was still slightly in the clouds, and his arms and hands felt warm from where they had been pressed against Theo. So far, this second ball was just as wonderful as the first had been.

He was alerted that he was no longer alone at his table when a polite cough and swish of skirts told Elle that someone wanted to speak with him. Elle turned his head in the direction of the noise.

"Prince Drin looks handsome tonight," a woman said in a bland and emotionless voice. She sounded like an older woman, someone of his stepmother's age, and Elle couldn't help wondering why she wanted to speak with him.

"Yes, my lady," Elle replied politely. He certainly wouldn't know what the prince looked like, but he couldn't be rude and not reply.

"And those sapphires you're wearing are gorgeous. Wherever did you get them made?" she asked, a touch more interest in her voice. A chair squeaked as it was pulled out across from Elle, and the woman took a seat.

Elle reached up to touch the intricate band of metal and stones around his neck, feeling the delicate work that had gone into the swirls of metal holding the precious stones in place. "They were my mother's," he answered softly.

"And do you know where your mother got them?" the woman asked, her voice suddenly cold and intent. "Because," she continued before Elle could speak, "the last time I saw those sapphires in that particular setting, they were worn by my sister-in-law, Lady Olivia, when she married my brother. You will tell me how you got them, girl."

Elle's hand clenched around the necklace in surprise at her words. He was wearing something his mother had worn when she married his father? He'd had no idea how important the necklace had been. But, wait, her brother? Elle refocused all his attention on the woman he could feel glaring at him.

When had he last seen his aunts? The only time he could remember was when his father had married his stepmother. There had only been one aunt who had been as brusque as this woman was currently being.

"Aunt Adel?" Elle guessed, hoping his assumption was correct.

"Adelina, if you please," she snapped. Her frigid tone had not faded in the slightest.

Elle shook his head. "But you told me it was okay to call you Adel because I couldn't pronounce 'lina. You said so when you came to stay for a week after my mother died."

Elle heard the woman's sharp intake of breath. "What is your name, girl?" she snapped. "And how do you have such information?"

"Because I am a boy," Elle answered softly. His aunt had no love for his stepmother, Elle remembered. Elle didn't think there was any harm in letting her know who he was. "And my name is Elle, Elleron, after my father."

Elle heard skirts rustle as Aunt Adelina moved, but it was only when she blew in his face that he realized she was so close. Elle jumped back, surprised.

"You fit the description," she said softly, much of the malice gone from her voice. "I will have to find an old family portrait to be sure, but you look like the woman my brother married. You're certainly blind like my nephew. But why are you wearing a ball gown?"

Elle felt himself blush and ducked his head. "Theo said he was invited to the ball and wanted me to come," Elle explained. "But my stepmother would recognize me if I came as a boy, and without an invitation I would be turned away at the door. Since every eligible lady was invited, by pretending to be female, no one stopped me."

Aunt Adelina spluttered in her seat for a moment. "No invitation!" she gasped. "You're the Duke of Marchcant! Your invitation came embossed with gold and was hand delivered by the king's courier himself!"

Elle laughed, but it was a cold, sad sound. "My stepbrother, Silvester, has taken the roll of the duke since my stepmother declared me unfit and turned me into a servant. I clean her fireplaces."

"Such an affront! Their Majesties will hear of this, never fear," she snapped.

"But, Aunt!" Elle gasped, reaching out for her before she could rise and stomp away. "I am blind. I'm unfit to run the dukedom."

She snorted. "Blind doesn't matter. You'll just hire someone to read and write for you."

"There's no money for that," Elle disagreed. "My stepmother has already spent it all."

"No money?" Aunt Adelina asked, incredulous. "With your father's merchant enterprise being the richest in the kingdom? Aside from the king, you're the wealthiest man in this room, Elle." There was a pause, before Lady Adelina continued musingly, "No, that woman wouldn't have access to that money; it's only available to the rightful heir, not the spouse. Unless—" She paused ominously. "—unless her eldest son were to marry and the king named him as the Duke of Marchcant…"

"That's what she's after," Elle gasped in realization, suddenly understanding why Lady Sadia was so insistent in urging Sil to marry.

"Their Majesties will not be pleased when I tell them," Adelina said with satisfaction in her voice. "That horrible woman will suffer for what she's done to you." Elle heard her rise to her feet. "If you'll excuse me, Elle," she said politely.

"Lady Adelina," Theo's voice called as he neared the table. "It's so rare to see you at court."

"Yes, well, I do like to leave the countryside occasionally. My youngest son is being presented at court this year, so I thought I should make the journey." She sounded distracted, as if she weren't paying full attention to the conversation. "Ah, I see the person I need to speak with over there. If you will excuse me?"

Elle's aunt left, so Elle turned toward the clicking sound of plates being placed on the table in front of him.

"I've brought you a selection of finger foods," Theo explained. "And above your right hand is your wineglass." Theo settled into a seat next to Elle.

Elle's mouth watered. The scent rising from the plate in front of him was heavenly, and when he tentatively reached forward and wrapped his fingers around one of the small sandwiches and popped it into his mouth, Elle knew why. He didn't think he had eaten anything this good in his entire life. The bread was rich and buttery, and whatever was spread inside was creamy. There was a bit of a crunch that Elle recognized as fresh cucumbers, and the sandwich finished with a bit of a zip from some sort of spice sprinkled on top. Elle was quick to reach for a second sandwich.

Theo laughed at Elle's enthusiasm. "I'm glad you like it!"

"It's delicious. What's in it?" Elle asked as he reached greedily for a third sandwich. He paused for a sip of wine and felt his eyes nearly roll back into his head at the smooth, heady taste of what he assumed was a very expensive glass of red. The last time Elle had eaten this kind of luscious fare had been, like most of his last fancy opportunities, at his father's wedding. Fine wines and gourmet food selections were not offered to house servants.

They talked about the food and wine for a while, before heading out for another dance that had Elle smiling happily at Theo the entire time. When the music for the waltz ended, Theo led Elle off to the side of the room.

"When all the balls are over and things return to normal, would you like to continue spending more time with me?" Theo asked awkwardly. "We could go out drinking again, or I thought I might teach you to ride a horse?"

Elle remembered liking horses when he was a child. "It would be nice to learn to ride," Elle agreed with a smile on his face. It would also be nice to spend more time with Theo. Elle wondered if he should tell Theo about Aunt Adelina or what she had said... But Theo was in the guard. Knowing that Elle was technically nobility might scare him away, which was the last thing Elle wanted.

"Fantastic," Theo said happily, bringing Elle's mind back to the conversation. "Oh," Theo added, voice suddenly reserved. "Your friend is waving at us again."

"Macy?" Elle gasped. "I wonder why?"

They made their way over to where Macy was peering worriedly through a balcony curtain and stepped outside.

"Her Grace has just ordered her carriage," Macy said frantically as soon as the balcony curtain closed behind Elle and Theo. "She's dragged both her sons outside with her and is waiting in the castle drive. If we don't run, we won't make it home in time!"

"Run?" Elle gasped. "In these shoes?" They were good for walking and dancing, ornate and tooled, but soft soled. Elle would break an ankle if he had to run in them.

"It's not far to your cart, right?" Theo asked, his voice all business. "Elle, leave your shoes with me. The garden won't hurt your bare feet as much."

Elle was quick to toss off his shoes. He spun quickly and embraced Theo in a hug before grabbing Macy's arm and taking off at a run.

"Until next week!" Theo called after them.

"She got away again?" Elle heard someone laugh loudly behind him as he raced down the stairs.

"She left her shoes this time," Elle heard Theo reply.

"Three, two, one," Macy counted down, telling Elle when it was okay to lengthen his stride as the stairs ended. The bells started chiming midnight as Elle felt soft grass instead of stone beneath his feet. They made it to the cart in record time, and Macy clucked the mule into a grudging canter. She clutched the reins in one hand while the other began pulling at the laces holding up Elle's dress.

They careened around corners through the town as quickly as the mule and the aging farm cart could go, no doubt waking a few of the residents in their clattering rush. The dress was holding on by just a few strings and Elle's hair was hanging loose when they pulled onto the street the manor was on. Elle unclasped his necklace as they clattered through the manor gates.

The cart raced up the drive and stopped by the front kitchen gate. Elle was quick to dismount, clipping his shoulder painfully when he misjudged going through the kitchen doorway.

"Hurry!" Lucy gasped as she greeted them. "They're at the driveway by now!" Elle's dress was whisked off while he frantically braided his long hair. Lucy left the dress behind as she pushed Elle toward the kitchen fire. "Close your eyes," she warned before dumping a bucket of ashes on Elle's head.

Elle was quick to rub the ashes into his skin and hair even as he fought to pull on his clothing before his stepmother summoned him.

"The cart's hidden," Macy gasped for breath as she rushed into the kitchen. "I'll put the mule away later."

"Get to the front door!" Lucy hissed as they heard the sound of wheels creaking to a stop in the drive.

Macy rushed out of the kitchen again while Lucy gathered Elle's dress into a bundle and hid it in one of the cabinets and Elle finished tying up his breeches and rubbing the soot into his hair.

"She wants tea and a hot fire," Macy said as she reentered the kitchen on her way to the servants' stairs. "And she's in a frightful mood," Macy added before she vanished upstairs.

Elle gathered wood and kindling while Lucy made tea. They went up the stairs together and entered Her Grace's sitting room to find organized chaos.

Macy was helping Elle's ranting stepmother out of her coat while the new manservant, who had been dutifully waiting for his master to return upstairs, was helping divest Sil of his jacket.

Lucy set out the tea while Elle moved to build up the fire.

"That damnable woman!" Elle's stepmother was snarling. "How could Adelina Heathbridge come to court now? How dare she put such a wrinkle in my plans! Silvester, you will be married before that woman can interfere. You understand?"

"Yes, Mother," Sil agreed as he settled into a chair and picked up his tea. "One of the girls I was dancing with tonight seems a likely candidate. It's a shame we had to leave so quickly, but hopefully at the next ball she'll accept my proposal."

"We had to leave before that Adelina started asking questions I can't answer," Elle's stepmother snarled. "But she shouldn't be at the next ball; that woman hates to leave her grubby country home. Yes, Silvester, at the next ball, ask that girl for her hand. We'll approach the king the second she agrees."

Elle kept his focus on the slowly growing fire so no one in the room would realize he knew who and what his stepmother was so unhappy about. Such knowledge would get him into trouble; of that Elle had no doubt.

When the fire was steady, and Elle had control over his facial expressions, he went to help Everett remove his jacket. The jacket would be returned to his father's dressing room, but Macy had already promised to have another one ready for the next ball.

"How did it go?" Elle asked softly, voice pitched below Lady Sadia's continued cries about his aunt.

"Thank you so much for the jacket," Everett replied in an equally low voice. "We'll be speaking to her mother at the next ball."

"That's excellent news," Elle said encouragingly. "Congratulations."

"Yes," Everett sighed, "but then we have to somehow convince my mother. She'll never agree to have me marry better than Sil, let alone allow me to join the Estelveld family."

"Something will work out," Elle said fervently, thinking of his own hopes when it came to Theo, and his aunt's declaration of aid. Elle lowered his voice and bent closer to Everett before speaking again. "If you get the chance," Elle whispered, "try talking to my aunt Adel about it. She might be able to help."

"You're crazy," Everett gasped, but he kept his voice lowered and his head bent near Elle's.

Instead of answering, Elle pulled back and gave Everett a smile.

"What are you doing, Cinder-Elle?" Sil snapped. "Feeling fabric you'll never wear again? Nostalgia does not look good on a servant."

"There was a thread caught, brother," Everett replied as he slipped out of his jacket and handed it to Elle.

Elle turned away to fold the jacket properly. Someone stepped next to him, and he heard the manservant's voice whisper softly to him a moment later. "You're wearing earrings," he warned sharply. Elle jumped and his hands flew toward his ears. He had forgotten to remove his earrings in the rush! With nimble fingers, Elle pulled the gems from his ears and hid them in the pocket of the jacket.

"Thanks," Elle whispered back. Elle moved away to tend the fire while the manservant returned to his master's side.

*

Once the family was in bed, the four servants met in the kitchen for a late dinner. Elle handed the jacket and earrings to Macy, who promised to return them to where they belonged in the morning.

"Tell me what I can do to help," the manservant said as he joined them at the table.

"Well, Jack," Lucy said to the man sharply, "we can't really have you help if you're to be with Sil all the time."

"He's a horrible, spoiled boy," Jack grumbled. "If I didn't need this job so much! Well, I heard that Her Grace wants her son married, but there's a woman who keeps disappearing at midnight from the ball, taking attention away from her son. Her Grace isn't pleased. I saw Elle's earrings tonight, and I figured you're dressing him up to hurt Her Grace for some reason. I want to help."

"Not to hurt her, although that's a side benefit I admit I'm enjoying," Macy said, clearly believing whatever she saw on Jack's face. "Elle just wants to go to the ball. We've got most of it down to a science. Just do what you think will help, like telling Elle about the earrings before the missus noticed tonight."

"If we think of something," Lucy added, "we'll tell you. Elle!" She turned and said, "Off to bed with you."

Elle lifted his head from where he had been resting it on the table and sighed gustily. "It was so much fun," he said with a smile.

"And you've had too much to drink and not enough sleep," Lucy sniffed. "Here's your stick; now off with you!"

"Thanks," Elle said as he levered himself to his feet and headed off to bed.

Chapter Four

Elle couldn't stop giggling. It hadn't been funny at first, when he'd stepped on the trailing hem of a lady dancing nearby, who had then tumbled into her partner with a squawk. When Elle found himself on the floor, Theo sheepishly apologizing for landing on top of Elle, and the sounds of other affronted women and men on the floor around them, he had buried his head in Theo's shoulder in embarrassment. This third ball had certainly begun with a bang!

Now, though, Elle was remembering that woman's squawk and the sound she had made when she hit her dance partner, who had then stumbled into another couple, and the whole debacle had continued until Elle was underneath Theo's warm body, and he couldn't stop the smile that broke over his face or the laughter from echoing freely. Theo had bundled Elle off the dance floor before the lady could figure out who had stepped on her hem. A giggling Elle would make a perfect target for retribution.

"It's not my fault," Elle gasped out between sniggers. "I can't see, and she was dancing far too close to us."

"You laughing doesn't help all that much though," Theo replied with mock stiffness. Elle could hear the laughter hidden in Theo's voice but knew the man was too aware of the situation to allow more than a small smile to cross his face.

"I'm sure it doesn't," Elle agreed as he brought himself under control. "Well, this is a good time for a snack break anyway. Shall we go to the buffet?"

"Do you want me to bring you back a plate again?" Theo asked as he stood. When Elle stood as well, Theo courteously pulled Elle's chair back.

"I want to pick my food this time, by smell," Elle explained, excited to try more exotic food and drink.

"Of course, my lady," Theo said with a pleased touch to his voice. Elle felt Theo hold out his arm and pressed his hand there gratefully. This ball wouldn't be nearly as much fun without Theo present.

Elle started sniffing the air when they got close to the food and detected something delectable. The scent was sweet, but there was a strange bitter hint in the air as well. "What's that delicious smell to our left?" Elle asked as he pulled Theo in that direction.

Theo turned to look, laughing softly at Elle's eager expression. "The dessert table is over there," he answered. "You're probably smelling the chocolate."

"Chocolate?" Elle asked softly. "I haven't had chocolate in years." Not since the party after his father's marriage to his stepmother.

Theo laughed gently. "Then you should have some now." He steered them in the direction of the wonderful smell. "Do you want milk chocolate or dark chocolate?" Theo asked when they came to a stop.

Elle's mouth watered. "Dark please."

"All right, open your mouth," Theo teased.

Elle did as he was instructed and felt Theo carefully place a morsel of chocolate on his tongue. Then Elle closed his mouth and let the wonderful, heavy sugariness of the dark chocolate melt there. The taste filled his mouth, a bitter sweetness that made his tongue tingle and wish for more. Ecstasy.

Theo laughed at the very pleased expression on Elle's face. "Let me grab a plate, and we can bring all the different types of chocolate to a table."

Elle felt Theo pull away and hoped that he had been left far enough from the buffet so he wouldn't get in the way of other people. It wasn't as if Elle could safely move away without the chance that he would knock into a table or person like he had stepped on that woman earlier.

"I was advised to ask Lady Adelina for advice," a familiar voice said from Elle's right.

"Hmm," a woman's voice replied. "That might be a very good idea. Adelina has been speaking quite angrily about your mother in court over the past week. It is a good thing Lady Sadia does not frequent those political circles often," the lady added with a wry laugh.

The voices seemed to be coming closer. Elle hunched his shoulders to hide his face. He thought he had a very good idea of who was coming in this direction.

"Oh, I hope she'll be able to help, Everett," a younger woman's voice whimpered next to Elle.

Elle flinched and wished he could run and hide. Sneaking Everett a couple of jackets and advising him on what to do with the Lady Marina did not mean that Everett wouldn't tell his mother that Elle was sneaking into the balls.

"Pardon me, miss," the elder woman said sharply as she tried to politely push past Elle.

"Sorry," Elle replied as he took a small step backward, directly into someone's tall, muscular side. "Sorry," Elle repeated and tried to sidestep Everett before his stepbrother recognized him.

"Oh, it's all right," Everett began cordially. "It's my fault really, so if you'll accept my apolo—" Elle heard the catch in Everett's breath when he recognized Elle. "Elle?" Everett gasped, shock making his voice sharp. "What are you doing here? And why are you in a dress?"

Elle bit his lip and lifted his head in Everett's direction. "I was invited by a friend. And your mother won't recognize me in a dress," he answered and bit his lip worriedly.

Everett groaned. "She'll kill you when she finds out. You're crazy for trying this."

"I think my nephew is very brave," Aunt Adelina's voice snapped from behind Everett.

"Lady Adelina," the older woman with Everett said, relief in her voice. "I was just planning to search you out. Everett here is quite seriously courting my daughter, and I have agreed that they should marry. However, his mother will never allow it." She paused. "Everett is not your nephew. Whom were you speaking about?"

Elle could hear the smug tones in Adelina's voice when she replied. "My nephew, Elleron. The one wearing a dress? But I have a perfect solution to your problem! If the Duke of Marchcant were to recognize your right to marry, then you would not need to speak with that horrible woman."

"The duke?" Lady Marina gasped in a worried, high-pitched voice that made Elle grit his teeth. "Sil would never allow it, and he would tell his mother who would also never allow it."

"But..." Everett said slowly. "Sil isn't the duke, is he? He's not the proper heir."

"He is not?" Lady Estelveld snapped. "Then who is?"

Everett didn't respond. Elle couldn't tell if Everett was looking at Elle, but he did feel his aunt's elbow in his side a moment later.

"I am," Elle said softly.

"Preposterous!" Lady Estelveld began, but Elle heard her mouth snap shut a moment later.

"There you are, Elle!" Theo's voice called. "I filled a plate with those sandwiches you liked last time. Let me choose some chocolates, and we can find a place to sit."

"Thank you, Theo," Elle said with a grin.

"You'll have to carry one of the plates back though," Theo called. "Oh, hello, ladies, sir."

"If you give me the one with the chocolates, I'm not sure if there will be any left by the time we get to the table," Elle teased. He heard Theo laugh from over by the buffet table.

"What is going on?" Lady Estelveld demanded softly with quite a bit of surprise in her voice.

"I'll explain it all later," Adelina replied quickly as Theo returned.

"Pardon me, sirs, madams, but the Duchess Marchcant requests her son at her side when she approaches the king," a small voice said suddenly, making Elle jump in surprise.

"Sil's found a woman willing to marry him, then," Everett said with a sigh as the pageboy ran off once his message had been received. "I'll meet back with you when this is over, my lady," he said with a rustle of fabric that told Elle he was bowing. Lady Marina giggled.

"You'll keep your mouth shut about Elle, boy, if you want your marriage plans to go through," Adel snapped.

"Yes, ma'am," Everett replied diffidently before walking off.

"Elle, hold your hand out," Theo said. Elle did and felt the edge of a plate brush his palm. He carefully took hold of it. "That's the one with the sandwiches, so I can get some chocolate too."

Elle reached out and found one of the sandwiches and popped it into his mouth. The same buttery, creamy, zippy flavor exploded on his tongue, making Elle smile.

"I hope you didn't want any sandwiches then," Elle said with a full mouth and a laugh.

Theo laughed back. "I've got a second plate of them, don't worry. If you'll excuse us, ladies?"

Elle put his arm on Theo's and was happily led away.

The rest of the ball was spent in equally high spirits. They ate and danced some more, pausing for drinks around midnight. The potent wine, rich food, and lovely dancing all had Elle quite happily smiling and enjoying himself along with Theo. When Macy didn't poke her head around the curtain at the usual hour, they returned to the dance floor. This was turning out to be the very best of all the balls. Elle's feet were tired and his muscles ached from all the dancing, but it was all worth it to be spinning in Theo's arms or sitting next to him chatting freely. After this ball, they would be back to their short walks in the morning through the market, and they would feel painfully short when Elle had the memory of hours spent together to compare them with. Still, any meeting was better than not meeting at all.

"Ah, darn," Theo sighed about an hour later.

"What?" Elle asked, worried that their night was coming to an end.

It was. "Macy is waving by the curtain again," Theo said, the first note of sadness entering his voice that night. "It must be time for you to go."

"Oh," Elle said, sounding equally sad as they began walking in Macy's direction. "Thank you so much for inviting me, Theo," Elle said politely, suddenly hyperaware that the end of the night loomed closer with each step they took.

"Thank you for coming, Elle," Theo said, equal parts happiness and resignation in his tone. "I will see you in the market, though. And now that these balls are over, I'm sure you'll be able to get out of your house at night to meet with me more often."

"I hope so!" Elle agreed fervently.

*

"The nerve of the king," Lady Sadia snapped as she carelessly tossed a pair of costly earrings onto the floor. "Such offhand congratulations and a request for an invitation! As if we were some sort of entertainment," she scoffed and stomped over to her dressing table, where she promptly knocked over a tray of brushes and combs.

"Yes," Sil agreed with a haughty sniff that showed his own dislike of the situation. "But, Mother, does that mean he plans to attend?"

"Ah," the woman hummed, the anger dimming from her voice and movements at this new, happier thought. "Well, we shall have to be as lavish as possible, as only a duke can be, in anticipation of his attendance," she added with a calculating smile in her voice.

Elle crouched closer to the fire, hoping Lady Sadia wouldn't notice him. She was talking about making Sil the duke right in front of Elle, and the last thing Elle wanted was to be noticed eavesdropping on their scheming and sent away permanently.

"The king was probably distracted by his son," Everett cut in with a placating tone to his voice as his mother knocked her jar of hairpins to the floor. "He's probably found his bride as well."

"That awkward woman?" she said with a cruel laugh. "I guess the king would be preoccupied. I would be spending my hours planning how to make such an odd-looking girl disappear too. Sil, I am quite pleased that your bride is not so gangly and uncultured as Prince Drin's."

Elle sighed quietly in relief. Lady Sadia was back onto safer subjects, and Macy had returned to the room, bustling about to clean up after her ladyship's various messes. He was sure it was safe for him to get up and help Everett with his clothes now.

"Don't worry," Everett said softly as Elle helped with his jacket. "My mother is just jealous."

"Of what?" Elle asked, lifting his head toward Everett, no doubt with confusion on his face.

Everett just sucked in a small breath of surprise before chuckling slightly.

"And what is so funny, Everett?" Sil asked coldly.

Elle could feel Everett shrug and waited to hear what his response would be. Why had something Elle had said garnered that reaction?

"Oh, I'm just looking forward to tomorrow's gossip. Sil getting married, a girl being deposed—it does promise to be interesting."

"True," Sil agreed. "I am getting married after all."

"And we will have to begin wedding plans at once," Elle's stepmother agreed. "This can't be too rushed, of course, but the sooner you're wed, the better." She paused to harangue Macy for a moment before turning back to her son. "We'll begin sending your manservant around to start arranging things properly in the morning. The rest of the house servants," she added, turning to Macy as she spoke, "are to return to their regular duties until I say otherwise."

"Yes, Your Grace," Macy replied courteously. Elle was firmly ignored where he was folding Everett's jacket in the corner.

"And start cleaning one of the disused wings of this manor," his stepmother added. "We're to have guests soon, after all."

Elle winced. Keeping just the few rooms currently in use clean took almost all of Lucy's time, what with Elle and Macy working in town all day. Having to clean a dozen more rooms and hallways would be near impossible. Elle foresaw some very late nights in the future for all three of the household servants.

Despite that, Macy just curtseyed and replied, "Yes, Your Grace."

"Very good. You're all dismissed for the night," Lady Sadia said offhandedly. Elle, Macy, and Jack left the sitting room to head to the kitchen as quickly as they dared. It wasn't safe for Elle to remain in that room while his stepmother plotted, and the other two weren't particularly interested in being berated again by the equally irate and pleased duchess.

"That horrible woman," Macy snarled as soon as they were safely away from Lady Sadia and her sons. She threw herself into a chair at the kitchen table, but jumped back to her feet a second later to gather bowls for their supper.

"What's she done now, dear?" Lucy asked from where she was stooped over their late dinner heating on the hearth. She and Macy served the weak stew, and they all sat at the table for a quick meal while Macy explained the extra work they now needed to do.

"She desperately needs the money from what we make in the market," Macy said as she tried to explain Lady Sadia's reasoning for sending them on their normal chore duties. "But she also needs the house cleaned. How can she expect us to do both?"

"We'll make do," Lucy sighed tiredly.

Jack leaned forward. "I'll do everything I can to help. My lay-about of a master won't need me every second, so feel free to put me to work too." He ate a few spoonfuls of his dinner before turning to Elle. "It's you who has to worry, you know, Elle."

"I know," Elle replied with a sad sigh of his own. "I'm just waiting to hear whether she'll try to sell me, send me away, or finally have me killed."

"She can't!" Macy gasped, dropping her spoon into her bowl with a splash.

"I can't be around when she's trying to get the king to declare her son the duke, can I?" Elle replied stoically. "I've always been in the way of her ambitions." Ever since Elle had been old enough to understand that his stepmother did not have the right to force a blind child into servitude, he had wondered what her ultimate plans were. Elle needed to be out of the way for any of her ambition to flourish. Having him in the manor was good only as long as she wanted to keep him under her thumb. When Elle's existence became a threat, Lady Sadia would want him gone, perhaps permanently.

If the plan was to have the king declare Sil the Duke of Marchcant at his wedding, having Elle around had just become a threat.

"Well, the second we get wind of that happening, we squirrel you away to Theo's side," Macy said firmly.

"You'll not be sold off like a common slave," Lucy agreed.

"Thanks," Elle said with a smile for his friends.

"And what are we doing still talking?" Lucy cut in suddenly. "You two need to be at market early, and Jack and I will be cleaning all day. You especially need your sleep after the ball tonight, Elle."

Elle laughed. "It was a grand ball," he sighed happily. "I didn't want it to ever end."

"Well," Macy said with a grumble, "one day you'll get to go to a ball where you won't be forced to run at the sight of your stepmother."

"And it will be magical," Elle agreed as he rinsed his bowl and set it to dry.

Chapter Five

"My mother is plotting again," Theo sighed as he helped Elle unload the last of the cabbages. Three days had passed since the last ball, and they had resumed their morning walk together. Now, though, they held hands, and Theo always gave Elle a polite kiss hello and a not-so-polite kiss goodbye.

"Last time it was something to do with the ball. What's your mother up to now?" Macy said from across the stall where she was helping a customer.

Theo sighed again. "I don't know, but she's been plotting. It's worrying."

"I'm sure it will turn out okay," Elle said softly as he found and gripped Theo's hand. "It did last time, right?"

Elle felt Theo nod and sigh. "And it will this time," Theo agreed firmly. "I'll figure out a way to fix whatever they're plotting." They finished unloading, and Elle and Theo waited while Macy took the cart and mule to the local stables.

"You're sure you'll be okay by yourself?" Elle asked worriedly when Macy returned.

She laughed. "Of course! Enjoy your date," she added with a sly giggle.

"We will," Theo agreed, happiness coloring his voice so much so that Elle couldn't help smiling too.

"Well, get out of here, you damn lovebirds!" Macy called over her shoulder as she moved to help a customer.

Theo led Elle away from the market, chatting idly as they walked. When they stopped walking, Elle tried to place where they could be in the city.

"This is a riding park," Theo explained softly. "I thought you might like to ride a horse."

"Can I?" Elle gasped, wonder making his voice shiver. It had been years since he had been let near a horse, and even longer since he had ridden one. As a child, he had had his own small pony that he had been learning the finer aspects of riding on. But his favorite times had been when his father had held him on his gigantic horse as they rode together.

Theo laughed. "Of course you can! I've brought you a set of riding clothes so you don't return home smelling of horse. There is a clean stall in the stables you can use to change in."

Elle fingered the fabrics in his hands as Theo closed the door to the stall. The weave was tight and the cloth soft, but stiff, and he could feel delicate embroidery tooled into the material. He slipped his sackcloth shirt off and replaced it with the fine one with a small, pleased sigh. When he felt the stiff leather of the riding pants, he had to fight back tears.

It had been so long, so very long, since he had been able to wear good clothes—since he had been able to wear riding clothes! When Elle walked out of the stall a few moments later, he immediately wrapped his arms around Theo in a hug.

"Thank you," Elle said softly.

"You haven't even been on a horse yet!" Theo laughed. "Thank me after."

"I will," Elle promised.

*

Elle fought hard to keep a wide smile off his face as he walked up the servants' stair from the kitchens; his stepmother would notice if he seemed unduly happy about something. A properly sober servant would go unremarked on, so Elle made sure his face was blank when he pushed open the door to the dining room.

"Well, that hussy did it somehow," Lady Sadia snapped as Elle moved into the room.

"That hussy, Mother?" Everett asked his mother curiously as Elle set down the heavy tray he was carrying.

"That girl the prince spent all the balls dancing with," she explained tartly. "She left her shoes behind, apparently, and by royal decree, the prince will be visiting every household that attended the ball. All eligible ladies will try on the slippers, and if the shoe fits, the prince will marry her."

"He must really love her," Everett said gently as he shifted out of Elle's way to allow him to place the plate on the table. He ignored Sil's snort of disbelief.

"Love?" Lady Sadia laughed. It wasn't a happy sound to Elle's ears. "No, it's a ploy. There must be dozens of girls who attended the balls who will fit those slippers. But now the prince will be forced to marry the first girl the shoe fits, regardless of whether she's the one he danced with."

"The prince is being forced to marry?" Sil asked with a laugh. "That's hilarious. We must send them a congratulations card," he added with a snort.

Elle moved to stand quietly in the corner as the family ate, ready to fetch or pour anything they might need for their meal. When he heard his stepmother tapping on the side of her glass, Elle hurried forward with more wine. He groped for the cup and carefully filled it, but before he could walk away, he felt a rough tug on his hair.

"Such hair, boy!" Lady Sadia said snidely. "So much of it, and so long." Elle felt her fingers drop away and quickly moved out of reach. "Silvester, remind me to set up an appointment with the wigmaker. That hair should fetch enough to buy you a nice coat for your wedding."

"For what time, mother?" Sil asked, and Elle could hear the smirk in his voice.

"Sometime tomorrow afternoon, I think," was the woman's reply.

As the family continued to talk about wedding plans, Elle was happy to hide in the corner. Yes, his hair was unfashionably long for a man. But, in recent days, the long hair had become important to him. How else could he have managed to pretend to be a girl so he could successfully sneak into the ball? Besides, Theo liked his hair too. Elle would prefer to keep his hair uncut.

But his stepmother was even going to sell his hair so she could better the life of her oldest child. It wasn't like she hadn't sold his very life into servitude in his own home, so he shouldn't expect anything less from the woman. Still, Elle had to turn his head away so he wouldn't give either her or Sil the satisfaction of seeing any pain on his face.

Any remaining happiness Elle felt from his wonderful day with Theo had long since evaporated.

*

"So?" Macy asked eagerly when Elle brought the empty dishes back to the kitchen for cleaning, which he dumped in the sink before turning to face Macy. He heard Lucy go by with what must have been a tray of dessert; she would stay there for the remainder of the meal, so Elle knew he couldn't escape this interrogation.

"So what?" Elle asked dully. He didn't really want to discuss his hair being shorn until after it had already been done.

"So how was your date?" she responded with a huff, as if it were the most obvious question. Before dinner service it would have been, but not now.

Elle dredged up memories from the wonderful afternoon and gave Macy a wide smile.

"I got to ride a horse!" he said eagerly. "First Theo led from the ground," he explained, and much of the wonder from those first moments crept back into his voice.

Theo had walked them both around a track for a time while Elle got the feel of the horse under him. Elle loved the sounds of the hooves clomping over the hard ground, the feel of the wide, fuzzy horse's back under his hands, and the sharp smell of the leather of the saddle and the reins he had clutched in his fingers. Even the wind in his hair, a thought that now made him wince, had broadened his smile at the time. Theo had eventually mounted his own horse and led Elle's at a faster pace, finally leading them to a wide path that he described as straight and wide with no obstacles for at least three miles.

So Elle had ridden on his own for the first time since he had lost his sight. Even with Theo carefully shadowing him on his own horse, the exhilaration had left Elle breathless and smiling for long after.

They had taken lunch out in the field while their horses grazed, and Theo had kissed Elle until he was breathless again. Only when it was time for Elle to get back to the market stall to help pack up for the evening had they separated and headed back to the stables.

"It sounds so romantic!" Macy sighed dreamily.

"It was," Elle agreed, but of course his stepmother had to ruin everything for him without even trying.

Elle tossed and turned in bed that night, so restless that he beat Lucy to the kitchen the next morning. As he went about his morning chores, Elle's heart began to sink. Every brush of his long braid down his back reminded him that in a few hours the length would be gone. He really didn't want to be forced into getting his hair shorn off.

As Elle walked through the market, he thought of what to tell Theo, but the man had not appeared by the time Elle reached Macy and their stall.

The day passed normally, and as the sun finally dipped below the horizon, Elle and Macy finished hitching up their cart and headed home. It was only when they reached their street that Elle realized the day was going to be somewhat different from what he expected.

"What is this?" Macy grumbled to herself as the cart slowed and the noise levels on their street rose. There were horses and carriages and lots of people, from what Elle could hear, and they all seemed to find their street the place to congregate.

The curiosity did not raise Elle's spirits, although the sounds his straining ears picked up were able to distract him for the time it took for Macy to maneuver their cart through the busy street. Still, once he was done with his work and he was ready to report to Lady Sadia, his anxiety had not lessened any.

His stepmother just sighed when she saw him. "I had hoped to go quietly," she grumbled, "but with the prince's entourage in the streets, that's just not possible."

"You shouldn't go anyway, Mother," Everett called from the couch across the room. There was a soft thump of a book being put aside and the noise of Everett shifting to face his mother. "The prince is testing all eligible ladies who attended the ball. Who is to say that he won't visit you? You are an eligible lady."

"I am, although I am far too old for the prince." Despite her comment, Lady Sadia sounded pleased at the thought that the prince might consider trying her feet into the shoes. "Well, I had better change into a better dress, just in case." She giggled as she stood and walked by Elle as if he weren't even standing in front of her.

When the parlor door thumped shut, Elle finally turned to leave the room as well. He wasn't sure if it was relief or further dread he felt. Relief, certainly, because his hair would not be cut today, but dread because he had no doubt that day would come soon.

"You weren't meant to return from the barber shop," Everett explained quietly before Elle could open the door. "I've no doubt she means to sell your hair to pay for Sil's wardrobe, but she planned to take you to a shop that specializes in making bodies vanish as well."

Elle shivered. He had known his death was inevitable; as long as he was around there was still the chance that Sil could be denied the dukedom. Having Elle killed was the best way to ensure his claim to the title vanished entirely.

Elle left the room before his morbid thoughts had him curling up in a corner in fear. He was quick to enter the warmth of the kitchen where an early dinner was waiting for him.

"You're okay!" Theo cried the second Elle stepped into the kitchen. "I was so worried when I heard."

Elle jumped, startled. "Worried?" he asked, wondering what Theo was doing there.

"Of course I was!" Theo exclaimed as he helped Elle find his chair. "When Everett went to see Duchess Estelveld this morning, he told her your stepmother's plans, and she went to see Lady Adelina at once. Lady Adelina spoke with my mother, and suddenly I'm organizing an entire afternoon here, carrying around the prince's missing lady's shoes. Which reminds me, Elle, I have your shoes here too."

"Thank you," Elle said dazedly, taking his shoes from Theo. He wasn't sure if he was thanking Theo for having a hand in saving his life or for returning the shoes, but he was thankful either way.

"Tomorrow's a holiday, so nothing will happen to you then. We'll get everything fixed up, don't worry," Theo added gently.

"Is it the fall equinox already?" Elle asked absentmindedly.

"Yes," Theo said happily. "The castle isn't holding a ball this year, as they just had three, but the city is supposed to have good entertainment."

"Speaking of entertainment," Lucy said as she plunked Elle's food in front of him, "I've been hearing some interesting stories of the prince and his shoes."

Theo laughed. "Oh, yeah. You wouldn't believe what some women are doing. You see, the prince actually knows exactly who his mystery lady is; most of this is just a scheme to make the romance sound more intriguing. So we switched the lady's real shoes with a child-sized pair, just in case someone did have the same-sized feet. We've had women try to switch the shoes." He paused before continuing in a somewhat horrified voice. "There was a woman who cut off her heel, and another her toe, to force their feet into the shoes. That was quite gruesome."

"I bet," Macy said with a gagging sound. It sounded like she and Lucy were busy making the formal dinner for the family. Elle reluctantly tried to eat faster. He didn't want to leave Theo, but he needed to set the table and begin his other nighttime chores.

Theo groaned. "Women crying, begging, there was even one who tried to bribe me! It's a bit of a disaster, really, but the prince should be happy when everything concludes."

"He'll be happy, no doubt," Macy said with a giggle. "Right, Elle?"

Elle looked up, surprised to be asked such a question. "I guess?" Elle asked. "I don't know the girl or the prince, so I couldn't really say."

Before anyone could reply to Elle, Jack rushed into the room. "They're looking for you out there."

Theo groaned. "All right, I had best be on my way. Time to visit more houses, I suppose."

Theo left and Elle hurried to finish his meal so he could get to his own chores.

"Ah, don't forget, Elle," Lucy called as Elle headed to the cabinet where the fancy dishes were stored. "Tomorrow is an early morning because Her Grace and her sons are leaving to attend a number of parties all day."

Elle had forgotten. He would have to hurry his chores so he could get to bed at a reasonable hour. "Thanks, Lucy," Elle said with a smile before he headed out of the kitchen.

Chapter Six

Lady Sadia and her sons left the manor with the rising sun. There was a grand gathering at one of the country estates they were attending, but it would take at least two hours to get there. The family rose early, much to Sil's disgust, in order to arrive in time for morning tea.

That meant that Elle, Lucy, Macy, and Jack were left to their own devices for the entire day. Of course, the duchess expected them to spend the time preparing the closed-off rooms for the impending marriage, but it was a holiday, and none of the servants felt all that inclined to listen to the woman for the entire day. Taking a few hours of their own here or there wouldn't be noticed. There were street parties to attend, after all.

Jack left while Elle was still yawning into his breakfast bowl. Elle usually spent the holidays relaxing at home, glad to have the opportunity to be lazy for once.

This year, things were a bit different.

"Hurry up, Elle," Lucy chided. She whisked Elle's bowl out from under him the second he took his last bite, and while he was still chewing, Macy dragged him upstairs.

Instead of walking to his mother's rooms, as Elle assumed, they walked farther down the corridor and turned into his father's old room.

"Macy," Elle began in a worried voice as Macy let go of his arm and headed over to the wardrobe. "What's going on?"

"The Lady Heathbridge has requested an audience with you," Macy explained, "and she told me to see you dressed properly."

Elle heard the heavy scraping sound of something quite large being dragged into the room just as the door opened to admit Lucy. At the sound of water splashing, Elle realized he was getting another bath. The bath wasn't surprising; he was dirty from cleaning ashes out of fireplaces.

"Why are we in my father's room?" Elle asked curiously while Lucy and Macy worked quickly to fill and heat the tub.

"Lady Adelina said you were to be dressed to your station. 'No skirts,' she told me," Macy replied as she helped Elle undress and climb into the tub without slipping. "So you'll be wearing something of your father's."

He washed his body while Lucy and Macy worked on his hair, and he wondered why Aunt Adel wanted to meet him. Once his hair had been washed, the women wasted no time pulling the front strands away from his face and into an artful knot on the back of his head.

"At least my stepmother is away today, so the chances of my getting caught..." Elle trailed off pensively. Neither woman bothered to reply to his fears, instead busying themselves with getting Elle ready. Elle dried himself off while Macy returned to the closet and began selecting clothing and Lucy disposed of the bathwater.

Once Elle was dressed simply but finely in breeches, a delicately cut shirt, and a jacket—all just as expensive as the riding outfit Theo had let him borrow—they moved to inspect his father's jewelry. Unfortunately, most of the useful pieces had been moved with his father when this wing of the manor had been closed off. Anything his father had left behind, Lady Sadia had sold or given to her sons. However, there were a few elegant pieces remaining in this hidden room, including stud earrings and matching cufflinks, which Elle put on.

Elle couldn't help fidgeting in his borrowed clothes as he was guided from the room and down the hall by Lucy, unused to the feeling of fine cloth and properly fitted clothing. His sackcloth clothes were horribly ill fitting, loose and unrestricting, and it felt a bit strange to Elle to actually be wearing proper clothes.

Wearing a dress and all the finery that accompanied women's clothing hadn't felt as discomforting to Elle because he had known from the start that he was in costume. This wasn't just some costume—it was his birthright, and Elle was simply not used to having his life be as it should have been without his stepmother's interference.

When Elle was handed into an actual carriage, no doubt sent by Aunt Adel, attired in real finery, he almost started crying. For the first time since his father's death, Elle was doing things expected of his intended birthright. He finally felt like the Duke of Marchcant.

Elle held back his tears; he knew at the end of the day when he had to redress in his servant's clothing, it would be much harder to resist breaking down into sobs.

It took some time for the carriage to travel through the city. Elle could hear the beginnings of holiday celebrations; the sounds of laughter—drunken and happy—slipped into the carriage and made Elle feel a bit melancholy. The entire week had been one emotional extreme to another, from joy to fear at how strange his life had become, and the added burden of memories and dreams of what should have been. Elle heard when they passed through a gate, the noise from the street celebrations fading behind them. The carriage traveled up a long driveway before finally coming to a halt, where a footman opened the door and gave Elle a hand outside.

Elle stepped out into the sun and took a deep, bracing breath. He didn't know what his aunt wanted to speak to him about, although he had his guesses, but it wouldn't do to arrive showing his gloomy feelings to her.

"Elle!" Theo's voice called. Elle heard jogging footsteps as Theo rushed to his side. "I'm sorry I was late," Theo added as he reached Elle, brushing his arm against Elle's in a signal for Elle to take it.

Elle rested his hand against Theo's arm and smiled at him, his sadness fading as Theo's warmth enveloped him. There was no better cure for a bitter heart than having the one you loved beside you. "I wasn't expecting to see you here," Elle responded. "And I've only just arrived, so you're not late at all."

"I'm taking you to meet Lady Adelina Heathbridge and my mother," Theo explained as they walked into the building. "They both want to have words with you."

They walked for a while, chatting happily through the winding hallways. Elle only noticed how long the walk had truly been when they finally came to stop. Where were they, to be in such a large building? There weren't many buildings of this size in the city, as far as Elle knew.

Theo knocked politely on a door before opening it and guiding Elle inside.

"May I present Lord Elleron, Duke of Marchcant, my nephew," Elle's aunt said politely as Elle and Theo walked into the room.

"Such a handsome man," another woman replied, but Elle ignored her as he turned to Theo. Theo hadn't flinched or gasped or indicated any surprise when Elle's real title was given.

"You knew?" Elle whispered furiously. "All this time?" He pulled away from Theo and backed toward the door. "All of this was just to get me here?" He had shared kisses with Theo. Theo had taken him drinking and riding and was the only reason Elle had been able to enjoy the balls so much. The truth that Theo had just been digging out the true duke from the cinders was clear, and Elle didn't want to have anything further to do with him.

Elle drew one fist back and swung wildly in the direction Theo had last been standing. His fist connected with what felt like Theo's shoulder, and they both grunted in pain. Now that Elle knew exactly where Theo was standing, he pulled back his other fist and struck at Theo's face. He missed and swung again.

This time Elle's arm was caught and his body was yanked forward into Theo's warm arms. He struggled to get free, growling angrily at Theo, but Theo's arms were strong and Elle soon subsided when it became obvious he wouldn't be getting free.

"Now, Elle," his aunt admonished in the strict voice he remembered so clearly from his childhood, "be polite to His Highness."

"His Highness? The prince is here?" Elle gasped, his voice going high and squeaky in surprise.

"You see what I mean?" Lady Adelina asked brightly, as if Elle acting out was not horrifyingly common and rude.

"Your nephew certainly had no idea; I agree with that," the second woman's voice agreed. "However, we might wish to enlighten the poor boy before the guard decides to arrest him."

Arrest? Elle's thoughts scattered at this idea. Who was being arrested, and why?

"I'm sorry, Elle," Theo's voice whispered into the hair over Elle's ear.

"For what?" Elle snapped back coldly.

"For not telling you everything," Theo replied, his voice annoyingly calm. He gently drew Elle further into the room and guided Elle into a couch seat. Theo didn't let go of Elle as he joined Elle on the couch. "I didn't know when we met in the market that you were the real duke. I didn't!" he added when Elle opened his mouth to argue. "I suspected at the first ball that something had happened to you that demoted you into servitude, because you do know the basic forms of all the dances."

"And of course I needed to know everything about the girl my son was dancing with," the second woman—Theo's mother! Elle remembered—added sharply. "So I interrogated my son. The fool boy didn't want to tell me much, but I finally coerced him into telling me where you lived, and I sent a man to find out more."

Elle's head started spinning. If Theo wasn't lying, then none of their morning walks, or their time out drinking, or even that first wonderful ball were a façade. Theo's actions had been sincere—in the beginning at least.

"And then after the second ball," she continued, "my spy found out that it was a servant boy dressing as a noblewoman."

So, Theo hadn't known during the second ball that Elle was nobility? Elle shook his head, trying to clear it of any remaining sense of betrayal. Everything he was hearing sounded truthful, and Elle preferred to believe that Theo hadn't meant to hurt him.

"Of course, I then confronted my son about a servant boy masquerading as his love interest."

"I laughed at her," Theo interjected immediately, before his mother's words could hurt Elle's feelings. "I explained that I knew you were a servant and a boy," he explained. "I told her that you weren't trying to trick me."

"And then I had my audience with Their Majesties," Lady Adelina finally spoke up. "I told them everything! My nephew, the true duke, a servant in his own home! And that horrible Lady Sadia trying to steal your money and title for her own spoiled son."

"To attempt to deceive the crown in such a manner is a serious accusation," Theo's mother added. "But the story soon became clear. With my man reporting on Lady Sadia's actions, and Lord Everett coming forward to warn of your impending demise, we devised a course of action to intervene on your behalf.

"But we must clear up the last discrepancy in the story, Elleron. You must know the entire truth of the matter before we decide how we are to proceed." She paused, as if waiting for someone else to begin speaking.

Theo's body stiffened, and his hand dropped away from holding Elle in place, but he didn't speak.

"I am Queen Margaret," she said gently. "And my son, Prince Theodrin, appears to have fallen in love with you."

The queen? Elle's frazzled mind supplied the words, but he didn't quite understand.

"Theo?" Elle asked, turning to him for answers.

"I'm sorry," Theo said. "I should have told you from the start, but it was so nice to have a real friend. And you were so wonderful I had to invite you to the ball." His voice trailed off when Elle did not show any response.

Elle's mind was still whirling. "You're the prince?" he asked Theo.

"Yes," Theo confirmed, voice gentle. "I am sorry."

"You were wearing a military jacket," Elle said, half question and half accusation.

"First son is the heir," Queen Margaret interjected. "Second son goes to the military, and third son to the monastery. I doubt you were ever taught these social customs, as you were removed from society at such a young age."

"I'm a captain," Theo explained. "And, on formal occasions, I wear my dress uniform."

"None of it was fake?" Elle asked softly, almost afraid to hear the answer. "The horseback riding, the dates?" Elle hesitated to mention their kisses in front of his aunt and Theo's mother in the room, unsure how scandalous it would be.

Theo heard what Elle didn't say aloud. "None of it, Elle," he said, with such conviction that Elle sighed and relaxed back into Theo's side. Theo wrapped an arm around Elle, who reached up to clasp the hand resting by his shoulder.

Theo might have held back information, but his purpose had never been malicious. He had never intended to take advantage of Elle. Any lingering sense of betrayal was quick to fade forever, nestled in Theo's arms.

"Well, I believe that settles that," Aunt Adel said briskly. "I assume you are satisfied that my nephew is not trying to hoodwink your son in any way?"

"No, no," Queen Margaret laughed. "Duke Elleron was clearly innocent of any trickery! And I am satisfied that my son is truly in love with your boy. It's an advantageous match, at the very least, so I certainly cannot complain about your choice, Drin."

"Thank you mother," Theo replied wryly. "That was, of course, one of my chief concerns," he added with even more sarcasm in his voice. "I love him, so your support means a lot to me," he finished in a much softer voice that made Elle melt a little inside.

"Yes, yes, love is important. But to the court? A man marrying another man must have a purpose behind it to so flout tradition. Tying the powers of the Marchcant family with the royal family is a wonderful excuse. Now, let's forget about politics and move on. We must free Elleron from servitude and make the duchess and her son pay for what they have done to you. Summon my husband!" she called imperiously. A responding set of retreating footsteps told Elle that one of the servants or guards also in the room had left at a quick pace. "And, Theo, where is that engagement ring?"

Epilogue

"The wedding of His Royal Highness, Prince Theodrin and His Grace, Lord Elleron, Duke of Marchcant... All are invited to attend the auspicious ceremony...and may they live happily ever after." Adel read the wedding announcement aloud, satisfaction in her voice. "Oh, how lovely."

Elle couldn't agree more...usually. Right now, however, being stuck with pins as his first properly fitted formal outfit was sized put a damper on his enthusiasm. He also couldn't help feeling morose about the occasion the outfit was being sewn for. The official trial of Lady Sadia Vellei and Lord Silvester Vellei was to start at the end of the week. Elle needed proper clothing for the event, as Lady Adelina had so adroitly pointed out, despite the fact that the conclusion was forgone. The king had already heard all he needed to order the executions, but removing a peer of the realm, even a traitorous one, required a touch more delicacy, so the trial had been arranged.

To Elle's relief, the tailor and his assistant finally started pulling off the pinned pieces of cloth. Macy had declared herself in love with the young tailor a few weeks back when they had first met to begin designing Elle's wedding outfit, so Elle knew he was a good man. Still, he was glad when the tailor and his staff finally left. Elle walked behind his desk and sighed happily as he sank into the soft chair.

"You will have to choose a flavor for your wedding cake," his aunt added. She was flipping through papers in the visitor's chair on the other side of his desk.

"Chocolate," Elle responded without hesitation.

"He never stops eating it," Patrick, Elle's new secretary, grumbled. Since Patrick was usually the one sent to fetch Elle's favorite treat, he had a right to complain.

Elle heard a notebook snap shut and skirts ruffle as his aunt rearranged her dress. "I'll take care of it," she sighed. "Now, Elle, we do need to talk about the trial. You will have to speak about what occurred."

"The guard saw Sil hit Theo!" Elle gasped. "Why do they need me?"

Lady Adelina laughed, but there was no humor in the sound. "This isn't about what happened when we apprehended Lady Sadia or her idiot son. You spent fourteen years in servitude while she did everything possible to steal your birthright. You don't have a choice."

Elle grumbled. The day Lady Sadia and Sil had been arrested had been fraught with stress, but the planned goal of having both culprits incriminate themselves had gone off with only a small hitch—Sil had tried to kill Elle.

*

They had decided the best way to gain access to the house was by pretending to try the infamous shoes on Lady Sadia's feet. Sadia had been all aflutter at the idea, immediately summoning her sons to watch as Elle knew she would. The family, Theo, and the prince's small entourage of guards and personal servants all retired to a small parlor off the entrance hall in the manor.

Aunt Adel had been waiting outside while Elle had been standing around the corner where his stepmother could not see him. They were both waiting for the hall to clear so Lady Sadia would be surprised at their appearance. The hope was Lady Sadia would be less calculating when she spoke because of her shock, and they could coerce her into confessing. Both Elle and Aunt Adel stepped forward once everyone was settled in the parlor.

"Ready, Elleron?" Adelina asked.

Elle took a deep breath and nodded. It had to be done. They had talked and argued about the best way to go about their plan, and everyone had agreed that without Elle's involvement there was very little chance of success.

That morning, after he had served the family breakfast, Elle went upstairs to his father's room. Macy had handed the market cart off to a palace servant at the manor gate and had snuck back inside. While Lucy and Jack helped the family get ready for the day, Macy had been helping Elle bathe and dress in another of his father's old outfits. Elle could tell by the amount of embroidery in the jacket and just how soft yet stiff the cloth was that he was wearing something his father would only have worn while in attendance with the king. Elle knew the outfit made him look like the duke, but even when Aunt Adel fixed his collar in the entrance hall, he still didn't quite feel the part.

Still, he was the duke. Elle put on a strong face and delved deep inside. He was the true duke, and no one—not his stepmother or his stepbrother—could take that from him.

"I'm afraid the shoe does not fit, Lady Sadia," Theo's voice said through the open door. "Are there any other eligible ladies in this household who might wish to try?"

Elle didn't need Adelina's shove in his back to remind him of his cue. He stepped forward into the parlor.

"Lady Sadia is currently the only woman residing in my home, Your Highness," Elle said in as noble a tone as he could dredge up. He stood straight with his shoulders back, because Queen Margaret had told him it would make him seem more regal, and looked straight ahead. In his hands was his new walking stick, a thoughtful gift from the king and queen themselves; it had fanciful carvings across the surface, the lacquer feeling silky to the touch. Elle was glad not to have to worry about splinters any longer, and he knew the elegant staff made him seem more authoritative.

"Thank you, Duke Elleron," Theo replied in his own imperial tones. Elle could hear suppressed mirth at the staging of the scene in Theo's voice, but he knew only those who knew him well would recognize what that tone actually meant.

"What is this farce?" Lady Sadia snarled. This time Elle heard Adelina snort under her breath; she had been so sure that it would be Sadia instead of Sil who would speak out first.

Elle ignored her. "However, there is someone else who wore a dress to the ball and lives in this household."

"Is there really?" Theo asked. "Well, bring them forward."

Lady Adelina touched Elle's arm, and Elle followed her to a seat away from his stepfamily. Elle took off his shoe and held out his stocking-clad foot.

"Me, Your Highness," Elle replied with a smile.

"Adelina, you have quite the audacity, coming here!" Lady Sadia snapped as Theo bent down and touched Elle's foot with the familiar ballroom shoe. "Dressing a servant in fine clothes and pretending he is the duke? How dare you malign my family in such a way?"

"A servant?" Theo asked, carefully practiced tones of disbelief in his voice. The shoe slid easily onto Elle's foot.

"Yes, a servant!" Sil finally jumped in, his cold voice a strong counterpart to his mother's slightly panicked tones. "I'd know my own servant, even when you put him in nice clothing. That boy has been cleaning our fireplaces for almost fifteen years. I demand you arrest him at once. How dare he impersonate a peer of the realm!"

"Impersonating a peer of the realm?" Lady Adelina asked sharply. "My lord, allow me to prove just who the impostor is." She clapped her hands together sharply to call a servant.

"My lady?" Elle heard Lucy ask politely.

"Bring me the wedding portrait of Lord Elleron and Lady Olivia. There will be no doubts after today."

Elle had been so very excited at this point. He knew he looked like his mother, but there was enough of his father in him that there would be no mistaking his lineage. Fear had quickly replaced it, however, when Sil snarled and jumped across the room, shoving Elle's chair and sending him flying backward. Theo had immediately moved to Elle's defense, and the guardsmen in the room had to forcibly stop Sil from continuing to pummel Theo.

The arrests had gone quickly after that. Sil was taken away swearing and struggling; Lady Sadia had gone demurely while giving quiet threats to all involved.

Everett had clearly expected to be abandoned to his own devices upon the arrest of his family, penniless aside from whatever dowry the Duchess Estelveld had arranged for her daughter. Theo and Elle had made it clear this was not the case—especially as Elle would prefer having someone he trusted to care for the manor as he would no longer be residing there.

Everett could only bow with a rustle of fabric as Theo led Elle from the wrecked parlor.

*

Could Elle speak about his years as a servant in his own home, culminating in the arrest of his stepfamily? He wouldn't enjoy it, but he would do it.

Lady Adelina saw Elle's decisive nod and stood up from across his desk. "You'll do right by your family and your heritage," she said firmly with a proud note to her voice before turning and leaving the office.

"The caravan's packing list has arrived," Patrick announced with a rustle of paper after the door swung shut again.

"The one carrying the goods for the local market?" Elle asked as he sat up in his seat. "Lovely. Please read it to me."

"Twenty bolts of fine silk, five spools of silver wire, five of gold…" Patrick read while Elle listened intently. Patrick had been hired soon after Elle had moved into the palace with Theo and had proved to be honest and hardworking. Patrick had helped Elle understand the workings of his merchant network and was always available to copy letters and notes Elle dictated as well as read anything Elle needed.

"And thirty-eight wooden spoons," Patrick finished, adding an exasperated sigh for the last item on the list.

"Where are the last two spoons?" Elle asked sharply. "I ordered forty."

"Ah… There is a note that the caravan has bought two of the spoons from you at the bottom here," Patrick answered, still using the same tone. He had fought bitterly against adding wooden spoons to the buying list for this particular caravan, but Elle had been insistent. The caravans usually bought and traded for high-quality goods that steadily increased the size of Elle's coffers, and wooden spoons had seemed too incongruous for Patrick.

"Oh, stop complaining," Elle said with a smile. He pushed back his chair and stood. "Those spoons will be incredibly popular in the local market. Trust me, I spent enough time there to know what is needed. Make sure the caravan is paid properly, and tell them to be on the lookout for decent cooking pots on their next trip north."

"Yes, sir," Patrick said with a sigh, used to Elle's strange requests. The spoons would sell though, Elle knew, and once Patrick saw that, he would stop complaining.

"Thank you. I have another meeting to go to now, so I'll leave it to you," Elle said as he gathered his walking stick.

Elle made his way into the palace corridor where two wind chimes jingled to his right, the sounds sharp and clear. Elle followed the one with the higher pitch as it led him unerringly to Theo's office. The other chime hung outside his and Theo's bedroom door down a side corridor.

Adding the chimes had been Theo's idea after Elle had gotten lost in the twisting palace corridors one too many times. Each of the half dozen chimes now hanging around the palace had a different pitch, and Elle rarely found himself lost since their addition.

Elle made his way to Theo's office and tapped politely on the door before letting himself into the room.

"Right on time, Elle!" Theo said happily. A chair scraped on the floor, and Theo's arms encircled him moments later. Elle rested his head on Theo's shoulder, listening to his heartbeat. When Theo pulled away, Elle tilted his face up to accept a gentle kiss.

A knock on the door finally pulled Elle and Theo apart. Taking Elle's arm, Theo guided him to a love seat with his usual confidence and gentleness.

"Enter," Theo called once he and Elle were settled on the couch.

"Your Highnesses," Dr. Barington greeted, bowing. Elle inclined his head politely, as he had been taught, and felt Theo gesture for the man to take a seat. He was the most renowned doctor the king could find, and he had been hired to take a look at Elle. The king wanted a professional to check Elle's blindness and see that Elle's years of hard living had not been detrimental to his health.

"I have the results of my tests," Dr. Barington continued once he was seated comfortably in the chair across from them.

"And?" Theo asked. He tried to keep any sharp, anxious tones from his voice, but Elle sensed his worry. Elle was fairly nervous himself.

"Unfortunately," he began slowly, "I can state unequivocally that there will not be any biological children resulting from your union." Dr. Barington chortled to himself.

Neither Elle nor Theo found his jest particularly amusing, however. They might at a later time, but currently they had more pressing concerns.

"Firstly, I would like to state how lucky you are to be alive," Dr. Barington continued. "A tumble like that can be quite deadly, and the damage you sustained could have been far worse."

Elle nodded. He had always wondered why Sil had pushed him down the stairs. Sil had made it quite clear during interrogation that he had meant to kill Elle that day. Apparently, Sil had been ordered by his mother to remove the competition for the dukedom at the first possible opportunity. That Sil had failed was unfortunate, according to Sadia, but it had served as some amusement to see Elle forced to clean cinders from the fire.

Sometimes it surprised Elle how truly cruel his stepmother had been.

"I cannot say if immediate, proper care would have saved your sight," Dr. Barington explained. An investigation had proved that the doctors his stepmother had hired while Elle's father had been away were little better than actors. "As you cannot distinguish light or form with your eyes, even while under external stimulants, there is very little I can do now either. It is my saddened opinion that I must advocate no further care."

"Thank you for your time, Doctor," Elle said politely, pressing into Theo's embrace.

"I am sorry I cannot do more," Dr. Barington repeated, sounding truly upset. Elle heard him excuse himself and leave the office. Theo remained silent at Elle's side, although his arm had tightened considerably around Elle's shoulder.

Elle tilted his head toward Theo. "Are you upset I can't have children with you?" he asked cheekily.

Theo puffed out a laugh. "I'm sorry, Elle," he whispered, his breath rustling Elle's hair as he spoke.

"I'm not," Elle said firmly. "I have a good life now. I don't need my sight to have that, do I?"

"No," Theo agreed. "No, you don't need your sight to live happily with me."

"I didn't think so," Elle said as he snuggled deeper into Theo's warm and loving arms.

THE CURSE

Chapter One

He could hear the screams farther off, and closer, the clash of steel on steel. Footsteps of at least a dozen men pursued him as he dashed along the corridors, but Gabriel knew the way, whereas they did not. Sean knew the way just as well, so they ran in step down one hall, into another, and finally into the back near the closest entrance to the escape tunnel.

Gabriel pushed the correct switch, and a door that had previously looked like wall paneling popped out. He hurried through, then spun around to hold a hand out to Sean.

"Come on," Gabriel hissed when Sean hesitated. Then Sean shook his head. Gabriel had never seen Sean look so unkempt. His blond hair, usually combed and braided neatly, fell in messy rivulets halfway down his back. Sweat dotted his forehead and his green eyes were wide with fear.

"I can't, Prince," he said softly. "Someone must lead them away from this hall so they don't find this passage."

"It's a hidden door! Even if they do find it, it will take them more than enough time for us to get safely away on the other side."

Sean shook his head again. "They must believe you are hiding somewhere inside the castle. It is the only way to foil their plot and to keep you safe. Go!"

Gabriel could hear their pursuer's footsteps quickly approaching, likely just one hall away, but that didn't stop him from lunging forward, reaching desperately for any part of Sean he could grasp to pull him to safety. He couldn't lose Sean, not now after all he had already lost. Not with what Sean meant to him.

Sean dived toward him, and for a moment Gabriel felt relief, but after the briefest press of lips against his own, Sean's hands landed on his shoulders, shoving him deeper into the passageway. The secret door clicked shut a moment later, throwing Gabriel into darkness.

"No, Sean!" Gabriel didn't quite dare raise his voice, but somehow, he knew Sean heard him, just as he somehow heard Sean's reply:

"Run and live, my prince. My love."

And then Sean was gone, running away to draw off their pursuers. There wasn't a catch on this side of the door, a safety precaution in case someone tried to sneak into the castle by traveling the wrong way down the escape tunnel. The only way out was deep in the forest. If Gabriel wanted to save Sean, he would have to traverse the tunnel and return above ground.

Gabriel set his chin and spun away from the door. So be it. He would assail the castle from the outside, storm it somehow, and rescue Sean. If he had to kill every single one of the invaders, he would do it. He had to, because losing Sean...

He had already lost his sister, and his father had not escaped the castle either. He could not lose Sean too.

Gabriel hurried his feet, walking as fast as he dared in the near-perfect darkness. He knew this tunnel, had walked it dozens of times, as did every member of the royal family. The floor was flat and even, sloping gently downward at this point as the branch he was in headed toward the main tunnel. Once he got to the main tunnel, there were torches and matches. It took a while before Gabriel's footsteps began to echo as he stepped into a larger space. It took another few minutes of fumbling awkwardly until his fingers brushed against the waiting torches, and then he fumbled around a bit more to strike a match and get it lit. Gabriel squinted against the light, but didn't wait for his vision to adjust before continuing on his way. He had to get out of the tunnel so he could go save Sean.

No one really knew when the tunnel had been built. Rumor said the tunnel predated the building of the castle, that a wizard's tower much like Wizard Rap's in the Zel Mountains had once stood where the castle was now and the tunnel had been part of it. Other rumors said the first Queen Gabby had the tunnel built after the second war with the mindless hoard of Faltiken, when the hoard had come almost too close to winning, and she had feared for her children's safety.

Regardless, the walls were dry and the ceiling secure despite no maintenance being conducted on it for as long as Gabriel could remember. At least with the torch lit, Gabriel felt safe to move at full speed. He covered the last mile in only fifteen minutes and stepped out into the forest only twenty minutes after Sean had locked him away.

Gabriel doused the torch in a pile of dirt just inside the mouth of the tunnel, then peeked out into the woods. He heard birds chirping to each other as they began to settle into their nests for the evening. It was too bright for the frogs and crickets to begin sounding, but the setting sun filtering through the leaves said it was about dinnertime. Gabriel had been dressing for dinner when word had come that the castle gates had been breached and an army was invading.

What he didn't hear were sounds of fighting. The fact that the birds were willing to make noise said there wasn't an army hiding out here, waiting to grab him. Still, it wouldn't do to get caught easily by taking one of the many paths through the forest. Gabriel started walking back toward the castle, but through the underbrush. He would leave a trail for a skilled tracker to follow, but wouldn't run into anyone lying in wait along the paths.

It took another twenty minutes to reach the edge of the forest. The castle was just ahead, its sprawling, ancient structure a welcome sight. Now, how to sneak back inside? Gabriel knew better than to try the main gate, but perhaps one of the smaller servant's gates weren't as well guarded. He would have to try one of those.

All Gabriel had to do was get inside, find Sean, and together they would kill the invaders and save his father. Then they could return to figuring out the cure to his sister's mystery illness, and once that was solved, everything would return to normal.

That's all Gabriel wanted. No more fear, no more sadness. Just love, of his family and of Sean. And the sooner he got to work, the sooner it could be fixed.

The south servant's gate was the smallest and most likely to be overlooked by soldiers new to the castle grounds. He would try there first.

Gabriel had barely taken one step south when he spotted movement at the top of the central tower. The flag there, proudly flying his father's crest, was lowering.

"No."

It didn't stop at half mast, just continued to dip lower and lower until it reached waiting hands and vanished. A moment later a new flag appeared, slowly rising into the setting sun. Gold and blue, the colors of the northern invaders.

"No," Gabriel whispered again and felt his knees hit the ground as all strength left his legs. "Father! Sean! No."

Removing his father's flag could only mean one thing: the king was dead. Sean wouldn't have let Father die, not without fighting tooth and nail, and if Father were dead, then Sean... No, Gabriel couldn't even think it.

"Please, Sean..." Gabriel gripped his necklace, the one Father had given to him at his birth along with the name Gabriel, and felt the first hot tear slip down his cheek to splash against his clasped hands. Any minute now Sean would come bursting out of the top of the tower to slash down the enemy's flag and return Father's to its rightful place. Then Sean would lead the charge into the woods to find Gabriel, so they could all go home safely together.

But the gold and blue continued to flap, shining in the reddening light as the sun began to dip.

"Sean, no, please," Gabriel whimpered one last time, with one last hope-filled plea. When it, too, went unanswered, his body went limp, and he fell to the forest floor, sobbing his pain into the dried leaves and pine.

Chapter Two

FOURTEEN YEARS AGO

"This is my pond! How dare you invade without my permission!"

The boy—the invader—stood from where he had been sitting on the banks, staring into the calm brownish-blue water. Gabriel was immediately entranced. His eyes were the same green as the vibrant grass that so lushly bordered the pond, and his hair practically glowed in the noon sun.

"I'm sorry. I didn't realize this pond had an owner," the boy said, and his voice was soft and lyrical, like birdsong.

Gabriel pretended to think for a minute, frowning and rubbing his chin. "If you're nice, I can share it with you. Ponds are really at their best when you have someone to splash with."

It wasn't like his silly big sister, what with her dress fittings and tea parties, was interested in playing with him anymore. No, this beautiful, wonderful boy was perfect to play with.

And play they did. All summer, every day, Gabriel would sneak away from lessons and luncheons, and every boring thing his parents wanted him to do. There Sean was waiting. They swam and fished, and romped through the grass. Sometimes they went off into the royal forest to play at being bandits in the trees. Other times they explored the reeds at the far end of the pond where they caught frogs for Gabriel to take back to the castle to torment his sister with.

"My master says if I don't pay attention to my lessons, one day someone will turn me into a frog," Sean joked every time, but he never hesitated to dig in the mud to get the largest, slimiest frog that would really make Gabriel's sister scream.

After seven weeks, however, it all came to an end.

"My master says we are leaving for the next city in the morning, now that summer is over," Sean said on that terrible day. "We will

winter on the other side of the mountains, and we must leave now before the snows block the pass."

Gabriel knew his mouth was hanging open and his eyes filling with tears as despair quickly set in.

"But, I convinced my master. This city, your home, is the perfect place to spend the summer," Sean continued hastily. "We will be back. I promise you. Next summer, let's meet at the pond."

It hurt to say goodbye as the sun set that afternoon, but Gabriel bravely watched Sean's back as he headed towards the city that lay below the castle. Only when he couldn't see Sean any longer did Gabriel turn and head in the other direction, up to the castle where his neglected lessons waited.

The summer, he told himself firmly. He only had to make it to next summer, and Sean would be back.

Gabriel half expected it to be a lie, all those months later, as the summer finally really began to settle in after a hard winter and wet spring. Still, he went down to the pond and there, waiting for him as if he had never left, Sean stood.

The pattern repeated itself for seven years straight. Sean would appear at the start of summer, and for seven weeks they would play, growing close as only best friends. Gabriel was thirteen by then, but he still loved to play in the mud as long as Sean was smiling happily at his side. His mother had passed away two years before, but that only seemed to make his father all the more strict. Lessons, lessons, lessons, and then getting yelled at all summer for skipping out on his tutors and coming back covered head to toe in muck. As long as Gabriel could see Sean, he didn't care.

And Sean was wonderful. He was shorter than Gabriel and still had the rounded face of a child. Gabriel was pretty certain Sean was older than him, although he didn't look it, but that didn't stop his smile from growing even more beautiful as the years went on.

Then that seventh summer drew to a close.

"My master has decided we should head overseas, to see some of the countries on the other side of the world," Sean said softly, all cheer gone from his face and voice. Gabriel's heart sank. He knew from his lessons that it would take months for a boat to reach those foreign lands, and it could be years, if not a decade, before Sean was able to return.

"Don't leave me," Gabriel forced out from between stiff lips, knowing his face and body were frozen in fear. "Please, Sean."

Sean shook his head. "I'm not. I told my master I'm staying here. I'm going to become a knight and serve you for the rest of my life." He reached out and clasped one of Gabriel's hands in his, pulling Gabriel close so they stood with their shoulders brushing. "My master yelled at me. Told me I was giving up everything she had taught me, but I told her... I told her you were worth giving it up for."

And then Sean was leaning close, and although Gabriel didn't know why, he found his own chin tilting. Their lips met in a firm but chaste kiss. Gabriel groaned. He wanted more than this, but he didn't know what more entailed. Sean knew, because he pressed closer so their bodies touched in just the right way.

The next seven years passed in busy happiness. Gabriel actually attended his lessons, learning how to be third in line for the throne, a role that would have him supporting his sister in keeping the kingdom peaceful. Sean worked hard as a page, then a squire, as he trained to be a knight. It only took two years before Sean was taller than Gabriel, and he kept growing until he was well over six feet tall. Thanks to his sword training, he had shoulders to match his height.

They had to spend their days apart, but their nights they spent together, exploring where that first kiss eventually led. Everything was almost idyllic, until the moment his sister suddenly collapsed and their troubles began.

*

It was on that unhappy thought that Gabriel opened his eyes, blinking against the late-morning sun filtering through the trees overhead. Day seven had already begun.

Seven days of lying here, broken. Gabriel knew he had eaten. There were stores of jerky and hardtack kept in the tunnels for emergencies, and he had a vague memory of finding berries one of the times he had headed to the river for some water and to bathe. Mostly, though, he just floated through the day as if he were sleepwalking. He lay in the little hollow among the roots of an ancient tree and watched the sun move across the sky, and then watched the stars emerge and twinkle overhead. He couldn't think, just curled up around the constant pain radiating through his chest.

"The signal is coming from over here, I think," a voice said off to Gabriel's left. He knew he should have felt alarm. If the enemy had finally found him, he would be captured and executed, but he couldn't find it in him to care. Sean should have been curled between the tree roots with Gabriel, but he wasn't there. He wasn't anywhere, not anymore.

"You said that five minutes ago and we're still walking," another voice replied without ire.

"No, I've got it this time. See, the magic is starting to pulse as we get closer. Last time we were just in the right vicinity, but this time he's got to be within sight of us."

The first voice kept talking, blathering on about something. Gabriel didn't bother listening, tuning out the words and the voice, until a shock of purple hair suddenly appeared in front of him.

"Found him!" The purple hair turned, and a face appeared with lavender eyes set wide over his cheekbones and a bright smile stretching his cheeks. "Told you," he told someone over his shoulder.

"Great. Move back so I can get him out of there."

The purple hair disappeared and another man moved into view. He reached down and gripped Gabriel under his arms, gently pulling until he was freed from the roots and out on flat ground. This second man had dark hair, shaved on the sides with a thick braid running down the center. The tail ended somewhere down his back.

Gabriel opened his mouth to complain about being moved, but then the dark-haired man turned and looked at him, and Gabriel's mouth snapped shut in surprise.

"Your eyes." His voice croaked from disuse and tears, but the words were clear enough.

The man smiled wryly and touched his cheek with his fingers. "It's nice to see after all these years the eyes still hold true in the family." Gray shot through with blue streaks, exactly the same as Gabriel's eyes—eyes he shared with his father and sister. Any other similarities were absent— Gabriel was fair with golden hair and light skin where this stranger was dark—but that eye color didn't lie.

"Who—" Gabriel swallowed, trying to make his voice work. "Who are you?"

"You don't know? You summoned us with your necklace," the purple-haired man cut in.

Gabriel looked down at the necklace hanging around the collar of his shirt. It was silver in the shape of a tower, with amethysts studded along the walls. Father always said it was Wizard Rap's tower, but Gabriel had never made the trip all the way out to the border to see it in person. Could one of these men be Wizard Rap?

"Of course, he doesn't know. It's been a hundred and seventy years since I gave that to Gabby," the dark-haired man said. "I'm sure its purpose was lost, and it simply became a family heirloom passed down through the generations."

"My father gave it to me when he named me Gabriel," Gabriel said softly, looking down at the charm as his eyes filled yet again.

"Ah," the dark-haired man said, his voice full of understanding. "Come on. We caught a hare on our trip here. Let's set up camp and start a fire, get you fed, and then we'll see how we can help."

"No fire!" Gabriel said, grabbing the dark-haired man's arm. "They'll see and they'll come looking. Sean saved me. I have to hide for Sean. For Sean." His hand fell back to his lap as he curled back up around the throbbing pain in his chest.

"It's okay. We can keep the fire hidden. Come on now, Gabriel. We just need to get to the clearing over there."

Hands helped him to his feet and steadied him as he stumbled where he was led. It felt like only a moment later that Gabriel found himself seated on a log, a cup of water in his hands, and the warmth of a fire bathing his face.

"Come on now. Drink."

The dark-haired man waited for Gabriel to obey, and the cold liquid felt nice on his parched throat. Gabriel took another sip as the man sat on the ground across from him.

"I'm sorry we're late. Zel and I got a letter from an old friend asking us to come help solve a curse. We felt your call from the necklace just as we crossed the border into Monrath and came as fast as we could."

"Zel? I thought the wizard was named Rap?" Gabriel couldn't help asking.

The purple-haired man let out a laugh. "I guess that is one thing that will never change. No, my name is Zel, and I'm the wizard of your famous tower. This is your...well, I guess you can consider him your uncle, Ishiah."

Ishiah? Gabriel knew that name. Everyone knew that name and the story that went along with it. The bastard prince who had bravely taken on the Rapunzel Tower tasking, noticed the mindless hoard was about to invade, summoned the Monrath Army, and was instrumental in defeating the enemy. Then, when his time at the tower came to an end, Prince Ishiah resigned his commission and vanished. Some said he had gone off with his lover, the Wizard Rap; others that he had enough of war and had wanted a peaceful life in the south with his mother's people. Some said the royal family could still call on his immense strength in times of dire need.

It was a name revered in Monrath. None of the royal family had dared name their children after him, not like they used Gabby's name every few generations, and yet it had never been forgotten.

The purple-haired man—Zel—was still talking. "We're here to help you, Gabe. Ish and I meant to get back this way sooner than we did, but there was this interesting new spell we found while traveling through the desert, and we were waylaid by a few years. That's probably why some of our protection spells are starting to unravel."

"Gabe, why don't you tell us what happened? That way we'll know what we can do to help fix it," Ishiah cut in.

"You can't fix it. Sean's gone. You can't fix that," Gabriel said, practically yelling directly into Ishiah's face. "Sean's gone."

"Tell us what happened. Start from the beginning." Ishiah didn't seem perturbed by Gabriel yelling at him. He held out a hand and gently rested it on Gabriel's shoulder. The weight of it grounded Gabriel to the here and now, and he found his mouth opening.

The beginning. The moment Sean burst into Gabriel's room, sword unsheathed in his hand, telling Gabriel to run, now. No, the story started six months beforehand, when his sister's illness began; that was the moment when their troubles first started.

"My sister, Rory—Aurora—was walking in her garden one morning. She collapsed suddenly. As far as we can tell, she's asleep, but no one dares get close enough to check. One of her maids rushed to her side when it happened, and the second she touched Rory, she fell asleep too. It kept spreading. Everyone who touched one of the sleeping victims fell victim themselves. Father had a glass roof put over the garden, then locked the door so no one else could get hurt. All the best scientists and theorists across the country have been searching for a cure ever since, and nothing has worked. The castle and Father were consumed by grief, to have the crown princess struck down like that. We worked hard to keep everything running smoothly, Sean and I. I signed orders for farm relief and to collect taxes. Sean sat in criminals' court and met with the generals. We thought we could keep it together, but then the rumors started to fly."

Gabriel paused to take a sip of water and to square his shoulders in preparation for this next part, but he couldn't quite make himself look up at Ishiah.

"The kingdom was cursed, just like Rory, the rumors said. Backers pulled out of construction projects, our neighbors pulled out of trade deals, and even the eastern barbarians retreated behind their walls and refused to come out. And then rumors of salvation. Our northern neighbors knew how to release the curse. We just had to sign over all of Monrath. Give up our kingdom, become vassals of their so-called empire. We call our eastern allies barbarians, but the truth is the unconquered North are the true barbarians. Sean and I refused, and Father refused, too, when he could be pulled from the scientists' sides.

"And then, seven days ago, someone opened the gates and let them in. Sean grabbed me and we ran. Sean made sure I got to safety, and he went to draw them away from me, left me behind, and he's... Now he's..." Gabriel broke off with a cry, burying his face in his hands.

"Interesting that the rumors actually used the word 'curse,'" Ishiah said. His hand had moved from Gabriel's shoulder and was instead rubbing his back in comfort.

"It means either the forgetting spell is starting to fray—unlikely—or it really is a curse," Zel replied.

"What do you mean?' Gabriel had to ask. He wiped his cheeks dry with the back of his hand, but that didn't stop his eyes from continuing to water.

"I mean that a sleeping sickness like the one you described sounds awfully like a curse-type of magic spell," Zel answered. "And the way you described those rumors flaring up so suddenly could be another spell too. Clearly the protections you and I left on the castle are beyond frayed."

"Or they were removed," Ishiah added. "The wizard would have to be strong, but it's not impossible." Ishiah moved away from Gabriel, walking over to the fire where he pulled something free and began cutting into it with a knife. "Here, Zel, Gabe. Food's ready."

A plate was pressed into Gabriel's hands, and he mechanically began eating, barely tasting the hare and dried vegetables. All the talk of magic and spells, of what might have happened to his sister was meaningless. It was too late to save anyone. The castle was overrun. They had killed Father and Rory, too, most likely. And Sean—no, Gabriel wasn't going there.

The plate was taken away when he was done, and Gabriel let himself be led to a bedroll.

"Sleep," Ishiah said gently. "We'll go take a look at the castle in the morning."

The sun was just beginning to set, the light starting to weaken as it filtered through the leaves overhead. It was hardly time for bed, yet as Ishiah left him to go sit by the fire next to Zel, Gabriel felt his eyes drifting closed as the first real, deep sleep in seven days dragged him under.

Chapter Three

Was it weird to notice how blue the sky was, or how green the leaves? Leaves the color of Sean's beautiful eyes. It was certainly weird to feel as alert and well rested as Gabriel did. He hadn't felt this good in months, yet the hollow emptiness in his chest said he would never actually feel whole again.

"Oh, good. You're up. Come have breakfast."

Gabriel looked over at Ishiah and saw he and Zel still sitting together by the fire. This time Zel was stirring a pot, and he spooned something into a bowl Ishiah held out. Their movements were choreographed in such a way that said they had done something similar in front of a fire thousands of times. Gabriel and Sean could move like that. They had always somehow known where the other would be and could move to support each other without really thinking about it.

"Here. Sit up and eat," Ishiah said. He held out the bowl for Gabriel to take, so Gabriel pushed back the bedroll and sat up.

"Why are you doing this for me?" Gabriel asked, staring down into the rough camp porridge.

Ishiah let out a breath and sat down next to Gabriel. "You're family," he explained softly. "I chose to leave Monrath with Zel, to make a different path for myself, but I promised to always come home when my family needed me." He reached out and tapped the necklace resting below Gabriel's collarbone. "That promise is important to me. Now hurry up with breakfast. It's time to see what we can do about retaking the castle and bringing everything back to rights again."

Ishiah patted Gabriel on the back, then stood. He went over to Zel, and Gabriel watched their dance as they put out the fire and packed up the camp. They left their packs tucked against a tree with their bedroll. Gabriel ate. He wasn't hungry, but it was there and it was warm. When he was done, he took the bowl and went down to the nearby stream to wash it out. He splashed some water on his face while he was there, just trying to wake up and see about facing the day.

Maybe Ishiah and Zel could retake the castle, but even if they did, they couldn't put everything back to rights again. It just wasn't possible. Too much was gone forever.

Gabriel also knew he would be a terrible king. He was too flighty, and now too hollow. Everyone also already knew him as the younger brother who had fallen in love with the titleless knight. While Gabriel had a place and a role in the kingdom, it was only as support to Rory, and that was all he would ever be respected as. Even if he retook the castle and kingdom from the invaders, he would still face an uphill battle for the rest of his reign. It wasn't a battle he was interested in fighting, especially not alone.

He walked back to the campsite in silence, trying to keep his thoughts as quiet as the rest of him. It really was a lovely day. The birds were out in force, chirping happily through the trees as sunlight dappled the ground below. A lovely day to start a war. Terrible king he might be, but Gabriel still had to save his people. It was his duty as part of the royal family. The rest of it he would figure out afterward.

When he walked back into the clearing, Ishiah and Zel were waiting for him. Ishiah took his dishes and tucked them away in one of the packs sitting under a tree next to both of the bedrolls. He muttered something under his breath, and the gear suddenly faded from view, replaced by an odd sort of sparkle Gabriel could only see out of the corner of his eye.

"Shall we?" Ishiah asked them as he stood and brushed off his hands on his thighs. He didn't wait for an answer, instead leading the way toward the castle. He was wearing a sword, too, which he hadn't been earlier.

It didn't take long to walk to the edge of the forest, and before long they were looking at the castle. It hadn't changed in the week Gabriel had been away. The towers and parapets still stood as they always did, and that hated gold-and-blue flag still flapped from the tallest point.

"How do we get in without being seen?" Zel asked as they looked across the manicured lawn. The grass was kept short by an army of goats to prevent an enemy from sneaking up on the walls, which meant any guards patrolling would see them long before they could get to a gate or try to climb the rough stone.

"The south servant's gate," Gabriel replied, remembering his original plan. It was still viable, even a week later. The single doorway was tucked away and hard to find, and Gabriel was certain the invaders had a few other things to take care of that were more important than finding a hidden door.

"What south servant's gate?" Ishiah asked. "Did they construct a new gate?"

Gabriel shook his head and waved for them to follow his lead. He stuck to just inside the tree line, heading toward the point where the forest was closest to the wall.

"It's a really, really old gate. I think most people have forgotten it, but Sean and I found it when we were kids." It was how Gabriel had been able to sneak out to the lake every summer without getting caught. When he had been old enough to understand the danger, he had pointed the gate out to his father, but by then he hadn't needed it any more to see Sean because Sean had moved into the castle page's barracks. More than once, the page master had arrived in the barracks in the morning to find two heads sharing Sean's pillow. When Sean achieved squire rank, and therefore the liberty of his own small room and considerably more autonomy, the quartermaster had complained about wasting a room that wasn't being used. By then, Sean had essentially moved into Gabriel's rooms, and when Sean was knighted no one had needed Father or the knight master to declare Sean was assigned as Gabriel's sworn protector.

And now, all Gabriel could do for Sean was find his body and give him a proper burial. He had done his duty as knight protector; the one duty Gabriel had wished he would never have to perform. To die in protection of his sworn liege was the ultimate sacrifice, and Sean hadn't understood that his death had taken half of Gabriel with him. Without Sean, Gabriel knew he was as good as dead anyway. It would have been better for them to have escaped together, to try to live on at each other's side for as long as they could. Now they would never have that chance.

They reached the point where the wall was only fifty feet from the royal forest without any sounds of alarm erupting from the castle walls. Of course, Gabriel was traveling with Zel and Ishiah. No doubt one of them had used magic to shield them from sight. Still, Gabriel also hadn't seen anyone on the walls, patrolling. It was odd to see the walls so empty. The captain had used a mix of stationary soldiers and roving guards along the walls. Even if the invading forces had a different sort of defense in mind, they still should have had someone patrolling the walls.

"Where's the gate?" Zel asked.

Gabriel pointed just to the left, where thick ivy covered the door. He studied the wall one last time, searching for any hint of movement, but still saw nothing. He darted forward as quickly as his feet could take him, scrambling to get into the shade cast by the wall. It took a moment of fumbling under the ivy to find it, but a second later he had his hand on the latch and was pushing the door open.

A rush of sweet, perfumed air gently blew out of the open door. The smell was odd, and definitely didn't belong, so Gabriel waited for Ishiah and Zel to catch up.

"What is it?" Gabriel asked after they had both taken a sniff. The door should have opened into the queen's outer garden, the area where soldiers could patrol, but courtiers could also still walk through the carefully manicured hedges and flowerbeds. There was a second, smaller wall inside the garden that belonged to the queen's garden. The last time Gabriel had seen that garden, the construction for the glass roof had just been completed and the door locked until a cure could be found.

"It smells like flowers," Zel said.

Ishiah nodded in agreement. "Roses. Are the old rose gardens through here?"

Gabriel had to think for a moment, trying to remember what flowers were planted where. "I think the queen's inner garden had a few rose bushes, but that's where my sister is. Father completely enclosed the garden to make sure she would be safe until we could find a cure. There shouldn't be anyone there unless the enemy did something to hurt her." Which Gabriel expected. A sleeping woman protected by a measly locked door and a glass ceiling? She would have been the easiest of the entire castle to kill.

"Interesting," Ishiah replied. He rubbed his chin thoughtfully while looking at the open door. Despite the flowery scent, Gabriel still hadn't heard any sounds of alarm, so he wasn't surprised when Ishiah placed one hand on his sword and stepped through the doorway.

"Roses," Ishiah called back, his voice incredibly loud for someone supposed to be sneaking into a castle. "Come see. It's really incredible."

Zel followed immediately and Gabriel stuck close to his heels. They stepped out into a forest of red and pink roses with gigantic petals and equally gigantic thorns. They were everywhere. Gabriel barely had space to put his feet, and he was practically on top of Zel and Ishiah in the small space allowed by the doorway.

"That explains why there weren't any guards," Gabriel said, craning his neck to see if he could spot where the massive thicket ended.

"It's one of the most beautiful spells I've seen in decades," Zel agreed.

"Spells?" Gabriel asked, not because he was surprised—What else could cause rosebushes to grow like this aside from magic?—but it didn't seem like something the enemy would do. They were more of the blast-the-gates-open-and-kill-everyone-in-sight style of magic users. Not that Gabriel could really generalize about magic since the only two wizards he had met were standing next to him, and he had barely seen them use magic yet.

"It's got to be the kid," Ishiah said. He turned to look at Zel for a brief moment, as if he were reading a silent message that Gabriel couldn't interpret; then he turned toward Gabriel. "Try walking forward, see if the roses notice you. Please," he added when Gabriel stared at him incredulously. Those thorns were huge!

Still, Ishiah hadn't steered him wrong yet. Gabriel took a tentative step forward, reaching out with one foot more than taking a full step, and gasped when the roses pulled away from him.

"What's going on?" he asked and had to stop a grimace from forming when Zel and Ishiah shared another look.

"Lead the way into the castle, and we'll tell you on the way," Ishiah said. He waved in the direction of the castle doors, right where Gabriel was hoping to go anyway, so Gabriel obeyed and started slowly walking through the roses. Each bush pulled aside as he grew close, then returned to its spot after they had passed. It was rather unnerving, so Gabriel instead focused on Zel as he started explaining.

"There was once a baby, maybe six months old, who was found floating objects over his bassinet. His mother didn't know what to do, but luckily Wizard Bessie happened to be passing through the area and came to investigate the commotion. Bessie eventually took charge of the child and began to teach him magic. It was a delicate process, you have to understand," Zel told Gabriel. "Using magic halts aging and the child had to grow up, but he also had to learn enough control to keep it from leaking out everywhere. I believe it took about fifty years before she was confident enough to start traveling with him again."

"Yeah, I think it was fifty years," Ishiah added in agreement. "We met him once, and as you can imagine he was a strange kid. Fifty years old, but still with the body and the mind of a child. At least, as much of a child's mind as he could have."

"Then, one day he told Bessie he wanted to give up magic entirely to live a normal life here in Monrath," Zel continued. "How could she say no? The child never had a choice about becoming a wizard, and that is a choice wizards take very seriously. The child would never be entirely normal as he still had to use a little magic to prevent him from spilling out, but without working spells regularly, he would finally grow up and live a normal life. She had to let him go."

Gabriel could see some stone starting to peek through the roses, so they had to be getting close to the door into the castle. He didn't slow his steps, but he wanted to hear the rest of the story. Was it possible this wizard had been working with the enemy and that was why the castle had been taken so easily?

"That's where it gets interesting," Ishiah continued. "Zel and I received a letter, magically delivered right into our hands, asking for our help unravelling a sleeping spell. The wizard who sent the letter said he didn't have the training to do more than ascertain that there was magic involved. He couldn't break it on his own. Zel and I, of course, started traveling here immediately. Unfortunately, sea voyages take time, and we were late in arriving. However, we knew the child wizard was still here somewhere. These roses are more confirmation."

"He might not have been able to stop a sleeping spell, but these roses are a nice bit of magic," Zel added. "If your sister is somewhere in the middle of this, I'd say she's probably safely sleeping still. The invaders wouldn't have been able to get through the roses so easily."

Rory might be alive? Gabriel's knees shook, and he firmly planted his feet to keep from collapsing. The wizard might have saved his sister. Then what about everyone else in the castle? Could they be saved too?

No, Gabriel knew he couldn't think like that. He couldn't get his hopes up. He was here to avenge Sean, not look in every nook and cranny trying to find someone who no longer existed.

Gabriel kept walking, letting the roses move out of the way before each step. The castle's stone wall was completely visible now, but it was hard to see the doorway. Gabriel thought the top of the arch might be poking through some of the oversized flowers to the left, but it could also be an imperfection in one of the stones.

"I need to get inside," Gabriel said aloud, trying not to feel silly about talking to roses, especially since they were moving for him already. The roses rustled for a moment in a nonexistent breeze, as if they were speaking to each other in a voice Gabriel couldn't hear. A moment later the roses started moving, opening up a path to the left that led directly to the archway in question. "Thank you," Gabriel said as he hurried forward, Zel and Ishiah right behind him.

Chapter Four

Gabriel had never felt this uncomfortable in his own home. His steps echoed along the stone walls, a sound he had never heard before. Usually these halls were full of the laughter and chatter of dozens of people. There should have been guards at every corner, servants bustling around to get the day's events situated, and the first of the morning's courtiers should have been filtering out into the halls to start their day of being seen. No one was in sight, and the only noise at all was their three sets of footsteps.

"What's going on?" Gabriel whispered, and even that seemed to reverberate strangely.

Ishiah shook his head. He looked around and shook his head again, as if he were as incredulous as Gabriel to not see anyone around.

"Let's try the throne room," Ishiah finally said. "If anyone is in this castle, they'll probably be there. Or at least we might find some clue left there."

He led the way, as familiar with the layout of the castle as Gabriel. How many years had Ishiah spent living here, and how many times throughout what was apparently a very long life had he come back? Gabriel touched the tower necklace hanging around his neck. It was some sort of charm that let Ishiah and Zel know when one of their family was in trouble. This was Ishiah's home, too, just as Gabriel was his family, and Ishiah was going to get to the bottom of this attack for the same reasons as Gabriel.

It was nice to know he wasn't alone.

That thought did nothing to fill the gaping hole in Gabriel's chest, of course, but it did lift his lips in a wry smile.

With no one to stop them, it didn't take long to reach the throne room. This was another room that was always bustling, particularly with courtiers, but instead the place was empty and strangely dark. None of the sconces were lit, and somehow the bright morning sun wasn't penetrating through the stained-glass windows on the far side. The room was left in a dim, almost foggy gloom.

They carefully edged inside, staying close to the wall by the main door to prevent an ambush, yet nothing moved. The throne room was as empty as the rest of the castle. There was a long, dark lump lying on the stairs leading up to the dais where the thrones sat. Gabriel glanced at Ishiah and then slowly moved forward to investigate.

After only a few steps, the rancid, rotting smell of death told Gabriel what he was going to find. The scant light revealed a body with bloated flesh, but the face with the carefully clipped beard was still recognizable.

"Father," Gabriel whispered, his voice choked as tears quickly began to slip down his face. He fell to his knees, his hands limp at his sides. The king was dead. His father was dead.

"I'm sorry," Zel said.

Ishiah's hands landed on Gabriel's shoulders, squeezing comfortingly. "Come away, Gabe. You don't need to see him like this."

Gabriel groped blindly behind him and ended up grabbing Ishiah's knee where he buried his face. Ishiah knelt and pulled him into a proper hug.

"It's okay, Gabe. We'll figure this out. Come on, let's stop the tears for now. We can cry when it's all over." Ishiah gently lifted Gabriel's chin and used the pads of his thumbs to wipe Gabriel's cheeks dry. The pressure made something sparkle off to Gabriel's left.

"It's not okay. My father's dead, my sister's trapped behind rosebushes, and Sean... If my father's dead, then Sean... Sean has to be too. Sean went back to draw them off, but he must have been going to save my father. Sean wouldn't have let this happen." Gabriel shook his head, then used his sleeve to dry more of his face. The gaping hole in his chest had burst, and now he was bleeding out everything that had kept him somewhat together over the past week. The strange numbness was gone, but feeling again... No, Gabriel didn't want to feel any more. It hurt too much. He would never again feel his father's hand on his shoulder, praising him for doing some task well. His sister would never smile her impish, mischievous grin. And Sean's kiss, the warmth of his body as he held Gabriel close, that was gone too.

"Let's finish this," Zel said firmly. "We can find who killed your father and make them pay. That's our duty now."

Zel was right. Gabriel staggered to his feet, leaning on Ishiah for strength. Everyone might be gone, but the ones who had taken it all away were still hiding somewhere in this mess. Gabriel could find them. He would find them, and then he would ask them why they had done this to his family. Why they had chosen to destroy his happy life.

There was no army here. No invading forces set to take control of the country, or to fold Monrath into the northern empire. Gabriel pulled away from Ishiah and pressed his palms to his eyes to try to stop the tears. He had to think. What was the point of all of this if it wasn't a real invasion?

Because it wasn't an invasion yet.

That had to be the answer, and it was so ridiculously simple. Send in a small advance force with a wizard. Kill the king, completely destabilize the ruling elite, and there wasn't a need to invade. The enemy was probably marching uncontested across the Monrath border right now, secure in the knowledge that Monrath had been rendered incapable of defending itself.

"The castle is empty because the invaders haven't arrived to fill it yet," he said, testing his theory aloud to see if it felt right. Unfortunately, it did.

Gabriel dropped his hands to his sides, blinking against the sudden sparkle on the dais as his eyes readjusted to the strange half-light of the room. Except, the sparkle didn't fade away even after his eyes were fine.

The dais only had three short steps, and Gabriel leapt up them.

"The castle isn't empty," Zel replied. "It's sleeping. Where are you going?"

"I want to know what keeps sparkling up here." Gabriel ignored both surprised gasps behind him and took the last few steps to the thrones at a jog. He skidded to a stop in front of a black birdcage sitting on a side table in between the two thrones. Inside the cage was a toad. "Why is there a toad in a cage?" he asked. A second later both Zel and Ishiah joined him in looking down at the toad, which had begun hopping up and down frantically.

"A transfiguration spell?" Ishiah asked Zel, frowning thoughtfully down at the cage.

The toad used to be human? Gabriel wondered. He reached out to inspect the cage and see if there were a door to let the toad out, but the black bars melted away before his fingers could touch them. The toad hopped eagerly into his hands.

"I think so. I think this is probably our missing wizard." Zel stopped looking at the toad and instead focused his purple eyes right on Gabriel. "Transfiguration spells work because they run in a continuous loop, constantly refreshing themselves to hold the spell in place. To break it, you need to shock the loop out of sync. A kiss should do it," he added pointedly.

Kiss a toad? Gabriel looked from Zel to Ishiah, hoping to get a better explanation, but Ishiah was also looking at Gabriel expectantly. Well, the toad did used to be human, and it certainly wasn't the strangest thing Gabriel had done today. At least it wasn't particularly slimy-looking.

Gabriel lifted the toad to his lips and pressed a kiss to the top of the toad's warty head.

Light exploded around them with a whoosh of air. The toad writhed in Gabriel's gentle grip, and then suddenly started expanding rapidly. Gabriel let go of the toad when it grew too big to hold, but then he had a man leaning against his chest as the last of the green skin began to fade away into the pale peach of a naked man.

The man was warm, and muscled, and as he breathed against Gabriel's chest, Gabriel's arms wrapped around the man's naked back, instinctively moving to hold him close. The body was familiar in a way that said Gabriel had held this man close dozens of times. Gabriel looked down and saw beautiful long blond hair hanging in messy rivulets down his back.

"Sean?" Gabriel asked, but his voice cracked. He swallowed and tried again. "Sean?"

Sean groaned and shifted in Gabriel's arms, turning so he could look up at Gabriel. "I'm sorry I couldn't save your father. I tried, but I'm out of practice. I used too much magic protecting your sister, and I didn't have enough left to stop him. I'm so sorry."

"Sean," Gabriel forced out, but the tears were back, sliding down his cheeks and choking his voice. "You're alive."

"I'm sorry," Sean said again, and then his eyes slid closed and his body slumped in Gabriel's arms, unconscious.

Gabriel looked up at Zel and Ishiah, frantic to know how to make Sean better, but before they could answer a door slammed somewhere above them. A sound that normally wouldn't reach beyond one hallway echoed through the empty castle. Stomping footsteps followed, and Zel and Ishiah stood tall in preparation for the coming confrontation.

Someone started yelling just outside the throne room. "I told you, you break the spell, and it will leave you weak and completely helpless. I promised I'd turn you into something worse than a toad, and since you woke me up this early, it's going to be something disgusting."

A man stomped through the back door, a door that was usually heavily guarded as it led exclusively to the royal wing. He sparkled even in the dim light of the room, but not with magic like the toad had. He was wearing a lot of jewelry: multiple rings on each finger, a thick collar of gold and gemstones, plus at least four heavy gold necklaces studded with even more gems, chunky, glittering earrings in each ear, and a thick crown over his thinning hair. Aside from the jewelry, all he wore were a pair of loose sleeping pants.

Gabriel recognized the jewelry, of course. It all belonged to his father, although his father had never worn so much of it so ostentatiously. Gabriel also recognized the man.

"Ambassador Jelkins," he snapped. Gabriel didn't stand; he was much more interested in keeping Sean close than confronting the ambassador from the northern empire. Still it was gratifying to see Jelkins's neck snap in an awkward double take as he abruptly turned from the empty thrones to look at Gabriel and the rest of the room.

"Prince Gabriel. I thought you had run off. This makes it so much simpler for me. Now I don't have to explain that there's a prince somewhere out there, likely orchestrating a coup when the new king arrives." Jelkins smiled, and it was his familiar snide, slimy grin that had always made Gabriel stay away from him at events. "Let's make this all so much easier for us all. You sign over your rights as heir, and I'll let you live. I'll even let you keep your little plaything. Collared, of course, since we can't let him do magic, now can we?"

"Still as unobservant as ever, Jelkins," Zel said before Gabriel could snarl at Jelkins. "I would think after five hundred years, you might have learned something. Apparently not."

Jelkins whipped around again. "Zelimir, what are you doing here?"

Zel shook his head in mock humor, his usual good-natured manner gone. "You're unobservant again, Jel. I've been living with Prince Ishiah for well over a hundred years. Surely you must know what that means in terms of my association with Monrath?"

"You used magic to destabilize this country, to hurt my family," Ishiah continued sternly. "We're here to make sure you can't do anything else."

"You think you can take me?" Jel asked, his voice as snide as his smirk. "I'm a wizard of the empire. You two measly magicians can't compare!" He threw out one hand, and Gabriel flinched and ducked to cover his eyes as bright light suddenly filled the room. When he could see again, Jel was gone.

Ishiah snorted. "And yet he runs away?" He turned to Gabriel. "Stay here. We'll hunt him down and take care of this." He jogged off through the door leading into the royal wing, Zel right behind him. Which left Gabriel with Sean, who was breathing softly into Gabriel's shoulder.

Chapter Five

Gabriel couldn't stop the gentle smile that lifted his lips automatically when he looked down at Sean. He softly ran his fingers through Sean's hair, pushing it off his forehead. Sean looked awful. His skin wasn't green like the toad's, but it was sallow and clammy. Dark circles made his eyes look cavernous, and while Sean had always been thin and fit, his ribs stood out in a way that said he had missed more than a few meals. Despite all that, he was still beautiful. He was breathing; he was alive. Gabriel rested his hand along Sean's cheek and felt his warmth seep into Gabriel's skin.

Sean's eyes blinked open, the green vibrant even when he looked so ill. He smiled at Gabriel immediately, and his own hand lifted to rest on top of Gabriel's. "You should have run."

"I did, but help came so I could come look for you. I'm so glad you're alive. So glad."

A boom shook the castle, and the crash as something shattered overhead made them both jump.

"They can't beat Jelkins, not like this," Sean said. He struggled to sit up, gripping Gabriel by the shoulders to get upright.

"Sean, don't!"

"Gabe, he's tapped into everyone in the castle. He put them to sleep and has been drawing on them to power himself and his spells. Even the two you brought with you won't beat that kind of power. We have to break that connection."

"How?" Gabriel asked, hoping he didn't have to kiss everyone in the castle.

"By waking your sister. I tied a solution to her illness into the protection spell. We have to pluck the heart flower. That'll wake the entire castle and break Jel's control." Sean grimaced and tried to stand, but his knees gave way after barely an inch. "You have to go. It's in the garden with your sister."

"I can't leave you—not again!" Gabriel gasped.

Another boom shook the castle. "I'll need a few days before I'm strong enough to walk again. We don't have that long. Go, Gabe! I'll be fine here. You have to go."

Gabriel squeezed Sean tightly to him, gratified when Sean's trembling arms lifted to hug Gabriel back. It took a moment to lay Sean comfortably on the floor. Gabriel didn't look back as he rushed from the throne room—he wouldn't have had the strength to leave if he had, and anyway, the sooner he got this task finished, the sooner he could return to Sean's side.

He traversed the familiar halls back in the direction he had just come from, stepping out into the queen's outer courtyard and into the fragrance of the roses only a few minutes after leaving Sean's side.

"I need to get to my sister, please," he told the roses, hoping they would still be willing to listen to him. They were. With a rustle, a new path opened as the roses moved aside. "Thanks," Gabriel called as he hurried down the path. It led him right up to the wooden door of the inner garden.

Gabriel grabbed the handle and yanked, and it didn't move. "Locked. Of course, it's locked."

He had to get inside, but how? Could he climb the wall, break through the glass roof, and climb down on the other side? Gabriel shook his head. It would take too much time, but he didn't have any other options.

"Please, open," he gasped, yanking one last, desperate time at the handle. Something tingled in his fingertips, and suddenly the handle turned. He stumbled forward through the doorway, and into a barren wasteland. Outside were the roses; inside every plant had withered and died as if they had chosen to give their lives to the protection of what lay at the garden's center.

Rory lay where she had fallen. The maid who had rushed to her side lay almost on top of her, and the guard who had tried to catch them both was sprawled there too. No one had dared touch them since, yet the lone living plant had somehow curled vines over their bodies as if to shield them in one last protection attempt. That plant had bloomed one vibrant red rose the size of Gabriel's hand. That had to be the heart flower that Gabriel needed to pluck.

He didn't hesitate, although he was careful not to touch any of the sleepers so he didn't catch the sleeping sickness.

"I'm sorry, pretty flower, but you're the key to ending all of this." One of the thorns jabbed his thumb as he gripped the stem, but it snapped in two as easily as any other flower.

Utter silence dropped over the castle like a blanket; then a violent scream of defiance echoed out of the castle and through the garden, only to suddenly be cut short with another earth-shaking boom.

A soft gasp came from below Gabriel. He looked down and let out a gasp of his own. "Rory!"

"What— No, I know what happened," she said softly. "It was the northern ambassador. He gave me something to drink, and...please tell me my dreams weren't real, Gabe. Tell me Father isn't dead."

There was no way to break it easily, not something like this.

"You are the queen, Aurora," he said softly.

She nodded, but her lips were pressed together as if she was trying not to cry. "Right, then." She got to her feet with Gabriel's help, and then as the guard also staggered up, he and the maid both helped Rory and each other stumble out of the garden. Gabriel followed, hoping to get back to Sean, but not daring to let the weakened Rory out of his sight just yet.

Where before entering the castle had been odd for the quiet, this time it was the opposite. Too much noise filled the halls as the guards' barracks emptied frantically, servants rushed around, and courtiers wandered into the halls to find out what was going on. The great bell on top of the tallest tower began pealing, signaling the mournful fact that the king was dead. A wail broke through the noise as the realization of what had happened to the kingdom broke through the shock, but Gabriel was just glad to know someone had gotten to the tower and removed the enemy's flag. The queen's flag had to be sewn, so a black flag to honor the deceased king would fly until then.

Rory went straight to the throne room where Gabriel found someone had draped a sheet over Father. Someone had also apparently found a pair of pants for Sean, who was sitting propped up against one of the thrones. Rory dropped into the queen's throne, a chair that had remained empty in the ten years since their mother had passed. Now the king's throne would remain empty until Rory married.

"Thank you," Rory said to the soldier and maid who had helped her. "Please, go tell your families you're okay. Others will help me from here." They both bowed and hurried off, and Rory turned her attention to the guards who had begun filtering into the room to take up their posts. "Bring me the captain of the guard and the general," she told one of them.

Gabriel sat down next to Sean and gladly held out one arm when Sean shifted to lean against Gabriel instead of the hard throne.

"I see you found it," he said, nodding toward the rose Gabriel was still holding.

"That is quite the spell," Zel said as he approached them from the direction of the royal wing. Ishiah was with him, but off to the side where he could safely wipe down his bloodied sword with a handkerchief. "A real piece of beauty. You know this means you can't escape the magic anymore, Sean."

"I know. If I had more training, I could have stopped this before it ever got this bad," Sean replied. "But my reason for leaving my master hasn't changed."

"It doesn't have to," Ishiah said. He slid his sword back into his sheath before walking over. He knelt in front of them, then gripped Gabriel's chin in gentle fingers. "You have the eyes," he told Gabriel. "I can count a good dozen spells you've either accidentally cast, or seen completely through in just the day we've been together. I'd say you've already extended your life a good fifteen years just on the magic you cast today alone."

"Magic? Me?" And yet, it made sense. He had managed to open a locked door just now, hadn't he? And he had found Sean the toad when no one else had noticed him. "But what about Sean?"

"That actually makes it easier," Sean replied. "We can both learn magic together. I stopped so I wouldn't outlive you, but now we can be together forever, just like Ishiah and Zel."

Together forever certainly sounded nice to Gabriel, but as the general and captain rushed into the room Gabriel was reminded of who he was.

"I can't just leave, especially not now." Not with his father's body still lying there, his sister not yet coronated, and the northern army about to descend on them.

Zel nodded. "Ish and I have something in the North to take care of first anyway. We need to figure out if the forgetting spell on magic was tampered with, or if it might be fading, and then we have to fix it. Plus—" He plucked the rose from Gabriel's fingers. "—if you don't mind, I would like to use this to teach a northern beast how to be a man."

"Take it," Gabriel said, half-hoping to never see a rose again. "But, if I stay, how will I learn magic?"

"Sean will teach you," Ishiah said easily. "He can teach you the introductory basics; he's probably the best wizard for that, since he spent fifty years just learning it. We won't be gone more than seven months. By then, everything should have stabilized and you can come travel with us to learn more."

"Although, we're not leaving tonight," Zel added. "We'll go find a guest room to sleep and then head out to see about the North in the morning."

"I should get Sean to bed too," Gabriel said, looking down at Sean, who had fallen asleep against him.

"Until the morning, then," Zel said with a smile. Ishiah smiled as well, and then they both headed in the direction of a servant who could show them to an open room.

The priests had arrived while Gabriel was distracted. They had Father on a litter so they could take his body to begin treatment for proper funeral rites. Gabriel nodded his thanks to them as they passed him. Two knights approached him once the priests had left.

"Prince, we will take your knight protector to your rooms," one of them said as they both bowed. It took both of them to lift Sean, and they carried him carefully from the room. Gabriel followed. He glanced once back at Rory, but she was head to head with the general and captain. She didn't need her little brother's help, and Gabriel wanted to stay with Sean anyway. He followed the knights up to the room he had shared with Sean for so long now. They laid Sean in bed, and Gabriel crawled in afterward, once they had gone again.

He settled against Sean's warmth and felt like he was letting out a breath held too long. The gaping wound in his chest still stung, but every moment pressed against Sean's side—feeling his chest lift with each breath and hearing the firm beating of his heart—healed it just the slightest bit more. Gabriel drifted off to sleep, secure in the knowledge that this time Sean would still be there when he woke.

Epilogue

The tree roots where he had curled up were deep, so deep he couldn't seem to crawl out of them. But Gabriel knew he had to; it was the only way to rescue Sean, so he had to keep climbing and climbing.

"Sean!" he called, hoping Sean might hear him and know Gabriel was coming as fast as he could.

"Gabe, I'm here. You can wake up now. It's okay, I'm here."

Gabriel blinked, then blinked again until the familiar ceiling of his bedroom came into focus. Sean leaned over Gabriel, his bright green eyes concerned.

"A nightmare again? I'm so sorry, Gabe."

"It's not your fault," Gabriel replied as firmly as he could. They had had this conversation so many times, and every time Sean still blamed himself for Gabriel's nightmares. He never listened when Gabriel insisted it was Ambassador Jelkins's fault, or it was Gabriel's fault for having so little faith in Sean. After all, he had assumed Sean was dead instead of trusting in his strength.

Gabriel rolled over so he was half lying on Sean. He propped his chin on Sean's chest so he could look up at him. The black circles were gone after four weeks of nothing but sleep. Sean had enough strength to take short walks, and he was doing his best to turn those walks into some sort of training, but he wasn't anywhere close to his full strength yet. Gabriel was busy with the war council during the day, handling the reports his sister and the general sent back, as well as the day-to-day running of the country while Rory was away leading the army against the North. That only left the late night and early morning for them to spend together, except most mornings were spent making them both feel better after Gabriel had a nightmare.

It was time to change that negative cycle.

Gabriel grinned up at Sean, then tilted his neck so he could lick a long stripe down Sean's chest, relishing the salty-sweet taste of Sean's skin and the firm hardness of Sean's muscles. He rolled a little more so they were pressed body-to-body and he could feel Sean's entire length against his own. The move brought his head in line with Sean's, and Sean was already there, his own head tilted perfectly to take Gabriel's lips with his.

Heat flared between them, much like the magic Sean had barely begun to teach Gabriel, but this heat was so much more intense. Sean's arms held Gabriel close as their lips pressed together. It was slow, leisurely, as they took the time to reintroduce their bodies to each other. The heat built as their bodies shifted, pressing close, then drawing away.

The intensity and focus in Sean's eyes as he lovingly took in every inch of Gabriel eventually did Gabriel in. Sean didn't take long to follow Gabriel's lead, and they cuddled together under the blankets afterward.

Why would Gabriel worry about nightmares when he had this to wake up to? Sean's slowing breaths in his ear reminded Gabriel he was still alive. Sean's every touch, so gentle, yet firm enough to show he knew Gabriel was strong enough to take everything he could give, was full of love. A nightmare had no power against this.

Gabriel draped one arm over Sean, ready to take a nap and enjoy a lazy morning. Sean let out a soft, happy sigh and snuggled close.

The horns blowing outside were easy to ignore when he had Sean's long, beautiful hair to play with. It was so easy to braid, and so silky between his fingers. Sean's laughter as he happily let Gabriel play was the real reason Gabriel could be so carefree.

Until the moment was shattered by frantic banging on the door. "Prince Gabriel, Knight Protector Sean! The horns!"

The horns? Gabriel listened for a moment, hearing the particular cadence of the horns blowing outside, and then he fell out of bed at a sprint, scattering blankets everywhere as he rushed to the washbasin to clean off, before hurrying to the wardrobe to throw on some clothes. Somehow, he managed to not get in the way of Sean, who was getting ready as well. The door banged open, slamming against the wall as they dashed out together.

Footsteps of at least a dozen people ran with them as the courtiers rushed from their rooms in the public halls and servants followed behind. When Gabriel and Sean reached the front hall, the crowd that had beat them there made a path for them. They spilled out onto the front courtyard en masse just as the loudest horn blast sounded and the main gates were thrown open.

Rory rode in at the head of the army, resplendent in her armor. She looked like a queen, and everyone around Gabriel seemed to see it too. They all stood straighter for a brief moment, as awe of her brilliance settled on them, and then they bowed to her.

Gabriel strode across the courtyard as Rory dismounted. He waited while a hostler took her horse, and then he bowed to her as well.

"Welcome home, Queen Aurora!" he called loudly enough for everyone in the courtyard to hear. A roar erupted from the onlookers and from the soldiers that were still streaming in through the gates.

Rory held up her hands until silence slowly descended. "We, the soldiers of Monrath, are proud to bring home victory!" she yelled in her best parade voice. She was drowned out a moment later as cheers erupted again, so she didn't try to say anything else to the crowd. "It's still early morning, so I think planning a banquet for tonight wouldn't be too difficult?" she said to the maid who had already come to her side. The maid nodded eagerly and ran off. Rory turned to Gabriel and Sean next, and her look said she had something to say to them in private. They fell into step with her as she headed into the castle.

It took much longer to return to the royal hall than it had to leave it not ten minutes prior. Everyone had to stop Rory to tell her something, and she took the time to listen to them all. When they did reach her rooms, Gabriel and Sean settled together into a love seat in her sitting room while she went with her maids into her bedroom to wash and change.

Gabriel was happily napping with his head resting on Sean's shoulder, who was in turn resting with his head on top of Gabriel's, when she emerged.

They waited until tea and a light breakfast was served and the maids had left before she started explaining.

"They all saw a bright-red rose in their minds and then forgot what they were doing there," Rory said over her teacup.

"Who saw what?" Gabriel asked. He picked up a tea sandwich and bit into it, glad to assuage his growling stomach.

Rory grimaced. "Sorry. It's all muddled weirdly in my head. I know the antidote to the poisoned needle I touched was brewed from rose petals, so maybe I'm mixing up my stories. All I know is we were encamped for the night, preparing for battle to begin at first light, when all of a sudden all of the scouts came running in. The entire northern army was wandering around aimlessly, and when we captured them to question them, none could remember why they were there. One or two with that story I could understand, but we found dozens. They all spoke about some sort of red rose vision, but that faded from their memories quickly too. I swear, it was the weirdest thing I have ever seen."

Rory took a long sip of tea and then ate two of the sandwiches ravenously. Gabriel looked up at Sean, who shook his head slightly, so Gabriel kept his questions to himself for the moment.

"After seven days of talking to people who didn't remember leaving their mother's house, let alone joining an army, we broke camp and came home. I also sent scouts north, and the empire is gone. It's as if it never existed."

"Then we should celebrate our victory and mourn our dead," Sean replied easily. "Let's leave it up to the historians who will write down this victory to decide how it was won."

Rory laughed. "They'll decide that regardless, but you're right. Let's celebrate today, mourn tomorrow, and figure out the rest later. Finish your breakfast, and then go get dressed. Today's going to be a busy day!"

Twenty minutes later, Gabriel and Sean headed back out into the hallway, walked two doors down, and entered their room. Only once the door was firmly closed behind them did Gabriel turn to Sean and fix him with a glare.

"Rory thinks she was poisoned by a needle?" he asked sharply.

Sean nodded. "It's the forgetting spell. I think that's what happened to the northern empire too. Zel and Ishiah must have broken whatever Jelkins did to keep the army of the North from forgetting about magic, and the soldiers immediately forgot the magic that had gathered them together."

"So why didn't I forget?" Gabriel asked.

Sean grinned. "How can you forget about something coursing through your blood? You remember how it goes? From your head, to your feet—"

"Back up to the head, and out," Gabriel finished, throwing his hand outward to focus the magic. The bedroom door swung open a half second later. He grinned over at Sean, who laughed. "Shall we get ready for the day?" Gabriel asked him.

Sean walked over and pecked Gabriel on the lips. "Let's."

HAPPILY EVER AFTER

"Every eligible maiden! Can you believe it?" Rainier spun once around the room, his arms akimbo and completely graceless, in his patched breeches and nothing else.

"And?" Mabli was sprawled on zir back on the lone throw cushion in the room. Zi was in zir small form of about three inches tall, and the shapeless robe zi was wearing glimmered with every movement. Zir wings were squished under zir back, but that didn't appear to bother Mabli, who rolled over onto one wing with a sprinkling of fairy dust to look directly at Rainier.

"So you magic me up a dress and some boobs, and I can walk right into the castle with the rest of the maidens in the kingdom. With that many people wandering around, it'll take me a few minutes to find something to steal. I get the right item, we'll be set for life."

"I'm your fairy godparent, not your magical assistant at thievery," Mabli replied with a pout. "There are very few people in this world who have been assigned a personal fairy. My job is to see you to your happily ever after, not help you steal stuff from the castle."

"Oh, come on, Mab!" Rainier said with a groan. "You've helped me find plenty of happiness. I'm safe from my stepfather, I have this lovely attic room, and if I can steal something really good from the castle, I won't have to worry about money for the rest of my life. That's happiness to me."

Mabli scoffed and rolled over onto zir other wing so zir back was facing Rainier. "What about true love? The happiness to be found when the love of another person surrounds your every moment?"

It was Rainier's turn to scoff. He turned away from Mabli to look out the small attic window at the sprawl of rooftops of the capital city. Far in the distance, Rainier could see the stone towers of the castle.

"My mother thought that way too," Rainier said softly, unable to put any force in his voice. "After my father died, she thought she needed to find someone new to take care of that need. She found my stepfather, and for the first year or two, she thought he loved her. She didn't know he was abusing me behind her back. Then she finally changed her will to leave everything to him if she died, and not even a week later she had her heart attack. If you hadn't come for me, Mab, I'd be dead. Relying on love to give my life purpose is a waste." Rainier rubbed at his chest, feeling the physical scars under his fingertips and knowing that most of his scars weren't visible to the eye.

Mabli didn't answer for a long moment, but then zi sighed. Rainier heard the gentle flap of wings and felt Mabli settle onto Rainier's left shoulder. Mabli's hand gently stroked against Rainier's neck, brushing away Rainier's raven's wing-black hair. His stepfather had forcibly shaved his head once when he was six, and Rainier hadn't been able to cut it since. The braid fell halfway down his back, the ends ragged from lack of care, and strands of curls always escaped.

"I just don't think stealing from the castle is going to make you happy," Mabli said softly, "but it will certainly help distract you from all this." Zir small fingers gently ran down the lurid red scar that curled from Rainier's back over his shoulder. The whip hadn't been kind that day. "I can't magic you breasts, but I can certainly get you a dress with a padded brassiere. You want to go to the ball; I'll make sure you go to the ball. Just...if someone worthy of loving you appears there, do me a favor and dance with him?"

That wasn't a difficult promise to make, since Rainier had zero intention of going anywhere near the actual dancing. There would probably be food and drink—and he wasn't one to turn down a free meal—but he planned to spend the rest of the ball wandering around the castle, filling the padded brassiere with small items that would net him a fortune on the black market.

"Then I will get to work fabricating a dress and some jewelry. You figure out where you're going to get a proper bath and how you're getting your hair done."

"Thank you, Mab," Rainier replied. Mabli jumped off Rainier's shoulder and flew across the room to the scarred wooden table that had come with the rent. The cushion flew through the air after zir, and Mabli settled onto it on the table and began muttering magical words to zirself.

Rainier walked over to the small mirror he had hung from a peg on the wall, fingering his hair. With it properly washed, his natural curls would serve. Maybe a small braid to keep it out of his eyes, and it would be done. His eyes were bright blue, in sharp contrast to the darkness of his hair. He ran his fingers down the white scar over his forehead that had somehow, miraculously missed his eyes. Maybe he would skip the braid to hide the scar. The hard part would be finding a bathing facility that would let him in without coin. Although, he could probably afford to splurge just this once, since he was going to be independently wealthy after the ball.

He pulled the mirror off the peg, revealing a small hole in the wall behind it. His coin purse was hidden there, and Rainier pulled out the coppers that would get him a warm bath with mostly clean water. He replaced the mirror and went over to the chair where he stored his clean clothes. He found a pair of breeches and a long-sleeved shirt, quickly put both on, and then hurried out of the attic in search of his bath.

*

Rainier was no stranger to the castle, which he knew was odd for a thief, but his entire life had been odd so far. Mabli's parting admonition to "stay away from the library" was one Rainier was more than happy to obey. His stepfather was still a librarian in the main library, as far as Rainier was aware. The bastard had been aiming for the head librarian position and had thought he needed to prove his worth via a large purse and by marrying the wife of the previous head. The position had remained vacant for years after Rainier's father died.

His stepfather had been like his mother: part of the wealthy middle class able to purchase a proper education for their children and to be eligible for good work in the castle. Most ended up as secretaries for the various lords and ladies, or low-level officers in the military, but there were always some who ended up in the library.

The head librarian position—much like any position in the castle that required work, but was still high level enough that the king or queen might interact with whomever held the position—was always filled by someone of noble birth. Usually it was a second or third son or daughter of a noble family. Someone born to privilege, but who would not be inheriting any title and would not have anything to pass down to their own children.

Needless to say, Rainier's stepfather had always derided Rainier for being of noble blood but lacking a title to go with it. Looking back now, Rainier knew it was jealousy talking, but at the time he hadn't understood what he was being blamed for. When his stepfather hadn't gotten the head librarian position because it was instead assigned to the fourth son of a marquis, things had gotten even worse for Rainier. Luckily, it was only a year or so later that Mabli appeared and a year after that when Rainier finally found his freedom.

And he was going back to the castle he had so happily fled from.

Well, Mabli was correct. All he had to do was avoid the library, and his stepfather would never know he was nearby. There was no way an ordinary librarian would get an invite to the ball. Besides, Rainier was wearing a dress, and it had been five years since they had last seen each other. Stepfather wouldn't recognize him.

Rainier took a deep breath and firmly told himself to stop stalling. As the next carriage came to the drawbridge and the horses slowed to a walk, Rainier slipped into the shadow cast by the torches shining over the carriage and walked through the main gates and into the castle courtyard.

He could hear music playing through the open windows, even though the fancy ballroom was at the back of the castle. Every door was flung open, and people were milling about the courtyard gardens off to the left. Rainier moved away from the carriage before the footman noticed him, and joined the throng in the gardens. There he stood straight, brushed his hair off his shoulders so it hung down his back in a curtain of curls, and strode deeper into the gardens, his steps sashaying in the delicate heeled shoes Mabli had also magicked up.

The dress he was wearing was not in current fashion. Necklines were low with breasts threatening to spill free from all the women he passed, while the neckline of his dress came to a stop just above his collarbones. Rainier didn't have the breasts to pull off a low-cut dress anyway, but since his chest was just as ugly as his back, he always kept his body concealed in public. That was why he was wearing long sleeves when current fashion was a wide strap hanging off the shoulder. Still, his dress looked the part of a ball gown. It was a deep blue as close to the shade of his eyes as Mabli could manage, with silver embroidery stitched to artfully enhance his assets without the need for skin showing. Small diamonds were sewn into the fabric as well, and a massive white diamond sat in a necklace just above his fake breasts. His skirts were wide and full and rustled as he walked. White diamond-encrusted pins kept his hair out of his face, although he had managed to braid the front so it still covered that scar. He didn't look out of place at all in the garden, and he thought the ruse would stand up in the rest of the ball as well. The magic would last for about four hours, so he needed to be gone by midnight to avoid discovery.

Torches and braziers all the way around the side of the castle lit the path he was following in the garden, which let out into a backyard of low-cut grass and hedges below the wide patio at the rear of the ballroom. The music was louder here, as were the voices. As Rainier stepped closer, he could also smell the alcohol. The party had just begun—carriages were still arriving in front—but the alcohol was apparently flowing. Rainier couldn't help the smile that lifted his lips at that realization. If everyone was drunk, the chances of him being noticed were that much slimmer.

Rainier climbed the artful stone steps that led up to the patio and stepped into the ballroom.

The place was absolutely magnificent. Rainier stood in the doorway for a long moment, blinking and trying not to let his awe show on his face. Crystal chandeliers soared overhead with thick tapers lit on each branch to light the space. The walls shone with gold-framed mirrors hanging over expensive cloth wallpaper thick with gold-threaded embroidery. The floor was magnificent golden-brown hardwood, no doubt imported from some faraway country. But it was the ceiling that had Rainier completely captivated. It was painted with clouds the color of the most magnificent sunset, and hidden amongst them dancers even more extravagantly dressed than those around him in the ballroom frolicked.

"Pardon me, miss," a man said from behind Rainier. He slipped past before Rainier could apologize, but Rainier did finally gather his wits and move out of the doorway. One wall was completely filled with tables straining under the weight of the platters of food and drink. Most people were still milling about the gardens or chatting amicably by the food, so it wasn't a hard decision to walk in that direction. Rainier filled a plate with some of the delicacies and stood along the wall to eat while he waited for his chance.

On the other side of the room was an empty dais with three thrones as ornate as the rest of the ballroom. The ball wasn't officially started until the royal family joined them, so Rainier couldn't slip away to start stealing until after that. Instead he people watched, and he quickly came to a happy conclusion.

The smell of alcohol that permeated the air so thickly even in the open space of the garden should have tipped him off, but the drinks were flowing fast and strong. Harassed-looking servants were constantly refilling glasses and flutes on the table, and other servants were circulating among the crowd with even more trays. The nobles were getting completely and utterly drunk, and those same nobles were dripping in gemstones and precious metals.

It would be laughably easy to slide next to the woman a few feet away and unhook the ruby bracelet hanging precariously around her wrist. That gentleman still by the door with the opals sewn into his jacket wouldn't notice if Rainier cut a few threads with the very small knife in his pocket, nor would he miss the opals once they were safely in Rainier's hands. Why bother with the danger of being discovered wandering through the castle when a lifetime of riches were here in the ballroom for his taking? It was an easy decision to make.

Rainier had just stepped away from the wall to go relieve that woman of her bracelet when horns blew and the room immediately quieted. Rainier settled back into place to wait.

"Announcing His Majesty, King Richard the Fifth and Her Majesty, Queen Isabella the Third!" the crier yelled into the room. A door on the side of the dais opened, and the king and queen regally stepped into the room. Rainier didn't dare approach them, but their outfits outstripped every single other person's in displayed wealth. Just getting one of the queen's bracelets would have meant he wouldn't need to steal anything else that night. The door closed again, and this time the hush in the room was anticipatory as every eye eagerly turned in the direction of the doorway.

The room was filled with women hoping to be the lucky one the prince chose as his bride, as well as the fathers and mothers hoping their daughters would be chosen. All of them eagerly awaited the arrival of the prince in the hopes of attracting his attention.

The horns finally blew again and the doors opened. "His Majesty, Prince Henry the Third!" the crier called. Prince Henry stepped into the room, but Rainier's eyes caught on the man standing guard at Prince Henry's back. Rainier would know Peyton anywhere.

Peyton's skin was the rich light brown found in the noble families from the southern regions of the kingdom. He had been fostered to the captain of the royal guard—the only brother of the current Duke Del

Martinene—at the age of five. As two lonely children in a vast castle of far more important people, Peyton and Rainier had somehow found each other. They had been friends until Rainier's stepfather had started keeping Rainier confined to the library, ostensibly so Rainier could keep up with his studies, but in reality, to hide the often bloody injuries that had been inflicted on him. Rainier hadn't seen Peyton since he had fled from the castle.

Apparently, Peyton had achieved the posting of captain of the prince's guard, which meant when Prince Henry became King Henry, Peyton would become captain of the king's guard. As much as Rainier wanted to go say hello to his old friend, he knew he couldn't. Peyton would try to bring Rainier back into the castle, most likely as a librarian like his stepfather, and Rainier wasn't going to let that happen. Besides, if he was going to steal himself to an easy life, letting the captain of any guard know he was about was utterly foolish. No, Rainier would stay as far away from Peyton as possible and be content with the knowledge that his friend was doing well.

"The prince will now choose his partner for the first dance of the night!" the crier continued. A receiving line had already begun forming to the right of the dais, and at the crier's words, the line began to firm up and snake through the ballroom. The crier took calling cards from the first group in line and began saying names while bows and curtsies were exchanged. It would take at least two hours before the dancing started, and now all the people Rainier wanted to relieve of their jewelry were waiting impatiently in line. He sighed and went to get another plate of food.

Rainier had just settled back into his spot by the wall, happy with a plate full of food, when a gasp rang through the room. Prince Henry had jumped down from the dais and was making his way through the room toward the patio doors. Rainier turned to look along with the rest of the crowd and couldn't help rolling his eyes.

The girl's dress was also blue, but a shade lighter than Rainier's— probably because her eyes were a lighter shade as well. The skirt was even fuller, and the fabric seemed to glow in the candlelight. Her hair was blonde and pulled delicately off her bared neck. She was too busy blinking in surprise at the sight of the ballroom—much as Rainier had done moments before—to notice Prince Henry heading her way, but when she looked down and finally saw him, her lips immediately lifted into a welcoming smile. She knew Prince Henry, that much was obvious, and as musicians scrambled into place on their balcony high above the ballroom, Prince Henry swept her into his arms for the first dance.

What wasn't obvious was the sparkle of fairy dust that hung around her. Rainier had been with Mabli for over five years now. He would recognize the mark of fairy magic just about anywhere, and it was all over that girl.

Rainier could already guess her story: a poor servant girl abused by the stepmother and stepsisters who had forced her into servitude, but on a night when she had escaped to the forest for some much-needed peace, she had accidentally encountered Prince Henry out on his horse and their hearts had become ensnared.

It was perfect fodder to attract a fairy. The girl would go to the ball, Prince Henry would ask for her hand in marriage, and they would live happily ever after. Except, fairy magic only lasted a few short hours, and Rainier didn't know whether she would be able to accomplish all of that before her time was up.

None of that really mattered to Rainier. He was sure her fairy had everything well in hand, and it was time for him to get his act together and make certain his task was accomplished before his own magic dress faded back into fairy dust.

He finished his plate and set it on the collection tray, then meandered into the crowd.

*

Rainier stepped back into the ballroom after a visit to the washroom where he had emptied his hip pockets into the hidden slots between the thick padding in his breasts. He would be a cup size larger by the end of the night, but it was oh so very worth it. The hour was starting to get late, so Rainier decided that one more pass through the ballroom and a stop by the food table where there were chocolates would be enough.

He was chewing on a berry-crème-filled chocolate and relieving a lady of some seed pearls stitched onto her puffy sleeves when he felt something burning on the back of his neck. With instincts honed by years of working the streets, Rainier immediately stopped what he was doing and started heading toward the door. He could feel the eyes on his back as he walked, but going any faster would attract additional attention. The back door was just a few steps away when someone rested a hand on Rainier's shoulder.

"Miss, might I ask you for this dance?"

Rainier slowly turned around, hoping the familiar voice that had only deepened with age didn't actually belong to Peyton. The hand on his shoulder slid down Rainier's arm until he gripped Rainier's hand. Peyton pulled him back onto the dance floor, and his grip was so strong—no doubt from wielding the sword currently at his hip—Rainier didn't have a chance to pull away.

Except, Rainier wasn't certain he wanted to.

Peyton was a few inches taller, and his shoulders were broad with muscle. He was even more beautiful up close, especially in his formal whites with ribbons and pins decorating his chest. He slid his hands into place at Rainier's waist and shoulder, and then started leading them into a simple waltz.

"You're supposed to be dead, Rain," Peyton said softly. His brown eyes were soft and slightly sad as he looked down at Rainier. "Max held a funeral for you and everything. I'm also certain you were a man then."

Rainier's responding smile was equally sad. "I am dead, Peyt. My stepfather killed me. If it helps, you can believe I'm back as a woman to say goodbye." It was the only thing he could think to say that might help him get away. He couldn't stay here for much longer or the magic would end. Still, he couldn't help enjoying the feeling of Peyton's warm arms surrounding him and pulling him close, or the intensity in Peyton's eyes as he looked down at Rainier.

"See, I think you're a thief taking advantage of the ball. Rain, what happened to you?" The hand on Rainier's waist dipped lower, slipping into his pocket to pull out a delicate lady's belt of woven golden strands with a heavy emerald at the end to weight it properly. He quirked an eyebrow pointedly at Rainier.

It was definitely time to go, but Rainier didn't have any idea how to escape from Peyton. He wasn't exactly certain he wanted to, except he knew that he didn't have a choice. He needed to come up with something to say that would convince Peyton to let him go, but his mind was coming up blank.

The clock from the tower high above the castle rang once, the first bong to signal midnight had come, and Rainier knew it was too late. He had the mere minute it would take for the elderly tower to get through the last eleven bongs before the magic on his dress vanished.

"Wait! Miss, please, wait!" Prince Henry's voice rang out over the music, grinding the dance to a halt. Peyton immediately spun around to see what was happening to his primary charge.

Rainier got the barest glimpse of the girl in the very blue dress dashing across the floor away from Prince Henry, whom she had been with all night. She vanished through the door leading into the castle and no doubt straight to the front door.

Rainier didn't wait to see what happened next. He yanked free of Peyton and headed toward the garden door he had entered from as fast as his skirts would allow.

Peyton's shouted "Rainier" vanished behind Prince Henry's desperate "Miss!" and then Rainier was outside and quickly hopping down the ornamental steps off the patio and into the garden.

Bong!

Ten bells left and Rainier could hear footsteps following him. Peyton would catch him in the garden, but if Rainier could get back inside without Peyton seeing, he could get to the front door and escape that way. There! He saw the side door he was looking for and dodged left around a leafy tree. Rainier threw open the door, dashed inside, and shut the door behind him before hurrying into the hallway.

He knew where he was. The door had been a servant's entrance, and the hallways were simple and familiar to the child who used to play here. It only took a few seconds to dash toward the stairs he knew would lead him directly to the front hall.

Bong!

"Rain! Please stop running!" Peyton called behind him. Rainier suppressed a vocal swear and kept running. Peyton hadn't been fooled and was still behind him. "I don't care about the thieving. I just want to know you're okay." Rainier ignored him and kept running.

Bong!

He dashed up the staircase, knowing he was at least out of sight of Peyton. Maybe Peyton would continue running through the servants' hall, not believing Rainier would dare reenter the castle proper.

He flew out of the servants' door and into the marble-floored entrance hall, and right into the girl in blue.

"Sorry!" she gasped as she scrambled back to her feet. There was a commotion from the hall behind her, likely of courtiers and other ladies hoping to catch Prince Henry's attention while he was trying to run after her.

Rainier got back to his feet as well and joined her in running to the front door.

Bong!

"Damn," she swore and kicked of her shoes so she could run faster. She scooped them up as she went, but Rainier saw they looked like they were made of glass. "I'm not going to make it."

Rainier knew what Mabli would do in this situation, but then Mab had always been softhearted. He also knew what Mabli would say if zi found out Rainier had left the poor girl in the lurch when he could have helped.

"Fairy magic fades too damned quickly," Rainier agreed, panting out the words as he ran. She was clearly in much better shape than he, given she wasn't having any issue with talking and running at the same time. "You have to get out of sight so the magic can fade, and then in your street clothes, no one will recognize you and you can go home safely."

"I've got to get my carriage out of here before it turns into a pumpkin," she replied. Which meant she would need extra time to escape. They dashed out of the open front doors just as Prince Henry and Peyton finally entered the hall at the far end. An ornate carriage was waiting for her on the drive just a few feet down the courtyard, but she would never make it out the gate if Prince Henry or Peyton had the chance to call out to the guards there.

Luckily, Rainier had an idea.

Bong!

"You need to fall down and drop a shoe when you do," Rainier explained quickly. "They'll have to stop to see what you left—they won't be able to help their curiosity—and that will give your carriage the time to get out."

"Miss!" Prince Henry had reached the door.

The girl didn't hesitate, falling to the ground in an awkward flop of skirts. Rainier dragged her back to her feet and practically threw her into the carriage. It took off with Rainier still on the footstep jutting from the side, so he grimly hung on to the door as they rattled through the gate and past the guards belatedly scrambling to stop them.

Bong!

The carriage hurtled over the drawbridge, which began lifting when they were halfway across, and bumped heavily out into the wealthy streets of the city. Rainier almost lost his grip as they flew over the end of the lifted drawbridge before hitting the cobbled street below. He was surprised they hadn't broken a wheel or axle in the impact, but then the carriage was fairy-made.

It was also shrinking, Rainier noticed with some horror as his already precarious grip began to slip. One of the four horses was also growing a set of very mouselike whiskers.

Bong!

Rainier couldn't believe how fast they were moving. There was definitely magic involved in their speed as the wealthy quarter of the city flashed past. They didn't even need the extra time they had gained when the soldiers chasing them had gotten stuck behind the lifted drawbridge.

The carriage took a sudden right turn, and Rainier realized they were going to leave the city for the fancy manors in the countryside.

"I need to get off here," he called, knowing the girl couldn't afford the time it would take. Still, Rainier had zero interest in trekking all the way back to the city from way out in the country.

Bong!

The carriage slowed, although it didn't actually come to a stop. The girl poked her head out of the window and smiled at him. Her pretty dress was already gone, replaced by a simpler pink one that looked as if someone had tried to turn it into rags while she was still wearing it. A ripped sleeve hung from her arm as she held out her remaining slipper.

"I can't keep it," she said softly. "They search my sleeping quarters regularly to make sure I'm not stealing from them." She shook her head sadly, likely because she knew that they were really making sure she didn't have money or travel clothes hidden away that would allow her to escape them. "Will you keep my happiest memory safe for me?"

Bong!

The carriage was still shrinking, and they were still driving slowly while they waited for Rainier to get down. He didn't have time to argue with her, and he somehow could sense the will of one of their fairies involved with her request. He took the shoe, nodded politely to her, and carefully jumped away from the carriage. Rainier stumbled slightly, falling back against the wall of a nearby building, and the carriage sped up again. It vanished into the distance amazingly fast.

Rainier didn't have time to watch it go, although he did hope she made it home safely. He tucked the shoe into his already-full pocket and started running in the other direction, back into the poor quarter and toward his attic room.

Bong!

The clopping sounds of horses moving quickly over the cobbles had Rainier darting into the nearest alleyway. He hunkered down behind a trash bin and started pulling the pins from his hair. He also unraveled the braid and used the ribbon from that to pull his hair back into a simple tail at the back of his neck.

Bong!

With the last ring of the bell from the clock tower, the magic faded away. His dress vanished, leaving him back in his patched breeches and long-sleeved shirt. The two bags of stolen jewelry slid down his chest until they were stopped at his stomach by his crude rope belt. As long as Peyton wasn't out there, no one would recognize him.

Rainier carefully strode to the mouth of the alley, and when he didn't see anyone, he continued walking along the street in the direction of home.

"Ho! You there!" A group of soldiers on foot patrol came around the corner and immediately spotted him. "Have you seen a carriage come through here?"

"No, my lord," Rainier replied truthfully since the carriage hadn't come anywhere near this particular street.

The soldier preened for a moment at being called a lord before one of his fellows elbowed him. "Very well. Go about your business." The soldiers continued on their patrol, and Rainier was happy enough to continue heading home.

He needed to be quick and careful with what he had stolen. Right now, the girl in blue was distracting everyone. Hopefully, Prince Henry would be keeping Peyton busy as well. If Rainier could sell the loose gems he had gotten to various brokers around the city tonight before the courtiers got home and looked at their clothes, he could get an easy payday. The gems actually in settings would have to wait. Either he would have to disassemble the jewelry and sell it in pieces, or he would have to hold on to it until the lookouts for each individual piece were forgotten. That would take years, but he thought he had enough in loose gems that he could afford to wait that long to cash in the rest.

Rainier climbed the stairs to his attic room. It would only take him a few moments to sort his catch and get back out there.

Mabli was asleep on zir cushion—no doubt still exhausted from all the magic zi had done at the last minute—so Rainier tiptoed past and started emptying everything onto his bed. His hand found the shoe first and he pulled it out to look at.

His memories weren't the ones associated with the shoe, but it still brought back the ball and that last dance. Peyton had looked good. Really, really good. Rainier had never gotten the chance to look at Peyton as anything more than a friend when they were both living in the castle, but that had definitely changed now. Peyton was everything Rainier had ever wanted in a man in terms of looks, but Rainier also remembered the sad, almost pained look in his eyes when he realized what Rainier was doing. There had been so much compassion there. Rainier knew he wanted to see what other emotions Peyton could show him. He particularly wanted to see how Peyton would treat him when Rainier wasn't in the middle of stealing the nobility blind.

"I told you to dance with him when he asked," Mabli said smugly, albeit tiredly, from zir cushion. "Now do you see how wonderful love can be?"

"I'm pretty sure he wants to arrest me for stealing," Rainier replied with a heavy sigh.

"Or he found it adorable, if slightly annoying," Mabli answered smugly. "Now go get your money before the black-market traders close their doors for the night."

Rainier reluctantly put the shoe aside so he could dig out all the jewels and get to work.

*

"I could hardly get a word in at the market. Everyone was too busy talking about the mystery princess who left behind her shoe. Apparently, Prince Henry put out an edict. He's going door to door to try the shoe on every single maiden in the kingdom. Every. Single. Maiden. They were trying it on a milkmaid two blocks over on my way back."

Mabli flittered down from the rafters overhead to sit on zir cushion. Zi was grinning at Rainier as zi leaned back on zir hands and crossed zir legs. Mabli looked coy and far too knowing.

"What's going on?" Rainier couldn't help asking. He set his purchases down on the scarred table and started sorting through them.

He had bought a new shirt, since the one he was currently wearing was getting threadbare at the elbows, and enough food for a few days.

It wouldn't do to be seen in the market and around the city as having suddenly come into money. He had sold all of the loose gemstones to seven different black-market dealers so no one person knew exactly how much he had stolen, and he was being careful not to appear too eager to buy things he never could have before. Eventually he would have to buy a real winter coat, his first since leaving the castle, and a few other things like a better pillow for Mabli, but to do it all at once would attract unneeded attention.

Thieves would be eager to steal from him, of course; however, the real problem would be a well-meaning citizen alerting the guards about him. Most of the word on the street had been about the shoe fittings and speculation on the girl, but Rainier had also heard quieter whispers about nobles angry that they had returned home with far less jewelry than when they had left. The nobles were ostensibly looking for restitution, yet Rainier knew they would really be after blood.

A better idea would definitely be to leave the city entirely, but Rainier also knew it was far too late for that. The guards were checking the bags of every single person leaving, so he wouldn't be able to take the pieces he hadn't sold. Those were his insurance policy to sell in a few years so he would never have to worry about money again; he couldn't leave without them.

And then there was the damned shoe.

It was sitting innocuously on the table next to Mabli's cushion, throwing rainbows across the room from the ray of sun shining directly on it. Rainier couldn't help admiring just how beautiful it was every single time he looked at it. The problem with the shoe was the memories of Peyton it also brought up whenever he looked at it. As much as he wanted to run as far away from the damned city as he could—and now that he had enough funds for travel, that was actually a possible dream to achieve—it would mean leaving behind far too much. Rainier just couldn't do it.

He quickly ate a roll from the bag of freshly baked bread he had bought and then pulled his old, threadbare shirt off over his head. He laid the new shirt on the table next to the bread. It was soft with cloth and stitching that would last a year or even two before he needed to start patching and fixing seams. He fingered the hem between two fingers happily as he ate another roll and then picked it up to finally put it on.

The door to his room was flung open violently, banging against the wall so hard it took a nick out of the wood. Rainier let out an involuntary yelp and dropped the shirt as men in guard's uniforms piled into the room.

How had they found him?

"He's got a shoe!" one of the men gasped.

"He's also got a small treasure of stolen goods," another man replied. As the man stepped forward, Rainier noted the patch on his shoulder, denoting him as a sergeant.

It wasn't like there were any hiding spots in his room large enough to conceal everything he had stolen. The hole behind the mirror was just large enough for his coin purse. There was also zero reason why someone would ever come to his room, including the absent landlord, since Rainier always managed to pay his rent on time, so hiding it hadn't been a priority. Now Rainier wished he had made the effort.

"Here I am, searching every nook and cranny for some whore that will fit the damned shoe, and I instead find the thief of the ball. A thief who apparently also stole a glass slipper." The sergeant waved his men forward, and Rainier abruptly found himself with his arms bound at the wrists behind his bare back. Another man gathered the jewelry into a bag while a third delicately lifted up the shoe to place next to its companion in a padded box. "I think there's been enough shoe fitting for today, men," the sergeant continued. "I say we drop this ruffian off in the dungeons and bring the rest of our finds to Prince Henry." He sounded happily smug, but then he would probably get a promotion for what appeared to be a purely accidental find.

Rainier's only consolation as two men led him out of the room, their gloved hands tight around Rainier's bare, scarred upper arms, was that Mabli had managed to get away.

The soldiers made him walk the distance to the castle while they rode next to him on their horses. The sergeant continued to look smug as he turned Rainier over to the guard manning the castle dungeons.

"Got caught thieving, eh?" the guard said as he guided Rainier into a thankfully empty cell. There were enough seats for a dozen, and the stone walls echoed Rainier's footsteps. "You'll be here awhile, unfortunately. This month's court ended yesterday, so you'll have to wait till next month's for your hearing. Don't worry; I'm sure you'll have company soon," he added as he removed Rainier's bindings and then stepped back out of the cell. "Thieves always get caught eventually, and they all end up here." He closed and locked the cell door and walked off, whistling happily as he went.

Rainier slowly sat on one of the long, wooden benches that lined the wall. The cell was big enough to pace in at the moment, but that wouldn't be true when it was full. It was dry, but cool, and the only light was from a tiny, barred window high in the wall. Once the sun set it would be pitch-black. Rainier shivered and rubbed his arms, wishing they had let him put on his shirt at least before dragging him away.

"Mabli, what do I do now?" Rainier called softly, aware that the guard might still be in hearing distance. Mabli didn't answer, but Rainier hadn't expected zir to pop into sight just because Rainier had spoken to zir.

The only hope Rainier had to cling to now was the fact that Mabli wouldn't let him rot in here. Mabli's entire existence as a fairy godparent hinged on finding a way to get zir charge to that vaunted happily ever after. That couldn't happen if Rainier was hanged for his crimes or sent to a work farm to slowly die from abuse. Mabli wouldn't abandon Rainier now, not when Rainier's need for safety was the most desperate it had been since Mabli had first found him, bleeding and near death after another session with his stepfather.

An hour passed and then two. It began to darken in the cell as the sun started setting. Rainier knew it would be completely dark in the cell long before the sun was actually gone, as the surrounding buildings would block it from the window. The temperature was also dropping, and Rainier found himself shivering. He huddled on the bench, his knees tucked under his chin with his arms wrapped around his legs. After a few days of this, he wouldn't have to worry about a hanging; the flu would get him first.

The light at the end of the row was a welcome addition when it came into view. It took his tired mind a few extra seconds to realize it was moving closer, and he blinked stupidly at the friendly guard when he stopped outside of Rainier's cell with a torch in his hand.

"Don't know what you did, boy, but someone's pretty upset. You're heading up to the courtroom now." He gestured with his free hand for Rainier to stand and then took a second to put the torch in a holder outside the cell before pulling out his keys and a set of bindings for Rainier's wrists.

Rainier let himself be bound and went where he was directed. Anything had to be better than sitting in that cold and dark cell. At least, that was what he was telling himself as he was taken across a rutted dirt yard and into a side door of the castle.

The dungeons and courtrooms were somewhere Rainier hadn't dared go near as a boy. It was a potentially dangerous place for a child to be exploring, for one, and interrupting a court session would have been just as bad as getting in the way of an irate criminal trying to escape. The guard brought him to a smaller courtroom and forced Rainier to his knees in the center of the floor, then stood ominously over him. The dais at the front of the room had a long table with a half-dozen chairs along one side. Only the centermost one was occupied. Prince Henry sat there, glaring down at Rainier. On the table in front of Prince Henry sat both glass slippers.

"I have been informed that you were in the possession of a number of stolen goods, in particular the mate to the glass slipper of the woman I have been seeking these last four days. If you want to live to see the sunrise, you will tell me where you stole it from."

Telling the truth wouldn't satisfy Prince Henry, given Prince Henry already believed Rainier had stolen the shoe. A story about helping the poor girl escape before her magic pumpkin carriage was discovered and her dress vanished in a poof of fairy dust, and being given the shoe in thanks, wouldn't fall onto receptive ears.

"Where?" Prince Henry roared out, his voice echoing against the bare walls of the courtroom.

The door opened before Rainier could decide on an answer, and Peyton stepped into the room. He held the door politely for an elderly gentleman to step through, then closed it firmly before looking up.

"Captain, what is the meaning of this?" Prince Henry said sharply.

Peyton's eyes immediately fixed on Rainier, and Rainier saw his eyes widen in shock when he caught sight of the mess that was Rainier's bare skin, but if he allowed emotion to govern his actions, Peyton wouldn't have made captain. The surprise in his expression vanished as quickly as it had appeared, replaced by a blank face. He jogged past Rainier and hopped onto the dais where he picked up a chair and brought it back down for the old man to sit on.

"I am clearing up a misunderstanding," Peyton said to Prince Henry once the old man was situated.

"You are Rainier Osbundsman, are you not?" the old man cut in softly, his voice firm and strong despite his apparent age. At his words, Prince Henry shut his mouth with an abrupt snap and leaned back in his chair with a groan.

"Captain, what is going on?" Prince Henry asked, although this time his voice was much politer.

The old man and Peyton both ignored Prince Henry, which Rainier didn't think was particularly smart, but Prince Henry didn't appear to be annoyed. Rainier turned his attention to the old man. The hair on his head was cut short to just above his ears, and it was as white as snow without even a hint of gray to darken it. His eyebrows, on the other hand, were as dark black as Rainier's own hair. The eyes below those dark brows were the exact same color as Rainier's own eyes, and suddenly Rainier knew exactly who this man was.

He hadn't seen his grandfather since he was three years old, and he remembered the experience as only a quick flash of an older man smiling gently at him. Still, Rainier didn't have any doubts that the Duke of Canebria, Sebastian Osbundsman, was sitting there.

"Answer the question please," His Grace said softly, his voice still firm with what felt like steel.

"That is my name," Rainier replied, trying and failing to make his voice sound just as strong.

The duke looked up over Rainier's head toward Prince Henry. A look over at Peyton showed that Peyton was also looking at Prince Henry, so Rainier joined them. Prince Henry had one hand covering his eyes as if he were trying to stave off a headache.

"You didn't have to make a big production of this, Captain," Prince Henry finally said as he removed his hand and sat forward in his seat. His gray eyes fixed on Rainier, and this time, the sharpness in them wasn't dangerous to Rainier's continued health, although it was certainly not a pleased look. "I suspect you know the first part of this story, but if you already knew the ending, you would not be sitting here in chains," Prince Henry continued to Rainier. "The Duke of Canebria had two sons. The eldest was his heir, as is the tradition. He married the daughter of a marquis, and for the next twenty years they failed to have any children at all despite the efforts of multiple doctors. Two months ago, they died in a carriage accident. You remember the midsummer storm, I'm sure. They were caught out in it. It appears a wheel broke, their horses slipped on a muddy slope, and the carriage turned over. They were likely killed instantly."

Rainier did remember that storm because it had flooded the city. Anyone with a basement or first-floor home had lost everything, some even their lives, and the markets had needed to be rebuilt completely. Commerce had ground to a halt, and Rainier had been unbelievably glad of his attic room, as it had kept him far away from the riots that had resulted. Of course, during the storm, he had been certain the wind would tear the roof off at any moment and he and Mabli would be carried away to their deaths.

"The duke's younger son had died years earlier from a fever that had swept the castle, but he had managed to have a son before that. Except, to my knowledge, the son died when a section of shelving in the library collapsed five years ago." A touch of suspicion entered his voice as he said the last bit, but then he glanced behind Rainier to the duke and Peyton and his expression cleared again. "You would not have the support of my captain or the duke if you were not, in fact, the heir apparent."

All of a sudden what Prince Henry was saying hit Rainier, and his mouth dropped open. His uncle was dead without an heir. His father was dead, and Rainier was his only child. Somehow he, a lowly thief, was the heir to an entire duchy. There were only two of them in the entire kingdom, and one was going to be his someday.

It was a completely ridiculous, utterly preposterous notion, and yet there his grandfather sat looking sad but firm in his conviction.

"I would like to get Rainier a proper shirt, some dinner, and into bed," his grandfather said after the room remained silent for a long moment. The guard immediately stooped to remove the restraints and helped Rainier stand on his numbed knees.

"Wait, please," Prince Henry said, his voice pleading. "Please, I need to know where you got this slipper. I need to find Ella. Please."

"She gave it to me as a thank-you for helping her and because she couldn't keep it safe where she lives," Rainier said, and this time the words flowed easily.

"So you don't know where she is." Prince Henry shook his head and collapsed back into his seat like the air had been let out of his body.

"I don't know exactly, but when we parted ways, the carriage was traveling toward the countryside properties of the wealthy nobles that don't wish to live in the city. You should check those." Prince Henry was on his feet and heading toward the door with the shoes in hand before Rainier finished speaking, but Rainier knew there was more to say. "Your Majesty," he called after Prince Henry before he could run through the door. "She is likely a servant."

That stopped Prince Henry in his tracks. "What do you mean? The way she spoke, her ability with the waltz... She was far too educated to be a servant." The yearning in his voice told Rainier that Prince Henry didn't really care whether she was a servant or a queen. He was simply trying to piece the facts he already knew together with what Rainier was providing.

"I feel she might be like me, Your Majesty," Rainier said as he tried to explain. "She was born to privilege and raised correctly for a good portion of her life, but thanks to the machinations of a conniving stepparent, she was forced into servitude. Please, you should be careful how you approach her family. They may try to harm her if they think it will benefit them."

Prince Henry nodded at Rainier to show he understood, but he turned to Peyton. "Captain, ready your men. We will search every single house in the countryside tomorrow until we find her."

"I have one last question to ask, Your Majesty," Peyton said before Prince Henry could try to leave the room again. He looked at Rainier and then said, "Who whipped you? Who gave you those terrible burns?" Rainier's chest, back, and arms were bare, revealing the worst of the damage done to him, to everyone's eyes.

There was only one answer to give: "The man who killed me. The one who pushed over an entire set of shelving in the library in an attempt to silence me, and then, no doubt, dressed some poor, dark-haired servant's body in my clothes and claimed I was dead."

"Max did all this to you?" Peyton said, his voice low and dark with promised retribution.

"He married my mother when I was six, and I didn't escape him until I was sixteen. Ten years is a long time for a bad man to do a lot of bad things."

"And here I am, your supposed closest friend, and I didn't even notice." This time Peyton's voice sounded anguished.

"Of course you didn't," Rainier answered firmly. He walked over to Peyton and tentatively reached out to touch Peyton's shoulder. "You had just begun the real training as a guardsman when things became really bad. Your days were spent learning to fight, and any free moment you spent passed out in your rack from utter exhaustion. There wasn't anything you could do, Peyt, I promise you that."

"Maybe not then, but there's certainly something I can do now," Peyton replied with an angry growl in his voice.

"I give you my full permission. Get that bastard behind bars, and then get your men ready. We depart at 0600 hours." Prince Henry finally completed his exit of the courtroom. The guard from the dungeon followed after.

Peyton gently rested his own hand over the one Rainier had left on his shoulder. "I want to make amends, and I want to actually talk to you, but my duties have to come first this time."

"I understand." Rainier had always understood. That was why when he was desperately hoping that someone—anyone—would save him from his stepfather, he had never blamed Peyton for not coming to the rescue.

"Thank you," Peyton said softly. He carefully squeezed Rainier's hand once before pulling away and hurrying out the door.

That left Rainier in the room alone with his grandfather. "I believe we also have a lot to discuss," his grandfather said, "but I also think we both have had enough surprises for one day. Some fresh clothes, food, and a good night of rest should come first. We will speak tomorrow. Until then, I could use your strong arm to help me get back to my room." He held out a hand for Rainier to take, and when Rainier obeyed, he helped lift his grandfather to his feet. Together they slowly left the courtroom and headed to the main halls of the castle.

*

Rainier couldn't believe what he was wearing. His breeches were of thick cloth suitable for the coming autumn. He had on proper stockings and shoes that actually fit his feet. His shirt had embroidery that enhanced his jacket. Rainier didn't remember the last time he had owned a jacket that matched the shirt he was wearing.

The ensemble had been waiting for him when he finally convinced himself to roll out of the sinfully soft bed he had been given in a second bedroom of his grandfather's suite of rooms. He had gotten dressed quickly and come downstairs to the front hall, unable to help wanting to be part of the party going out to search the countryside that day.

Rainier knew there were probably dozens of other things he needed to do. For one, this heir-apparent business no doubt needed to be smoothed over, or at the very least spoken about. As the child of the second son, Rainier had only technically been in line for the role. He had expected to follow in his father's footsteps as a librarian—although he probably wouldn't have been given the head librarian position, as that would have gone to someone else's second or third son who was lacking even a courtesy title. He didn't know what his responsibilities entailed, nor did he have the proper training to undertake them.

He also needed to know what had happened with his stepfather. Peyton had gone to likely arrest Max, and Rainier would probably have to speak or write some sort of statement about that.

And yet, instead of staying in the soft bed that was still calling his name, instead of waiting for his grandfather to wake so they could speak, and instead of working to figure out his role in his stepfather's case, Rainier was standing awkwardly in the front doorway, looking out at the soldiers and horses waiting patiently in formation. There was no sign of Peyton or Prince Henry, but it wasn't quite six o'clock yet.

"Lord Rainier! How was the rest of your evening?" Prince Henry called as he and Peyton descended the staircase from the second floor and joined him at the door. Peyton was wearing another formal-looking uniform in dark burgundy red that brought out the tan color of his skin in the scant dawn light. Rainier had to tear his eyes away to bow politely to Prince Henry.

"Still rather overwhelming, Your Majesty," Rainier replied.

Prince Henry smiled at him, and his eyes were kind with understanding. "You will learn your new role, just as we all did." He turned to look at Peyton, who hadn't taken his own eyes off Rainier in his new clothes that actually fit. "It seems my captain likes the sight of you in men's clothes as well as in a dress. I suspect we will soon be calling him Lord Peyton when he marries you, Lord Rainier?"

Peyton's cheeks darkened in a blush as he dropped his eyes to the ground. A moment later he looked back up at Rainier, and there was a slight smile tilting up his lips that told Rainier Peyton was certainly interested in the idea of having a relationship with him. Rainier couldn't help smiling back.

"There are logistics of your having an heir, of course," Prince Henry continued, "but I'm sure the duke and you will figure out some sort of arrangement." He grinned at them both before striding toward the door. "It appears you are interested in joining us," he added when he was standing next to Rainier and looking out at the assembled soldiers. "Given Ella gave you her second shoe to hold for safekeeping, it seems only right that you be the one to return it to her." He clapped Rainier companionably on the shoulder before walking outside. "Bring another horse for Lord Rainier."

Peyton stopped where Prince Henry had been standing a moment before and looked down at Rainier. "You do look better like this than in a dress," he said softly. He gestured toward the three horses being brought up the drive, so Rainier started walking with him.

"I was only in a dress to sneak into the ball," Rainier explained. He couldn't help ducking his head down in shame for a brief moment, but then he firmed his resolve and stood tall. He had done it to survive, and there was no shame in that.

Peyton let out a low chuckle. "Yes, well, the nobles will have their property returned, so the whole matter should be ended."

"What are you going to tell them about the thief?" Rainier asked as they reached the horses. He patted the nearest one on the neck.

"The truth, of course," Prince Henry said. He was already sitting in the saddle and the box of shoes was in his lap—although Rainier hadn't seen him carrying it earlier. One of the soldiers must have been holding it for him. "The thief was apprehended and the crown is satisfied with the results. No one else needs to know more. Now, let's be off."

Technically, Rainier knew how to ride a horse, but the last time he had been on one was before his father's death. He got his foot into the stirrup and his butt onto the saddle and was glad when one of the guards attached a lead rein to the bridle. He must have looked like a sack of potatoes sitting on the horse's back, but the potential indignity of being led like a child was better than trying to figure out how to ride and falling off.

Peyton dropped back to give him helpful reminders as they rode through the city and out the gate toward the countryside. By the time they reached the first house about a mile or so from the city, Rainier thought he had it figured out. He stayed outside while Prince Henry, Peyton, and a handful of guards thoroughly searched the property and then tried the shoe on every maiden they located, be she servant or noble. It didn't matter how slim or wide the women's feet were, the shoe magically did not fit any of them.

The guard removed the leading rein as they rode on to the next house, and Rainier was able to guide his horse on his own. Admittedly, he was in the middle of a formation and it would have been difficult for the horse to get free and wander off, so he wouldn't call himself suddenly proficient, but he was improving.

At the fourth house, however, he had to dismount so he could wander away from the soldiers for a moment to discreetly rub his bottom, which was starting to get sore, and to stretch out his thighs. The house itself was an old manor that looked like it had recently suffered some hardship. The ivy on the walls was overgrown, but not so much it was starting to destroy the mortar. What was once likely a manicured lawn had been turned into rows of vegetables, which were no doubt meant to feed the family and to sell in the market for some extra coin for the household. Rainier appreciated the practicality of it.

"See, I told you true love always wins out," Mabli said as zi flitted down from a tree overhead. "You're much happier now with the prospect of love in your life than you were on your own. You have your grandfather whom I'm certain you will learn to love, and you have your Peyton."

"Mab!" Rainier gasped quietly so he didn't alert the guards that he wasn't alone. "I could have used some of your magic last night."

Mabli laughed, zir body shaking in the air, although zi didn't drop from zir position in front of Rainier's face. "A little bit of magic might help get things started, but what really matters isn't the magic. It's what's already inside you and inside the people who matter to you. See, you stayed strong and look at where you are now, and Peyton loves you, so he made certain you were safe when he somehow found out you were stuck in a dungeon."

"Somehow?" Rainier asked, but he knew Mabli wasn't going to answer.

Mabli flew toward the garden at the side of the house, then turned around to wave at Rainier to signal him to follow. "It's time to get this girl's happily ever after completed as well."

"Were you her fairy godparent too?" Rainier asked as he carefully walked down the dirt path that had been maintained between two rows of leafy pumpkins.

"Goodness, no," Mabli replied instantly. "We can only handle the magic for one child at a time. Unfortunately, the fairy that was here thought the ball would be enough and didn't stay to ensure her task was completed. It's always the young ones that are so flashy, you know. I'll have to track her down and explain everything she missed."

They stopped outside of a small storage shed that was likely where the wheelbarrow and other farming implements were kept. There was a padlock on the door. Rainier hadn't been able to leave his lock picks behind—a force of habit he appreciated as he carefully knelt and began fitting them into the lock.

"Are you going to leave me now that I've found my happily ever after?" he asked Mabli. He kept his attention firmly on the lock because he didn't want Mabli to see his sad expression. Mabli was his friend, and Rainier would sorely miss zir.

Mabli let out a sigh and drifted down to land on Rainier's shoulder. "I've been around a very long time, and I've never stayed with a charge as long as I have you. I will have to go help other children in need, you understand, but I think I might like to return to your side in between jobs. I can make sure your children and your children's children don't need a little bit of magic to help them on their way too."

"I'd like that, Mab," Rainier replied, his voice slightly choked with suppressed tears. The lock popped open, so Rainier quickly composed himself before pulling the door open.

The girl—Ella, he believed her name was—was sitting in the middle of the dark shed. She stood as the door opened and carefully stepped out into the light. Ella might have been wearing a drab blue servant's dress and she might have had what looked like dirt, soot, and tears streaked across her face, but somehow she still managed to look regal in the middle of a pumpkin patch.

She blinked at him for a long moment before recognition lit her eyes and she smiled at him.

"Your prince has been looking for you," Rainier told her. Ella's head was already turned toward the noise being made by the horses and soldiers waiting at the front of the house. Rainier held out his arm, and she placed one delicate hand on his wrist, and together they walked down the path through the pumpkins.

Rainier could see Peyton shaking his head to tell the soldiers that they hadn't fit the shoe at this house as he and Ella drew closer. Prince Henry was descending the front steps.

The mistress of the house said, "No, Your Highness. There are no more maidens living in this household," just as Peyton looked up and saw them. He waved toward Prince Henry, who also turned to look, and they both hurried over.

Prince Henry knelt in the middle of the front drive while Rainier and Peyton steadied Ella, and Prince Henry removed her rough country shoe himself.

The glass slipper slid onto her foot like it had been made for it—which, technically, it had—and Prince Henry stood to take Ella into his arms. Rainier and Peyton politely looked away and their eyes caught.

Rainier immediately knew that while they might not be kissing in the yard with a magical shoe on one of their feet, their happily ever after was just as certain.

THUNDERBIRD

The rumble of thunder far off in the distance made Haven's heart beat just a little faster. Swallowing hard, he wiped beads of nervous sweat from his forehead. The sky had been clear when he left work ten minutes ago. The bright beauty of the setting sun on the first really warm spring day of the season had convinced him to forego the five-minute bus ride in favor of a fifteen-minute walk in the warm air. Apparently, he should have paid closer attention to the weather instead.

A second roll of booming thunder sounded, this time closer. Haven jumped slightly and started walking faster. A glance over his shoulder showed towering, black storm clouds building ominously a few miles away. The wind was picking up, which meant the clouds would be moving swiftly overhead.

Haven absentmindedly fingered the white stripe of hair amid the rest of the black strands growing over his right eye as he tried to keep his breathing even so he didn't pass out. He wasn't afraid of thunder; rather he feared what the thunder gave voice to: the vibration of molecules caused by an electrical discharge. A lightning strike.

He'd been struck on a day almost exactly like this one. The thunderclouds had gathered in the distance, the wind quickly blowing them overhead. Haven had foolishly decided to make the dash across the quad from the building his classroom was in to his dorm. He had another final to study for and didn't have the time to wait around for the storm to pass. He hadn't made it.

When he woke up in the hospital, the doctors told him what had happened. Lightning had struck the classroom building just as he reached the foot of the stairs. Students said a metal flagpole sticking out of the building attracted the lightning. Haven had been hit with a side flash, a bit of electrical current that branched off from the main bolt. The doctor said he only suffered minor burns and showed him a photograph of his skull where a light feather pattern of broken capillaries was visible through slightly crispy hair. He probably wouldn't have even passed out from the strike, the doctor marveled, if he wasn't already overstressed and exhausted from finals.

It was a very minor strike—lightning could kill or cause permanent brain and organ damage, so Haven knew just how lucky he was—but that didn't stop Haven from flinching every time thunder rumbled overhead.

The storm was coming faster now. Haven could taste rain in the air even though he couldn't yet feel the drops on his skin. He probably only had mere minutes before the storm let loose over his head, and he would much prefer to be inside before that happened.

There were two options for getting home. The first was to stay on the sidewalk. He had two more blocks to go before he crossed the street and turned right. Then he had another two long blocks to walk to his house. The second option was to take the path just ahead. It led through the reservoir: a bit of undeveloped, low-lying land set aside by the town solely for the purpose of collecting excess rain in order to prevent floods and water damage to the nearby neighborhoods. The trees in the reservoir were still bare, their buds only beginning to show baby green leaves poking through, but the path was clear. Taking shelter underneath a tree during a storm was idiotic, but it would shave off minutes to his travel time, and the path ended across the street from his house.

When he reached the path, Haven took it. He was hustling as quickly as he could in slacks and shoes. Running was out of the question, but he could and did power walk. The path itself was winding, created to show off the most scenic parts of the forest and to stay on higher ground. Haven had to stay on the path to avoid the small rivers and lakes that filled the reservoir every spring. He clattered across an old wooden bridge, five feet long and the only way across the winter snowmelt that wouldn't also soak his shoes.

The sky overhead was getting darker, and the first droplets of rain were penetrating the branches. It was getting harder to see the path clearly as the sunlight faded and the wind picked up even more. The old leaves still composting from last fall made slithering sounds as the wind blew them around. Haven thought he heard rain hissing against the leaves, too, like the loose pipe letting steam out of his hot water heater had done a few weeks back.

Haven's foot caught on something suddenly, and he lurched, falling to the ground hard. He scrambled to his hands and knees, brushing leaves off his front as he stumbled back to his feet.

Haven had tripped right over a big rock in the middle of the path. Lightning flashed overhead, quickly followed by a boom of thunder. Haven let out an involuntary squeal of fright as he instinctively huddled low to the ground. He had to get home. Now.

He used the rock for leverage to get back to his feet a second time. It was warm under his hand and slightly textured. It didn't feel like any rock Haven had ever held. He bent closer, and in the fading light, he could make out what looked like raised veins of gold crisscrossing the entire surface. It almost looked like a gigantic, minimalist Faberge egg.

Haven carefully picked it up, grunting slightly at the weight. It was about the size of a large melon and shaped like an egg, oval with one pointed end and one more rounded. It fit snugly into the curve of his elbow as he curled one arm around it. Maybe it was just an oddly colored rock, but it also looked like someone's heirloom. Personally, Haven didn't understand why someone would prize what amounted to a gigantic, albeit very fancy, egg. Still, there was probably a child getting a scolding right this moment for taking the Faberge egg out of the house and losing it. He could get a better look at it once he had stronger light and would call the police to find the owner.

Another boom of thunder made Haven jump. He fumbled the egg for a second before he got his fingers locked around it and took off at a jog. His toes cried out from the abuse his shoes were causing, but he didn't care anymore. He probably only had seconds before the storm exploded over his head.

He reached the end of the path without tripping over anything else just as a light drizzle began to soak the ground. He dashed across the street and up the steps of his porch as another gigantic boom of thunder shook the ground and a downpour started. Haven got his keys out of his pocket and fought with the lock one-handed. He dashed inside, panting for breath and shaking, and slammed the door behind him.

He made sure the door was locked and hurried downstairs into the basement where there weren't any windows and he could play loud music to drown out the sounds of the storm. He switched on the lights and music first, then grabbed a couple of the blankets he kept on a nearby cot. He made a quick nest for the egg, so it wouldn't roll anywhere and get damaged, before taking off his shoes and tie and wrapping himself up into another blanket. He huddled in on himself and waited for the storm to pass.

*

The egg was a warm, albeit uncomfortable pillow. Haven didn't know when he had fallen asleep or why he was curled around the egg, but it made for a stiff back and a bruised cheek.

He found the remote and lowered the volume on the music, then listened intently, hoping the storm was over but ready to flinch should he hear something. The blinking clock across the room told him that sometime while he was sleeping the house had lost and regained power. It was resolutely showing midnight on the screen, but a quick glance at the clock on his phone told Haven it was actually almost three in the morning.

After a few too-tense moments waiting and failing to hear an ominous rumble, Haven sighed in relief and turned the music off. He rolled his head side to side as he stood up, trying to work out the tension making his muscles ache. Haven walked two steps away from the cot, planning to head to his own bed, before he turned around to look at the egg still tucked into its nest of blankets.

It was gorgeous, black with jagged lines of gold shot throughout. It almost glowed in the low basement lights, although after Haven blinked a few times he thought the glow faded away. Haven felt ridiculous for feeling bad about leaving the egg behind. He couldn't help laughing at himself for being silly, but he walked back to the bed and gathered the egg into his arms anyway.

Haven lived in a split-level ranch-style house that he could afford thanks to the bank and a recent raise. The basement door was in the lower level where his living room and guest bedroom were located. He walked up the three short steps into the small entryway by the front door. To the left was his small dining room and kitchen; to the right was the hallway that led to an office and the master bedroom. He walked down the hall to his bedroom in the dark. The sky outside the windows didn't show any stars, so it must still be cloudy. He really hoped there wouldn't be any more thunder that night.

The bedroom was mostly neat. He was a bachelor living on his own, so some mess was inevitable, but it was much cleaner than some of his single coworkers' houses. Haven was able to navigate around the small piles of discarded clothes and find his unmade bed without mishap. He fell into the soft covers with a tired groan. It was too much work to get up again to change into pajamas or build a new nest for the egg. Besides, even though the egg was hard it was also warm and somewhat comforting. It was a very strange sort of security blanket to cling to, but Haven didn't want to give it up.

He wriggled out of his dress pants and swiftly unbuttoned his shirt. Once he was left in only his boxers, he pulled a blanket over his head, curled around the egg, and fell quickly back to sleep.

*

It was Saturday. Haven's alarm should be off. Gloriously, he had no plans, which meant he could sleep in and enjoy the day. Thunderstorms might be awful, but the day afterward was always gorgeous. Haven was looking forward to a leisurely breakfast on the back porch, maybe a nap under the warm spring sun, and a chance to walk around his small garden and see how things were budding. Unfortunately, he would have to enjoy all of that on his own. He had a beautiful house and a nice weekend morning, but no one to share it with.

Haven mentally snarled at himself to stop thinking like that. He was going to have a good morning, and sad thoughts like the fact that he hadn't had a boyfriend in years weren't allowed to interfere. Haven pulled his blanket up to his nose, intent on going back to sleep, but the damned alarm sounded again.

The alarm wasn't set to go off on the weekends, but Haven still heard the buzzing and rustling, as if his phone was on vibrate and had gotten stuck underneath a heavy blanket when the alarm went off.

Haven peeled his eyes open with a groan, needing a few more hours of sleep after the late night but also needing to shut off that damned alarm so he could sleep in peace. Light was filtering in through his closed window shades. It made the gold in the egg he was still curled around sparkle slightly. There might be precious stones carefully hidden among the gold, which only made him feel odder about the fact that he was cuddling with a giant shiny rock.

The rustling sound continued, and Haven forced his body to roll over. He blinked in surprise for a few long moments when he saw his phone resting quietly on his nightstand. He rolled over again, toward the noise, and let out a shriek. There was a snake crawling through his blankets!

It looked like a garter snake, small and green with a red stripe down its back, except it also had horns jutting out from the top of its head. In response to Haven's shriek, it lifted itself as high into the air as its small body would allow. Then it hissed, and what looked like a cobra's hood flared behind it. Two fangs jutted out from the snake's mouth, glistening and dripping.

Haven let out another screech and tumbled from his bed. The egg was knocked free in his scramble, and it landed in his lap as he hit the floor and crab walked backward to the door. The snake gently soared off the bed, landing on the carpet with a muffled thump. That wasn't a hood on the back of the snake; it was a pair of wings! Did snakes have wings? Haven couldn't think of any snakes that had them as he kept desperately shuffling away.

The snake appeared to be taking its time, weaving back and forth threateningly as it moved slowly closer, and hissing as if it were laughing at him. Haven left the bedroom and entered the hallway, his back impacting painfully with the wall. He didn't dare turn his body to go down the hallway; if he took his eyes off the snake for even a second, Haven thought that might be his last second alive.

"Give me the egg!" a voice yelled. Haven's eyes were still fixated on the snake; he didn't have time to look at who was shouting. "The egg! Give me the egg!"

Haven fumbled for the egg resting in his lap, lifting it clumsily into the air and toward the insistent voice. The snake's eyes glinted, and the hissing turned from stuttering laughter to a low and ominous threatening hiss. It lunged at Haven, mouth wide and teeth glistening.

The flash of lightning and the window-shaking boom of thunder echoed through the house. While the leaping snake had made him freeze in fear, the thunder had him screaming and curling into a ball around the egg still inexorably clutched in his arms.

It took a few long minutes of shaking and gasping for breath after the thunder before Haven felt safe enough to slowly uncurl. The egg was warm and buzzing faintly, almost as if it were sentient and trying to comfort Haven. He reflexively patted it in thanks, trying not to feel silly for thinking such odd things when the day so far had been beyond odd.

"The child likes you," the voice said sharply, sounding surprised. "But then, you are lightning-kissed."

Haven looked up. There was a burnt spot in his carpet just a few inches from his feet in a slightly serpentine shape. No other sign of the bizarre snake remained. A man was standing next to Haven, frowning at the burnt mark. He was wearing what looked like a cloak of feathers, tied around the neck with a heavy hood hanging down his back. His hair was long, the ends lost in the hood, and black. It looked like it had been streaked blond with bleach by a very inexperienced hair stylist; the streaks were jagged and uneven, some starting midway or ending nowhere near the end of his hair. His cheekbones were very prominent and his skin lightly tanned. He was absolutely gorgeous, Haven's libido supplied eagerly. His smirk, as he quirked his lips upward when Haven continued to stare at him, was even and slightly haughty.

"The child?" Haven asked, scrambling to gather his fear-scattered wits. He was still sitting on the floor, and the stranger had broken into his house and somehow a flying snake had been zapped with lightning. Haven pushed to his feet, the egg still in his arms.

The stranger's nod indicated the egg. "Zephyr and I were bringing the child to the hatching grounds when we were attacked. We lost the child briefly in the melee. Zephyr remained behind to battle while I started searching to the east. Zephyr was going to look in this direction, the west, but when I sensed the child here, I came to join him. Has Zephyr told you where to meet him?"

Haven gaped for a moment. "Who?" he asked, trying to get his thoughts in order in the face of such an odd story. "Who are you and who is Zephyr? What child?"

"You are holding the child, the egg that Zephyr gave to you to protect!" the stranger exclaimed, his scowl deepening as he spoke. "I am Dae, Zephyr's partner!"

"I found the egg in the woods last night when I was trying to beat the thunderstorm home. No one else was around."

"Zephyr wouldn't abandon his most important charge!" Dae sounded incensed at the very thought. "What have you done to him?"

The cloak on Dae's back fluttered as if a stiff wind were blowing through the hall. A rumble of thunder sounded, low, still far off in the distance, yet it was very clearly emanating from nearby. Haven automatically flinched as if lightning had flashed to cause the thunder. It hadn't, but he couldn't help the shiver of fear.

"Where is Zephyr?" Dae hissed. There was thunder in his voice and lightning in his eyes. Haven stared, transfixed, as flash after flash of lightning eerily lit his corneas and outlined his pupils. Dae's eyes were gray, like a cloudy sky, yet they darkened like clouds filling with rain. Every bolt of lightning that flashed made them grow even darker.

When Haven couldn't answer, Dae apparently took it as he wouldn't. He reached out with one hand as more thunder rumbled down the hallway, and gripped Haven around the neck. The hand tingled, and then shot what felt like lightning into Haven's body. Haven gurgled for breath. It felt like he had stuck his finger into an electrical socket and had gotten the cord of whatever he had been trying to plug in wrapped around his neck. He would have screamed if he had breath to do so.

"Where is Zephyr?" Dae repeated with a snarl. He loosened his hand enough that Haven could gulp down small breaths of air, but when Haven didn't have an answer, he tightened his grip again.

It was too much for Haven: the fear making him shake, the electricity running through him, and the lack of air all combined. His head felt woozy and stars exploded behind his eyes. Darkness came slowly, and even Dae's curse as his grip loosened couldn't stop Haven from fainting.

*

Haven was flying. He could see trees soaring past far below him as well as the occasional fluffy cloud. The wind whistled in his ears as he rushed past. It was a decidedly odd sensation, and he wondered why he was having such a weird dream.

There was something clamped around his chest and stomach. If this were a dream, he'd wake up and find his blankets wrapped around his body. Haven looked and didn't find blankets. Instead, he found claws. They were gigantic and scaled, like what he imagined a dragon's would be like. There were talons on the end. He could feel their points poking against his side. Haven was still mostly naked, so it hurt a lot.

In the other claw, which was hanging to Haven's right, was the egg. He twisted around to look up, but only saw a lot of huge black feathers rustling in the wind attached to the claw. A gigantic bird was carrying him!

Haven let his weight drop back into the claws, which made one of them prick harder into his side. It hurt like he was being pinched, which was supposed to wake someone up from a dream. The scene didn't change though. Nothing changed. He was still being held in the air by a giant bird flying over a forest. He wasn't dreaming!

Terrified, Haven let out a scream and thrashed in the talons holding him tight. He didn't want the creature to let him go, because he would fall to a horrible death, but at the same time he couldn't stand being held like this for much longer.

"Put me down!" Haven yelled helplessly. "Please, put me down!"

"We're almost there," Dae's voice growled. "Stop squirming." Dae wasn't anywhere Haven could see, and yet he sounded close enough they could both have been held in the same scaled grip. It startled Haven into freezing for a moment, scared that he might knock a companion free to plummet to the ground below.

A pair of huge wings flapped above, pumping the air and angling their flight slightly to the left. A crack of thunder sounded out of the blue sky, making Haven shiver for yet another reason. They started descending. The tops of the trees slowly grew closer as the wings beat over Haven's head. Every downbeat was accompanied by a crack of thunder. The wings were so large they were displacing the air in much the same way a bolt of lightning did. It still made Haven flinch, but he was also growing used to it. Thunder on a day that was cloudless and blue just wasn't so scary, especially when compared to being carried in the air by a giant bird. Haven was pretty damn freaked out about that, and the thunder couldn't compete.

"Wind Rider, you made it!" A second bird flew into view, lifting up from somewhere in the woods below. His wings made the air crack beneath them, too, but it sounded more like gunfire in comparison to the bird carrying Haven. "And you're carrying a human?" he gasped. "We need to bring him to the chamber!"

"There's no time, Breeze Watcher," Dae disagreed. "The egg is hatching. I must go directly to the hatching grounds."

Breeze Watcher nodded. "I'll inform the elders." His wings dipped and he turned abruptly, flying back into the depths of the forest below.

Haven looked over at the egg and saw that it was quaking in the bird's grip. The jagged streaks of gold were glowing slightly, although it could have been the wind in Haven's eyes that made it look like that. He hoped it was the wind, but nothing about any of this was normal. He was still shaking, and without the distraction of the movement of the egg, he would probably also still be screaming.

What he had foolishly thought was someone's lost Faberge egg was actually a living egg belonging to the gigantic bird carrying him. The egg was apparently about to hatch, and Dae was bringing it to safety. Perhaps Dae was riding on the back of the bird. Maybe the bird was the missing Zephyr?

They were dropping quickly now. Haven's ears popped and the rushing wind stung his eyes. He could have reached out and touched the tops of the trees if he wanted as they swooped low over the forest. The trees were tall and leafy, already fully bloomed despite the early season. The bird tucked its wings and pulled its feet closer to its body. Soft feathers brushed against Haven's face and body. The bird dove and Haven let out an involuntary scream of fright. They slid through the trees easily, barely a branch cracking in their passage, and through a wide cave entrance that appeared suddenly as they broke through the tree line. They emerged from the cave a few minutes later into bright sunlight. The forest had vanished, replaced by high walls of stone with cave openings spaced evenly around.

It looked similar to the pictures of dormant volcanoes that Haven had seen in a nature magazine once. There was a blue lake in the basin below, and the cone was blasted open. It was an unwelcoming place for humans, but there were so many black birds flying idly around that it must be a perfect home for them.

The bird flew toward a cave opening slightly larger than the rest, again tucking his wings to dart through. This cave was even longer, and the bird was losing momentum. Haven was worried they would have to stop and walk, but they burst out into sunlight just before that could happen. They were inside what looked like another dormant volcano. This one had a thick layer of sand in the basin. Six birds were already sitting in a circle in the sand. The bird carrying Haven flapped its wings twice to stabilize and then gently circled until he awkwardly landed, the ground hitting him in the butt directly underneath his tail feathers so he didn't crush the cargo in his feet. The bird's feathers thankfully blocked the resulting spray of sand, but Haven still flinched at the impact.

A zap ran through Haven, much like the electricity Dae had zapped him with earlier. The claws around him began to shrink, as did the bird above him. Haven's feet touched the warm sand, but his legs didn't have the strength to hold him up. He sank to the ground in a boneless heap, panting in fear.

The electricity faded away as the bird let go of Haven. He was still twitching slightly, but the buzzing was gone from his ears and behind his eyes. Haven looked up and watched as the bird shrank to human size, shivered, then split down the middle. Dae's arms poked through the seam, and his hands pulled his cloak away from his body and the hood off his face. His cloak of feathers settled into place on his back. No sign of the bird he had been remained, but Haven knew what he had seen.

The egg had landed on Dae's other side. He quickly bent and gently buried it in the sand. Once that was done, he reached out and gripped Haven's wrist in one hand. He yanked Haven backward, out of the circle of waiting birds and farther back until hard rocks began to take over from sand underfoot. Haven stumbled over a rock, his feet crying from the abuse. He fell into Dae's side and involuntarily wrapped his arms around Dae's middle to catch his balance.

Dae's body was warm and tingly, as if lightning ran through his veins and passed via his skin to whatever he was touching. There was muscle there, firm underneath Haven's hands as Haven scrambled to push away and get his feet underneath him. His traitorous hands wanted to cop another feel of that soft skin over muscle, but luckily he stepped on another rock and sense returned with the onset of pain.

"What's going on?" Haven asked softly, aware that everyone, Dae included, was staring raptly at the lump in the sand where the egg was buried. "Where am I?" His voice was shaky with nerves, and his heart was beating heavily with a combination of aborted lust and fear. The fear was winning, however, as he glanced around at the place to where he had been kidnapped.

The egg was shaking in the sand, pieces of it being revealed as the sand was knocked off the top. Haven didn't know what the point of burying the egg was because the first cracking noise only occurred once all the sand was already gone. All of the birds including Dae started humming, each letting a different, complementary note reverberate. The noise echoed around the sandy basin, combining and growing until Haven couldn't hear the egg cracking.

A bolt of light—of lightning, Haven realized—flashed from the egg. Haven didn't even flinch; he was getting so inured to things that had scared him the most only mere hours ago that he almost didn't recognize himself. He was barely even shaking anymore at being taken from home by a bird that shape-shifted into a human.

All of a sudden, the humming stopped. In the abrupt silence, Haven could finally hear the egg creaking and groaning. There was only quiet for a brief moment before another flash of lightning lit the space. With an almighty crack, a large portion of the egg broke free and fell to the sand below.

Two tiny human hands popped out and gripped the edge of the egg. A small bird's head followed after. The baby tumbled out of the egg, hitting the ground hard. The hood from the cloak of feathers hanging down the baby's back lifted away from her face, revealing a human head. To Haven's eyes, the baby didn't look like an infant just born. Instead, if he hadn't known better, he would have pegged the child as a one- or two-year-old. The egg had been large enough to fill the cradle of his elbow, and the child was just a little smaller than that. None of the birds seemed surprised about it though, so this must be normal for whatever species they were.

The baby let out a peeping cry as she slowly levered herself off the sand and onto her hands and knees. The air felt expectant around her; each of the birds in the circle leaned forward slightly as if they were waiting for something. The baby crawled, still crying, toward the side of the circle closest to Haven. The birds on the far side of the circle slumped back when it became clear the baby wasn't going to crawl to them.

She drew close to two birds and they both reached an expectant wing forward so she could grab on, but the baby continued to crawl without noticing. She passed underneath those wings and beyond the circle. The baby was crawling directly at Haven, he realized. The sand quickly became rocky underneath her knees, and her peeping cries grew louder with the hurt.

Dae knelt so he was eye level with the baby. "The Elders are over there, youngling," he insisted. "Go choose your Tribe."

The baby ignored him. Haven was forced to kneel, too, when she reached his bare feet and flopped down in front of him in exhaustion. She peeped imperiously up at him, and Haven couldn't help reaching out and scooping her gently into his arms.

Her body was warm, but it lacked the tingling electricity he felt from Dae. Haven would have said she was running a fever if he didn't know better.

"Should I take her back over there?" Haven asked.

"It is instinct," an old woman said. Her cloak of feathers was thrown back, and she was struggling to her human feet on shaky legs. "The younglings are born, and they already know which Elder to approach to begin their training in that Elder's Tribe. We have never had a youngling purposefully not choose a Tribe, but there must be a reason for it." Her back was bent severely to the point that one of the other Elders, a man not much younger than she was, had to help her across the sand.

When she finally reached Haven, she studied the baby slumbering peacefully in his arms and then Haven himself. Her eyes were clear and focused despite her age, a deep brown color that seemed to see everything.

"You are lightning-kissed?" she asked, her eyes on the white streak of hair falling over his forehead. "At least Dae and Zephyr did not bring an ordinary human to our nest." One knobby and shaking hand reached out to tug on that specific bit of hair. "The youngling has chosen you; that is clear. Very well, you are welcome here to raise your child. Accommodations will be made for your flightless status." She turned to Dae. Her eyes grew even more piercing for a moment as she studied Dae, but they gentled after a long moment. "You did what you had to do by bringing a human to our nest. You are forgiven for the transgression. Now, tell me, where is Zephyr of Tribe Storm Fighter?"

"I request permission to go in search of Zephyr," Dae said formally. "My duty to the Tribe has been completed." He sounded strained, as if regardless of the answer he would be flying away to locate his missing partner.

The Elder no doubt saw that. "I grant permission, but you must take this human with you. Zephyr must have disappeared in the human territories, and the human will provide direction and instruction."

"I can't take the youngling with me!" Dae gasped, looking at Haven like he was a bug that needed to be stepped on. Haven's lingering libido was crushed on the spot.

The old woman laughed. "Ah, Dae, you know as well as I that a wet nurse is waiting. She will care for the youngling until the child is strong. All we need from the human at this moment is a name for the youngling, and then you can be off."

All of the Elders and Dae turned to look at Haven expectantly. He had to name the child? She was sleeping peacefully in his arms, her human face pressed into his elbow and her cloak of feathers pressed softly against his chest. She was cute, for a baby, and she had apparently chosen him to raise her. Was he now her father? Haven had never expected to have kids. After his parents died, his father from cancer and his mother from a car accident a few years later, there hadn't been any further pressure for grandkids. As a gay man, Haven hadn't really given any thought to his future family or if he might eventually choose to adopt a child or find a surrogate mother. He would need a long-term partner or a husband before those thoughts could even begin to manifest. Yet, in his arms was the baby girl that was apparently his.

"My mother's name was Aira. It means 'of the wind.'" Aira was an American name—it hadn't come from Europe or anywhere overseas. It seemed appropriate for whatever First Nation species the bird shape-shifters were.

"Aira is a beautiful name," the Elder woman agreed with a smile. "Now, we will bring Aira to the wet nurse, and you and Dae shall be off. Do bring Zephyr back to us. He is my grand-nephew by blood and by Tribe, and I would not like to see him lost to the horned scourge."

"Thank you, Elder Storm Fighter," Dae said. He sounded far too relieved for someone just interested in finding his work partner. Haven forced the last lingering vestiges of attraction away from his heart. Dae was clearly already spoken for, and Haven wasn't interested in getting between someone else's relationship.

They walked slowly through the tunnel Dae had flown so quickly through just a few minutes earlier. Haven looked down at Aira, bemused. He was a father, as simple as that, and he was still totally flummoxed about it. Aira was still sleeping peacefully; her workout reaching him across the sand had exhausted her. She was nestled in her feathers, using them as both blanket and pillow.

"What are you guys?" Haven asked, wondering how a human creature could be born with feathers and shape-shift into a bird.

"We are Thunderbirds," Elder Storm Fighter replied.

Thunderbird was a Native American term, one Haven had only heard of maybe once in his life in a high school American history class. He thought they were gigantic birds that brought thunderstorms, but he had little doubt that he was woefully undereducated on the subject.

Elder Storm Fighter apparently read his ignorance on his face because she started explaining. "Long ago, the Sun became angry with the people of Earth and sent an illness to kill them all. The Sun halted the rain and blazed strongly so nothing could quell the disease running through all the human Tribes. The Tribes prayed to the spirits of the water for aid, and a horned serpent emerged from the depths. He promised to vanquish the Sun and bring life back to the Tribes. He failed. A simple rattlesnake took his place and succeeded where the mighty horned serpent was impotent. So the serpent retreated to the depths of the waters, and hate festered within his heart. When he again felt the strength to emerge, his goodness had faded entirely. His very breath brought back the illness to the Tribes, and he killed with impunity. Again the Tribes prayed, and this time the Thunderbirds heard them.

"The Thunderbirds were once human before we found our feathers and took to the skies. We swore to help our flightless brethren defeat the great horned serpent and bring peace back to the Tribes. The first of the Storm Fighter Tribe struck a mighty blow of lightning against the serpent in the battle, hitting the seventh spot below the head where the serpent's heart is located. Yet, the serpent's heart had turned to stone in his hate and he was merely wounded. We retreated to our separate nests to recuperate until the battle might recommence. Small skirmishes, like the one you encountered, occur often, and we hope that one day the great horned serpent might be vanquished."

Elder Storm Fighter finished her story just as they emerged from the tunnel. The sun was bright, reflecting off the clear water filling the basin below. Birds flew overhead and basked in the sun on large ledges in front of the numerous cave openings. A woman was waiting by the cave entrance, her feathers carefully pulled backward so her arms were free. She held them out for Aira without even the slightest hesitation when she saw who held the baby.

"Mona Breath Giver, welcome," Elder Storm Fighter said formally. "We present you Aira and her father..." She paused and then chuckled to herself. "I never asked for your name, Lightning-Kissed Human."

Haven shrugged. He hadn't expected her to ask, considering he was just a human in her eyes. "My name is Haven Winnow."

"Her father, Haven Winnow," Elder Storm Fighter finished with a nod.

"I take upon myself the responsibility of Aira of the Winnow Tribe," Mona Breath Giver said formally. "She shall grow strong and hale under my care."

Haven passed Aira over to Mona with a pang. She had been named his daughter, yet he had barely even held her before having to give her away. He was surprised at how attached he had become to the idea of being her father in such a short amount of time. As much as Haven might have liked to see where Aira would be staying or to learn more about Mona and the Thunderbirds Aira would be staying with, Dae was grumbling low in his throat with impatience. He wanted to find Zephyr badly, and Haven was holding him up.

Aira would be well taken care of, but there was no guarantee that Zephyr was. Haven nodded his thanks to Mina and turned to Dae.

"We should go back to my house. I need clothes if we're going around the human world, and I found the egg in the forest right near there. There might be a clue of Zephyr's whereabouts."

"Fine," Dae grunted. He stepped back to get enough room before pulling his cloak around his shoulders and the hood over his head. A smaller bird, slightly misshapen for its human height and thinness, appeared where Dae had stood. It grew in size quickly, filling out until width matched height and the gigantic bird stood in front of Haven again. Dae held out one clawed foot. "Climb on. It's easier to carry you if you can hold on yourself."

Haven stepped onto Dae's clawed foot, found a grip in his thick feathers, and pulled himself up onto Dae's back. It took a little situating before he found a spot that didn't impede Dae's wings, but once he had, Haven buried his fingers in Dae's soft feathers to hold on.

Dae flapped his wings twice, stirring the dirt below them and forcing Mona to turn her back so Aira was protected, and then he threw himself into the air. Haven gasped and tried not to pull on the feathers in his hands. He huddled close to Dae's back as wind buffeted him.

They rose quickly and flew through the tunnel leading out of the mountain swiftly. The blasted volcano vanished beneath the forest until all Haven could see was the original image he had woken up to just a mere hour ago. Flying was totally different this time. For one thing, he knew what was going on. Somewhat. The entire Thunderbird concept was still defined a little shakily for him, but he had seen Dae change from a human to a bird. He was touching Dae's soft feathers, sitting on his back, and feeling the air rush past his face as Dae flew. He knew he was on a mission to help another Thunderbird named Zephyr that Dae had a deep relationship with. The other side of the coin was that he had woken up hanging from a gigantic bird's claw like prey snatched away to be torn apart for dinner. Luckily, he had been welcomed by Elder Storm Fighter and was hoping to help the Thunderbirds. It made a big difference.

Flying back to Haven's home didn't take nearly as long as he thought it would. Dae's wings were strong, cracking with the power of thunder with every beat, and they soared through the air like a rocket. Haven didn't know how many miles they traveled, but it wasn't more than an hour before he started to see the tops of the skyscrapers of the city ahead.

It took another twenty minutes before they were flying low over familiar neighborhoods. Haven didn't see anyone below pointing incredulously at the sky, which confused him for a few moments until he realized there must be some more magic at play keeping them hidden. Still, the thunder from Dae's wings had the few pedestrians Haven could make out clutch at their umbrellas and glance instinctively up at the few clouds in the sky even if they couldn't actually see Dae.

"You found the egg in the forest?" Dae asked, twisting his head around until Haven could see his human gray eyes peeking out between thick feathers. His beak didn't move as he spoke, but the words were clear.

Haven located the reservoir near his house, the budding trees still bleak and bare below. "That's mine, the small one there," he explained, pointing over Dae's shoulder. "I found the egg right in the middle of the path. It wasn't hidden or anything."

Dae growled under his breath. "The damned snakes must have been carrying it when you interrupted them. They can't have gotten far with the weight of the egg and of Zephyr. I'll drop you off at your house. Get dressed and meet me in the woods." He turned abruptly, dropping hastily and landing in the small yard in front of Haven's house. Haven quickly climbed down, and Dae took off with a gust of wind and a crack of thunder.

The front door was unlocked, which was good because Haven didn't have his key tucked away in his boxers. It was dark and quiet inside. Haven hurried to his bedroom, carefully stepped over the burnt spot in the doorway, and found a pair of jeans that were mostly clean lying on the floor. He yanked the pants up his legs and did up the button fly. All he had to find was a T-shirt and his keys and he could join Dae in the woods.

A sharp pain radiated from Haven's left ankle. He staggered and his vision fluttered. He didn't feel his knees hit the ground, but he saw the tiny snake that slithered out of his jeans cuff before everything went black.

*

A thump and a pained groan woke Haven. His head felt fuzzy, and it took a few blinks for his eyes to clear of gunk before he could see. Haven was lying slumped on his own basement floor, legs and arms akimbo as if he had been unceremoniously dropped and left where he lay. It took a few uncomfortable seconds for Haven to untangle himself. His limbs didn't quite want to cooperate, as if whatever he had been drugged with hadn't entirely worn off. He would manage to get one leg situated only to have to start over again when he kept falling over while trying to move the other.

Soft chuckling off to Haven's right made him freeze in place and turn his head.

"Don't stop now," the man lying on the floor next to the small cot Haven had slept in not even twenty-four hours ago said with a grin. His teeth were bloody and his face swollen. One of his bright blue eyes was almost totally obscured by a heavy bruise over his inflamed cheek. "That's the best damned thing I've seen in hours."

"Wha—" Haven coughed, trying to clear his throat and move his vocal chords, which were obeying about as strongly as the rest of his body.

"It'll take at least twenty more minutes before the muscle relaxer in their venom wears off," the man continued. "You're lucky you were only bitten by a small one. The bigger ones can kill just by licking your skin." Haven let out a shudder. "So, how did a human get mixed up in all this?" he asked, then paused sheepishly. "Wait, you probably still can't talk. Tell me later."

Until the man had described Haven specifically as a human, Haven hadn't paid any extra attention to the black mass half lying across the man's legs. It wasn't a blanket like Haven had assumed; rather a very ragged cloak of feathers lay there. Some feathers were missing and others were broken, but it very clearly belonged to a Thunderbird.

"Zeph—" Haven tried to speak again, hoping to force out the name of who he thought he was speaking with.

"Zephyr, that's me," Zephyr said with another grin. Even with the bruises he was a gorgeous man, easily the equal of Dae in looks. Haven had to remind himself they were a pair before he said or did something stupid. "If you know that, then Dae must be nearby. That idiot. I'm the Storm Fighter; he's only a Wind Rider. I fight while he flies. Did he at least get the egg to the nest?"

"Egg fine," Haven forced out. "Dae looking—"

"The idiot's looking for me. Of course, he is. I don't know if I should kiss him or kick him. He's not cut out for rescue missions. Didn't Elder Storm Fighter send someone to help?"

Haven slowly shook his head and shrugged.

"Well, damn," Zephyr sighed. "We'll have to get out of this one on our own, then. Look, the snakes have no sense of time. They'll come in five minutes or two hours after they left, thinking it's been an hour." He groaned in pain as he forced himself into a sitting position. A small dribble of blood rolled down his chin as he panted weakly. "I—I need you to distract them when they do come, just for long enough that I can fry them. I have one more good shot of lightning in me. We can kill some of the snakes, and Dae will hear it and know where we are."

Dae already knew where Haven was. Sort of. Dae was searching the forest while Haven quickly put clothing on. When Haven didn't show up, hopefully Dae would come looking. He wouldn't fall to the snakes as easily as Haven had, even if he wasn't a fighter like Zephyr had insisted. Haven had to tell Zephyr that, before his plans counted Dae out entirely. He was feeling stronger with every passing minute. Hopefully, he'd be able to speak properly now.

"Dae in woods," he forced out. "Waiting for me. Maybe come look here when I don't show."

Zephyr's grin widened, and Haven's heart gave an extra little thump. "Is he now? I bet he'll come stomping in, yelling for you at the top of his lungs. Dae's got a bit of a temper," he explained fondly. "I have a feeling a good distraction should come along shortly. Can you move yet? I'll need your shoulder to walk."

Haven was able to straighten both his legs in front of himself and with a bit of struggling was also able to push into a sitting position. His muscles still felt uncoordinated and weak so he rested there. Zephyr was leaning against the side of the bed, slumped, as if he didn't have the strength to hold himself up. He might have the power for one more good lightning strike, but Haven had doubts he would be conscious afterward.

The front door slammed open upstairs long before Haven felt like he was strong enough to stand. He curled his legs underneath him and pushed upward so he could stagger to his feet.

"Where are you, damned human?" Dae yelled, stomping around so hard the floor overhead creaked. Zephyr grinned and rolled his eyes.

"Come over here and help me up," Zephyr called. Haven hurried to his side, every step a little stronger than the one before it. He wasn't scared, Haven realized as he bent down so Zephyr could wrap one arm over Haven's shoulder. Maybe after everything that had already happened to him, he couldn't find it in himself to still be scared. There was also something about Zephyr's constant smile, bloody as it was, that made being afraid impossible. Zephyr's confidence in the situation's outcome helped too.

The basement door creaked open, and Zephyr froze in place with a hiss. "Don't look into the light." With that cryptic statement, Zephyr turned them both toward the door. Injured and frail he might be, but he was still stronger than Haven.

There was a gigantic snake standing in the doorway. It was black skinned with a wide yellow stripe down the middle. It had human arms and a snake's tail instead of legs. The human face was oddly flattened, and a pair of long fangs poked out of the top lip. In the creature's forehead was a gemstone that glowed slightly. It was so very pretty. Haven didn't want to look away from the gentle glow as it brightened. It was all he could see; it was all he wanted to see.

Distantly, he heard Zephyr snicker, and then a hand came down over his eyes. "Don't look at their light," he repeated, whispering it into Haven's ear as if he were a lover. Haven shivered, but when Zephyr removed his hand, Haven was able to look away from the light. It was still there, easily the brightest thing in the basement room, but Haven had other things on his mind. Like reciting the alphabet backward because the beginnings of an erection was a terrible thing to have when a snake-man was hissing like that.

It honestly hadn't been that long since he'd slept with another man! Haven didn't understand why he kept having these feelings around two men, especially two men who were in a relationship with each other. It was beyond wrong to interfere, so Haven told his body to shut up and pay attention to more than the heavy tingling warmth of Zephyr's arm over his shoulder.

The hissing actually contained words, Haven realized once his brain had checked back in.

"The bird man will find your dead body and will cry," the snake hissed with what sounded like gleeful laughter. "Once he is sad, we'll kill him too. Then we'll eat all your flesh."

"He's a lot bigger than the other snakes I've seen," Haven murmured, unable to listen to the hissing diatribe any longer.

Zephyr snickered. "The bigger ones are more venomous, but I think it affects their brain detrimentally. How about we find out for certain?" His skin started buzzing where it touched Haven's bare skin. A bolt of lightning seared across the room, hurting Haven's eyes. The responding crack of thunder shook the house. Haven felt Zephyr's weight increase where he was leaning on Haven. It took a few more seconds before the spots faded from his eyes and he could see again.

The snake was nothing but smelly char, smoking on the basement floor.

"Always aim for the seventh spot from the head," Zephyr mumbled. A second crack of thunder resounded from upstairs. "That idiot," he added fondly.

Haven's knees were wobbly, but for the very first time in his life since the accident, they weren't wobbly because of the lightning. He hadn't even flinched when Zephyr killed the snake. It sounded like a minor thunderstorm was ravaging the upstairs, but he still turned toward the staircase. He wasn't afraid of thunder and lightning any longer.

It could be because all of the lightning he had seen in the last day was used to protect people. Haven hadn't been harmed; even when Dae lost his temper, it wasn't the lightning that caused Haven to faint. Dae and Zephyr themselves were probably the other reason Haven was no longer afraid. When the lightning came from two handsome men that Haven had formed an instant crush on, it was difficult to be scared.

The venom in Haven's system was beginning to fade, so he felt confident on the stairs. He half carried Zephyr, who, despite still being conscious, was having difficulty moving his feet. It was slow going. Haven would walk up one stair, then pause to heft Zephyr up too. When they finally reached the landing, Haven was exhausted and Zephyr was shaking. Haven guided them into the nearby kitchen where Zephyr thankfully sank into one of the chairs. It was still thundering down the hall, closer to the bedroom, so Dae was still busy. Zephyr kept looking in that direction worriedly, but he didn't have the strength to go help. He would probably end up getting in the way instead. They really should leave the house entirely, but Zephyr needed the break and they had to meet up with Dae.

Haven filled a glass of water at the sink and brought it over to Zephyr. "I'm going to find Dae, if you think you'll be all right for a few minutes on your own."

Zephyr's grin was weak, but still devastating. He held up one hand and let a little spark travel between his fingers. "I probably can't take another big one, but if any of the little ones try to ambush me again, I'll be ready."

Haven nodded. "I'll be quick."

Kitchen knives were a terrible weapon to use against an enemy. Without a cross guard, Haven was as likely to slice open his own fingers as stab a snake. He took the largest knife off the butcher block anyway and peeked around the corner into the hall. It sounded like Dae was in the bedroom fighting off a large number of the snakes, judging by the different-sounding hissing noises and the sheer amount of thunder still echoing through the house. The hallway was empty, so he crept from the kitchen. The carpet underfoot smelled slightly burnt, and the hairs on his arms and head were standing up from the ozone-scented charge that fought for dominance around him.

The house wasn't large, so it only took a few anxious moments for Haven to reach the bedroom area where he found Dae. He had probably stormed there after stomping into the house, blindly looking for Haven, and been cornered just like Haven had. The doorway was open, so Haven boldly stepped into his room.

There were two larger snakes, their humanlike features set in snarls as they tried to advance on Dae. At least half a dozen smaller snakes of various colors and shapes, some with wings and some with fangs, all with pointed horns on their heads, were also trying to break through Dae's defenses. Dae himself was leaning against Haven's dresser, wheezing for breath. One of the smaller snakes lunged, and Dae zapped it with a bolt of lightning that flashed so quickly only the afterimage and the roll of thunder let Haven know what he had just seen.

"Hey, snake-monster thing!" Haven yelled. He didn't know what he was doing or why. Well, he knew why. He had to save Dae. He never wanted to see Zephyr's smile dim or Dae's scowl fade. Haven might not be able to have either of them for himself, but at least he could ensure they had each other. The what portion of his actions had his brain asking if he was being crazy.

Both of the big snakes hissed and turned in his direction. They glanced at each other, appearing to converse for a long moment while Dae zapped two more small critters, before one of the big ones advanced in Haven's direction.

"You're ugly, you know that?" Haven gasped out, backing away into the hallway. The gemstone embedded in the snake's forehead glittered, but Haven resolutely kept his eyes trained on the snake's nose. "And you're not welcome in my house!"

There were spots on the snake's bald head, just as Zephyr had said. He counted for the seventh one as the snake slithered into the hallway and hissed at Haven. Its fangs were long, dripping venom and menacing. Haven would have looked away if it hadn't meant taking his eyes off that one damned spot.

As if sensing Haven's fear, the creature took its time sliding closer across the abused carpet. Haven let himself shiver in response. It wasn't feigned—he was panting for breath and the knife was shaking in his hand—but it galvanized the creature into laughing cruelly.

"Watch as the bird dies first," it hissed, turning its body sideways so Haven could see the other snake also advancing on Dae. It took its attention from Haven for one crucial moment to admire Dae's impending death. Haven tried to steady his hand. He wanted to take a deep breath, but there wasn't time before the snake's attention would return. The knife wavered in the air as his arm shot outward. It wasn't a direct hit; the blade sank into the creature's leathery skin, cutting deep into the seventh spot just to the left of center. The snake gave a choked gasping groan full of pain and the burble of death—Haven didn't think he would ever forget that sound—and then collapsed to the ground.

A great crack of light and thunder shook the house, and the smell of charred meat filled the air. Haven forced his fingers to let go of the embedded knife, leaving it inside the body of the dead snake. Dae was sitting on the ground, holding one hand to a bloody nose. Haven couldn't see any more snakes, but there were a bunch more burnt patches in his carpet. It would all have to be ripped out and replaced, he thought distantly. Haven was still shaking, but not from fear. He felt cold and shivery as if his body wasn't firing on all cylinders. Dae's eyes were sunken and tired and blood was still dripping from his nose, but he was alive.

"Zephyr's in the kitchen," Haven explained, knowing that was the most important thing to say.

Dae's eyes lightened immediately. He used the corner of Haven's dresser to lever himself to his feet and then tottered toward the door unsteadily. Instead of passing by Haven and going to his partner, Dae looped his free arm through Haven's and pulled Haven along with him. They walked around Haven's dead snake, which Haven tried not to look at too closely, and back down the hallway.

"Zephyr?" Dae called, his voice muffled thanks to his fingers still pinching his nose shut.

"I'm here!" Zephyr called back.

They hurried into the kitchen. Dae let out a strangled noise of pain when he saw how beaten Zephyr looked. He hurried to Zephyr's side. Haven let their clasped arms drop and headed to the counter where there were paper towels instead.

"You're all out of lightning seeds, aren't you," Zephyr stated. One of his arms was around Dae's waist as if he couldn't be so close to his partner without touching him. Haven wordlessly held out the towels and tried to keep his envy at bay. Zephyr took the towels, but he also gripped Haven's hand in his for a long moment before letting go so he could tend to Dae. Haven's hand felt warm and tingly for a few long seconds afterward.

"I'm tapped dry," Dae agreed. "Do you have anything left?"

"Just a spark," Zephyr groaned. "We should get moving before any more damned snakes try their luck."

"Dae Wind Rider? Zephyr Storm Fighter?" There was a woman yelling outside. Dae looked up, his bloody nose apparently contained.

"That's Tempest Storm Fighter," Dae exclaimed. "What is she doing here?"

"Elder Storm Fighter probably sent her after us," Zephyr replied. "Let's go meet up with her."

It took some doing to get Zephyr back to his feet. They both had to cling to Haven's shoulders for balance, and Haven had to cling back as they left the kitchen and Haven's house behind. Tempest was standing in the middle of the street, repeating the two names over and over again.

None of Haven's neighbors, quite a few of whom were outside in their yards, had taken any notice of her. Since there weren't any police officers or people looking concerned in the direction of Haven's house, he guessed there had been more than storm magic at play during the fighting.

"Here, Tempest!" Zephyr called.

She hurried to their side and reached them at the same time as a second Thunderbird landed next to them.

"Rescue mission successful, I see," she said happily. "We were following the thunder, but it stopped before we could pinpoint the house. Glad to see you're all right. We've got a hammock to take you all back to the nest if you haven't got the strength to fly the distance."

"Thank you, Tempest," Zephyr interjected quickly before she could continue speaking. "We would appreciate the ride."

Tempest threw her cloak on and assumed her bird shape. Her partner was carrying what looked like the rope and knots of a collapsed hammock. Together they straightened out the rope until a rough hammock appeared. They each took one end, pulling it taut so Zephyr could gratefully drop into it. Dae followed, leaning against Zephyr as soon as he was situated.

Haven hesitated to follow. He was a human, and even with a partially destroyed house, this was where he belonged. Aira should be raised by her own people, not a human she had no doubt accidentally chosen, and Dae and Zephyr should return to their own nest together.

"Come on," Dae called, his scowl firmly in place. Zephyr shot them both an automatic smile at Dae's hard tone and then waved for Haven to join them. Haven couldn't say no. He climbed into the hammock next to Zephyr.

Two pairs of wings cracked overhead as the hammock lifted into the air. Haven was thrown into Zephyr's side. Zephyr gasped in pain, but before Haven could scramble away, Zephyr rearranged Haven's body so he wasn't leaning on sore ribs. Zephyr wrapped one arm over Haven's shoulder and held him tight.

Haven held himself stiffly for the first few minutes, his neighborhood quickly vanishing below as they flew over the city. He didn't want to hurt Zephyr again, and he didn't want to read more into the situation than he ought. Zephyr was just being kind, Haven reminded himself even as he slowly relaxed into Zephyr's gentle hold.

The long and difficult day coupled with how comfortable Haven felt and the gentle rocking of the hammock soon sent Haven drifting off to sleep.

*

Haven was dreaming. He must be dreaming. It was the only scenario that explained why he was curled in bed with two other people. Zephyr was bandaged and bruised on Haven's right side. One of his arms and part of his soft cloak were thrown across Haven's chest. He was breathing deeply and evenly despite how much pain he must still be in. On Haven's left was Dae. He also had his arm and part of his cloak thrown over Haven, arranged in such a way that his cloak didn't overlap with Zephyr's while their arms were still pressed together. It felt like Dae and Zephyr were trying to hold each other, but Haven was in the way. Yet, instead of moving him, they had embraced Haven willingly. That was why Haven knew he was dreaming. Why would Dae and Zephyr feel any need to include him when they already had each other?

Haven let his eyes slide shut again. He was selfish enough to enjoy the dream while it lasted, so he settled back into the bed and let the dream take him away.

When Haven woke again, his body felt heavy. It was the same feeling he got whenever he overslept. His brain felt sluggish and his limbs too weighty to move. It took a few minutes for his mind to start thinking properly and even longer before his arms and legs agreed to attempt sitting up. He was alone in the bed, and a pang of disappointment that his wonderful dream had ended lanced through him.

Two gigantic feathers fell off his chest and into his lap when he sat up. They were each the length of his forearm and as black as the feathers of every Thunderbird Haven had ever seen. They could have belonged to anyone, but as Haven ran his fingers gently over the soft plumes, he knew which one belonged to Zephyr and which one belonged to Dae. He held the one that felt aggressive, as if it were just waiting for a moment to zap him with its pent-up electricity in his left hand. That was Dae's feather. The other felt much more mellow, almost like it could fly out of his hand and start laughing just like Zephyr. Haven didn't know why he had the feathers, but he stroked their plumes for a long moment before deciding it was time to get up and find out whether he was going home or not.

He held the feathers in one hand as he climbed out of bed. Someone had removed his jeans and put him into a pair of loose black sleeping pants, he noticed, as he pulled the blankets off and swung his legs off the bed. He was in a darkened room. There were heavy curtains hanging over a doorway, which blocked most of the light. Haven headed for the door and pulled the curtain aside. He was blinded momentarily by sunlight, forcing him to blink to clear his eyes as he stepped into an outer room.

There were three people sitting on two wide couches, talking softly among themselves. Mona was sitting alone. She looked up first and smiled widely at him.

"You're awake," Mona said happily.

The other two people jumped to their feet immediately, turning around to look at him. Zephyr's cloak was still a little ragged-looking, his face was still swollen and bruised, and he had bandages visible underneath his shirt. Dae looked fine despite having black circles under his eyes. He was holding Aira tucked into one elbow. She was sleeping with her cloak twisted around her, one foot scaled and clawed while the other was still human. She cracked one eye open at the sudden movement, caught sight of Haven, and let out an excited chirp.

Dae hurried forward at Aira's insistence, and Haven found his arms automatically extending before conscious thought could take over. Aira shifted around a few times in his arms, cheeping contentedly. She was still warm to the touch in a slightly frizzy way, as if the hair on Haven's arms was standing up wherever he was touching her. She continued to peep and burble, her wide brown eyes looking around and missing nothing.

"We think it's because you protected her so fiercely in the egg that she's chosen you," Dae said softly. He was still standing just in front of Haven where he had come close to pass Aira over. Haven looked up and was caught in the intensity in Dae's eyes. His usual scowl was gone, but the blank face and burning eyes that replaced it was just as ambiguous.

"We've chosen you for a different reason," Zephyr added as he walked up to stand next to Dae. He still had a small smile on his face, but his eyes were just as intense. "You've shown us the strength in your heart, which has called to the lightning in ours. We want to offer you our flight feathers."

Haven looked down at the two feathers he still held in the hand that wasn't keeping Aira secured to his side. They were giving him their flight feathers? What did that even mean? They could simply be expressing their admiration for how Haven had helped rescue Aira and save Zephyr. Haven's libido wanted something a little more personal than that, and it soared in want as he looked up from the feathers to the two men still earnestly looking at him.

Before he could give an answer, Haven had to be sure what they wanted from him. "What does that mean?" he asked, his voice soft with a hopeful note to it that he couldn't suppress. Dae scowled, but Haven thought it was just reflexive.

Zephyr smiled sheepishly. "I had forgotten that you wouldn't understand what we were asking. I believe for humans it is customary for the one asking to present a ring? For Thunderbirds we exchange flight feathers."

"But you already have each other!" Haven gasped, looking between them wildly while hoping this wasn't a cruel joke or a misunderstanding.

"One, two, or even three. The lightning doesn't care how often it strikes as long as it strikes true," Dae insisted. "We have each other, but that never meant we wouldn't eventually find you too."

"But why me?" Haven gasped. He was just a human. Dae and Zephyr were glorious Thunderbirds. What did he have to offer them?

Zephyr laughed. "Because you're beautiful," he insisted. He gently reached out to run his fingers through Haven's sleep-tangled hair, tugging playfully on the strip of white. "Because you make Dae smile in happiness and me frown in thought. Because from the moment we met you, our lightning insisted we were connected." He let the palm of his hand rest against Haven's cheek. Haven felt the same buzzing under his skin that he always felt whenever Dae or Zephyr touched him.

Mona reached past Zephyr and softly placed her hand on Haven's arm for a brief second before gathering Aira and stepping away. Haven felt nothing from her touch. Her skin was soft and warm, but he didn't feel any of the buzzing or lightning he expected from a Thunderbird's skin. Mona left the room before Haven could ask for clarification. Dae stepped into the empty space at Haven's side now that Aira was gone and placed one hand on Haven's arm. His skin buzzed again, only double because they were both touching him.

"Just give us a chance to prove to you what our lightning has already proven to us," Zephyr insisted, his voice soft, but his eyes still burning.

There really wasn't a way for Haven to say no. Dae and Zephyr were everything he had ever wanted. He was tired of curling up alone with only loud music to drown out his fears. He wanted them both, and it appeared they wanted him back. "Okay," he whispered and let himself be drawn back through the heavy curtain that led to the bedroom.

Haven had a feeling as he looked at their strong backs and cloaks of feathers as Dae and Zephyr pulled him toward the bed that he would never be alone again. This was everything Haven had ever wanted, and he couldn't help smiling happily as they fell into the soft bed together.

THE BEAST

Prologue

If Kiki had ever thought about strange visitors coming in the middle of the night to curse him, he would have assumed the night would be stormy and cold, the visitors ugly and mean, and he would have valiantly fought them off. He, the Great Emperor of the North, would never be felled by something as measly as a curse, after all.

He knew better now.

The visitors were two beautiful men, and the rose they carried was such a vibrant, deep red, Kiki demanded they give it to him at once. He hadn't bothered asking their names or why they had come. Kiki's eyes focused on that rose, and once he saw something he wanted, he took it. That was his right as emperor, and no one had dared gainsay his claims before now. The two strangers hadn't denied him either. The taller one with the oddly shaved dark hair had smiled at him and handed over the rose without argument.

Kiki should have seen something in that smile, and looking back he certainly noticed something strange and almost smug in the tilt of those lips. He didn't at the time, though, and grabbed the rose without any forethought. It was the one with the purple hair who actually spoke.

"You are a beast in the body of a man, and we are here to rectify that discrepancy," the purple-haired one said, and his voice seemed to resonate even as the rose began to pulse in Kiki's hands. "Your outside should match your inside."

The rose exploded, plastering him head to toe in bloodred petals and wrapping him in a thorny stem that pricked and scraped along his skin. Kiki remembered screaming, remembered feeling both squeezed, as the thorns dug in, and stretched, as his body was yanked apart and put back together.

"True love will break the spell." He somehow heard through the pain, the words imbedding themselves directly into his brain. "If you can learn to love someone other than yourself, and if they can find some way to love you in return, the spell will be broken."

When Kiki woke, he was alone—only the red rose still clutched in his hands a reminder of what had happened.

Kiki had called for his servants to help him up, to get him cleaned and dressed, but no one came. The manor he had chosen to call home while the troops were heading south into Monrath was empty. The servants were gone, the guards were gone, and even the baron he had commandeered the place from had vanished.

Worse, the empire was suddenly gone too. Everything he had worked so hard for, had spun so much magic into, had completely ended. With the rose's touch, all of the spells tied to him to control the lands and the people he ruled were broken, and they then left him behind. He wasn't an emperor or even a king. No, Kiki was nothing now, and the utter silence of his home only served to emphasize how much he had lost.

Except, Kiki hadn't realized just how much was gone until he staggered to his feet and happened to look into the mirror hanging in the front hall. He didn't have the voice left to scream, but his knees collapsed. Even from the floor, Kiki could still make out his face in the mirror. His fingers shook as he reached up to touch, running his fingertips across his forehead, over his nose, and down his cheek along the path the scar took.

His skin, once so smooth, thanks to daily applications of aloes and lotions by his parade of servants, was pocked across every inch where the thorns had taken out chunks of skin. Where he wasn't pocked, he was scarred. His face was twisted to one side. The skin on the fingers he trailed along his cheeks was also scarred, so tight with scar tissue it was difficult to straighten them fully. He didn't look like the same person any longer.

Kiki was a beast in image, just as the wizard with the rose had said.

He could still make a fist, luckily, and the mirror shattered with one punch. Kiki let the glass fall all around him. It didn't matter if it cut his skin any longer. He was ruined and alone. Nothing mattered anymore.

When Kiki finally staggered to his feet, bits of mirror dropped off his clothes. He needed to change. Kiki opened his mouth to demand his servants prepare a new outfit for him, as he had done thousands of times throughout his life, but the silence of the manor reminded him. He had to change his own clothes and probably had to wash and repair the ones he was wearing now too.

It was all the fault of those wizards. How dare they do this to him, the emperor. Kiki tried to be angry, but it fizzled as he stared down at his crabbed hands.

That was the point of the spell, though. He could read the spells of fate and feel them wrapped around him. Kiki hadn't become the emperor by being a weak wizard himself. The rose had blasted through his defenses, but he could still see the spell that had been written so violently on his flesh.

And there was the rose, lying where he had dropped it in the middle of the foyer. Kiki left it there and limped past. First, he had to break the spell, and then he would make those wizards pay.

Chapter One

There was a vibration in Kiki's spell web. He sat up in bed, already grimacing. It was two in the morning! Couldn't they have waited for a decent hour? Except, the vibration suddenly stopped.

"Magic," Kiki hissed. He threw back his blankets and levered his body out of bed. The scar tissue stiffened when he lay down for a while, so it always took time to really get moving in the morning. He didn't have that luxury now, not if he wanted to catch the wizards.

No one had come to see him in fifty years. It was past time for those damned wizards to come check up on their rose spell, and this time he would be ready for them.

Kiki ran magic through his body, bouncing it from feet to head until he had enough power ready for a big blasting spell. He limped through the halls of his manor, heading to the kitchen where he had last felt the wizard. It was an odd place to hide, but maybe they thought to ambush him first thing in the morning when he went to make breakfast.

If that was the case, then Kiki had the advantage now. He walked as quietly as his limp would allow, sneaking into the kitchen where he followed the rustling sounds of someone moving about in the dark.

Kiki gripped a piece of the magic he had gathered and threw it into the air. Light flared brilliantly bright in the night-dark room, and someone let out a surprised shriek.

That someone sounded young, which had Kiki frowning even more. He yanked open the pantry door, blasting spell ready to go, and froze in place at what he saw. An urchin was huddled there, hands up above his head to protect himself from Kiki. The kid was maybe ten years old and in one hand was a small loaf of bread.

It was just a hungry kid. Kiki let his blasting magic fade away and let out a sigh. His hands lowered, and Kiki was about to step forward to speak with the kid when the fingers of the kid's free hand flicked. Magic flared and shoved Kiki backward. He went flying into the kitchen, and the kid rushed past, heading toward the doorway into the neglected herb garden.

Kiki could deal with magic. He flicked his own fingers, and the door slammed shut, the handle yanked from the boy's hands, locking him inside. The boy spun and lifted his hands again.

"Don't try magic with me, boy," Kiki said in his firmest voice. He knew what he looked like, his scars still faintly red even after all these years, and his voice still had a ragged edge left over from his screaming when it had happened. Besides, he really shouldn't be calling the kid a kid at all. Using magic likely meant the kid was probably much older than he looked. The magic was definitely untrained and raw, so Kiki estimated the kid was probably closer to fifteen or twenty, rather than ten, but he still looked so young and vulnerable.

His hair was blond, although it was even more unkempt than Kiki's. He couldn't really tend it with his hands as crabbed as they were, and in fifty years his beautiful brown curls had turned into a terrible rats' nest. The kid's just needed a good bath and a brush. The kid looked up at Kiki, his eyes huge and a dark gray that would be utterly captivating when his body matured.

"I'm sorry," the boy said softly, his voice shaking. "They said— They said all the extra food in the village was sent up here, so if I wanted to eat, I had to come get it myself."

He was thin and shivering, in addition to needing a good bath, and he was probably homeless as well. The fact that he could use magic was likely a detriment in a world that had forgotten about magic again. In Kiki's empire, his abilities would have been a prized jewel to be cultivated. Now, though, whenever something strange happened around him, it had probably only caused him to be ostracized.

Kiki wasn't used to the odd twisting feeling in his chest. He didn't have the words to describe it. Regret, maybe? Either way, he found his feet moving back into the pantry before his brain caught up with his intentions. It took a moment to find the bread—now missing one ripped end thanks to the kid—and to pull some eggs and milk from his spelled cold box.

The kid hadn't moved while Kiki was distracted, which was good. A quick spell had the fire flaring back to life. Kiki set a fat-treated pan to heat while he pulled a bowl down from the shelf. He got the eggs cracked and the milk poured, but his hands weren't strong enough to hold a fork to mix so he set a spell on the fork to mix it for him.

"Magic," the boy whispered. "You can do magic." There was awe in his voice, but also shock, as if he had never met someone who could do what he did. The forgetting spell had done that to the world. It prevented kids like this boy from realizing who they were truly meant to be, and often they were deeply hurt in the process.

Fifty years of hindsight had taught Kiki a few lessons. He hadn't been in the wrong, lifting the forgetting spell to allow others to use magic as he did. Kiki firmly believed that, and he honestly didn't think that was why he had been afflicted with the rose spell. No, it had been his using magic to further his own personal agenda—to make himself and his empire even more powerful—that had gotten him in trouble. Because he had learned that just because someone could do magic didn't mean they should actually learn how. Too many wizards in his empire had been all too eager to emulate his bad example, and while he had been the first wizard to be punished for his transgressions, Kiki doubted he was the last.

It was a hard-learned lesson, one he wasn't about to ignore with the boy, but it was also true that when magic spilled out of a child on its own, the child didn't have a choice but to learn.

And it was a wizard's duty to teach a student when he found one. Whether the student would be willing to stay with a man who looked like him...that Kiki couldn't answer.

The pan was hot enough, so Kiki poured the eggs into it. They immediately started sizzling, and a flick of his fingers had a spatula heading to the pan to start scrambling. Another flick had the bread knife flying over to start slicing the loaf. Two more things he couldn't do with his mangled hands, but Kiki tried to ignore that as he went to get plates and silverware from the cabinet.

"Sit," he said as he set two places at the kitchen table. "We'll eat, and then we can discuss your schooling."

"Schooling?" The boy scrambled to his feet, his fright at being caught apparently forgotten. "You mean, you'll teach me magic?"

Kiki couldn't help laughing lightly at the boy's eager tone. "We'll get to magic eventually. First, I'll teach you reading and writing." And hopefully the time away from magic would allow the boy to grow up and reach an age where he was capable of making adult decisions in an adult's body. He had to choose whether he was okay with the extra years of life magic brought to a person. Not everyone was suited, and Kiki could just as easily teach him how to shut the magic away permanently and let the forgetting spell take hold, as he could take him on as a student.

The boy pouted. "Why do I have to learn that?"

Kiki smothered another laugh. "So you can read other wizards' spell books to learn from, and so you can eventually write a spell book of your own. All wizards-in-training start with reading and writing, and you will too."

"Makes sense," the boy replied, but Kiki could still hear remnants of that pout in his tone.

Kiki put a piece of bread on each plate and then grabbed a cloth to protect his hand before pulling the pan from the fire. He divvied up the eggs between both plates and sat down across from the boy to start eating.

"What's your name, and why're you up in this old place, anyway?" the boy asked with his mouth full as he shoveled more food inside. Manners would also be in the lesson plans, Kiki immediately decided, although those would have to be gently taught to the boy to prevent Kiki from coming across as patronizing.

"My name is ridiculously long and overcomplicated. My friends call me Kiki." He didn't admit how few people he had ever been able to call friend. Kiki also ignored the second half of the boy's question; that was a story for another day a long, long time from now. "What's your name?"

This time the boy swallowed before answering, although Kiki was inclined to think that was a coincidence. "I'm Nicole. I'm an orphan, I think. I'm not sure. The patronage house in the village took care of me when I was really little, and now I beg for scraps in the market."

"Well, there will be no more of that," Kiki said firmly. "Now, finish eating and I'll show you to your bedroom. We'll start your lessons in the morning."

Nicole shoveled the last few mouthfuls of food into his mouth as if the plate would disappear. He then bounced from his chair and stared eagerly at Kiki, as if daring Kiki to take back what he had just promised. Kiki took his time, carefully pushing the eggs onto his fork with his knife and chewing and swallowing. When his plate was empty, Kiki picked it up and took it over to the sink. Nicole let out a soft gasp and rushed forward a second later with his own plate.

Nicole held it out for Kiki to take, but he was looking at the ground shamefully as if to apologize for messing up by not clearing his plate. He cringed when Kiki took it from him to stack in the sink as if waiting to get hit. Kiki ignored him. Making a big deal out of the terrible life Nicole had apparently led up until now would not help with anything.

Kiki left the plates in the sink to wash in the morning and gestured toward the door leading into the rest of the house. Nicole meekly walked in that direction, and Kiki followed, hoping Nicole would quickly learn that life wasn't always going to be so hard.

Chapter Two

ONE HUNDRED YEARS LATER

"Get out of the larder!"

"But I'm hungry, Master!"

Kiki let out a heavy sigh and scrubbed his face with one hand. He reached through the larder doorway, grabbed Margo's collar, and yanked him out.

"Lunch is in an hour, and you're skipping out of lessons." He shook Margo gently, then pushed him back in the direction of the main ballroom where the classroom was set out. After one hundred years of harebrained kids, Kiki would have thought he'd be used to this, but they somehow always found a new way to drive him nuts.

He escorted Margo back to his seat and then stood over him menacingly for a few seconds to ensure the brat got the message. If he had to wear this scarred face, at least he could make it useful for something.

Speaking about kids breaking into his larder, Kiki glanced up at the front of the room where Nicole was pointing at something he had written on the chalkboard. Nicole sent him a quick grin and a wink, before calling on a girl sitting in the front row.

Nicole had grown into a beautiful young man. His blond hair had deepened into a luscious shade of gold that glittered in the ballroom lights. His gray eyes were still big in his face, and they were bright with intelligence. Nicole was quick to smile and had a sly side that made his grins often seem mischievous. The kids loved him and Nicole enjoyed teaching them.

Kiki turned away before he said or did something inappropriate in front of the kids. Besides, he knew what he looked like. Every year only seemed to make everything worse: his scars deepened, and his body became more crabbed and bent. There was no way Nicole would ever look at Kiki as more than a mentor who had brought him out of poverty and then given him a job.

Well, technically the school had been Nicole's idea. Kiki had thought up the spell that drew homeless kids to his home, but it was Nicole who had created the curriculum to teach the kids their letters and numbers. The homeless kids grew up educated, and were able to venture on to the rest of their lives with a benefit usually only the wealthiest children in society could boast. They got good jobs working in often high-level posts, and most would send money or supplies when they could in thanks, which allowed Kiki to take in even more students.

And, every once in a while, a child like Nicole would appear with the ability to learn magic.

Evaluating the children for magic was Kiki's job. He was good at assessing which children had to learn magic because it was already escaping their control, and which had the ability but could safely go through life ignorant of it. The latter he usually left alone—they would be happier living a normal life, he knew. The former, however, were always a trickier story. Children knew how to be power hungry, and how to take advantage of all their abilities to come out on top. Luckily, they mostly lacked subtlety, and it was easy enough to figure out which ones could be bad apples. If they couldn't learn humility—and with Kiki's face glaring at them they also had all the opportunity to learn the cost of lacking humility—Kiki and Nicole sealed their magic and allowed the forgetting spell that covered the world to remove all memory of magic from their minds. For the genuinely good children who were interested in learning, Kiki taught the magic classes in the afternoons while the other students had their own subject-matter-focused curriculum to follow.

It was time to stop daydreaming, Kiki told himself firmly. Dwelling on the past and on the things he would never be able to get in the present or future was a waste of time. He needed to get lunch ready before the hoard of kids descended on the kitchen.

Kiki hurried back down the hallway, returning to the kitchen and calling all the spells he had frozen when Margo wandered in back to life. Spoons stirred themselves, the fire gentled to keep the stew he was also making for dinner at a simmer, and the pot pies he had made for lunch turned themselves in the oven to get their crusts toasted evenly. Out in the dining room, dishes flew through the air as the table set itself.

It wasn't long before Kiki heard the stomp of many feet and the chatter of excited voices as the kids rushed into the dining room and took their seats. Nicole swept into the kitchen a minute later.

"Smells good, Master," he said with his usual grin. He wiggled his fingers in the air and a large tray flew toward him. The pot pies slowly slid out of the oven and onto the tray, and a second later, Nicole swept back out of the room, food in tow.

Kiki let out a soft sigh. "Master." Why did Nicole insist on calling him that? Nicole knew Kiki's name, had eventually wriggled Kiki's full name and his story out of him, yet when Nicole had chosen to stop using magic for long enough to allow his body to grow into adulthood, suddenly it had been "Master" instead of "Kiki."

It was a distancing term, one that kept Nicole a step away from Kiki at all times, and it burned in Kiki's chest every time it fell from Nicole's lips. And Kiki didn't understand why. Nicole could leave at any time, had been proficient in magic since the day he chose to pause his magic use in order to grow up, and was therefore more than capable of making his own way in the world. Instead he had chosen to stay and create their school together, and yet he maintained a purposeful distance at the same time.

Kiki couldn't blame him, of course. There weren't many mirrors left in his manor, but he knew what he looked like and what he sounded like. He knew the children were always afraid of him when they first arrived, clinging to Nicole and the other kids out of fear every time he entered a room. Even once the kids slowly got used to him, they still never sought him out for their little troubles like they did Nicole.

There was one pot pie left in the oven. Kiki floated it out onto a plate and settled into a kitchen chair to eat on his own. The fingers of his right hand couldn't bend enough to hold a knife, which meant if Kiki had to cut something he either needed Nicole to do it, or he had to use magic. The former was demeaning; the latter meant he had to eat alone.

Still, the steam as he cut into his pot pie bathed his face and the scent of chicken, vegetables, and warm spices melted together perfectly was slight consolation. Cookbooks and a lot of trial and error had taught Kiki how to cook. He refused to subsist on premade or dried foods. Kiki's palate was used to far more sophisticated cuisine, and if he wanted to eat like his body craved, he needed to make it himself.

Kiki blew on the pie, trying to cool it down so he didn't burn his mouth, and scooped up a bit with his fork. He blew on it some more, watching the steam billow, until it finally began to dissipate. The bit he put in his mouth melted, the flavors making his tongue sing, and Kiki couldn't help the happy hum.

Laughter rang out behind him. Kiki swallowed and spun around to find Nicole grinning at him. He went over to the sink to fill a pitcher with water, still smiling to himself.

"What?" Kiki ground out, his voice more gravelly than normal as embarrassment deepened it.

Nicole shook his head. "The pot pies are really good," he said, and there wasn't any judgment in his voice. Kiki spun back around to eat some more before it got cold, hoping the scars on his cheeks hid the fact that he was blushing. "The kids will be in here in about ten minutes to begin their afternoon chores. I'll have them clean up from lunch, and then I'll send them out back to work on the garden."

Kiki nodded to show he heard, but his mouth was full, so he didn't have to respond. Nicole laughed and swept out of the kitchen, back to the kids and leaving Kiki alone again. Kiki hurried to finish eating and was just savoring his last bite when the kids swarmed into the kitchen with stacks of dishes. They headed to the sink to start cleaning, and Nicole returned with them to supervise.

Kiki stood in the corner, watching as well. He particularly kept his eye on Michel, a lovely dark-shinned girl from the East who had only been with them for three months. She was the only one with them at the moment with mage potential, and she appeared to have the temperament for it, but she wasn't spilling like Nicole had. She seemed happy as a regular human, so Kiki had so far decided to leave her alone, but he would watch her carefully for any evidence of spillage. It would almost be worse to send an untrained mage out into the world than an evil but trained one. Michel had at least five more years with them, though, so Kiki knew he had plenty of time to decide what to do with her.

The kids never took long cleaning the kitchen, since there were so many of them. Once they were gone, outside into the garden to work on the herbs and vegetables, Kiki returned to working on the stew for dinner. He poked his nose outside while the bread he was making kneaded itself. The kids were mostly playing, rather than weeding, and their cheerful laugher brought light into the old manor in a way it had never felt back in the day when it was packed with servants, courtiers, and soldiers.

Nicole stepped into view. He sternly redirected the kids back to their chores, but his beautiful face was still bright with laughter. Somehow even weeding became play under Nicole's gentle hand. Kiki looked down at his own hands, at the scars, and at the blood he had spilled that those scars represented, and he turned away from the garden and went back to his kitchen alone.

The rest of the day passed like normal. Nicole took the kids back to the classroom to work on math. Kiki wandered through the room, helping the kids figure out how to make the numbers on their personal chalk boards do what Nicole was teaching them at the front of the room. He left early to get the table set and dinner finished. After dinner, the kids cleaned up, and then Nicole took the girls to supervise baths and bedtime while Kiki took the boys to their dormitory for the same.

Kiki collapsed onto a couch into the sitting room he shared with Nicole, exhausted from another long day. He did like the school—he wouldn't have opened his home to the kids if he didn't—but it was draining keeping track of all of them. Nicole joined him a few minutes later, dropping into one of the chairs on the other side of the coffee table from Kiki. The distance hurt, but in a way that was far too familiar at this point.

"I think Robbie is going to leave us soon," Nicole said after a long moment of silence they both relished, being free from kids for the first time all day.

Kiki nodded. "He's seventeen, the oldest, and I don't have much more to teach him. I think it's time he start looking for employment somewhere and begin his own life."

Robbie would be a staggering loss. Kiki had only been able to get the younger kids to bed as easily as he had thanks to Robbie's help. Still, it wouldn't be fair to Robbie to keep him here.

"I'll send out a few inquiry letters for him to some of our alumni. Hopefully one of them will be looking for an apprentice."

Nicole leaned forward in his chair after he finished speaking and held his hands out across the coffee table. Kiki didn't hesitate, leaning forward to place his hands into Nicole's. He relished these moments, as infrequent as they were becoming, because it was a fleeting connection to another human being. Nicole didn't even flinch at the touch of Kiki's crabbed hands, but then he wasn't actually looking at them. Instead, his eyes flared as magic poured into them.

"I almost had it last time," Nicole murmured to himself, his fingers tracing the lines of the scars as he read the spell within Kiki's skin.

He was interested in the puzzle of unravelling the spell on Kiki, not in Kiki himself. Kiki had to remind himself of that, even as Nicole's gentle fingers brushed up and down his hands and made Kiki think thoughts he had no business thinking about his first student.

Kiki didn't have the heart to tell Nicole that studying the spell wasn't going to provide an answer for how to break it. Nicole insisted he could at least push the spell back so Kiki could regain full use of his hands, but Kiki knew better. This was his punishment, and it was a well-deserved one. Nicole messing with the spell wouldn't do anything except waste magic.

Ten minutes later, Nicole let out a heavy breath full of defeat. He gently released Kiki's hands and sank back into his chair.

"I'm sorry," he said softly.

Kiki clasped his hands in his lap, trying to preserve the remnants of Nicole's warmth for just a moment longer.

"No, I'm sorry," Kiki replied. "This isn't a spell you can break just by studying it. I shouldn't let you keep trying." Kiki stood and walked past Nicole on his way to his room. He clumsily patted Nicole on the shoulder before turning and walking through the right-hand door into the bedroom.

When Nicole had been so very young his first few days in the manor, Kiki had given him the other bedroom that shared this suite, and Nicole had never moved out. Kiki would never make Nicole move out, but some evenings it was definitely awkward to be sharing the space. The door closed behind Kiki with a soft click, and Kiki ignored the way that sound made something in his chest ache. Instead, he walked into his dressing room to find his pajamas.

Hidden in the back of the closet, where Nicole would never see it, was the damned rose. It glowed, and floated about a foot in the air over the dressing table Kiki had eventually left it on, but the stem had begun to wilt and some of the vibrant red petals had fallen off and turned black where they lay on the tabletop. Kiki didn't know what it meant that the flower holding the spell on him was dying, but he could guess it wouldn't be good for him when the last petal fell off and the flower was no more.

He turned his back on the flower so he could instead start fighting with the buttons on his shirt with his uncooperative fingers. Twenty minutes later Kiki gratefully slid into bed, letting soft feathers cradle his aching body and ease the pressure from a long day.

Chapter Three

An insistent tugging poked at Kiki, and he woke with a jolt as his spells poked at him again. Someone with magic had just walked in the front door! Kiki tried to lever himself upward, but his arms locked as the scars refused to stretch. He fell back onto the bed with a yelp and scrambled to get his hands underneath himself again.

Nicole flew into the room, and a second later he wrapped an arm across Kiki's back and gently pulled him upright. "Who tripped the spell?"

"The kids," Kiki said instead of answering, panting slightly from the ache in his torso from moving so suddenly. "I'll be fine. Go protect the kids."

Nicole gave him a sharp look full of disbelief, but he nodded and ran out of the room again. Kiki felt Nicole rush down the hall, heading in the direction of the kids' dorms. The intruders were still in the front entry, but Kiki knew that wouldn't last for much longer. He got his feet underneath himself and used a side table to force his body to stand. By the time he shuffled to the bedroom door, his muscles were starting to stretch out again, and he hurried down the hallway in the opposite direction, his legs almost at a full stride.

Kiki reached the top of the grand stair leading down into the entrance hall and was surprised the visitors were still waiting by the door. He had expected to run into them as they ventured farther into the manor, not for them to wait while he struggled down the steps. Light flared from overhead when he reached the ground floor, and Kiki could see two men waiting for him.

The closer man was tall, with long blond hair, green eyes, and had a sword hanging from his hip. The other...the other had the eyes. Gray shot with blue streaks. Kiki knew those eyes, although he didn't recognize the rest of the man they were attached to. His nightmares remembered lavender-colored hair and eyes belonging to one of the men who had cursed him. The second man in his nightmares had dark skin, dark hair shaved at the sides with a braid down the middle, and those piercing, judging eyes.

"Go away," Kiki snapped, already knowing how ineffectual his words would be. If these two were related to the men who had cursed him, in his current state, Kiki knew he had no chance.

The one with the long blond hair grinned at him, but it wasn't a friendly sort of expression. More bloodthirsty, and yet he somehow managed it without a hint of aggression. He must be a knight or a lifelong soldier, as those were usually the men who had seen enough terrible things to have learned that look. At least, that was what Kiki remembered from so long ago.

"Imagine my surprise," the man with the eyes began, "when I returned home to Monrath for a visit and found one of the finest scribes in the land working hand in hand with the queen. I asked the scribe where he grew up, and he explained about this wonderful school up in the northern territories that takes in homeless and desperate kids and gives them a future. And, of course I found it curious that kids somehow all managed to gather at one location like that, so I went looking for the magic. Which led me here, Emperor of the North."

"Are you training spies, to infiltrate countries and governments so you can bend them to your will?" the man with the long blond hair asked sharply. "Or assassins, ready to destroy the ruling families to let you take over without an army, much as you tried to do a hundred and fifty years ago?"

"They're just kids," Kiki forced out through lips frozen in shock. He never would have imagined his little school might be seen that way, but Kiki couldn't help admitting if the school idea had come to him within the first decade or so of his being cursed, he might have done just that. Luckily, Nicole had come along first, and the idea of using his kids to further asinine political ambitions had never even crossed his mind.

From the tilt of the blond guy's eyebrows, Kiki could tell they didn't believe him.

"When Zel cursed you," the man with the eyes said, "Zel gave you a way to be saved. I can see he wasted his magic."

They both studied Kiki, as if waiting for him to profusely deny all their allegations, but Kiki wasn't having it. They could believe all they liked; Kiki knew the truth, and he also knew better than to waste his breath.

The man with the eyes nodded firmly, and then his hand waved almost indolently in Kiki's direction. Kiki hadn't even seen the flare of magic as the man primed it, flashing it from head to toe and back, but he felt the pressure as the spell built in the air for the few brief seconds the man's hand was in motion.

"No!"

Kiki whipped around at that exclamation, throwing up his own hands as if he could prevent Nicole from coming any closer.

"Don't!" Kiki forced out, but Nicole dashed into the entryway and dove in between Kiki and the spell. It hit Nicole with a brilliant flare of light, blinding Kiki and making him stumble back a step. When the spots faded from his vision, he saw the shocked faces of his unwelcome visitors and Nicole, lying on the floor, unmoving.

"Nicole!" Kiki gasped, scrambling forward and dropping painfully to his knees at Nicole's side. "Nicole, wake up! Please, Nicole!" His shaking hands reached out, then hesitated to touch. Nicole just lay there, limp and pale, and Kiki's heart burned in his chest. Finally, he let out a shuddering breath and let his fingers bridge that last gap of air. Nicole's cheek was still warm, beneath his closed eyes. Kiki knew that warmth would leave soon, just as those eyes would never open again. He gathered Nicole into his arms as the first sob forced its way out of Kiki's mouth.

Kiki didn't know how long he sat there, sobbing into Nicole's hair, clutching Nicole's body tightly to him, only that his face was stiffer than normal from tears when a hand intruded. It pushed beneath Nicole's hair and rested on his neck for a long moment, before pulling away. Kiki looked up at the man the hand was attached to and saw it was the one with the eyes, kneeling at his side.

"There's still a heartbeat," he said softly, his face a picture of contrition. Kiki didn't care if the man was sorry now, and he opened his mouth to voice a scathing reply, when the words filtered in.

A heartbeat.

Kiki stiffened and drew back from Nicole, studying Nicole closely, and—there! There was the tiniest movement in Nicole's chest as it expanded with his breath. A faint puff of air from his lips as he exhaled.

"Your spell hit him. I saw it." Kiki's words were more garbled than usual, thick with tears, fear, and heartbreak.

The man shook his head. "The flash of light wasn't my spell. That was the impact between my spell and whatever spell your friend here cast. They combined somehow."

"What spell did you cast?" Kiki asked immediately. As long as Nicole still lived, there was a chance Kiki could remove the curse.

"Permanent sleep. You would have gone to sleep and therefore been forced to stop using magic. Once the extra years magic use provided you ran out, you would have peacefully passed away."

That was actually an elegant spell. No violence, no fear. Just sleep and death.

"And the spell on Nicole?" Kiki asked. He couldn't help brushing Nicole's hair off his face.

The man sighed. "Since he dove in to save you, I would guess he also cast something protective or preventative. In cases like these, usually the two spells combine somehow, but your friend's protective intent could provide a key to break the spell entirely."

A way to break the spell on Nicole. Kiki let out a heavy breath. "How do I break it?"

"No idea," he said with another shake of his head. "We'll have to study the spell and see. We should move him somewhere more comfortable though."

The other man with the long hair stooped at Kiki's side. "Will you allow me to carry him?"

What was with this abrupt turn around in attitude? They had broken into Kiki's house, accused him of terrible things, tried to kill him, hurt Nicole, and now they were being friendly and offering to help?

"Who are you?" Kiki had to ask.

The man with the long hair sat back on his heels and shrugged awkwardly. "This is Gabriel, and I'm Sean. We're both wizards."

They were more than that, and who they were explained so much to Kiki. The man with the eyes was Prince Gabriel of Monrath, although he had given up his title when he had chosen magic instead. Sean was Gabriel's sworn knight protector. And Kiki had sent the operative tasked with subduing the castle and the royal family so Kiki could bring Monrath into the Northern Empire.

Kiki had gotten word the king—Gabriel's father—was dead and the castle his, and had sent his army to complete the takeover. Next thing Kiki knew, he was being handed a rose.

Although, Gabriel's identity also explained just who—and why—he had been cursed. Those eyes were clearly a family trait, and Prince Ishiah and Wizard Zel were famous in wizard circles for their power and ingenuity. Knowing those two were protectors of Monrath had kept the mindless horde of Faltiken within their own borders for over two hundred and seventy years—a lesson Kiki had stupidly ignored. Zel had come with the rose and with a furious Ishiah and had cursed Kiki in retaliation for attacking Monrath. Now, Gabriel and Sean had come to stop what they perceived was him committing more wrongs against Monrath.

And Kiki's litany of mistakes and stupid actions had caused Nicole to be cursed too.

"We can bring him to his bedroom," Kiki finally said, breaking the patient silence in the entrance hall.

Sean nodded and carefully slid his arms underneath Nicole's knees and shoulders, then lifted him in one smooth movement. Kiki stumbled awkwardly to his feet, and for a second, his aching knees almost didn't take his weight. He clenched his jaw and began shuffling toward the stairs.

"It's this way."

They didn't comment on how long it took Kiki to make his way up the stairs, nor how slow he was forced to walk through the halls. They eventually made it into Nicole and Kiki's shared sitting room, and Kiki held open Nicole's door so Sean could bring him inside and lay him on the rumpled blankets.

"To understand the key to breaking the spell, we need to analyze the individual spell components," Kiki said, mostly to himself. He flooded his body with magic, bouncing it from his head to his feet over and over again until it built up enough he could barely contain the power. It erupted from his fingers and gently bathed Nicole in a soft golden light. The light sank into Nicole's body until it was completely absorbed; then Kiki made a pulling motion with his hands, as if he were grabbing a rope, and yanked the magic back out. The golden light flooded into view, but this time there were distinct patterns visible inside. Kiki immediately bent forward to begin reading those patterns.

"Whoa," Gabriel said, but softly as if he didn't want to break Kiki's concentration. Kiki felt Sean give him a sharp look, but Sean didn't comment and Kiki allowed himself to sink into a semi-meditative state that would allow him to begin mapping out those patterns into the full spell.

Chapter Four

The light in the room was slowly growing stronger, but the golden glow around Nicole hadn't changed in intensity. Kiki blinked and sat back in his chair; the aches from sitting, unmoving, for hours now landed on his back and shoulders with pounding intensity. He glanced out the window and saw the sun just starting to rise over the horizon. Kiki knew it meant it was time to start his day; he had to go take care of the children, to deal with his responsibilities, and yet, all he wanted was to stay just like this.

Kiki thought he had a grasp of some parts of the spell, but they were all muddled together. Gabriel's spell of sleep mixed with Nicole's spell of protection. Kiki had to figure out where one spell ended and the other began, which would allow him to isolate only the parts Nicole had inadvertently added to the spell. Somewhere in there was the key to waking Nicole.

But the children needed chasing out of bed and breakfast had to be served.

Kiki reached out and gently rearranged Nicole's hair so it fell to the side of his face rather than over his forehead. He really was beautiful, even asleep. Still, Nicole had been pulling away lately. Kiki knew it was only a matter of time before Nicole moved to his own suite of rooms, rather than sharing Kiki's, or Nicole left the manor entirely. At least Nicole would be alive and awake to make that choice, Kiki told himself as he got his feet underneath his body and levered himself up.

If he had been hobbling at two in the morning, it was nothing to now. His joints burned, the scars pulled, and it seemed even his bones ached. Every step was a challenge, but Kiki ignored the pain and forced his body to move. He found Gabriel and Sean curled together on one of the long couches in the sitting area, no doubt where they had gone when they'd realized they couldn't help Kiki unravel the spell. He left them to sleep, instead, going into his own room to find clothes for the day.

Twenty minutes later, he made it down to the kitchen. The magic was slow in coming this morning, but the massive pot he needed, as well as the bag of oats and the bag of sugar, did eventually come to him. Kiki measured out the correct amount into the pot, added water, and set it to slowly come to a boil. Kiki popped the bread he had left to rise overnight into the oven before sending his still-sluggish magic toward the dining room where the table began to set itself.

"You know exactly how to break the spell on yourself, don't you?" Sean said softly from the kitchen doorway. "You figured it out almost immediately after you were cursed."

Kiki gave Sean a crooked smile full of self-deprecation. "I didn't need to look. Your Zel told me when he cursed me. Someone had to be able to look past all this"—he waved a hand down his front—"and fall in love with me. I double-checked, of course, but Zel is considered a genius wizard for a reason. He must have known the spell would never break."

"But your Nicole?" Sean asked leadingly.

Kiki let out a rude snort and pushed past Sean to head to the dormitory part of the manor. "He doesn't need to know how I feel about him. One day he'll find someone better than me and move on with his life. He's still here because I raised him when everyone else had thrown him away, and I'm still willing to provide for him now."

Sean followed Kiki, but he was shaking his head as if he disagreed. He would learn better soon enough, Kiki knew, so he ignored Sean and marched into the boy's dormitory.

"Time to get up," he called. Kiki fought with the heavy curtains for a moment, before he was able to draw them back and let morning sunlight fall onto the boys. He heard some groans, some of the boys rolled over so they weren't facing the sun, and only a few slowly began to sit up. Kiki went to each bed and started yanking blankets back. "Up!"

Robbie was thankfully one of the boys willing to wake easily. He wandered in the direction of the washroom and came out a few minutes later dressed and ready for the day. He joined Kiki in prodding the rest of the boys up and out of bed. Only once Kiki was certain all the boys were going did he head for the door.

"Make sure your beds are made and your bedclothes are put in the laundry," Kiki called after them.

He hurried down the hall to the other dorm, where he went through the same routine as before. The girls were just as irritable as the boys for being woken, but there wasn't an older girl to take charge of them so Kiki stood over them as they slowly emerged from the washroom in fresh clothes. He made sure every bed was made and everything cleaned, before urging them out into the hallway and down toward the kitchen. They met the boys on the way, and Kiki nodded his thanks to Robbie. It wasn't fair to keep Robbie here much longer, but for today, Kiki was glad for the help.

The kids rushed into the kitchen, grabbing their supplies, before hurrying outside to complete their morning chores. The animals needed to be fed, including the donkey and cow in the stables, which would also need to be mucked out. The cow needed to be milked and the chickens fed and eggs collected. Somewhere in the manor their mouser was skulking, and the kids refilled her water and food bowls without being reminded. Kiki just had to watch and to make sure they all washed their hands when they finished and went to the dining room for breakfast.

Kiki's timing was perfect. The oats were cooked and the bread soft and crusty. Sean and Robbie helped Kiki fill bowls and bring them out to the kids, and then Kiki filled his own bowl and actually joined them. He took a seat in Nicole's usual spot and saw Sean and Gabriel had taken seats at the other end of the table.

Once everyone had a chance to eat for a few minutes, Kiki rapped softly on the table with the heel of his hand.

"Nicole's sick this morning," he said when he had everyone's attention. "He doesn't want to get any of you sick, too, so he's staying in bed." If only it were that simple, but it was an explanation the kids would understand. "I've called in some friends to help out," Kiki continued with a wave toward his guests. "Gabriel will take over your morning lessons. Sean's a knight. If... If," he repeated pointedly, "you do well in your lessons this morning and all your chores are completed, Sean will teach you some knight lessons this afternoon."

That brought on an excited clamor. "Can we play with swords?" Margo asked eagerly.

Sean shot Kiki a sharp look, as if asking what hell Kiki had just volunteered him for, but he smiled at Margo.

"Not for a first lesson," he told the room. "We'll start smaller today, but only if you pay attention to your morning lessons."

That got the kids moving. Dishes were brought to the kitchen and washed. Even Kiki, Sean, and Gabriel's dishes were grabbed. There was half the usual bickering, and all the kids were sitting in their seats in the classroom in record time.

Kiki dug Nicole's notes out from the teacher's desk at the front of the room and handed the day's lesson over. "The kids know where they left off. Yell if you need me." Kiki shot the room one last warning glare before heading back to the kitchen. With the kids suitably distracted, Kiki called on more magic. He needed double bread for lunch and a good-sized loaf for dinner. Magic wasn't the best way to knead dough, but it was the only way Kiki could manage it. He was planning to use the rest of the chicken from the pot pies for chicken salad sandwiches for lunch, and there was more than enough leftover stew for dinner tonight. He just needed to give the bread enough time to rise.

Only once the bread was set aside did Kiki do what he had been craving for what felt like forever. He hurried back to Nicole's side and the unravelling of the spell keeping him captive. Kiki set an alarm for forty-five minutes before lunch, sat down at Nicole's side, and got to work.

Chapter Five

Two days. Three days. Four days. Kiki left Nicole's side only long enough to ensure the kids were where they were supposed to be throughout the day. Instead of his normal routine, he spent all his time picking apart the spell on Nicole, trying to analyze the various components and understand how the two separate spells had combined.

Five days. Six days. Gabriel and Sean had almost totally taken over watching the kids at this point. They woke the kids up, got them to and from lessons, and oversaw chores. Kiki still organized meals, but he didn't eat with them. He needed, needed, to be with Nicole.

Kiki was making progress. Since he knew what Gabriel had cast, process of elimination had isolated Nicole's spell. At its most basic, Nicole had cast a protection spell meant to redirect Gabriel's spell away from everyone. It had instead morphed into the key to break the spell, but that key was still eluding Kiki.

Day seven dawned without an answer. Kiki couldn't remember the last time he slept. Had it been two days ago? Maybe. He did remember a vague nightmare where Nicole was begging Kiki for help, screaming from down a dark hole deep underground, but no matter what Kiki did, he couldn't reach Nicole. Sleeping hadn't really been an option after that.

A soft knock came from the open door behind Kiki. "Any luck?" Sean asked gently.

"Not since the last time you asked," Kiki replied and was surprised how much his voice creaked with disuse. "It doesn't seem to have any correlation with Gabriel's spell, but we know it must somehow. A spell to put someone permanently to sleep, a protective key to wake them up, and yet they just don't seem to match."

Sean frowned. "There must be something. How would you wake someone up normally? I saw you wake the kids. Gentle calling, sunlight, sometimes a push to get them moving."

"All of which I inadvertently tried about thirty seconds after the spell was cast," Kiki replied, half scathingly to himself because he had tried them all again not so long ago. "Besides, what do those methods have to do with magic?"

"Magic is always about intent. It's intent that shapes the spells, and sometimes you can use gestures to help the magic understand your intent. Point to a door to tell the door to open, squint at a tree to tell the magic you want to see far into the distance. What intentional action would you use to wake someone up? Particularly someone you love?"

Kiki didn't have an answer to that. No one had ever loved him before, even prior to his curse. People had slept with him. Men and women, all of whom were eager for some favor or recognition, but love was out of his reach.

Sean apparently gave up waiting for an answer. "Take a break," he insisted. "Go get a bath and a change of clothes so you're presentable when the kids come down to the kitchen for breakfast."

A bath was probably a good idea, Kiki had to admit, but he was so close to figuring out Nicole's curse. He didn't want to leave Nicole's side until he had the answer, but Sean was right: a break might refocus his thoughts. Kiki forced his aching knees to take his weight, and after one last look at Nicole's sleeping face, he shuffled out of the room, through the sitting room where Gabriel nodded solemnly to him, and on toward his own room.

Kiki walked into his dressing room where he took off his dirty clothes, dropped them in the hamper for washing day, and pulled out a fresh set to leave on his bed for after his bath. The rose was still glowing in the back of the room, but another petal had fallen down and blackened. The loss of the petal coincided with the increased ache in his joints, and Kiki knew it was a bad sign for him, but it was a worse sign for Nicole. If Kiki didn't save Nicole before the last petal fell, there was no telling whether Sean and Gabriel would take over where Kiki had left off. Kiki was honestly surprised they had stayed so long, although they seemed comfortable enough in the guest room they had commandeered.

The bathing room was tiled and clean, mostly thanks to magic rather than Kiki actually cleaning it as often as he ought to, but it was almost a relief after all the time spent in Nicole's darkened room. He turned the taps to hot and gladly sank into the tub as it filled. It was wonderful to feel the grease and grime leave his hair as Kiki soaped it as best he could, then dunked his head under the water to rinse it out. He started cleaning the rest of his body next, and only once he was fully clean did he relax in the hot water and see about soaking some of the aches out.

What action did someone take to gently wake someone they loved? Sean's question echoed unhappily in Kiki's thoughts, circling now the distraction of holding onto a bar of soap with fingers that struggled to grip was over. Probably not throwing open the shades to let in sunlight, nor yanking the covers off their bodies to force them to get up. What would Sean and Gabriel do? They seemed like a happy couple, so Kiki wondered how Sean would wake Gabriel in the morning. Sex? No, there might be sex in the morning, but there were things that happened before sex to get the mood going that would certainly wake a person up prior to the act itself.

A gentle caress? But Kiki had done that every time a bit of Nicole's hair had slipped over his forehead. A hug? No, Kiki had hugged Nicole right after the spell had hit, and that hadn't worked. So, what then? What else did couples do?

They kissed. A kiss! Of course! Curses loved to have true love's kiss as their key. Finding someone who truly loved you, despite all odds against you, was nearly impossible. It was why Kiki was slowly dying as his rose died, because there would never be someone who loved him enough to want to kiss him. But Nicole was so easy to love.

Kiki erupted from his bath, barely remembering to grab a towel as he sprinted as fast as his legs could take him out of his room, through the sitting room, and back to Nicole's side. He sat awkwardly on the edge of Nicole's bed and stared down at Nicole's beautiful face.

Could it really be that easy? There was only one way to find out. Hoping Nicole wouldn't be upset with Kiki for daring to be so forward, Kiki carefully bent so he could press his lips to Nicole's in a chaste kiss. Kiki tried to fill the kiss with intent, as if he were using magic instead of body contact, pushing his desperate wish for Nicole to wake into the brief moment of lips touching lips.

For the first long moment nothing happened, and Kiki began to despair. Except, Nicole suddenly gasped. Kiki quickly drew back and let out his own happy gasp to see Nicole's eyes open and aware.

"You kissed me?" Nicole asked softly. His voice didn't sound like it had been a week since he had spoken, but he didn't sit up, so he must be feeling some aftereffects.

"I'm sorry. It was the only way to wake you up," Kiki admitted. He was prepared for Nicole to tell him off, to yell at him or force him to leave, but instead, Nicole smiled.

"You taught me intent shapes the magic. When I dove in front of that spell, I wanted to save you from the spell, and also from your curse. I knew intent would make it so when you found the solution to my curse, you would also find the solution to yours."

"True love's kiss is not so easy a solution for me," Kiki replied automatically, ready to explain that no one could ever love someone like him. Yet, something in Nicole's smile kept those words from being said out loud.

Nicole slowly sat up until they were face-to-face. "It really is," Nicole murmured.

Suddenly, Nicole's lips were pressed against Kiki's in a reverse of just a few minutes ago. Nicole was kissing Kiki! Kiki wanted to savor the press of lips on lips, wanted to push forward to beg for more, but his chest abruptly started burning.

It felt like his lungs were on fire. Kiki fell back from Nicole with a desperate gasp for air, but the burning sensation only spread. His arms and legs were tingling with it, the muscles contracting wildly, and he fell off the bed onto the floor where he could curl up into a ball around the flames trying to burst out of his chest.

It seared through his throat like he was about to spit fire, and then down his spine like a hot poker, and then his face started pulling like it was melting. Someone was yelling something nearby, and Kiki could feel multiple people kneeling at his side, but thankfully, no one tried to touch. He didn't want them hurt as the spell that had turned him into a beast completed by apparently killing him.

Kiki didn't know how long it took the burning sensation to ebb, nor when his muscles stopped making his limbs flail, just that one moment he was writhing in pain, and the next he was lying on the ground, panting for breath.

"Kiki!" Nicole's voice seemed to come from a long way off, as if Kiki's ears were down a long tunnel. "Kiki?" he repeated, and this time Kiki's ears worked because Nicole sounded like he was sitting right next to Kiki on the floor.

"Nic—" he stuttered, unable to get the full name out through a throat parched from screaming and fire.

"I'm right here, Kiki. You're going to be okay."

He was using Kiki's name. How many decades had it been "Master" instead?

"Wha—happ—" Kiki's throat closed up and he started coughing.

Someone scrambled away and then back. A cup full of water was thrust into view a second later. Kiki reached out to take it, his hands still shaking with the aftereffects of whatever the hell that episode was. His fingers gripped the cup, and he somehow managed to get it up to his mouth for a sip without spilling it. Kiki brought the cup back down, setting it onto the floor, and his fingers uncurled.

It took a minute for Kiki's frazzled brain to realize what he had just done. His mangled fingers had just gripped a cup without any issues! He brought his hand closer to his face, and this time it was shaking for an entirely different reason.

His fingers were straight, and Kiki made a fist and his knuckles closed all the way. The knobbles on each knuckle, the scars that had pulled the skin taut—they were gone! Kiki let out a sobbing breath, and his beautiful, perfect hand lifted slowly, hesitantly, as if he didn't quite dare, and yet Kiki had to know. His fingers brushed down a smooth cheekbone, then up over his nose and across his forehead where the largest scar had pulled the skin on his face sideways, but nothing except a bit of morning stubble stopped his fingers' progress.

Kiki looked frantically up at Nicole, knowing his own eyes were wide with shock and his mouth hung helplessly open. Nicole's eyes were shining with happiness and unshed tears, and he was smiling so widely his jaw had to hurt, but he was so amazingly beautiful.

"You—" Kiki began, but the words still wouldn't come. "I'm—"

Nicole reached out and gently gripped Kiki's still-trailing hand in his own. Nicole kissed the back, his lips soft against skin that actually had the sensitivity to feel the feathery brush.

"True love's kiss, Kiki."

"You love me?" Kiki finally got words out, and he hated that he sounded so incredulous when Nicole looked so happy. Yet, there was no denying that before all this happened, Nicole had been pulling away. A distance that had seemed unsurmountable had appeared between them and had only kept growing.

Nicole let out a tear-shuddery laugh. "I was so disappointed in myself, you see. I knew you wouldn't believe me if I told you my feelings, so I had to distance myself from you to keep from doing something that would hurt you. That's why I started calling you 'Master.' I swore I would break your curse, because only then would you be able to look beyond your cage and see me waiting for you."

Kiki let out his own broken laugh. "I believed you were worth more than a broken, defeated man. One day, I knew you would find someone better for you than me. I hated the distance, but I understood why."

"But that wasn't why!" Nicole cut in. "It was because I couldn't hurt you, not until I knew you would believe me. Do you believe me now?"

Kiki looked at his hand, still clasped in Nicole's. The smooth, youthful flesh unmarred by the scars of his curse, a curse that could only be broken by true love's kiss. The evidence was clear; Kiki had to believe Nicole.

"You love me?" Kiki repeated.

"I do," Nicole answered without pause. "Do— Do you love me?"

Kiki grinned at Nicole, and the feel of his mouth stretching like it was supposed to was almost as wonderful as Nicole's own smile.

"I do," Kiki replied softly.

This time when their lips met, there wasn't any pressure of ending a terrible curse. No one woke up suddenly; Kiki's body didn't burst into flames. Instead it was just the press of flesh against flesh, heated by the wonder of the knowledge that Nicole loved him.

Epilogue

"This really is an intricate spell you've got on this place," Zel said late one afternoon, two months after the curse had broken. He had shown up that morning, Prince Ishiah in tow, and had made himself at home. Kiki actually didn't know whether he wanted to stop Zel from invading again, but mostly he wanted to know why Zel had appeared after so long.

"It's a simple calling spell," Nicole replied, disagreeing with Zel's assessment.

Zel laughed. "Not even close. You managed to set a calling spell to a specific age group, socioeconomic class, and amount of desperation, and have it spread throughout multiple nations. It's master spell work."

"You're just jealous you didn't think of it yourself," Ishiah replied, and then laughed when Zel only flipped his long purple hair at him.

Gabriel and Sean joined them a second later, filling the downstairs sitting room to capacity. They passed out the tea they had gone to the kitchen to brew before settling into the lone empty couch together.

Zel and Ishiah had arrived during afternoon weapons practice, which had then been followed with dinner, evening chores, and bedtime. This was the first moment any of them had had to actually talk.

"The number of children we've received has suddenly doubled in the last two months," Nicole said. "I don't think the spell was designed to notice that we doubled our teaching staff."

Sean and Gabriel hadn't seemed interested in leaving, either. Despite their rocky start, Kiki had to admit he was definitely finding himself becoming friends with them, and he didn't really want them to leave.

"Intent. It's always about intent with magic," Sean explained.

"I know of a few retired or near-retired weapons masters who would be happy for free room and board in return for teaching your youngsters," Ishiah said. "That would allow you to continue traveling."

Kiki watched Sean and Gabriel exchange a look full of silent conversation, but it was Sean who answered aloud. "I don't think we're done traveling the world to enhance our spell craft just yet, but it might be nice to take a few years off to see where this school might go. I wouldn't say no to more teachers, though. If Kiki will have us, that is," he added hastily, turning toward Kiki apologetically.

Before Kiki could answer, Zel started speaking again. "Ah, yes. Kristopherson Kistingeir Kingsman of the Kron Keep, Emperor of the North."

Kiki couldn't help wincing at his full name. So much alliteration, and it was clear his parents had a cruel sense of humor. Besides, Kron Keep had fallen with the empire, so his title was beyond pointless now.

"Kiki, please," he said insistently.

"Kiki, then," Zel continued. "I received a letter stating you might be up to some of your old tricks again. Ish and I immediately started traveling north, but then I felt my spell on you break and I knew better. I know I forced you through considerable pain. I won't apologize for that."

Nicole opened his mouth in protest but stilled when Kiki reached out to grip his hand. He settled, his arm pressed against Kiki's shoulder, but his chin was jutted out slightly in anger.

"You desperately needed to learn a lesson about the price of power, and I admit, I was angry you had managed to accomplish such terrible things while I was distracted. Perhaps my spell was harsh, but looking at you now, I can't say I regret my actions."

"Then why are you here?" Kiki asked, since he knew if he left it for an angry Nicole to answer they might induce Zel to cast another curse.

Zel smiled. "To ensure the curse is well and truly gone. The rose has vanished forever, and I sense no traces of the spell remaining."

Kiki could have told Zel that. He remembered the morning after the curse had lifted, going down to breakfast with the kids and watching their initial reactions. Shock, surprise, and even some who didn't recognize him at all, but only for a few seconds. Kiki could practically see the forgetting spell rewriting Kiki's image in their minds, and suddenly the kids were asking him whether he was feeling better. The story of Nicole being sick in bed had changed almost immediately to Kiki being ill, and their vague memories of seeing Kiki bent and hobbling around were just times they had seen him while he was sick. The kids had continued on with their day without giving Kiki's appearance a second thought.

The forgetting spell wouldn't have taken effect so thoroughly if his curse wasn't completely gone.

"We won't stay more than a day or so before getting out of your way," Ishiah added.

"Stay as long as you like," Kiki said, his voice firm. "You're welcome here as long as you don't cast any more curses. Just be aware if you stay too long you'll probably get co-opted into teaching."

Ishiah shrugged. "I wouldn't mind teaching some of the knight classes. My training in the army probably gives me more range and understanding than one measly knight. I think I could bring a lot to that class."

"You wish, old man," Sean retorted. "I can spar circles around you."

Nicole let out a soft yawn. Kiki reached out to put his tea cup back on the table, trying not to visibly marvel at how effortless that movement was. He hoped he never lost that sense of wonder, but he had a feeling Nicole would help keep him grounded.

"We have an early morning ahead of us, so we're going to say good night," Kiki said, cutting into the budding argument before it could escalate. He stood and held out a hand for Nicole to take. "You'll show Zel and Ishiah to a guest room?" he asked Gabriel, who nodded.

"I'll show them somewhere far away from the kids' wing, so they might be able to sleep in tomorrow morning. Have a good night."

"Night," Nicole echoed. He followed Kiki out of the sitting room and through the halls to their shared suite.

They got ready for bed in silence, moving around each other without getting in each other's way. Kiki found his pajamas, noted he would have to do laundry this weekend, and cleaned his teeth in the wash room. Nicole did the same at Kiki's side, and Kiki couldn't help admiring how normal and comfortable they were together. Then again, they had been living together for a hundred and fifty years; it was only the last step in their nightly routine that had substantively changed.

Nicole pulled back the blankets from the bed and climbed in. Kiki walked around to the other side—to what had become his side of the bed—and slid under the covers too. Nicole immediately slid closer, forcing Kiki to wrap an arm around Nicole's waist.

"We got a letter from Robbie today," Nicole said into Kiki's shoulder. He let out another yawn and shifted around until he could use that shoulder as his pillow.

"How's he doing in Monrath? Is he enjoying learning to be a scribe?"

Nicole nodded. "Seems to be. Says he misses us, but Alex is taking care of him, and I think he'll settle in fine."

Kiki smiled, glad to have another success story for a kid that had only needed a bit of a helping hand to turn his life around. He awkwardly glanced down at Nicole and had to stifle a laugh when he saw Nicole had fallen asleep midconversation. Kiki waved a hand at the lights, which went out a second later, and closed his own eyes.

On the surface, it might seem like Nicole was another of Kiki's successes, but Kiki knew it was the other way around. Nicole had saved Kiki in so many ways, and as Kiki followed Nicole into sleep, he couldn't help also being glad Nicole had brought him a happily ever after as well.

The Fairy Tale Origins

The Tower is based on *Rapunzel*.

Cleanly Wrong is based on Scottish folklore brownies.

A Heart's Dream is based on *Cinderella* and *Heart of Stone*.

The Red Apple Witch is based on *Hansel and Gretel*, *Rapunzel*, *Sleeping Beauty*, and *Snow White*.

Cinder-Elle is based on *Cinderella*.

The Curse is based on *Sleeping Beauty* and *The Frog Prince*.

Happily Ever After is based on *Cinderella*.

Thunderbird is based on Native American Folklore—Thunderbird.

The Beast is based on *Beauty and the Beast*, *Sleeping Beauty*, and *Snow White*.

About Mell Eight

When Mell Eight was in high school, she discovered dragons. Beautiful, wondrous creatures that took her on epic adventures both to faraway lands and on journeys of the heart. Mell wanted to create dragons of her own, so she put pen to paper. Mell Eight is now known for her own soaring dragons, as well as for other wonderful characters dancing across the pages of her books. While she mostly writes paranormal or fantasy stories, she has been seen exploring the real world once or twice.

Facebook: www.facebook.com/MellEightFiction

Twitter: @MellEight

Website: www.melleightfiction.weebly.com

Other books by this author

Also Available from NineStar Press

Connect with NineStar Press

Website: NineStarPress.com

Facebook: NineStarPress

Facebook Reader Group: NineStarNiche

Twitter: @ninestarpress

Tumblr: NineStarPress

www.ingramcontent.com/pod-product-compliance
Lightning Source LLC
Chambersburg PA
CBHW051557100726
47898CB00001B/128